THE WONDER CATS MYSTERIES

Books 1-3

HARPER LIN

Harper Lin Books

This is a work of fiction. Names, characters, organizations, places, events, and incidents are either products of the author's imagination or are used fictitiously.

ISBN-13: 978-1987859546

ISBN-10: 1987859545

www.harperlin.com

BOOK 1: A HISS-TORY OF MAGIC

A Family of Secrets

I definitely should not be writing this down. It's private. Not secret—no. I didn't do anything wrong—at least, not in my opinion. It's been crazy and surreal. You would think that as a witch, I would be used to this kind of thing by now.

As I said, this whole experience is personal, for me alone to deal with, but I really need to let it out, you know? I can't just keep pretending that my life is normal, especially ever since this new hot mess blew up—literally.

I'm trying to make sense of all this, but I don't know where to begin, and my cat keeps trying to use my open notebook as a bed when the cat bed is right there in the corner. Now he's using my wrist as a pillow.

I'm thirty-three years old, and I don't know half of what I should about my own family.

Mystery. That's the word I'm looking for. Detective

Williams just calls it a "case" and files it away neatly, but I think his partner knows a mystery when he sees one.

My entire life has been a mystery. I don't know how to explain to myself the secrets that my family has kept all these years... let alone untangling them for nonwitches.

Also, there's the mystery of Ted Lanier and his vegan poutine, which tasted better than the real thing—why didn't we appreciate him more back when he was still with us?

What about the mystery of Min Park? How could he have changed so much as a person? He felt like both the old friend I had known, whom I could spend hours playing games with, and an entirely different person at the same time. Do millionaire entrepreneurs play video games?

The biggest mystery of all is my family. Some mysteries should remain hidden in the mists. This is "the wonderful town of Wonder Falls," after all.

My cousin and soul sister Bea could describe Wonder Falls better than I ever could. She's a lot more like her hippie mother than she thinks, and she's always getting on me to stop and smell the flowers blooming in the crisp Canadian springtime, to go with her on camping and fishing trips by the lake, and to see the waterfalls that the lake runs into.

The waterfalls are magnificent. Of course, they're big. Loud. Damp, eventually. There are three of them, and they generate enough electricity to power the whole town. Tourists come for miles just to look. As for me—well, I live close enough that I've just gotten used to them.

No, no, scratch that. I was getting nostalgic about the way

things used to be. Actually, I might never look at the falls the same way ever again.

My name is Cath Greenstone, and I'm a witch.

All the women in the Greenstone family line are witches.

Bea's hippie mother—my Aunt Astrid—owns the best café in town, the Brew-Ha-Ha. Bea and I grew up learning how to run it, and—I write this with all the love in the world for my beautiful and wise Aunt Astrid, who took me in after my parents died—Bea and I both think we'd run it a little differently than Aunt Astrid has.

The fact that we're witches is supposed to be a big secret, but Aunt Astrid is convinced that the best way to go about things is to hide in plain sight. She does fortune-telling for customers, and she talks a lot about the way "mystical energy" moves through the Universe. Yes, Aunt Astrid uses a capital U, and you can practically hear it when she pronounces the word.

Most of the time, I fear she's daring people to discover us. On a good day—and we'd been having so many good days until the fire—it's reassuring to know that Aunt Astrid has been a witch for longer than all the years Bea and I have spent on this earth combined.

Aunt Astrid can see the future, which is probably the best magical talent a witch can have because a muddy future can be dangerous and painful.

Speaking of "dangerous and painful," Bea's got injury and illness covered with *her* witchy magical talent, which is more easily concealed. People just assume that Bea's a naturally touchy-feely person. Then when they heal quickly, they don't make the connection that Bea had a hand in it and just assume they were going to get healthy again anyway.

It helps to know how the human body works, of course, so Bea's done a lot of reading on that. She's really smart, and she loves to study. She could have left Wonder Falls to go to university and come back with half a dozen Nobel Prizes, never mind a medical degree. Instead, she married Jake and took his name.

I didn't mean that to sound judgmental. Bea's not just my family—she's my best friend. Did I mention she was smart? I wasn't exaggerating. Well, as long as she's happy, I know her talents aren't going to waste.

Jake's a good guy, and everyone in town can't help but like him. He's a good detective too, at least for the quiet, small town of Wonder Falls. However, he hasn't detected that the Greenstone heritage involves magic powers and, therefore, his wife is a witch.

I can communicate with animals, especially cats. I was scared of my own special magical talent at first. Now that I'm older, I really appreciate being able to communicate with Treacle, who's become my best friend, next to Bea.

My skill certainly came in handy on the night of the fire.

Treacle's Warning

Treacle is a street cat. I picked him up from the animal shelter run by old Murray Willis. Treacle has a scar on his forehead, probably from a fight with another animal. It has healed into a shiny white welt in the shape of a star, and I doubt fur is ever going to grow over it again.

Whatever incident caused the big scar hasn't stopped Treacle from wandering at night. Neither has the fact that I took him in. I would've preferred that he didn't wander, but it's what he likes to do. Also, he's a black cat, so I worry that he'll find himself under the wheel of a car belonging to a driver that can't see him in the dark.

He'd call me if it happened. Not with a phone—I mean he'd call out to my mind, and distance wouldn't matter. We've got a telepathic bond now, and the communication is getting stronger all the time, but I still worry.

Treacle doesn't speak Human. I speak Cat. It's more of a mind-to-mind magical communication using ideas and images, not so much actual words. That's how I accidentally taught Treacle how to unbolt the cat door.

You'd think I'd have an easier time communicating mind-to-mind with humans because I'm human myself, but even with Bea, it doesn't come naturally—or at all, except under special circumstances. On the rare occasions that telepathic communication with women does work, I need several days to recover. Yes, magic can take a lot out of you. That's something they rarely depict in movies.

Anyway, that was how I knew where Treacle was the night he saw the Brew-Ha-Ha on fire. He got scared and bounded all the way back home at full speed.

When it was barely dawn, whatever I'd been dreaming was interrupted by a fiery nightmare as Treacle shouted into my mind, but I only woke up when he leapt onto the bed and started nipping at my face.

A full understanding of what had happened bypassed my conscious mind and got my instincts going. I jumped out of bed and grabbed the phone on the nightstand.

I was barely awake, completely panicking, and I almost let slip to the 9-1-1 dispatcher that I'd learned about the fire from my cat.

I cleared my throat of its early-morning roughness, shook off the just-woken-up mist from my mind, and tried again. "I can see it from my window," I lied. "That's my aunt's café, for sure, on fire. No, it hasn't spread to any other building yet, but please hurry."

I gave them the address of the café as I stretched the phone cord across the room, straining to reach into my closet to grab something to wear. The line snapped from its socket just as I finished talking.

Treacle nuzzled my ankle then pressed his head into it, purring anxiously.

"Do you think they got it?" I wavered between calling the dispatcher back and getting dressed.

Treacle pawed and nosed the closet door ajar and said, *"I can ask Marshmallow what's going on."*

Marshmallow was Aunt Astrid's cat, a Maine Coon. They had a bond, just as Bea and Peanut Butter had a bond. Marshmallow could even do some magic. When it came to communicating with the cats, however, it was pretty ordinary guesswork between human and cat for Aunt Astrid and Bea. The cats could talk with each other, and I could talk to the cats.

When they've bonded, as Treacle had with Marshmallow, then distance doesn't matter. So Treacle didn't need to go over to Aunt Astrid's place to check with Marshmallow and then come back to help me decide what to do.

Having a network of minds and being able to communicate instantly can be handy at times, as you might imagine. Although I'm a witch, I'm also a human, so if I do it too much or if I do it with someone whom I haven't formed strong bonds with, then I get headaches. Sometimes my attempts fail, and I only end up receiving mental static, or whichever animal I'm sending my thoughts to just doesn't understand clearly.

Treacle sent to my mind an image of Aunt Astrid in her bedroom. She was fully dressed except for shoes. The image was from the height of Aunt Astrid's ankle, looking up—Marshmallow's point of view.

Aunt Astrid's pear-shaped, slightly overweight figure was very well suited to her billowing drawstring peasant tops and gypsy skirts. Her hair had always been wispy and had never darkened from the dishwater blond of her younger days, although it was beginning to thin. She refused to dye over the pale streaks of gray.

That morning, she'd styled her hair into a French braid, but the locks still loosely framed her face like an ethereal halo. Aunt Astrid had a friendly face. The wrinkles around her mouth and blue eyes bespoke a lifetime of smiling and laughter—in spite of many tragedies.

I felt the ghost of a shift under my elbow as Aunt Astrid eased a pair of canvas flats out from under the giant Maine Coon. She brushed some strands of fur from the shoes before slipping her feet into them.

"You need another grooming," Aunt Astrid said to Marshmallow. "Just as well that there won't be any work today, I suppose, just dealing with the firemen. I'll be back soon."

The image faded. Aunt Astrid knew about the fire.

Treacle leapt to the windowsill, flicked his tail, and meowed. He didn't like fires. I wondered right then if that had something to do with how he'd gotten that star-shaped scar on his forehead. Treacle didn't want to think about it to himself, let alone to me. The fire at the Brew-Ha-Ha had spoiled his morning, and he just wanted to take a nap.

"I might as well go since I'm already up. It will just be insurance stuff and renovating the place, then," I said to myself. "No need to wake Bea, too."

I relaxed too soon, thinking that one of the perks of having an oracular aunt was being able to get a heads-up at times like that. As I said, I don't know half of what I should by now about magic. Every time you think you're in control of your powers or your circumstances, something comes at you from left field.

Nothing could have prepared my family for that morning.

The Humorless Detective

On a bench across the street from the Brew-Ha-Ha, I sat myself down beside Aunt Astrid. Wordlessly, Aunt Astrid nudged a paper bag toward me. I uncapped a large thermos I'd brought, poured some strong black tea into the cap, and passed it to Aunt Astrid. Then I poured myself some tea in the smaller, nested plastic cup that came with the thermos, and I reached into the paper bag for one of Astrid's homemade maple bran muffins. Aunt Astrid sipped her tea and sighed. I rubbed my eyes with the back of one hand and stifled a yawn.

Between the bench and the café, a fire truck's siren wailed in the otherwise peaceful morning. The warm glow of the dawn light had stiff competition from the pillars of lurid flames.

Wonder Falls was so small I recognized most of the firefighters even though I didn't know all of them personally.

Gillian Hyllis, the one shouting orders to coordinate the firefighting effort, had come from a family of elitist academics, whom she'd disappointed by following her passion into a more practical profession. Reuben Connors, who rushed to the scene without his gear, was an actual disappointment to the profession.

At the fire hydrant, lining up the hose, was one quarter of the town's support group for divorced fathers and one third of the town's support group for alcoholism recovery, Wayne Walter. I only knew him by name because he had the distinction of attending both groups. From the look of his hosing skills, he was on the ball. That was good to see. Gossip can be vicious, but I think most townsfolk, like me, were silently rooting for him to get his life back on track.

What a relief to see that most of the Wonder Falls fire brigade were in their best shape and getting their jobs done despite generally being unused to having to do them.

Eventually, some of our regular customers passed by and stopped to watch the fire. Some chatted with the firefighters, asking them for details. A few approached Aunt Astrid and me at the bench.

"...all right, there?" The wiry, petite woman spoke so softly that I caught only the end of her sentence.

I managed a smile. "No need to worry about us, Mrs. Park."

"If there's anything you need..."

I'd know where to reach her. We lived in a small town.

That didn't mean everybody was friendly, however. After

Mrs. Park wandered off, another figure cut into my line of vision. She had a loud, wheedling voice and smelled of artificial jasmine.

"I had a meeting scheduled here for later this morning!" she huffed.

A skittish part of me remembered my sixth grade again, and I flinched back a bit from the verbal bludgeon of entitlement that was Darla Castellan. Some schoolyard bullies never grew up. I remembered the names she used to call me and how she could manipulate the other kids into following her lead.

Aunt Astrid seemed to have woken up a bit. "I know," she exclaimed. "This is so inconvenient for everybody." She repeated, as a not-so-subtle reminder, "Everybody!"

Darla folded her arms over her chest. "Well, what are you going to do now?"

I took a gulp of tea and shrugged. "Apologize for the inconvenience?"

"And thank you for your continued patronage after we restore the Brew-Ha-Ha," Aunt Astrid said dryly. "It will take a few days."

Part of the café roof collapsed, sending firefighters scurrying to herd the spectators away, to a safer distance.

"Weeks," Aunt Astrid corrected. "A month, at the most."

"Continued patronage," Darla scoffed, "is an awfully big presumption." She stormed off in a huff. When she decided to snub or shun somebody, she meant it.

"Genius," I said, clinking Aunt Astrid's teacup with mine.

The residents of Wonder Falls loved the Brew-Ha-Ha—the location, the architecture (so we'd keep it as close to the original as possible when rebuilding the place, I thought), the impeccably polite staff, and the baked goods only a genuine French chef could make.

"Oh!" I gasped and realized aloud, "I should have called Ted!" Ted was our baker and cook. He came in to work at the crack of dawn, before everyone else.

"I left him a message on his answering machine," Aunt Astrid assured me. "I told him not to come in today and that we'll handle everything."

Another voice—from behind us, high, sweet, and raspy—added, "I wish I knew that! I called him just now too, but he's not answering."

It was Bea. Her dark-red hair was naturally styled in glossy waves. She'd inherited that from her father, along with the dark eyes. Our maternal grandfather must have been the one responsible for Bea's flawless, almost olive complexion.

"Good morning! I mean, better morning from now on." Bea put an arm around both of us and peered up at the building. "How did this happen?"

The fire had already been extinguished. I caught sight of Jake across the road, shaking hands with one of the firefighters. He glanced toward the three of us and gave something between a wave and a salute. He wasn't usually so cold, but I reasoned that I'd never seen Jake in action, so maybe he steeled up for his police work.

"Well," Aunt Astrid said, "I had a vision of the fire months ago, and since then, I've been so careful. After closing up, I'd see to it that Ted turned the gas off. Everything that had plugs in the wall sockets, I'd unplug myself." She heaved a sigh of resignation. "Sometimes, the future that I see is fixed."

"I refuse to believe that," Bea declared. More quietly, she suggested, "Senior moment yesterday, maybe?"

Aunt Astrid gave a deep belly laugh as I exclaimed, "Bea!"

"Mother knows what I mean. You could have told us. We would have helped. That's all I meant!"

"I don't have senior moments, Bea. I have ascended moments of omniscience."

"You mean precognition."

As they chatted, I watched as Jake intentionally stood between Gillian and a man I hadn't seen before. He couldn't have just been a visitor in town, judging from how Jake and the firefighter were both acting so tense. The strange man's strikingly handsome face was ruined by a squint when he turned and caught my eye. I returned his glower with an expression of confused stubbornness. Still, I didn't look away. Jake gave him a sharp word, and the strange man broke eye contact with me to acknowledge the argument he was almost having with Jake.

"That's Blake Samberg. He studied forensics in Boston," Bea told me. "He's Jake's new partner, been so these past two and a half weeks."

Aunt Astrid hummed as she considered the two men. "They seem to be getting along."

"Jake complains a lot about how on edge Blake is. City

slickers, you know." Bea rolled her eyes. "I bet he's accusing the firefighters of arson. He calls it his gut, but really he's just conditioned to be extra suspicious of absolutely everybody else in the world."

"What a shame," I said. "He's cute."

Bea drawled, "Give it time." She waggled her eyebrows at me. "Either he'll have you on edge too, or—"

"Wonder Falls will mellow him out." Aunt Astrid finished, confidently. She handed the thermos cap back to me and carefully folded up the empty paper bag.

As the fire truck began to pull away, Blake and Jake entered the ruins of the café, and Bea urged us off the bench to gather materials for the cleanup. She had the keys to her minivan, where the cleaning supplies waited.

The sun should've been up at that time of the morning, but the light from the overcast sky wasn't brightening the scene very much. "I hope it doesn't rain. The Brew-Ha-Ha doesn't have a roof anymore."

"Not over the customer area. We can go check on the kitchen." Aunt Astrid stood up to go, and Bea and I followed.

We went around back and met Jake on his way out.

"Don't go in there." Jake's voice was stern, his expression worried, with a hint of panic.

Bea looked confused for a moment. "What, do you think I had so much sentimental attachment to this café?" she asked with a laugh. "These things happen, sweetheart. We just do our best with whatever happens in business." Then she moved toward the kitchen anyway.

Jake interrupted her with a grappling sort of hug, trying to turn his wife away.

He was too late. Bea saw something inside the kitchen and screamed.

Blake strode up to the back entrance and blocked the way through.

"What is it?" I demanded of him.

Aunt Astrid handed me her broom and put her hands on her hips. "What is going on here?"

"This is a crime scene. Please"—Blake gestured toward the sidewalk—"wait here until we can call for backup." His voice was hoarse and deeper than I'd expected for someone with such a clean-cut look.

Aunt Astrid and I exchanged startled looks.

Arson. Some troubled teenager left rude vandalism that survived the building fire.

Bea, still in Jake's embrace, sobbed. She wouldn't have shed tears over a bit of vandalism.

"Wh—who was that?" she asked.

"We don't know yet," Jake answered at the same time that Blake said, "Théodore Lanier."

"Damn it, Samberg!"

I'd never heard Jake swear before.

"Ted?" I could barely get the name out. My nerves trembled with the looming sensation of something gone very, very wrong. "Théodore's his full name, Théodore Lanier." It's supposed to be pronounced "lan-YAY" in that Frenchy way, where the R is silent. "He's our baker. What about him?"

Blake turned to me again. "If the driver's license belonged to the body, ma'am, then it could very well be that Ted... is dead."

Aunt Astrid gasped in horror.

"There's a body in there, burnt to a crisp. Your baker's been roasted," Blake deadpanned.

Jake's jaw dropped. Bea released a wailing sob.

"Mr. Lanier"—Blake mispronounced the name "LANE-ee-yur"—"could now be that body that's layin' 'ere."

I squeezed my eyes shut and held up my palm toward Blake, to stop him. "I've got the gist of it, yeah! Detective... Punster, is it?"

"Do you think I have a sense of humor?" Blake growled the question, seeming offended.

I seethed. "I'll take any explanation other than the answer that this is really happening."

"We've got procedures to follow now," Jake said. "Samberg's right, at least on the point that this is a crime scene. We need backup to investigate before we know more."

He rubbed Bea's arm to comfort her. They walked back to the police car, and the rest of us followed.

I didn't notice it then, but Marshmallow must have darted from the alleyway at that moment and followed us.

A Lesson in Magic

Marshmallow later told me what had lured her out. I'll do my best to translate, beginning with the moment Aunt Astrid left that morning. Before I get to that, though, I need to explain something about witchcraft.

Basically, witches work with another dimension. Most people know that dimensions consist of height, breadth, and depth. Some people consider the passage of time the fourth dimension, and I don't know if that's true because I'm not a physicist, but that sure would make the next thing I'm going to explain a little easier to grasp.

The other dimension exists. It's obvious to us witches. We balance that world with the life in this world, which we share with nonwitches.

Imagine a square. Now, notice how a square can turn into a cube with an added dimension or just a few extra lines to suggest it. Time takes a different shape too, with an added dimension or two or three or more. That's why Aunt Astrid experiences time out of order: she lives the future in the present.

Every person, even nonwitches, has an extra body in this collection of other dimensions. It interfaces with one's physical body, locked to it for as long as life continues.

The bodies of the other dimensions get damaged more easily but heal more quickly than physical bodies, but because of the interface, the state of one body does affect the other. That's how Bea does her healing. Her body in the other dimension has a looser interface with her own, and her witchy senses let her see exactly what is wrong with the other person's "other" body. She works her magic, which these other dimensions are made out of, and she makes people healthy again or at least takes away their pain.

Cats know the other dimensions even better than witches do. I just happen to be in the same zone most cats are in, which is why I can connect with cats better than Bea or Aunt Astrid.

These other dimensions are like an ocean. It has zones of visibility, currents, quakes, and an irregular ebb and flow that makes it difficult to explore. That's why we witches have different talents from each other and also why a single talent might not work all the time.

Practicing witchcraft is like sailing a ship on an ocean. We can set down an anchor, as Bea can do with healing people's bodies; we can tether to a buoy, as I do with the bonds I make with cats; we can turn the sails when the wind changes, as Aunt Astrid tries to do in response to her visions of the future. However, if there's a giant tidal wave or an iceberg or a sea monster... Well, then it's all we can do to keep from sinking. When that happens, witches and nonwitches are in the same boat, really.

Okay, maybe not. We witches do our best, but that has never been good enough for nonwitches. Nonwitches have always thought that just because we know when some danger from another dimension is coming, we're also dangerous—that, because we're not strong enough to stop evil, we must be evil, too. No wonder we're neurotic about our privacy!

The Greenstones came to Ontario from Massachusetts. My I-don't-know-how-many-greats grandmother took the hint from the witch trials in Salem that the New World still had old problems. She might have run forever but never found a place where a witch could be accepted by other human beings.

She settled in Ontario because she found acceptance here from a being that's never been human. Among the generations of Greenstone women since then, this being has been known as the Maid of the Mist.

When I was at that awkward and insecure age of dealing with bullies at school—and growing into a magical talent I couldn't accept because magic had left me orphaned—I took frequent trips to the waterfalls where the Maid of the Mist was supposed to have first appeared to the errant Greenstones.

I'd been full of hope that the Maid of the Mist would appear to me and grant me some guidance, but she never did. Maybe she wasn't as connected to us witches as we'd thought. Or maybe the Maid of the Mist just wasn't interested in the emotional issues of adolescent humans.

But on the day of the fire, the Maid of the Mist appeared to Marshmallow.

Marshmallow Moans

I didn't want a grooming. I might like that it takes me back to my days in show, during which I won ribbons and was very proud to look so pretty, but that time is past. It's for no good reason now that Astrid takes me to that cold, bright place to get rained on, and I don't taste right afterward when I try to clean myself. Sometimes I get indigestion from whatever they put in my fur. I'm getting too old for grooming.

Yet I'm also too old to fight, scratch, and bite in protest. Besides, I know it will be over sooner if I don't make any trouble.

When the time came, instead of taking me to the groomer's, Astrid said she was going somewhere and told me to stay put. I took a catnap. Instead of being at the groomers for real, I had an uncomfortable dream about the grooming, a nightmare.

I wasn't sure if I was still dreaming when I heard a hissing sound. It made me curious because it was half like the sound of the rain that humans make and half like the sound of a cat warning everybody else away. Usually, I don't care, but this was a voice that knew me, and it wanted help.

I opened my eyes. I didn't know if the sound had woken me up or if I was still dreaming, but the room of the grooming salon disappeared and made way for a vast dreamscape of open sky and wild river waters. At what felt like the end of the earth, the wide river dropped. The hiss became a roar of water hitting water that made my fur fluff up with fright. I had already gotten wet and didn't want to drown.

Then I saw the falling water take the shape of a cat. She was a long-haired Persian—or at least she was shaped like one—but I think that was just a shape that she was taking so that I could understand her.

She told me that Astrid Greenstone should take "it" from her—but that she needed the other humans to help—and me, too.

"You have the wrong cat. I don't know the streets," I told her. "If they don't come fetch me, then I can't help them. I'm too old for this."

The Cat of the Mist told me, "No, it has to be you. Treacle can help get you there. Hurry, or else—"

I challenged her: "Or else what? What gave you the right to threaten me with anything?"

The Cat of the Mist turned into mist that wasn't shaped like anything, and I dreamed that the water covered where this giant misty cat used to be. It overflowed over everything. The bank of the river broke with all the water, which then filled the forest even to the top of the trees. I saw this as if I wasn't really there, as though I was flying. The dream changed so that I was in it instead of only watching, but the overflow didn't stop. I clung onto a branch, feeling like a kitten again, when I used to play in trees, climb too high, and get stuck.

I woke up.

The window was open because I never sneak out and sometimes Treacle sneaks in. I jumped out the window, leaving the cool and cozy familiar smells of my home.

I sent Treacle a message: "I'm outside. Now where do I go?"

Treacle was astonished. "Outside? You? Without a human?"

"I'm going to get to a human if you would just tell me. I'll tell you why later. I don't want to be late."

Treacle gave me some roundabout directions because he wanted me to stay away from the street gangs. When I understood where our humans would be, I ignored the detour and passed through street-gang territory to get there. Do you know, now, how much I put myself through for you?

Really, they weren't that bad. I'm a big cat, and my fur makes me look even bigger and tougher. If I moved right, they wouldn't even notice I was old. They were mostly surprised to see a strange new cat that they didn't know.

I didn't run, in case that would make them curious enough to chase me. One rude young calico that smelled like the Dumpster tried to rally the others to corner me, but many of them had stayed up all night hunting and weren't in a mood for surprises.

I could have used magic then. Not all cats can do it. Two things stopped me: First, I knew the magic would leave me for the next hour if I used it then. Second, I knew my humans would need my magic.

What was really bad was the dog out walking its human.

Oh, the dogs!

Dogs you should run from when they see you because they're loud and violent first. They don't think. They're not smart enough, not like cats. Humans only think that dogs are smarter because dogs are more likely to do as they're told. And even so, they don't do that all the time.

This one's human made noises like "No!" and "Come back!" after the giant St. Bernard broke the strap that kept them together. I had to run, duck into an alleyway, and climb over a wire fence. At my age, too!

I very much wanted to use magic then too, but I didn't.

When I finally found my human, Astrid, you can imagine my relief. I wasn't done yet, of course. The gods are annoying.

Five humans walked out to the banks of a dry river made of rough flagstones. I didn't know one of them, the one who was asking, "Did Mr. Lanier have any reason to come in early?"

Astrid answered, "Work ethic—that's the only thing I can think of. I had no idea he would come in so early, but he does that sometimes—or he did, if that corpse is really his. Oh, how awful!"

"He loved his job," Cath said. "A kitchen accident..." She shook her head. "That would have been a bad way to go."

The human I didn't know said, "We don't know enough to say that it was an accident yet."

Astrid and Cath stepped away from him, and my human said, "Just what are you implying?"

"Just that the police will be wondering what you could have done, too. It's our job."

I didn't like him. He was making my humans unhappy, so I ran in front of his ankle to trip him.

He stumbled. "What?" Then his voice sounded pleased. "Oh, what a pretty kitty!"

I gave him an annoyed sideways-and-upward glance as he ruffled the fur at the top of my head.

"And she's friendly! It is a she, right?"

"Yes," my human confirmed. I meowed up at her.

"This is yours?" The strange human picked me up comfortably, grasping my ribs behind my forelegs not too tightly, then putting an arm under my hind legs. I relaxed like a rag-doll cat, but when he had me against his suit, I pawed to show that I still didn't like him. His suit smelled like catnip. I don't care because I'm one of the rare cats that catnip does nothing for, but I wondered how much he actually liked cats.

"I was going to take her to the grooming salon," Astrid said to him, taking me from his arms. "Marshmallow must have escaped from Bea's car. I'll take her back now."

Astrid was lying to him for some reason.

"And these won't be needed for a while, either," Cath added, lifting the bucket of hay on a stick and the rope monster on a stick.

Treacle and even Peanut Butter liked to chase after the hay. I didn't. None of us liked the rope monster because it was usually damp and smelled too sharp and gross.

The strange human said, "Let me help you with that—"

"No, I can manage," Cath told him. "Shouldn't you be calling for backup? Jake's a little tied up right now, what with being a decent human being to his wife, and you've got to delegate the real work of investigation to other people so that you can make your accusations."

Astrid was holding me up to her shoulder, so as they walked away, I saw the strange male human's crestfallen expression.

Cats have sharp ears, and I heard him say, "I'm just doing my job..." And he walked away.

"We hadn't brought Marshmallow with us," Cath whispered. "Wouldn't he have noticed?"

"For now, we've got a more critical problem," Astrid whispered back. "We need to get back in there before backup comes."

Cath is a good listener. I told her, I can hide you—with magic, I can do it. None of the other humans will know that you were ever there.

Still, she was confused. "Why? What—and Marshmallow just volunteered to do her magic."

That's what I went there for.

"That's going to be a big spell," Astrid said. "It would be easier with Bea, but we need to be discreet, and we need to do it now."

We arrived at Bea's moving machine, which they called a "car," though it wasn't moving then.

Cath opened the door and pushed the things she was carrying into the car. She said, "Aunt Astrid, you're scaring me. What's going on?"

Cath knows about big spells, dangerous spells. She should have been allowed to go the rest of her life without being exposed to the dangerous repercussions of magic again.

"It's faster to show you," Astrid told her, as she moved me from her shoulder onto the cushioned surface covering the inside of Bea's moving machine. "And we do need to be fast."

Cath gave something like a human version of an anxious meow, then she surrendered. "All right. How do we do this?"

Cats can shift between this world, that world, and the other. We don't normally take up the gatekeeper role, but my human is a witch, so I did that. That's why I can use magic. Treacle and Peanut Butter are too young to do it like I can.

We cast three large spells. They would be a stretch of the two humans' usual talents. First, I would need to pull the other dimension over this one. Doing that would make witchcraft easier for my humans to do, but even then, the spell would not be easy.

Cath would pull some of this dimension around the dimension I pulled so that anybody nearby would not be able to pay attention to them, would not be able to remember, and would not even know they'd forgotten anything when the two ended the spell and joined the solid world again. That part would come from Cath's talent with minds even though she had never played with the mind of a human before and wouldn't want to do it ever again.

My human would do the same kind of magic, except with time. Any marks they left, footprints or strands of hair, would stay missing in that place until three days later. That would come from her talent with time and could work because the future is mostly not set.

None of those effects were normal manifestations of our usual powers. Casting those spells was going to be difficult for all of us.

Time Travelers

I was afraid I was going to die. Marshmallow and Aunt Astrid were obviously both worried that they wouldn't be able to pull the magic off, but still, they had a quiet determination that came from knowing why they would have to try in the first place. I didn't have that, and I still had to do a big spell—my first big spell since witnessing the one that took both my parents away from me.

When Marshmallow started to pull the other dimension—or some magic from the other dimension—in over this one, I felt like a little kid again, watching the monster come out from under my bed and feeling helpless as my mom tried to keep it at bay by waving her quartz-crystal wand. She'd drawn a protective circle on my bedroom floor and told me not to leave it. My dad had run into the room—

I forced myself to focus, telling myself, *That was then and this is now*. No evil beings were exploding out of a portal—we were just making a phenomenal effort to tweak people's minds.

Besides, Aunt Astrid was the one who had to do the magical heavy lifting, moving us into the Brew-Ha-Ha of the future just enough that we wouldn't leave a trace in it in the present but not enough to cause some temporal paradox that would collapse every dimension in on itself.

That wasn't as comforting a thought as I'd wanted it to be. First of all, a big spell was a big spell. Second of all, I wondered if we could really end the world by casting it. Bea would know the risks better because she reads about quantum physics. Aunt Astrid was just convinced that it was worth the risk.

Anyway, Marshmallow began to let the other worlds into our default one.

The sensation of that happening felt a little bit like standing under a waterfall as the numbingly cold water beats down on the top of your head. I forced myself to open my eyes against that flux and to move forward.

Aunt Astrid and I began to walk to the back entrance of the Brew-Ha-Ha. Bea caught sight of us, cloaked in magic. Jake turned toward us, and my breath caught, but he looked right through us and returned his attention to Bea, to my relief. Blake was in the police car, speaking into the two-way radio. He didn't take any notice of us either.

I gritted my teeth against the waves of magic as Aunt Astrid began to fold time in on itself. I saw a corpse in the kitchen with the same height and buff build that Ted had. As we took the next step, the body faded into a chalk outline, and in another step, it had become clean, new tiling. I began to feel dizzy.

Aunt Astrid led the way out of the kitchen and behind the bar, which was badly burnt but still standing. Behind the bar was a trapdoor. Aunt Astrid pulled it open just enough to squeeze through and make her way down to the stairs below. The trapdoor remained open at an angle that would have been physically impossible to maintain if it weren't frozen in time.

As I was about to follow, something on the ground caught my eye. It was a pendant on a chain, glinting silver against the soot and char. Because of the time manipulation, it flickered in and out of existence, but something about that necklace burned against the magic.

It could only do that if it were magic itself.

I took my phone out of my pocket and snapped a few pictures of the pendant. I don't know how physics and technology work when they're mixed with magic. Maybe Bea's developed some grand unifying theory, but I just do what I hope works out well in the end.

"Cath?" Aunt Astrid called.

I snatched the necklace from the ground, pocketed it, and then followed Aunt Astrid downstairs into the cellar.

The magic faded as we reached the bottom of the stairs. I leaned on the railing and waited for my nausea to pass.

"Marshmallow should keep the spell going on above us." Aunt Astrid's voice sounded frail in the pitch darkness. "I built this basement to stand up against a nuclear war. Fire wouldn't have touched it."

With a click, a flashlight flickered to life, the silver beam of light illuminating the room. It was a bunker—gray, concrete, and bare except for a shelf of dusty canned goods. I felt as if I hadn't slept in days. That's what magic burnout does to a person, and we were only halfway done.

"What was so important that we had to do this?" I groaned miserably.

Aunt Astrid beckoned and handed me the flashlight. "Hold this for a moment."

I shone it at the corner she was approaching.

"I needed to keep something here that was very important," Aunt Astrid told me as she opened one of the fuse boxes. "It's a spell book that we've kept in our family for generations. You know the spell that we're casting now? It's a cantrip compared to the weakest spell in that book."

She wrenched back a panel of switches and wires—a false display. I held my breath as she reached into the back of the fake fuse box.

She drew her hand back and exhaled sharply. "It's gone. Someone's taken it."

"Who would do that?" I asked, but I knew the answer to that. "Somebody who wants to do magic more powerful than we're doing."

"Somebody," Aunt Astrid added, "who knows that we kept it. Somebody who knows that we're witches."

I gulped. What could have given us away? We'd all been so careful, and Wonder Falls was such a safe town.

"Turn the light onto the floor."

I jumped back, startled, when I saw faint footprints leading from the stairs to the fuse box.

"Those are new," Aunt Astrid said.

"They don't belong to us," I observed. "The size of the shoe is too big."

I took note of the outsoles' imprints, too. They looked smooth, as though they belonged to formal shoes, not patterned like hiking boots or sneakers.

"Maybe..." My mind spun. "Maybe it was just an eccentric collector. Maybe they'll leave us alone now that they have what they want. It was a family heirloom, sure, but not one that we ever used, so—"

Aunt Astrid muttered a word, and a blast of magic shot out of the fake fuse box. It gave the air a fresh tang, like ozone or Freon.

"Protecting that book is a duty that I take very seriously," Aunt Astrid said as she reached into the fuse box once more. She drew out an old, leather-bound tome. "The thief stole a fake copy. I had this one hidden in a pocket dimension, guarded by the Maid of the Mist." She turned to me and said harshly, "We're all in great danger, Cath. Whoever found this set this whole place on fire, and now Ted is dead. Just remember that."

We made our way back outside to Bea's car, with Aunt Astrid tightly knotting time behind us. We wouldn't want investigators to walk onto the scene, disappear for days, and then reappear, insisting that no time at all had passed for them. We only wanted any evidence that we'd been there moved away somewhere safe.

When all that was done, Marshmallow flicked her ears and tucked the other dimension away, back where it belonged. Aunt Astrid and I raised a sort of magic wall that would prevent magic from coming through even though the wall itself was magic—it's easier to do if you don't think about it too much. I don't usually think about "How?" except when I repeat what Bea's figured out about how it works, but that day I was thinking about "Why?" and "Should we or should we not?"

So I didn't pull the spell off easily. Most magic walls that we cast are actually walls of spells—for example, to make a nonwitch afraid to go near a place for some unexplainable reason. Those walls take a long time to grow, but they tend to stay up for a while. We needed that sort of power in crunch time, which even Aunt Astrid—who had worked with time magic all her life—had difficulty with.

With a final burst of power, I felt the wall align.

Aunt Astrid clapped her hands and looked from Marshmallow to me. "Well done, team!"

I had to lean against Bea's car to keep myself from fainting.

Bea walked briskly over to meet us. "I convinced Jake to take his partner on their beat and interrogate us after."

She still looked visibly shaken by what she'd seen. That

much was no act. I gave her a hug. She looked as though she needed it.

As she hugged me back, she sniffled and said, "I want to go home. You can catch me up on whatever you just did when we're there."

"Just don't forget to lock your car doors from now on," Aunt Astrid told her as she got into the driver's seat. "This neighborhood isn't as safe as it used to be."

Bea's Books

Bea's house looked more like a library than a home. In every room except the kitchen and bathroom, she had bookshelves instead of walls. The shelves reached the ceiling and had side-rolling ladders mounted on them.

In the kitchen was a trolley—a trolley!—full of books, and they weren't even all cookbooks. I rolled them into the living room.

"I read over those when I have a midnight snack!" Bea objected when she saw me.

"What, all of them at the same time?" I furrowed my brow. "That's impossible. Besides, it's a fire hazard. I'm kind of concerned about that now, you know."

At that, Bea smiled sadly and laid out a serving platter of cold smoked salmon with avocado sauce and toasted crumpets. "When were you going to tell us about that spell book, Mom?"

"It's in my will," Aunt Astrid answered from the sofa, where she sat reading. "If anything happened to me, then it would go to you and Cath—technically. You'd be advised not to move it. You're both talented and intuitive enough that you would've been able to figure out the rest."

Bea munched on a crumpet thoughtfully. "Could the lawyer have caught on that this heirloom spell book was so valuable?"

Peanut Butter hopped up onto the sofa where Marshmallow sat curled up. They sniffed each other's noses and rubbed their heads together.

Aunt Astrid replied, "I only said that it was a book, that it was part of my collection. If it was a spell book of ultimate power, people would expect me to say so."

"My mother," Bea said, flourishing her hand, "master of the triple bluff."

"However, existence of the book got out. Why act on that information only now, though?" I wondered. "This is such a tiny, quiet town. What changed?"

Bea hummed, getting into bookworm mode. "I can only think of two things. First, somebody who was close to us, who could catch every moment that we slipped—who'd catch enough of those moments to wonder if there wasn't more going on—"

"You think Ted did this?" I asked with disbelief.

"Well," Bea said, "that's only one of my thoughts. How

nice was the author who wrote the fake book, the one that actually got stolen? Did she write spells that simply wouldn't work, or did she write spells that made sure that whoever tried them wouldn't get a chance to steal the real one? Try to conjure up a magic fireball, and it could backfire and..."

"There would have been a book beside the body," I said.

"And 'whoever thought up the fake spell book' was very nice—a downright tree-hugging hippie, as a matter of fact," Aunt Astrid said, pointing at herself. She shook her head. "I'm sorry, girls. I've only bought us time."

"Don't blame yourself," I told her. "The only one doing anything wrong here is this power-hungry thief, arsonist, and murderer who's meddling in things that not even we completely understand."

Astrid sighed. "I will blame myself if it turns out to be Ted himself—an accomplice might have double-crossed him and made away with the book. Ted didn't like to talk about his family or what was going on in his life, and in the decade he's been with us—I never pried!" Aunt Astrid heaved the spell book back into her bag and joined us at the dining table. Bea poured her mother a lemonade, and Astrid gulped it down.

On the sofa, Peanut Butter and Treacle curled up beside Marshmallow. Treacle could always find a way into the house. Marshmallow also seemed to have been exhausted by the spell.

"It couldn't have been Ted," Aunt Astrid said decisively. "He wasn't interested in magic—not at all. He'd always refuse my astrology readings."

"The other thing I'm thinking," Bea said, "is that it's a newcomer. Maybe a tourist pretending to have come to see the falls."

"Or..." A thought occurred to me, and I spoke it slowly. "A new detective in town, taking the perfect position to try to turn the tables and pin the blame on us?" I remembered the necklace I'd found and took it out of my pocket. "Could this have been a clue? I found it while we were walking through, and I thought it was magical."

Bea peered at it. "Weird, but not magical—not anymore, at least."

"We were covered in magic," Aunt Astrid pointed out. "Maybe you imagined that part."

"It wasn't there when I swept the place up yesterday," I said. "It was charred. This definitely wasn't Ted's."

"Maybe a locator spell—" Bea began, and Aunt Astrid and I interrupted her with synchronized groans of misery. "All right! All right. Not yet. Not like that's any of our talents, anyway."

Aunt Astrid told her, "There are no locator spells in the Greenstone spell book although there are other spells I'm aware of."

"But," I added, "if there were a locator spell in that book... If two out of three of us weren't recovering from magic burnout right now, would we be able to cast a locator spell? What about spells in this book that would help witches so their powers weren't limited to one or two talents?"

Aunt Astrid said, "That would mean that even nonwitches

wouldn't be limited. They would have magic as well. The words, the ingredients, the gestures—all were designed to create an intersection between this world and the worlds beyond, no matter what. So, yes, it also means that witches could work outside their talents. You see how important it is to keep this spell book out of the wrong hands."

I sent the clearest pictures of the necklace from my phone to Bea's, and I deleted the rest.

Bea leaned back in her seat. "So, then... All we can do is guess until we know more."

"No," I said. "We need to figure out what's going on. We can't just wait around—not with so much at stake!"

Bea added gloomily, "We're at stake... as witches have a historical tendency to be. Ha ha."

"It will be a witch hunt at best," Aunt Astrid agreed. "At worst... Well, that worst won't happen, not as long as they don't have the book. I'm taking this home with me to personally ensure its safety!"

"We just have to wait until we know more," Bea said. "Do you really want to go home, Mom? Are you sure?"

Aunt Astrid nodded. "The Maid of the Mist is more powerful than the three of us combined, but she wouldn't be able to move the dimension pocket. There are generations of protection spells in the old Greenstone house. That's the second-best option."

"Cath," Bea said, turning to me, "you know, we've got a guest room. You're welcome to stay overnight, and Treacle is, too."

I was just about to protest that the situation wasn't that bad when Treacle spoke into my mind.

"Well," I said instead, "Marshmallow says she's not going anywhere, and Treacle isn't leaving Marshmallow."

"And you don't want to go back to your place alone," Bea finished warmly.

It wasn't until she said it that I realized it was true, never mind what was going on with the cats. I'd inherited my house from my parents. I hardly ever think about what happened there because it was decades ago, but after the big spell that day, going back there would remind me of the monster under my bed.

Most kids have imaginary friends or monsters. In a family line of witches, those imaginary beings usually turn out to be real, which can be pretty disconcerting.

So Bea drove Aunt Astrid back to her place, and I stayed in the guest bedroom.

Bea spent the afternoon making calls and drafting letters to the insurance company, and Treacle kept watch over the sleeping Marshmallow. Peanut Butter pawed at the bottom of the guest room's door until I let him in, and we talked. Yes, I had magic burnout, but I'd guess it's sort of like waiting tables when you feel as though you're about to come down with the flu or feeling as if you've pulled an all-nighter.

Peanut Butter was so insecure that he really needed a chat, so I exerted the effort to do so even though I would be completely drained of magic for the whole next day.

Our talk was mostly just me reassuring Peanut Butter that

Jake didn't dislike him and that Bea and Jake weren't going to split up and abandon Peanut Butter in a cardboard box on the side of the road. I told Peanut Butter that the stereotypes humans have about cats being proud and independent just didn't fit him.

Neither Treacle nor I told Peanut Butter about the fire, Ted's death, or the big magical spell.

I did show Peanut Butter the pendant, though. He said it reminded him of the four-sided dice that Jake's nephew and his friends played with.

I remembered those. Min Park, who was Mrs. Park's son, had been a great fan of those fantasy-adventure tabletop role-playing games when we were back at school. Once Bea's brain ate up all the guidebooks, she became the most annoying player, a total stickler for the rules. She was better at running the game and telling the players what was what than she was at playing. When we tried certain actions, we rolled dice—six-sided, ten-sided, twenty-sided dice—to determine whether the characters we played would succeed or not. The four-sided dice were more painful to step on than Lego bricks.

Of course, those medieval fantasy games had magic, and I might have let it slip once that how we played out magic usage according to the guidebooks wasn't how magic "really" worked. Min Park was a good friend, but I think he dismissed that comment as my taking a fictional entertainment medium too seriously.

I realized then that I hadn't made a lot of friends since Min had left. I hadn't noticed because my family lived nearby, and I wasn't as much of a social butterfly as Bea. Maybe animal communication had spoiled me because, to me, nothing is clearer than a pure thought, a pure emotion, a memory, or a mix of the three just dropped into your mind. I wondered if I could try something new more often—meet new people or meet familiar people in new ways.

All right, maybe I didn't mull over all of that at the time. If I did, it would have been pushed to the back of my mind, considering the much bigger concern about who knew the Greenstone legacy, which we'd tried to keep so private.

When evening fell, Bea fried up some ground turkey and potato wedges. Jake called to say he would be working overtime that night. I gave Marshmallow some of the turkey just to get her to eat something. After taking the afternoon off to rest, I was feeling better, but Marshmallow still felt terrible.

The Unusual Suspect

The next morning, Marshmallow was too sick to get up. We weren't sure if Bea would make it worse by using magical healing for what could be a symptom of magic burnout, so Bea took her to the vet, and I took Bea's claim letter to the insurance company's office after Bea told me we'd gotten clearance from the fire inspector. I was still feeling tired too, and delivering a letter sounded like less trouble.

Oh, if I'd only known!

The rain that had threatened to break the day before had passed. That day, the sun blazed in an uninterrupted expanse of blue sky, and the wind blew just enough to keep the day cool.

Most of the townspeople seemed to be in a great mood that day, whether they were in Old Wonder Falls with the cobblestones and mom-and-pop shops or in the town square with the asphalt and the view of the franchise grocery store and the falls. The same chipper cheer, I imagined, would be prevailing in the fisheries and farms and where the fruit orchards met the forest.

That day, it would have been so nice to be one of those ordinary people instead of pretending to be one, even if I was just filing an insurance claim.

Inside the insurance office, I bumped into Nadia and Naomi LaChance, twin sisters who had been Bea's friends in high school: from mathletes and drama club, respectively. Nadia spoke at a much lower register than Naomi. Nadia had dyed steel-blue hair and a tattoo of a waterfall that blossomed over one shoulder and ran down the length of her arm, all the way to her knuckles.

Naomi—who used wooden pencils to keep her black hair in a bun and wore oversized button-down shirts belted around the waist as if they were dresses (hmm, I should try that out sometime)—was there to get money to repair her car.

Old Mr. Leary, who had driven into the headlight of Naomi's ladybug-patterned Volkswagen Bug the week before, was in the office with Mrs. Sutherland, the insurance agent—well, one of the insurance agents.

I asked if I could talk to someone who wasn't already with a client, and the office assistant—a lanky, swarthy boy in his late teens named Cody, very soft-spoken and formal—directed me to the office of Mr. Nguyen instead.

Cody knocked on the half-open door. "It's Miss Greenstone, sir."

Mr. Nguyen, a hefty man about Aunt Astrid's age, seemed momentarily relieved then tried to muster up some anger, but he wasn't a good actor. He craned his neck past his desk and past the man in the long, dark coat standing in front of him. "Cody, I thought I told you I was in a meeting!"

A familiar, gravelly voice replied, "Oh, no, this is a lucky coincidence. I should be asking you these questions directly"—the figure turned to reveal Blake Samberg—"Cath, isn't it?"

"What are you doing here?" I asked, too tired to be irritated.

"I was just asking Mr. Nungooyen—"

"'Ngwhen,'" Mr. Nguyen interjected.

"—what you stood to gain from a fire at the Brew-Ha-Ha."

I gave him a slow, disdainful blink. "Lost time. Days, maybe weeks, without customers to keep our business going —when, I might add, it was going great—"

"It *was* a very successful business," Mr. Nguyen said, backing me up.

"There goes your insurance fraud theory, Detective." Sarcastically, I added, "What a shrewd use of human resources too, killing our star chef. Great way to run a food business!"

Blake nodded to Mr. Nguyen. "Right." Then he nodded to me. "Thank you both for your time." He made for the door.

As he passed by, I asked, "What, that's it?"

"I believe you." Blake shrugged his shoulders, palms up and out toward me. "We're following every lead in this investigation. I just had to make sure this wasn't one."

And he left.

"Now, you wait just one hot minute!" I left Bea's letter on Mr. Nguyen's desk as Mr. Nguyen signaled desperately at Cody to send the next client in.

Blake Samberg just rubbed me the wrong way. He was presumptuous and insensitive. He wasn't the most unpleasant person I'd ever met, but he sure could find a spot in the top three. I couldn't have been more relieved that he would be out of my sight.

So why was I following him? Why was I stopping him?

Well, I still had questions. "Would you care to update a surviving victim of this crime? What other leads are you talking about?"

Cody lent an arm to old Mr. Cartwright, who had a prosthetic leg—the real one had been lost decades before in a mountain-lion attack—and they hobbled slowly into Mr. Nguyen's office. When the door shut behind them, Blake spared a glance at the LaChance sisters, who tried to look uninterested in our conversation.

"It wasn't asphyxiation," Blake murmured. "No, he burned. The fire started in the oven, and someone made sure that Ted was right in front of it."

I took that information in and exhaled the shock and horror. "Who would do that? Ted was a big, buff guy—who *could* do that?"

"He had a concussion before the fire started. That's a mercy. But someone really wanted to make sure that he was dead. Jake's running a background check on the victim as we speak, to see if he had any enemies back in... Quebec, was it?"

"Or his hometown in France. Only his dad was Canadian. His mother was from... I forgot the name, somewhere in France." *No. This couldn't be personal.* I could only think that Ted had come in early and caught the thief in action. The fire was just a way to get rid of a witness. *Oh, Ted, I'm so sorry you got caught up in this.* "Do you think that someone from his past could have found him without anybody in this town noticing?"

"We have a prime suspect," Blake told me.

"You do?" Every intuitive fiber in my body screamed that he was on the wrong track.

"Does the name Min Park ring a bell?"

The Park family managed the big grocery store that had the view of the falls. Min had gone away for university, and life just got in the way of letter writing. His mother had been at the café on the morning of the fire, making sure that Aunt Astrid and I were okay.

"He's in town?" I hadn't known that.

We used to be very close. My intuition clouded over, embarrassed, and curled up in the corner of my mind like a cat that had missed a mouse.

"In police custody by now—or should be. I got the text message from Jake while I was in Mr. Nguyen's office. Witnesses saw him at the scene of the crime, before the fire."

"No," I said. "No, there must be some mistake. Min Park left Wonder Falls fifteen years ago for university. Ted came to town a couple of years after. They couldn't have met—not here, at least."

Blake got a notebook and pen out of his coat pocket. "Would you testify to his character, then?"

"What's relevant to the case?" I asked. "The Min Park that I knew couldn't wrestle his way out of a wet paper bag. I know this because some schoolyard bullies"—more physical than Darla had been—"once trapped Min in a giant paper bag and threw him into the pool beside the gym. I can't even remember how that happened or why he literally couldn't punch his way out. It was so long ago."

"It was a long time ago," Blake agreed, scribbling something on his notepad.

I insisted, "Min didn't do this. I knew him in grade school. He's a good person."

"Well," Blake said as he folded his notepad again and pocketed it, "most people are good people in grade school. I'm not saying there aren't bad seeds, but life is hard for everybody."

I couldn't imagine Ted and Min facing each other down—what, in some gun duel at high noon, somewhere in the Mexican desert, with their cowboy hats on? *Ted's bullet grazes Min, who falls with a shout and plays dead as Ted saunters away in his chaps and boots. Min's fallen cowboy hat rolls away like the tumbleweed in the breeze, and then when he's sure Ted's gone, he picks himself up, clutching his wound, looks to the sky, and swears vengeance—*

Okay, maybe I could imagine it, but obviously that didn't

mean anything like it could have really happened. It just meant I was weird and crazy.

"I have to interrogate him anyway, now—just to be sure." Blake said, bringing me back to earth. "You've convinced me of your innocence. That only works on you. Do you understand?"

He delivered the last line with such grimness that I had to meet the sharpness and challenge of his gaze, and I wondered when I would get sick of our staring contests. "No," I answered. "This is about my family, my friends, in my hometown and my life. I don't fight just for my own innocence and protection. I fight for everyone's!"

"Good," Blake said, with a shade of... disappointment or maybe worry. "I'll just make sure that they're worthy of your loyalty."

"How can you possibly make sure of that?"

"It's my job. I work with the proof." He turned to walk out.

I almost stopped him, but I caught sight of Nadia's girlfriend coming down the hall. It was Ruby Connors, who'd been Darla's best friend at school, and—judging by her tailored blazer, hot-pink plaid A-line skirt, and stiletto heels—they still went shopping together.

I couldn't conceive of Min holding a grudge against Ted, but some people did hold grudges.

"Did you know about this?" I demanded, striding toward the three of them.

The twins began to deny too loudly, but Ruby objected at

just the right volume for someone who'd just come in and had no idea what was going on.

"Min Park." I told them, "He's back in town, and he's under arrest—or under interrogation, whatever—for burning down the Brew-Ha-Ha."

"That's ridiculous," Ruby said. Her manners always came off as just a touch too deliberate. She had a wide-eyed, expressive face and coquettish mannerisms that showed up in tiny ways: the way she walked, the way she flipped her hair. She had always gotten on my nerves. "I mean, you're like his best friend." Oh, and her presumptuous blanket statements.

"And your brother," I told Ruby, "was Min's worst bully. You'd think after fifteen years, Reuben would have given up on it and moved on, but if the first thing he does—"

Nadia got between us, saying, "Now hold on a minute—"

"—is call the cops on Min for some trumped-up charge. If he's still got Min in his crosshairs as if we all haven't grown the hell up—"

"I saw him!" Cody exclaimed, as if he'd been saying it in his own soft voice the whole time I was railing at Ruby. "I was at the Brew-Ha-Ha before the fire. I saw him. I told Detective Samberg yesterday."

I turned to Cody and tried to calm down. He was just a kid, after all. "How did you know it was Min Park?"

Cody twisted his fingers together nervously. "I didn't know. I just said who I saw: this tall Asian man in a three-piece suit and classy shoes. It didn't look like someone who'd caused an accident. It looked like he knew what he was doing."

I didn't want to call Cody a liar, but my tone might have been on the sarcastic, incredulous side. "What were you doing up and about at that time?"

"I was coming back from the lake."

"And why were you at the lake?"

"I was doing some research on glow-in-the-dark jellyfish and algae." Without my asking, Cody supplied, "Not for school. I just like it, even though I knew I had work today."

Glow-in-the-dark jellyfish and algae? I was sure that Ontario wasn't the climate for those things, even if they did exist, but I'd have to ask Bea later on.

Naomi hummed in the way she did when she wanted to call attention to herself without people realizing. "I was at the Parks' grocery store that morning, and Mrs. Park was saying something about heading over to the Brew-Ha-Ha to talk sense into her son." She flinched when I glowered at her. "I told Detective Samberg that yesterday, too. He asked who could have been there so early, and I answered! I'm sorry, I thought you already knew he was in town."

Ruby cleared her throat. "Can we get back to the part where you chewed me out for something my brother did? I am really not involved with his life anymore."

"Or any of her family," Nadia added, taking Ruby's hand.

"Not that that's any of your business," Ruby added primly. "You shouldn't just jump to conclusions and yell at people, Cath."

I felt like a jerk all of a sudden. "I'm sorry. It's been a really awful couple of days, and—that's no excuse, I'm sorry. It's just that nobody's telling me anything."

Ruby seemed to accept my apology. "After the stuff's been filed for Naomi's car, why don't you come with us for lunch? It doesn't have as many kinds of tea and coffee as the Brew-Ha-Ha, but there's the Night Owl café—you know, part of the Night Owl bookstore? And their shepherd's pie is pretty good."

"Thanks," I told them, "but that sounds more like Bea's thing, and she's taken my aunt's cat to the vet, where I'm supposed to meet her after this. Maybe next time?"

"Just call us when things settle down," Naomi said.

When I left the town square, the sun was still out. I pulled out my cell and called Bea.

"Mission accomplished," I droned. "How's Marshmallow?"

Bea answered, "I looked into healing her, but it just looked bad enough that I wasn't even going to try, so the vet just put her on a drip and started a round of antibiotics. Maybe all the stress yesterday lowered her natural immunity or something. She's an old cat."

"Guess who I ran into?"

"Oh! Umm, uh... Min Park!"

I was startled. How did everybody else know these things? "How did you know that he was back?"

"Internet. You should really get on a social network, Cath—any social network. Any at all."

"Well," I said, feeling in my pocket for the chain and triangular pendant. Most of the soot had rubbed off, showing symbols on the faces of the pendant. I rubbed my fingers along the chain to shine it even more. "Some welcome-home he got—Detective Samberg was at the insurance office, and he told me that Min's being taken in for interrogation."

Her first response was low, loud, and long with Bea's disbelief. "No!" The next was a chirrup. "Seriously?"

"I've got to go over there," I told Bea. "Would you check in on your mother for me after you're done at the vet's?"

"Of course I will."

"Great. I'm going to get to the bottom of this." I ended the call and stood up, then I sat right back down. Bea could explain better the connection among the physical, the mental, and the magical when it comes to health. Magic burnout had left me feeling dizzy if I moved too fast.

Sometimes those old feelings of being orphaned just come up again and overtake me. I don't even realize it, so I just take for granted that I have to go some things alone.

I thought I was going to be the one to solve this mystery. I thought, with my best childhood friend as the prime suspect, that I had to be the only one. I was swallowing my anxiety over the possibility that I really didn't have what it took.

I've walked a delicate balance all my life, and in two days, that tightrope had snapped over the edge of a waterfall. I thought I had to fix this.

Sometimes I forgot that I did have a family and that, with them, I'm never really alone.

Scratching Post

Peanut Butter doesn't do well alone. When he's alone, sometimes he tries to talk to me in his head and tell me what he's up to. He can get needy and lonely. It's a good thing, really, that Treacle always finds ways into Bea's place that the feral cats in the neighborhood can't manage. Treacle might only keep doing that because he considers Peanut Butter a lot of fun to mess with, but he's never gone too far with his teasing. Besides, Peanut Butter appreciates the company.

That day, Treacle stayed with Peanut Butter even though he would rather have been somewhere else. That wasn't usual for Treacle since he was a wanderer. Peanut Butter was content just to have Treacle around until Peanut Butter heard the scratchy popping of Treacle's cat claws against the carpet.

If they'd been humans, I could imagine this scene playing out with Treacle striking a punching bag with more grim determination than an ordinary fitness regimen would warrant—with the punching bag being a waterbed or something else breakable.

"Hey, hey—don't do that!" Peanut Butter told Treacle with a plaintive meow. The rest of the message would have been mind to mind: *"Mommy and Daddy don't like it. They only let me do it because I have blunters on my claws, and you don't even have those."*

Treacle replied, *"Good thing your mommy and daddy aren't here to stop me, then."*

Peanut Butter began to puff up his fur with fright. *"They're going to think your scratches are my fault, and they'll throw me out!"*

"You just said that you have nail blunters, so it couldn't be you. Go take a catnap."

"No! You stop that right now! Just stop it!"

"You can't make me." That wasn't a challenge but simply a statement of fact.

Well, it was a statement of what Treacle thought was a fact, anyway.

So Peanut Butter mauled Treacle.

Jake wasn't much of an animal lover at all, let alone a cat person. He wasn't allergic or, necessarily, cruel to animals—he'd just gathered that removing a cat's claws was a normal and sensible surgical procedure. He thought it was equivalent to neutering, without knowing, of course, that our cats couldn't care less about never getting to be fathers.

The declawing issue had been Jake and Bea's first really big fight, and with Peanut Butter's placid personality, all the arguments against declawing didn't apply as much. Peanut Butter was neither a hunter nor a fighter and was even willing to give up his claws to stop the arguing, but Astrid and Bea worried about muscular atrophy among other side effects, and the procedure would be something they couldn't undo. Preventing scratches on the furniture wasn't worth the risk of ruining the life of a living creature.

Jake had tried to get Peanut Butter to use a scratching post, and Peanut Butter did his own best to use the scratching post, but he wasn't always aware of when he started scratching at something because he did it out of anxiety most of the time.

I discovered nail caps for cats made out of vinyl, which stuck on with a nontoxic adhesive. Bea used them instead, and everybody was happy. Those were the nail blunters Peanut Butter was talking about.

For a timid kitty with nail blunters, Peanut Butter had quite the bite. He was no match for Treacle, who'd had a lifetime of street fighting the feral cats, but the attack came as a surprise to both of them.

Treacle's claw caught Peanut Butter's ear, enough to scrape the fur but not to draw blood. When Peanut Butter flattened his ears and gave a low, dangerous *mrrowl*, Treacle batted at Peanut Butter's head with a sheathed paw.

Treacle hissed. *"What's gotten into you?"*

Peanut Butter returned to his insecure anxiety for a moment but then steeled himself. *"You tell me. What's gotten into everybody? Is Marshmallow dying?"*

Treacle quickly hid his alarm. *"No. Marshmallow is just old and tired from doing magic."*

"Why would Marshmallow do so much magic?"

"I don't know! Because Marshmallow can do magic? We live with special humans. Magic is a part of life, and you and I will grow into it."

"I believe that's true"—Peanut Butter leapt onto the sofa and padded over to the window—*"but there's still something you're not telling me."*

Treacle leapt up to Peanut Butter and unnecessarily batted at his head again. *"Of course we never tell you anything! You're more prone to dying of fright than a rabbit!"*

"Ow! Stop it!" Peanut Butter leaped back a bit then licked his paw to clean his face. *"Are any of us going to die in some other way?"*

Treacle thought about it. *"I don't know. It's important that we all stay safe."*

Peanut Butter took that much better than Treacle expected. *"I want to know what's trying to hurt us."* Then he added, *"I'll fight to protect my family if I have to."*

"So would I," Treacle told him. *"But this is for our humans to find out. The best way that we can help them is to stay out of trouble."*

"You never stay out of trouble," Peanut Butter grumbled.

Treacle looked out the window and perked his ears up. *"You know what, P.B.? You're right. The best way to help would be to stay out of trouble..."* He bounded over to the cat door. *"It's not the only way to help, though!"*

"Wait for me!" Peanut Butter followed.

Outside, Treacle regarded Peanut Butter with apprehension. *"We need to go to the place where the bad thing happened. We have sharper eyes and better ears than humans. Maybe we can know something that they don't know."*

"Then I'll come with you. Two more eyes and ears should be twice as good!"

Treacle still didn't move. *"I might ask the street cats. They'll test us both harshly."*

"I'm a fast runner." That was a brave statement, coming from Peanut Butter.

"Stay away from the cars," Treacle advised before heading out.

A Doomed History

Meanwhile, Marshmallow and Bea returned to the old Greenstone house and spent the rest of the day there with Aunt Astrid. Marshmallow was still on her drip, in a cage, but she was feeling well enough by then to listen. That's how I know what went on that afternoon.

Aunt Astrid had been too exhausted to make herself a real breakfast, so Bea called to have a pizza and two liters of soda delivered and then basically threw together everything she could find in Astrid's pantry. Her resulting dish was a sort of rigatoni chicken stewed in white gravy, mushrooms, and parboiled root vegetables.

Aunt Astrid finished off the whole pizza by herself and still had room for a couple of bowls of what could be called Bea's accidental chowder.

Bea helped herself to a bowl while flipping through the spell book.

"For someone who loves books so much, you put them at risk a lot," Astrid warned from the soft armchair in which she rested. "That's one of a kind, bound by hand by Imogen Greenstone more than five hundred years ago. Every word in it brims with arcane power, and oh, the disaster that a single grease spot could cause—"

"All right, all right! I'm putting the soup away now, Mom." Bea set the bowl aside and smiled sincerely at her mother. "I'm glad that you have the energy to lecture me again."

She continued to flip through the supple vellum pages, reading the unfaded ink. It didn't feel like a magic book.

Whoever had written the Greenstone spell book took extra care to tie magic walls to the cover and pages. The spells would be powerful enough to break through the walls if they were read aloud or performed, but just reading them silently as Bea was doing wouldn't release anything too dangerous.

Bea read on with growing incredulity. Finally, she couldn't take it anymore. "These spells can't be real. Bringing the dead back to the prime of their life, using only a pound of bone from the deceased? Growing back all of the bones and the organs and the muscles, after which the resurrected would have eternal youth?"

"Keep reading."

Bea did. "Huh. This ritual required a coven of thirteen, and it sounds to me as if magic burnout took the lives of twelve of them—even though they took every precaution over the course of the nine months required to bring the subject back to life."

Astrid hummed an affirmative through a mouthful of chowder, swallowed, and chased it with a gulp of soda. "That's two of the reasons why we couldn't do that to Ted."

Bea flipped the page over again and found the other reason, written in a version of English older than standardized spelling. When Bea deciphered it, she balked. "They made a zombie! A violent undead cannibal!" She slammed the book shut and jumped back from it as if it were about to explode.

Aunt Astrid was unfazed. "Don't be afraid of the book itself, Bea. You know what they say. Those who don't learn from history are doomed to repeat it."

Bea objected, "When that doomed history is written out like a how-to manual, then it's more like those who do learn from history could have that problem! This is dark stuff, Mom. If it's at risk of falling into the wrong hands, we should destroy it—shouldn't we? It's not as if there's anything useful in there, anyway. It's all stuff that can cause fatal magic burnout and not one remedy for actual magic burnout! Not one!"

"No, no, no." Aunt Astrid beckoned her daughter. She took Bea's hands in hers and added seriously, "There are some good spells in there—if they aren't used the wrong way—and there are some blank pages, still. Those dark spells were written for a dark age, but you're an intelligent and kind young woman. You're a healer, too. You could be the one to add that magic burnout reversal spell, one day, to that book."

Bea shook her head. "I could never!"

Aunt Astrid peered at her in that amused sort of way that the wise gaze at smart alecks. "Only those who have lived forever and know the meaning of the word 'never' should be allowed to say it. Listen, Bea... Magic will always be around, lurking at the edges of the known world. It will always be powerful, but the question is whether it will also be wild. The book answers that question with, 'No, not if anybody in the Greenstone family can help it!' That's why we must keep it. When there's a disease, there's also an antidote. And what are the antidotes made out of? Disease. We need to know everything there is to know about magic so we can fight the bad part. This book is our antidote."

Someone knocked on their door.

"That might not be Cath," Bea said, taking the book and handing it to Astrid. "We need to keep this hidden."

"In plain sight," Astrid said. "You know my style."

"If it's Jake, remember that he likes books as much as I do. Also, he doesn't read silently."

"Oh. Right." Aunt Astrid shifted to hide the book under her seat cushion.

The caution was warranted, too, because Jake was indeed at the door. Bea greeted him warmly and asked about the investigation. He said he'd bring them up to speed, but first he asked after Aunt Astrid's health.

"Low blood pressure," Aunt Astrid lied. "It gets worse with age, but it's nothing serious."

Bea offered him a lunch of accidental chowder. "Sorry, sweetheart, you missed the pizza." She quickly finished her own bowl of chowder. "And I miss Ted already. He knew how to make a potage."

Even the simplest dish of his would have a dash of an herb or spice to make it something more than ordinary.

"The whole town will miss him," Jake said. "Anybody who'd ever been to the Brew-Ha-Ha, anyway. Darla Castellan was inconsolable."

"Histrionics," Aunt Astrid said dismissively. "That little tart."

"Oh, Jake wouldn't fall for that! Would you, sweetheart?"

Jake shrugged. "She might have been inconsolable for the wrong reasons, but I'd say that it was honest grief. You can't string along a dead man."

Bea blinked, processing that. "Darla... stringing along... Ted?"

Jake sat down with his bowl of chicken chowder. "Yeah. Apparently, they were dating—off and on. She must have preferred that kind of melodrama." He ate a spoonful. "This isn't bad." He caught the flabbergasted expressions on Astrid and Bea's faces. "He never talked about his life outside of work, then? I was hoping that one of you could confirm or discredit something I learned from Miss Castellan about Ted's troubled family history."

Aunt Astrid's eyes had widened in disbelief. "No," she said. "He never mentioned any of this to us. And Darla—that's a surprise."

"He must have known that Cath would never let him hear the end of it," Bea remarked. "Darla was so mean to Cath in school."

"I guess his good taste stayed literal," Jake said. At that moment, Bea's cell phone rang. Jake checked the number on the screen for her. "It's Nadia LaChance."

He handed the phone over to Bea, who answered with, "Hey, girl!"

"Please control your sister."

"Sis... You mean Cath? Is that what this is about?"

"Yeah. Cousin. Whatever! I hate her so much today. Do you know that she started yelling at Ruby for no reason, and my useless sister apologized to her? Ruby even invited her to lunch!"

Bea flinched. "I hate to break it to you, Nadia, but there's nothing to be done about Cath when she's on a mission. And this time, it's actually important."

Nadia swore and hung up.

Aunt Astrid groaned. "Cath wouldn't. Not in her"—she glanced at Jake and lowered her voice—"condition."

"Blood pressure issues run in the family," Bea told Jake, which wasn't a lie but wasn't an explanation either.

Jake accepted it anyway. "I'd rather Cath not interfere with the investigation, of course. Samberg will slap the cuffs on some poor kid for jaywalking—you know how I've been complaining about that—but when it's serious like this, he could be the best person on the case. If he could keep his mind on the case, that is." Jake smiled in something between amusement and veiled chagrin.

Bea read the expression instantly. "You think that Detective Samberg has a crush on Cath? They only just met yesterday!"

"Oh, no, not a crush. Samberg went to follow the money." Jake tried to gloss over the crush business. "Insurance fraud attempt took an unfortunate turn for the homicidal—that was Samberg's theory. That's how he thinks. I know it's ridiculous. He tells me that my personal life compromises my investigation skills, and we part ways. I have to say, if we had more detectives in this town, I wouldn't be working on this case, but I have to since Samberg is the only other detective now that Bill went to Montreal. He's new, and he'd mess up without me."

Aunt Astrid and Bea murmured their encouragement.

Jake held a hand up for silence, maybe partly out of humility but mostly out of excitement. "But Cath? She knocked him off that trail in under a minute. Samberg can only be head over heels in love with her."

Aunt Astrid gave a long, drawn-out "Ohhh..." the way mothers do when the young women they've always taken care of find someone special. She was probably imagining us walking down the aisle.

Bea waved her hands in refusal, almost laughing. "Enough!

Enough, please, no more relationship gossip! Tell us about Ted's family."

"I don't know how much I'm allowed to tell. It's only Miss Castellan's statement, but..." Jake sighed. "Ted Lanier might have gotten caught up in some organized crime syndicate and run up some debts, and maybe they took it out on his son."

"Is that why Min Park is your prime suspect?" Bea asked. "He's Asian, so he must be a member of the yakuza? That's so racist!"

"My wife is psychic," Jake remarked.

"No!" Bea's voice pitched high with momentary panic. "Cath called me while I was at the vet's, that's all. She'd heard from Detective Samberg that Min was being held there."

"Interrogated," Jake corrected, "not jailed. We've found no connection between Min Park and organized crime. None at all. We only have witnesses that put him near the Brew-Ha-Ha at the time of the fire."

Aunt Astrid objected, "The Parks have always been upstanding members of our community. Mrs. Park was the first person to check in on us when the fire brigade came."

"Was she?" Jake's voice sharpened.

An awkward silence ensued before Aunt Astrid answered, "Yes."

"That's interesting." Jake set his bowl down. He'd had only a couple spoonfuls. Distractedly, he said, "Well, that was delicious, but I've got to get back to work now."

"Jake, wait!" Bea said. "I have to tell you something."

Aunt Astrid kept silent.

Bea went over to embrace her husband. "Please stay safe," she begged, her voice muffled against his shoulder. "Don't get shot. Don't get held hostage in a warehouse somewhere by gangsters in suits. Please come back home safe to me."

"Of course I will. I promise." Jake returned her embrace. After a moment, he wondered aloud, "Would this thing that you're doing be equally convincing to Cath?"

"Nope," Bea answered accurately. She pulled away, more cavalier. "Cath's a force of nature. You've just got to deal with her as she comes. Good luck!"

They both said, "I love you," and then Jake left. Bea saw him out the front door.

When she returned, Aunt Astrid breathed a sigh of relief. "You really had me going for a moment there, Kitten. I thought you were finally going to tell him about our family secret."

"This is so wrong." Bea hugged herself and ambled to the window to watch Jake cross the street. "We can't throw the Parks under the bus, ruin their lives, and frame innocent people just so that we can keep our secret! Maybe if Jake knew, he could solve the case for real and make a cover story for us."

"Maybe," Aunt Astrid allowed. "Maybe not. Would you be so cruel as to burden him with the same double life as ours, and him without any magical talents?"

"I just wish I could do something."

At that, Aunt Astrid suggested, "Act normal. Call the LaChance girl, make amends, and go out with your friends tonight. Tell them about my low blood pressure and Cath's worrying penchant for vigilante justice." When Bea looked doubtful, Aunt Astrid added, "That will help us all more than you know. I'll be here with Marshmallow. Do you really want to be running around and yelling at people with Cath? How much of a good cop can you really be?"

Joy Ride

I didn't know any of this was going on as I headed toward the police station. Out of the corner of my eye, a black car slunk up beside the sidewalk with the passenger's window down. Blake Samberg peered at me and waved from the driver's seat. The car slowed to a stop as I approached and stuck my head in the window.

"So," I asked him, "Am I breaking some speed limit for pedestrians? Are you going to write me a ticket?"

"No," he answered. He really didn't have a sense of humor. "You're on the way to the station. Let me drive you."

"You know how townsfolk talk. I wouldn't want them to get the wrong idea, to see me picked up in a squad car." I silently noted that the vehicle was unmarked. I hadn't even known the Wonder Falls Police Department had cars like that.

"Nobody we take in for an interrogation rides up front."

I raised an eyebrow, mulling over how shady the entire situation could be.

Blake continued, "Besides, the way you were hollering back at the office? It sounds to me as if you can take care of yourself."

"You're not swinging by for Jake, then?"

"Jake?"

I stared at him before carefully enunciating, "Detective Williams."

At that, Blake gave the slightest of flinches and shook his head.

"What happened? Would your chief even let you just split up like that?"

Blake looked at me gravely. He looked serious all the time, from what I knew of him, but his darkness deepened. "I'll tell you on the way."

With my magic burnout, could I really take care of myself against Blake? But why assume the worst? I didn't know enough about anything yet. I'd only suggested that Blake had done it because I hadn't liked him when I'd first met him, which had been one day earlier.

I got into the car.

"Would you say that honesty with partners is important?" Blake asked as he turned down the sunny main street.

I looked at him sidelong. "Is this a date?"

"Williams thinks that I stick to the rules too much when I call him out." Blake gritted his teeth at the injustice of it. "He's too close to this case to be objective."

"Because of Bea?" Even though I knew Blake was angry—and even taking into consideration both my having just met him and his being in the driver's seat—I couldn't let that stand. "Oh, please! Have you met Jake Williams? Have you seen Jake Williams meet anybody else? He's close to everybody in this town. He's such a nice guy that everyone tells him everything. They can't help it."

"That didn't happen with me. When I told Jake everything that was on my mind, he went off alone and told me not to go near him. Let him explain that to the chief!"

"Stop the car right now!"

He didn't brake with a jolt, but he reluctantly slowed down and warily looked at me. No, not at me—past me.

The reason I'd told him to stop was that he'd been so busy ranting that he hadn't seen Cody about to cross the street. Now Blake eyed the poor kid the way Treacle eyes a mouse. Treacle, unlike many other cats, does not play with his food.

"This isn't a crossing area," Blake murmured.

I saw him moving to pounce and pulled him back by his jacket. "We're investigating a murder!" I snapped. "It doesn't count as jaywalking when everybody knows cutting across Main Street here is the fastest route to the grocery from the town square."

I was sure that would be wrong in Blake's book, but every driver in Wonder Falls knew it. Somehow, setting up the crossing lights and painting the pedestrian lane just kept getting passed over in the beautification society's itinerary.

Then Blake did something unexpected. He smiled, just for a moment. "You said we're investigating a murder. We."

"Separately." I was not disarmed by his smile. "I wouldn't want to interfere with the official investigation, but I can't sit back and do nothing." I added, warning him, "I'm not nearly as objective as Jake."

Blake nodded and drove on. "You know, I thought you'd stopped me there because you'd had enough of me after two seconds and wanted out, as if you'd rather walk the rest of the way. I'm glad that wasn't the case."

"I can see your elation."

I didn't mean to pick on him. The idea that Jake was nice to absolutely everybody in town except for Blake must have stung enough.

"As civil servants, Williams and I have got limitations that a citizen such as yourself wouldn't have. I wouldn't get in your way, either. But I'd like to be in the know."

"Oh, would you?"

"Jake plays nice. You're not afraid to speak your mind," Blake said. "I know this case is personal to you, and that's why you won't stop until you've found the truth. That's why I need you. I couldn't admit to being a confidant, though."

"Or an informant!"

"Do we have a deal, then?"

"None that either of us could admit to," I said.

We'd arrived at the police station.

Blake got out of the car first, came around to my side, and

opened the door for me. He muttered, "Williams thinks that I stick to the rules. He's wrong."

"Yeah. Real renegade, you are, letting that jaywalker go." I hesitated, but if I wanted him to think we were working together—and that I was getting anywhere—then I had to give him something. "I stole evidence from the crime scene."

Blake looked stunned then glanced around to make sure no one was listening.

I continued, "I'm sure that it belonged to the murderer, but I'm not sure if the murderer noticed that it was gone. If I show it to Min Park and he doesn't recognize it, then that would prove that he's innocent."

"Or it would implicate him, say, if he does know that he lost this piece of evidence and would deny anything that would tie him to the crime."

"That would still be something." Part of me was convinced Min wouldn't know what the necklace was, and he would be honest about that, too.

Blake nodded curtly. "Let me see what you took."

I shook my head. "Let me see Min."

I wanted to see Blake's reaction, too, when the pyramid necklace came out. I would have to be quick.

Lost and Found

The police station was entirely open, with no cubicle walls or even offices, only an empty holding cell in one corner. I saw the interrogation room with the one-way mirror, where I hoped Min was.

Blake told me to wait on a bench by the cooler while the police chief, old Talbot, took him aside for a talk. Blake explained that he and Jake still kept each other up to speed on important information despite having parted ways for the investigation. The police chief was more concerned about why they'd parted ways in the first place.

A third man emerged from the hall and approached them, and the police chief greeted him with respectful formality as "Mr. Park."

I barely recognized him, and not just because of the suit, the haircut, the pimple-free complexion, and the fancy shoes. The Min Park I'd known had a habit of hunching his shoulders protectively. He stammered everything he said as if he were breaking the worst of news to the listener.

Whoever this man was looked dismayed, even embarrassed—who wouldn't be when taken in for an interrogation? —but he had a serenity about him that comes only from being comfortable in one's own skin. His hair was gelled back neatly, and his eyes were warm.

I approached them cautiously, hardly believing my eyes.

Min recognized me instantly and shouted, "Cath! Cath!" Laughing, he pulled me in for a big hug.

Even though he'd never done that before, something about the way he did it reassured me that my old friend was still in there. The best way I can describe it was that Min was like a puppy. Min used to be a sad puppy, but he turned into a happy one.

I couldn't help laughing, too. "I didn't know that you were in town!"

"I wanted it to be a surprise." He looked around. "Not this kind of surprise."

"You are the silver lining in the nightmare storm cloud that the past two days have been," I reassured him. I turned to Blake and Chief Talbot. "Are we all done here?"

Chief Talbot kept a suspicious eye on Blake as he answered, "We wouldn't dream of keeping you, Miss Greenstone."

And Blake, keeping a steely look on me, answered, "Keep in touch, Cath."

Min looked at Blake, startled, and couldn't disguise his

renewed dismay. I used the opportunity to drop the pyramid necklace behind me as I took a step back.

"Cath," Min began, pointing at Blake, "is this—?"

"He's Jake's partner. You know Jake Williams?"

"Bea's husband." Min nodded.

"Jake and Blake are both working on the case with the fire at the Brew-Ha-Ha," I answered, hooking Min's arm in mine. "I'll show you around town for the rest of the day. It's been a long time. You'll be surprised at how little has changed."

I stepped on the necklace chain and pretended to slip a little. "Oh!" I said, leaning down and picking it up. "This must be yours. It must have fallen when you tackled me." I straightened up and dangled the pyramid pendant in front of us, looking sidelong at Blake.

He was good at not changing his expression, but I could see that the blood had drained from his face. Blake, the hard-boiled criminal detective, recognized the pendant as I held it up—and it scared him.

Caught you, I thought grimly.

Min said, "Huh, I thought I lost that. Thanks."

I turned my head toward him. "Wait, what?" The necklace dropped from my fingers in my shock. Min already had his hand stretched out to catch it. He wrapped the chain over his index and middle fingers and stuffed the bundle into his breast pocket.

He extended his arm gracefully. "Shall we?"

I mustered up some courtesy and took his arm. "So we

shall! Why do you have a four-sided-die necklace and keep it in your breast pocket?"

"Oh, I joined a club—kind of," Min told me. "It was boring. I don't miss anyone, and they didn't deliver on anything that they promised. But they gave that away as part of their new membership packet, and I think it looks kind of cool, so I kept it. It never matches with anything I usually wear now, though."

I still had a bit of magic burnout, but if Min had had a memory spell cast on him, or if what happened was magical in any way, I'd still feel it.

Hide and Seek

Meanwhile, Treacle and Peanut Butter had found their way to the crime scene. Treacle hadn't been to the Brew-Ha-Ha since he was a kitten. Ted hadn't allowed it after that first time, which Treacle remembered well.

Ted had claimed banning Treacle was for hygiene reasons. I'd argued that Marshmallow came into the café and even the kitchen all the time, but Ted had argued that Marshmallow would stay put, whereas street cats went all over the place and you couldn't stop them.

I'd almost argued that Marshmallow's hair got all over the place and nobody minded, or that maybe Ted had allowed Marshmallow because he thought Aunt Astrid had more clout than I did.

Really, Ted was afraid of black cats and particularly afraid of crossing their paths. I'd noticed he wasn't interested at all in Aunt Astrid's fortunetelling, either. Maybe a black cat with a star on his forehead was too ominously witchy.

Treacle had kept out of the way since telling me Ted's fear, or else he waited out front. The town had more interesting places for a cat to explore, anyway.

Aunt Astrid had been right. Ted wasn't interested because of a belief in magic. If he had been outright opposed to it, then he first would have stolen and destroyed Aunt Astrid's completely nonmagical tarot cards and slightly magical crystal balls. If he'd found the secret trapdoor into Aunt Astrid's nuclear war bunker, Ted would probably have ignored the book and used the space to store wines or something.

But that was all over, and the cats were at the Brew-Ha-Ha. Treacle hadn't been there in a long while, as I mentioned, and Peanut Butter had never been.

The place was also crowded with investigators.

Jake had dropped in to check on what his colleagues had turned up so far. The kitchen still had the yellow crime-scene tape cordoning off the area, and it was more crowded than it should have been because all the bagging of possible evidence and photographing of the scene should have been done the day before.

"I'd hate to say it," began Jason Boone, who was in charge of cataloguing, "but we're in over our heads with this. We could use someone more practiced, you know, dealing with cases like this."

Jake knew what he was talking about. "Blake Samberg's made up his own mind about what happened, and I'm letting him investigate that. Let's just do our best to get the evidence in."

Boone sighed. "Those damn strays." He waved a rubber-gloved hand toward Treacle and Peanut Butter, who were slinking in from what used to be the restaurant area.

Jake turned to look. "Those aren't strays!" He was surprised to see Peanut Butter out. He jogged toward them, as if skittish cats would keep still in a strange place—even being approached by somebody they knew. "Get back here, Peanut Butter! And you!"

"Leave it to Williams!" Boone called out to one of the investigators, who still wore their protective overalls, paper shoes, face masks, and white rubber gloves. "Don't contaminate the evidence!"

Peanut Butter hid in a corner. Treacle ran behind the bar, where the trapdoor was. Jake stopped at the door, realizing the cats would run if he kept going after them.

He crouched down in front of Treacle. "All right, come on... come on, kitty."

Peanut Butter calmed down a bit and came up to Jake, rubbing his head against Jake's knee and meowing.

"See? Peanut Butter's fine here with me." He picked up Peanut Butter in one hand, reached out to slowly and gently catch Treacle in the same way, lost his balance, and slipped. Treacle dodged the falling Jake as Peanut Butter leapt from Jake's grasp.

Boone poked his head into the room. "Are the cats giving you any trouble there, Williams?"

"No," Jake said gruffly.

Peanut Butter bounded over behind Treacle, who was licking his own paw. Jake pressed against the floor to push himself up, and the latch nudged ever so slightly, telling him he wasn't pressing on solid floor.

"No," Jake repeated quietly as he pushed himself up. "They're not giving any trouble at all." He found the handle, disguised as a missing floor tile, and pulled the trapdoor up.

Treacle, seeing the opportunity, bolted into the opening.

"Boone," Jake ordered, "get the rest of the team in here."

Jason looked at him blankly. "For a cat?"

"For an investigation! If Astrid Greenstone knew about this, then she forgot. Maybe the perpetrator didn't."

The only clue they found was a shoe print. They, like Aunt Astrid and me, didn't have Treacle's sharp feline senses.

To Catch a Fish

I wish I could say that I enjoyed that afternoon, spending time with Min Park after a decade apart. In all the ways that mattered, we'd stayed the same, still best friends. The stuff with Ted and the spell book had thrown me for a bad turn, though.

We dropped by the Parks' grocery store, and I saw the new Min Park rubbing off on his family.

Mrs. Park's wrinkled face beamed with joy as she loudly declared what an accomplishment her son was.

"My husband is a manager. He doesn't own this business, you know."

"I know." I'd known that since I was young, but I still thought Mr. Park had a decent job.

"Min owned his tech company. He sold it! He is... how do you say... set for life!"

Min gave an embarrassed laugh. "Let's not be too loud about that, Mom."

A lot of things had changed since our childhood. Being wealthy wasn't just a pipe dream anymore. A memory nudged at me, of Min and I wondering what we would do if money were no object. "I guess you can have that UFO built, huh?"

"I can say, with my degree in engineering, that this is completely possible. Give science just another three years to advance, and I'll bet sound waves and cymatics will bring us closer to a functioning tractor beam than magnetic force." Min tapped his chin thoughtfully. "We won't get to go into outer space, though—at least, not with the windshield-like clear panel—because of the radiation. Besides, we'd need to travel faster than light to get anywhere interesting. I'd rather invest in terraforming a planet."

"But it would look just like earth! There'd be no point!" I exclaimed with a laugh. We'd both known that since we were kids. It was part of the running joke.

"Seriously, though." Min Park put an arm around his mother. "I think it's time that I settled down and started taking care of my parents in their old age."

Mrs. Park hugged him back. "My son is ridiculous. So thoughtful! But no. That's your money. Your father and I love to manage this shop. We love this town."

Mrs. Park had the same warmth and reassuring presence as Aunt Astrid. Mr. Park tended to be steelier. He and Min weren't getting along by the time Min was in his teens. I'd always been intimidated by Mr. Park.

So that's why, when Min excused himself to go talk with his father, we both understood that would be a private conversation.

I needed to hold my own conversation with Mrs. Park.

"You could have mentioned that Min was back," I said to her.

"I am sorry." She did look sorry. Her voice became quiet again. It wasn't a whisper, but I had to lean close to listen. "I had my reasons. Please don't make me repeat them. Jake Williams has already interrogated my whole family."

I said to her, "If you won't tell your side, Mrs. Park, then other townspeople are going to. I heard one witness say that you wanted to talk sense into your son. Why didn't he have any sense in him already?"

Mrs. Park sighed.

"He was at the Brew-Ha-Ha before it caught fire, and you knew. Don't let me keep thinking the worst, Mrs. Park." I said sincerely, "Please."

"All right," Mrs. Park said. "Min hates this town. After he sold the business, he traveled all over the world, looking for nice towns and cities, sending Mr. Park and me postcards saying that we should move there with him. Mr. Park refused him, told him to quit showing off."

"Well, that's harsh. Did Min come back as a final act of persuasion?" I asked, looking across the grocery aisle at Min and his father. They were shaking hands.

"No. He knows his father too well." At last, Mrs. Park mustered up some strength behind her voice. "Still, he came back to this hometown of his, from his travels so far away. He couldn't sleep. What do you call it? Plane..."

I thought for a moment. "Jet lag?"

"Yes. Thank you. He wanted to go out for a walk. When the other detective came to arrest him, he said the whole thing was suspicious."

"Blake said so? Detective Samberg?"

"The nerve of that man!"

"He's suspicious of everything and everyone, though."

"What about the witness—that teenage boy who said that Min started the fire? What was he doing? Studying the glow-in-the-dark plants and animals in the lake, in the woods, alone? I can't believe it, but he... that detective—" She cut herself off.

I thought about Cody. When Bea had been his age, she'd been more interested in experimentation and travel than just reading about scientific facts and foreign places. After graduating high school, Bea had planned and saved up to go backpacking around Antarctica, of all things. There's a fine line between genius and craziness, and I sensed the same attitude in Cody. "I believe both of you. It's complicated. Cody must have been mistaken."

Mrs. Park, uncharacteristically, reached out to take my hand. "Thank you. This is the best life we could have hoped for, Mr. Park and I. Still, it's so difficult in this town! The way people talk!"

I couldn't tell her how much I understood. Being a witch

might have been a private subculture for generations, but you couldn't tell just by looking at us that we weren't like everyone else.

On the other hand, once nonwitches knew who was a witch... Let's just say history doesn't show that people have a good record of getting over and getting used to it so that witches could just be treated like people again.

At least Min had gotten the chance to shine, to change whatever people used to think about him.

"That's why," Mrs. Park told me, "I told him that I would rather he go find a nice Korean girl to settle down with."

I felt a brief twist of envy, which I tried to disguise as surprise. Min was a friend. Min was a good old friend. "If that's what Min wants, he shouldn't have any trouble! He's obviously a catch, Mrs. Park."

"It is difficult to catch a fish gone over the falls." Mrs. Park made no gesture to emphasize what she really meant, so figuring it out took me a while.

"So that's the real reason that you didn't tell me," I said to her. "You think Min likes me?"

Mrs. Park shook her head. "I don't think. A mother just knows these things."

"Min and I are friends," I said, as much to myself as to her. "We even need to get to know each other again. You've got the whole afternoon to see that we're just big kids, and it's just like before the fire. It's just like it was before this awful investigation started."

I wanted that to be true. I'd grown up with these people even if Mrs. Park didn't consider me an honorary family member. Everyone in every family has their... not secrets, not privacy, just boundaries. Expectations. The Parks didn't deserve the suspicion of other townspeople.

But I couldn't help harboring my own suspicions.

Respectable Accusers

At dusk, Bea called me on my cell. I could barely hear her over the background noise and electronic music.

"Bea, where are you?" I asked, standing on the grocery store's balcony. I guess it was meant for employees on their smoke breaks. It was empty and had a view of the town.

"I'm at the Night Owl. Decent book selection, terrible café. But that just might be today. Everybody who would be at the Brew-Ha-Ha came here instead. It used to be quiet enough to browse and do some reading."

"How's Aunt Astrid?"

"Well enough to shoo me outside for a night out with the girls."

The girls in question hollered their hellos.

I groaned, thinking about that morning. "Has Nadia forgiven me yet?"

"Nadia? I talked her out of reporting you to Detective Samberg for a hate crime, but I'll tell her that you're sorry—"

Nadia's voice rose above the background chatter to cuss me out: "Ruby's brother is a sore spot with her, you know. If you think he was unpleasant to you at school, imagine living with him."

"Let me go to the restroom where it's quieter," Bea said.

"He was so mean to Min at school," I said. "And Ruby's the best friend of the worst bully, Darla Castellan! The only friend, by now."

"With friends like Ruby, Darla doesn't need to antagonize anybody," Bea said.

The background noise became muffled. Bea must have found the restroom.

"Darla killed Ted for fun, then," I said.

"Oh, don't start! You know that I only have so much tolerance for mean, insipid gossip." Bea droned, "Clutch the pearls! Darla strung our Ted along, and that's why she didn't divorce until recently! Oh, my stars! Min Park's so handsome now—and a criminal! He's sexy now because he's dangerous! So much chatter in this town."

"No offense, Bea, but I thought your friends would have a better perspective after Naomi and Ruby got together."

"Apparently, if you can't beat 'em, then join 'em." Bea sighed. "The chef at the Night Owl is willing to stock our pastries once the Brew-Ha-Ha building is back up, by the way."

"That's great news."

"Now," Bea said, "you tell me something important."

I told her about a possible fraternity that marked its members with magical pendants.

"And Min was a member?" Bea asked. "You've got to bring him over here! We can ask him together! Discreetly, of course."

"With your friends treating him like an escaped felon when it was only an interrogation?"

"That'll show more people that it was only an interrogation. And an interrogation is just questions, like we'll ask him. Bookstore café, police department—just innocent, curious questions to find out the truth—"

At that moment, the balcony door swung open, and Min strode through, talking on his phone, sounding upset.

"No, today—tonight, whatever!" He paused. "I'm not going anywhere. You already know where my parents live and at which inn I booked a room. You should be the one to come to me for follow-up questions." He paused. "Fine." Then he hung up.

He told me, "This is just embarrassing. The chief wants me to meet with him for some follow-up questions. It's not as if they found new evidence in the past six hours."

"Ridiculous," I agreed, hanging up on Bea, knowing that she'd heard him. "I told Blake that you couldn't fight your way out of a wet paper bag. He probably wants to update that information since we aren't ten anymore." I laughed. "You know, I can't even remember that? What was it, a wet paper bag in a pool beside the gym?"

Min didn't laugh. "It was a burlap sack. Reuben Connors tied the sack shut, hauled me onto a boat, and pushed it downriver toward the falls. He called me 'pipsqueak.'"

I remembered then. Maybe I'd changed it to a paper bag because the reality was much more depressing.

I had chased after that boat, reached out with my mind for the Maid of the Mist, and begged her to do something. If she had had any part in it, I didn't see her, but I like to think that's when I awakened to my power. All the eels and fish and everything in the lake swarmed around to bump against the boat, pushing it away from the rapids and the falls. The boat found a riverbank instead, and I got Min Park out of the sack safely.

Maybe I'd thought it was a swimming pool because I confused myself with how Darla would steal my swimsuit or my clothes while we were swimming in phys ed class. The other girls in my grade, who tried to stay out of it, were probably even worse than the ones who laughed. I'd felt so alone.

All that had been a lifetime ago for me. Min's face, clouded over with an almost Blake-ish brooding, told me that —despite the wealth, the achievements, and all the new friends he'd met in foreign places—the horrors of his youth weren't over for Min. I felt terrible for him because I completely understood.

"Reuben wasn't just a bully," I realized. "He really liked to make people suffer, and it hasn't served him well in this town. He's a nothing, Min. He has no power over you."

"Right," Min said. I could tell he was forcing a smile.

"We've all grown up. Every encounter since high school ended is out of my mind. Reuben who?"

"That's the spirit!"

"I won't let him ruin this comeback!"

"Atta boy!"

"However, getting taken into police custody for arson and murder isn't something that I'd 'let' ruin my day so much as it's kind of a day-ruiner as a point of fact."

"He did accuse you, then?" I wondered.

Min replied, "He threw a shoe at the police-car window when it passed him, and I was in it."

"That's not a statement the cops would find worth considering," I said confidently. "No one in this town would bend an ear to such a lowlife."

"And my more respectable accusers?"

"They'll be proven wrong," I said with a simple confidence I didn't feel. I'd used magic for Min. Maybe he'd remembered those strange happenings when I'd let some magic slip or forgot that he wasn't supposed to know.

Maybe he'd come back for revenge, but he knew we wouldn't use our magic to help him with that, so he somehow figured out we had a spell book and took it.

I wanted to ask about his father and hear something good about how their relationship would proceed. A growing part of me even wanted to have a moment with him on that balcony, watching the sunset. He seemed so innocent, and I wanted to fight for that innocence if it was true, against all the lies floating around town.

But the truth was that I didn't know him anymore.

I didn't know anything anymore.

So instead I said, "Do you want me to come with you to meet with Talbot?"

Min shook his head, still looking glum.

It was on the tip of my tongue to say, "Too bad, I'm coming with you anyway," but I was too confused and had no plan.

Gone

So I went home. I took a detour to the falls to clear my head, though. I've seen enough photos and sunsets or sunrises over the falls to last a lifetime, but that time of day when drivers don't know whether to turn on or leave off their headlights just washes the world in soft blues. It's nature's own magic.

I might have accidentally discovered a cure for magic burnout right then. I wonder if nonwitches just feel magic burnout all the time. The static crackle that had been distracting me the whole day smoothed over until I felt more like myself again. My mind flowed out into the world and into all the connections I'd made—as it was meant to.

As my head cleared, an image entered my mind, of Aunt Astrid lying on the downstairs living-room carpet, and my body went cold with shock when I smelled blood through Peanut Butter's nose.

"Help! Oh, help!" Peanut Butter wailed in my mind. *"Treacle's gone, and Grandmommy won't move! I found her this way, and I didn't know what to do!"*

An image that felt more like one of Peanut Butter's memories appeared in my mind. He'd followed the smell of Bea's shoes to a loud place full of people—the Night Owl.

That was interrupted by an earlier memory—Min Park's formal shoes in an alleyway.

"I thought that Chief Talbot wanted to meet me," Min said. He must have been speaking to somebody.

"I said that to throw Miss Greenstone off our trail," answered a low, gravelly voice. "I really apologize for the inconvenience, Mr. Ark."

"It's Park."

"If things had gone differently, we would be calling one another 'brother.'"

"Mom!" Bea screamed in the present image. She fell to her knees beside Aunt Astrid's body. Sobbing, she checked for a pulse then for magic burn, and then she took about four deep breaths to calm herself. She needed a calm mind to do her healing.

The memory flowed back in. Peanut Butter was hiding in some old crate or box in the alleyway, knowing that Treacle was listening in from a nearby fire escape.

"I don't have any brothers."

"No. You don't claim to be part of the Order anymore, right?"

Treacle yowled as he fell to the ground. He landed on his feet, as cats do, and Blake swore and grabbed my cat.

"I didn't know what to do!" Peanut Butter wailed again. *"They went away together. They took Treacle with them!"*

I snapped out of it, reached for my phone, and dialed for an ambulance as I bolted home. The dispatcher kept asking me questions or giving me directions as if I were actually at the scene, which of course I wasn't. I could only see through Peanut Butter's eyes.

As soon as the dispatcher said the ambulance was on the way, I hung up and crossed Main Street into the town square. I didn't want the dispatcher to overhear the background noise of traffic and people milling about and realize I wasn't actually at home. Hiding these things had become second nature. I could only hope that was good enough because I might have been getting a reputation with the dispatcher.

The ambulance got there quickly, which was a minor relief, but I wasn't there with Bea and Astrid to know what was going on, which was a major anxiety.

When I arrived at the house, the door was closed and locked. I took the spare key from the flowerpot hanging on the trellis and went inside. I found Peanut Butter in the living room and Marshmallow still in her cage in Aunt Astrid's bedroom. All Marshmallow knew was that Aunt Astrid had gone to make herself dinner, and she'd taken the book with her.

Peanut Butter caught me up on Bea's cover story: she'd found Peanut Butter wandering around outside the Night

Owl and decided to take him home. On the way, she met with me. We decided to go to Astrid's place instead, where we found her. I called the ambulance and went upstairs, out of sight of the paramedics. Bea had called Jake to pick me up.

With a little of Peanut Butter's help and a lot of Marshmallow's, we searched the house for the book. The old Greenstone house had a few loose floorboards that Aunt Astrid would hide things under, and Marshmallow knew them all. Peanut Butter and I searched them all.

I had no doubt about it. The real spell book was gone.

The Order

Jake and I were silent as he drove me to the hospital. I kept reaching out to Treacle in my mind, but something kept blocking me—until suddenly, the blockage wasn't there anymore.

"Is it safe to talk now? I thought there was magic—bad magic, from somebody else." Treacle spoke in my mind, but I couldn't see anything from him but pitch blackness.

Contrary to popular belief, cats can't see in complete darkness. Their eyes just function much better than most human eyes do at low light levels.

"Treacle," I murmured. *"What happened?"*

"I'm not hurt."

"But where are you?"

"I don't know. It doesn't smell familiar."

I felt a steel grid through Treacle's whiskers and smelled dye and fabric that had been used to cover the grid.

Treacle asked, *"Why couldn't I talk to you? Was it because of magic burnout? You seem fine now. More than fine!"*

"No," I told Treacle. *"Not magic burnout. Something else."*

Jake cleared his throat as he drove. "Funny thing. Treacle and Peanut Butter interfered with the crime scene today."

"I keep telling Treacle not to go wandering off!" I whispered, hating the tremor of terror and regret in my voice. Then I bit my tongue. "I mean, I do what I can. Locking the cat flap door and all that."

Jake gave me a doubtful look. "They helped us to find evidence."

"Really?"

Jake nodded his head toward the dashboard, where I saw some fully developed photographs of the inside of Aunt Astrid's bunker. I picked up one of a shoeprint. Through Peanut Butter's eyes, Blake had some nice shoes, too.

"I think these animals really do know what's going on sometimes," Jake said.

I told Jake, "That's more than me these past two days."

AFTER THE HOSPITAL workers rolled Astrid out of the emergency room, Bea slept sitting on a plastic chair by her mother's hospital bed. That would make it easier for Bea to use her talent.

I warned her about magic burnout, but she turned her

despairing eyes to me and asked, "What use is my power if I can't save my own mother?"

I sat down on the armchair in the corner and didn't argue.

When she couldn't heal Astrid any more, Bea said, "I can't believe I didn't check for the book!"

"It was gone before you came in." That wasn't exactly reassuring.

"There were supposed to be protection spells in the Greenstone house. What happened?"

I said grimly, "The Order. They have magic."

"Min did this? Or Detective Samberg?"

"I don't know. Still, it's the Order that broke down the protection spells. Aunt Astrid's magic burnout was worse than mine. She and Marshmallow would both have been numb to the spells disintegrating." I massaged the sides of my head. "Something keeps stopping me from getting in touch with Treacle. It's either Min or Blake. They were meeting with each other while Aunt Astrid was being attacked. That much I do know."

Peanut Butter had bolted out of his hiding place in the alleyway the moment Min and Blake walked away. He'd gone to alert Marshmallow that Treacle had been captured.

"We need to know more about this Order," I said. "How many members could come to Wonder Falls? Is our town secretly being invaded by a secret society run by frat boys?"

Bea sat up. "What can we do? Look them up on their website? Run 'The Order' through a search engine? Ask Blake Samberg and trust he isn't lying?"

At that moment, someone knocked on the door of the hospital room.

I opened the door to find Blake waiting outside, holding a pet carrier hidden badly by his coat. Inside the carrier, Treacle put his paws against the grid of bars and meowed.

"I've made a mistake," were the first words out of Blake's mouth.

"No, I have," I said, taking Treacle from him. "Come in. Shut the door behind you."

I set the cat carrier down at the foot of the hospital bed.

Blake came into the room. I gently shut the door, turned, and slapped Blake across the face.

I was seething. "Confidant *and* informant, did you say? It was a huge mistake to trust you!"

Blake rubbed his jaw and flinched.

Bea stood up, trying to calm us both down. "I did not," she said, "just witness my cousin and soul sister assault a law enforcer!"

"As if he's to be trusted!" I was answering Bea, but my eyes were on Blake. That time, he lost our staring contest. "You're as crooked as they come, Blake Samberg."

Blake held his hands up as if he were under arrest. "Not usually. Only this time."

My jaw dropped. "Oh," I said sarcastically, "that makes it all better, then!"

"I thought I'd cracked the case. I thought that it was only about me." He glanced over at Bea. "Can I say anything more specific with her around?"

"You'd better," I said to him. "Because it's her mother who was getting assaulted while you had your showdown with Min."

Blake groaned. "I thought he wasn't going to say anything!"

Bea and I glanced at each other.

My outrage faltered as I remembered that he didn't know Treacle was my magically mind-linked pet cat—or, apparently, that I had any magic at all. I mustered up my outrage again and said, "Min Park didn't say anything about this club except that he was in it. I just figured some things out. So, tell us about the Order. No, wait, first tell us how you knew this was my cat."

Bea squatted to slide the latch open and let Treacle out of the carrier.

Blake answered, "Cats are the one thing Jake and I can talk about without fighting. He mentioned that if I saw a black cat with a star-shaped scar on its forehead, then he was probably yours."

"Right." I sat down on the edge of the hospital bed and gestured to an armchair in the corner. "Now, tell us about the Order."

Blake took his long coat off the carrier. From one pocket, he drew a palm-sized, leather-bound journal with a pyramid embossed on the cover.

"This is what they give to the legacy members of the Order. My father was a member, and he wanted me to join because he'd made some good friends there. He paid my dues at first. We host charity fundraisers, help entrepreneurs, give each other a leg up on the job network—that sort of thing. Country clubs. A few parties."

I said, "You did strike me as a party person."

"Never." He traced the triangle on the cover with his fingertips. "The pattern on this pyramid shows where in the hierarchy my father was. Until you get pretty high up, you usually only know who's immediately above you."

Bea asked, "How does the Order decide on hierarchy?"

"The higher-ups pick and choose who's going to be directly beneath them. If you progress in something called the Mysteries, then you get..."

"Higher up?" I offered.

Blake corrected me. "Deeper in. Attending solemn rituals in robes, drawing circles on the ground in chalk, dribbly candles, and saying the same thing as everybody else in the room at the same time in a language that nobody really speaks anymore."

Bea smiled. "The Mysteries! You figured out how to do magic!"

Blake's eyes flashed with resentment. "Mrs. Williams, there is no such thing. My father got too deep into it. I'm a man of science and reasoning."

I believed his last sentence. "So you don't mind if we keep that book?"

"Borrow it. I'd rather not forget how much it messed my dad up." He tossed the journal to me, and I caught it. Bea, with her magic burnout, edged her chair away. The Order journal wasn't like the Greenstone spell book, where every page and especially the cover had some seal that had to be unlocked for the magic to flow. Somebody had been careless in making it. The pulp of the pages twisted the physical world into the other worlds.

Blake continued, "I wanted out. After my father passed away, I quit paying my dues. The members would come to where I used to live and say something about legacy—how it means that you can never leave the Order. I filed complaints against them, even restraining orders, and finally I changed my name and moved here," he concluded, "where I thought that I could leave all that behind me."

"So," I said, "when you recognized the necklace—"

"I thought it was a warning from them. Min made clear that it wasn't just me who was from the Order. I met up with him in secret—I admit to that. I told Min to tell the rest of them that I was ready to barge into their chapter with guns blazing." Blake laughed. "Min's left the Order, too! They let him, though, because he wasn't a legacy. He didn't need any of their help to become a success, obviously."

I stifled a sigh of relief but still had to play it cool. "You said that you cracked the case."

From his other jacket pocket, Blake drew the chain and pyramid pendant. "Min gave me the Order's membership amulet you found. It isn't his. The pattern shows somebody too high ranking."

Bea suggested, "Could there be DNA on it still?"

"It's been passed around too much," Blake pointed out. "And Cath did say that she picked it up after the fire."

"Is it all my fault you can't catch them, then?" I demanded. "For tampering with evidence? What about the way you withheld crucial information pertaining to the case—and not for anybody else's sake but yours?"

"I'm saying that was a mistake! You don't have to forgive me, but just to start making it up to you, I thought you should be the first one to know what the next course of action is, and it won't be a DNA test." Blake stood up. "They—the Order—do have a website directory, and the Wonder Falls police force does have an IT team. We can cross-reference what I know about these patterns, what they signify, and narrow down who it might be. They might not categorize every member, but..."

I finished, "It's worth a try."

"The only problem is..." He heaved a sigh. "I'll have to tell Jake. And Chief Talbot, of course."

Bea and I started talking at the same time.

"Just do it."

"He doesn't bite!"

"Good luck."

Blake shrugged on his coat. "I just thought you deserved to know what this was all about."

I saw him out the door. "Thank you," I told him, "for trusting me with this after I slapped you. I really hope it turns out all right for you."

"I hope your Aunt Astrid gets well soon." Then Blake left.

Inside, Treacle batted at the journal with his paw.

"The Order stirs up trouble in more than the magical way," Bea remarked. "That could be all they need to get caught."

"But they have magic," I said. "They have *our* magic, and it's powerful!" I picked up the journal. "This has a blocking or privacy spell on it. That's why I couldn't get to Treacle when the carrier was covered. It's definitely effective, but whoever wrote the spell didn't put any safety catches on it so that it would only apply to somebody trying to read the journal. They don't know what they're doing."

"We can't get the Greenstone spell book back until we know which member of the Order came into Wonder Falls, killed Ted, and attacked my mom." Bea sighed. "You know this is the hardest thing for me to say, but we have to let them do their jobs—Blake and Jake and Talbot. Everyone."

"They can't do it properly if we don't tell them everything. They could be running out of time and not even know it!"

"Mom would know what to do." Bea brushed away a few stray wisps of hair from her mother's forehead. "I wish she'd wake up."

With that, Bea and I lapsed back into the gloomy silence we'd shared before Blake came in.

Trial by Fire

Jake urged Bea away from the hospital bedside, using the fact that he had a gun license and was in a better position to protect Aunt Astrid in case any agents of the Order tried to attack again.

"You think they'd attack again?" I asked him. They had what they wanted, the spell book.

Jake answered, "She might have seen something. The attacker wouldn't want to be identified."

I hadn't thought of that.

"Fine," Bea said, to my surprise.

Jake nodded. "Blake will drive you. He should be right outside."

I gave Bea a confused look.

She mouthed, "They have the book. They won't bother Aunt Astrid."

As we walked out, I whispered, "How can you be so sure?"

Seeing Blake, Bea adopted a more normal tone of voice. "They're in over their heads, drunk with power. Isn't that right, Blake? About the Order? They wouldn't hound Aunt Astrid like they did you since they don't know her personally."

"Better safe than sorry," Blake murmured.

So Blake drove Bea, Treacle, and me home. Marshmallow and Peanut Butter were already in the car. He said it would be safer if Bea and I were in the same place, and he'd stake out the house in case any members of the Order tried to attack us, just in case they were targeting everyone connected to the Brew-Ha-Ha.

The entire case had turned him and Jake into real partners again. Jake and Blake. The safety of innocent civilians was more important than arguing over attitudes.

"What makes our caution so important is that even I don't understand the motive," Blake said. "A couple of officers followed the gang violence that made up Ted Lanier's history and came to a dead end. Darren Castellan, Darla's ex-husband, has a solid alibi, and Jake says that the marriage had run its course for him—he wasn't jealous. So Ted's death had to have something to do with the Order. Why set one person on fire and leave another concussed?"

I played along. "You did say that Ted had a concussion. Maybe when Bea brought Peanut Butter home, she'd interrupted the arsonist."

"And nothing was burgled?"

I lied. "No, nothing."

Bea supplied, "It makes no sense."

"Well, Bea, Blake did describe them as basically a mob. Maybe they like to cause destruction, and they believe it's not that bad because they're all doing it together and laughing about it afterward." I reasoned, "They'll still go about it in different ways because they're different people."

The car pulled into my driveway. Bea carried Marshmallow in the cage into my house, with Treacle and Peanut Butter following.

Blake stopped me at the door. "I can't shake the feeling that you're holding out on me, Cath. After today, I swear I have no secrets from you."

"I don't have secrets, either. I never did! I have privates." That sounded really bad, didn't it? I blamed Blake's cheekbones and the composition of the rest of his face for distracting me. A hint of a smile appeared on his face; he wanted to laugh. Wearily, I added, "You know what I mean. Secrets. The day's not over until I've had some sleep. Then we'll talk. Yeah?" Without waiting for a reply, I patted his arm and walked past him.

Treacle walked me up to my room. *"In the cellar below the place where the fire happened, I smelled something."*

I wanted to theorize and think some more until everything fell into place, but I was too exhausted. I fell into bed without changing my clothes.

I DREAMED that Aunt Astrid and the Maid of the Mist were

one person, and I felt silly for not realizing that they were. Her braids cascaded in a loud hiss of flowing water that sounded like rain. From the balcony of the Parks' grocery store, I watched a meteor shaped like the pyramid pendant of the Order tumble from the sky and crash into the estuary of the three waterfalls.

Blake stood at a chalkboard like a teacher and said, "But you see, it isn't possible for this to happen."

From my school desk, I raised my hand so I could take my turn to talk. "It did happen. My Aunt Astrid is in the hospital now because of it. You said the Order did this."

Blake shook his head and looked around. "Does anybody else know the correct answer? The Maid of the Mist."

Aunt Astrid, in the seat beside me, wasn't raising her hand. She looked right at me and said, "I'm waking up."

"What?" I asked, confused and hopeful.

As if repeating herself even though she was not, Aunt Astrid said, "Sometimes, the future that I see is fixed."

"I refuse to believe that," declared a voice from my other side. I turned to see Darla Castellan as she'd appeared in high school. More quietly, she suggested, "Senior moment yesterday, maybe?" Darla swung her arm as if to strike me, holding a shoe with a strangely shaped heel—a kitten heel, they call it. I ducked, and the shoe flew past me.

"Aunt Astrid!" I shouted. I should have taken that hit. If only I hadn't been somewhere else...

But where Aunt Astrid had been sitting, Ted Lanier sat,

pressing star-shaped cookie cutters into a piece of rolled-out dough.

Bea took the seat on his other side. She gloomily added, "We're at stake. As witches have a historical tendency to be. Ha. Ha. Ha."

At her final "ha," Ted burst into flames. In an instant, the friendly face I'd known in life became the charred remains I'd caught sight of.

At that, I stood up. "I'm done with this." I turned to leave and entered a ballroom instead of a classroom. Everything was made of glossy marble. Walking was difficult in the ball gown I was wearing.

Min Park stood in the middle of the room, looking perfect in a white tuxedo. "Do you dance?" he asked, extending his hand toward me.

Music filled the room—but it wasn't music. It sounded like several people intoning the same thing at the same time in a language so old that nobody should speak it anymore.

"I don't know what this dance is called," I told Min.

He put one hand on my waist and held one of my hands with the other. "Trial by water," Min answered. "One, two, three. One, two, three. Repeating history."

"No." I laughed as we danced. "I'm pretty sure that this is called a..." *Waltz* was the word, but I forgot it in the dream. "A waterfall?" I looked down at our feet to make sure I wasn't stepping on his and he wasn't stepping on mine.

Our foot maneuvers looked strange. He seemed to be

stepping where I had just stepped. It didn't make sense. His shoes were nice, though.

I looked up to see that my dance partner was Blake, not Min.

"We were all under orders," he said to me. "Dress code. Bloodline legacy. What to say, how to think—it's a cult that takes over your life."

I didn't know what to say to that, so I asked him, "What's this dance called again?"

Blake stepped back and moved my hand in a circle, signaling me to spin around. I did so, and Reuben Connors in his fireman gear pulled me to his chest and answered, "Trial by fire."

I shouted in surprise and struggled to push him away.

I woke up struggling against the quilt.

The Social Network

As Bea filled the food and water dishes for all three cats, I made pancakes and eyed the morning sky suspiciously from the kitchen window. The sun shone bright over the neighbors walking their dogs, the shingles of the suburban houses, and the police cars driving by on their way to Aunt Astrid's home.

When the pancakes stacked higher than the distance between Bea's elbow and her wrist, she yelled at me to stop.

"What are they waiting for?" I wondered aloud. "They have what they wanted, our spell book. Why aren't they using it?" I ate my pancakes over the countertop by the sink so I could keep looking at the sky suspiciously.

Bea, at the table, spooned maple sugar over her pancakes and bacon. "I don't know," she admitted. "I've read that book from cover to cover—only once, but..." Bea didn't need to be so modest. She had a great memory for everything she read.

"I can only guess that every one of those spells comes at too high a cost for them. It isn't just a spell book. It's almost a how-to manual on different human sacrifices!"

"Between Ted and Aunt Astrid, the Order obviously isn't squeamish about hurting other people." I remembered what Treacle had told me the night before. "Treacle did some investigating, too. He smelled something in Aunt Astrid's nuclear bunker. Forensics probably wouldn't think to look for it, and I wouldn't even recognize it with my human nose."

Treacle and Peanut Butter sniffed each other's noses. Then Treacle, on a mission and tail up, stalked out the door.

The doorbell rang. I started, grabbed for something in the kitchen that I could use as a weapon, and bolted after Treacle.

"Cath, calm down!" Bea called after me.

Through the door, I could hear Jake's laughter and a voice that sounded like Blake's except that it was happy. I recognized it as Blake's for certain when he said, "Okay. Bye, kitty!"

I opened the door as Bea jogged up to me.

"Cath," she said, wrenching my weapon from my hand, "that's an egg beater!"

I had dripped pancake batter all down the hall. Peanut Butter was licking it off the floor behind me.

Jake looked from Bea to me and back. "Either way, Cath wasn't going to hurt us."

"Rough night?" Blake ventured.

"Good morning," I answered stubbornly. "I made too many pancakes. Please come in and eat some."

Blake and I went down the hall first.

Bea took her husband's hand and murmured, "They're both learning human ways!"

"I know! I'm so proud," Jake murmured back.

I turned to glower at them. "I can hear you!" Just because I wasn't a social butterfly like Bea, that didn't mean I was socially awkward.

We all sat at the kitchen table. Bea bustled about, being the good hostess, getting the extra glasses and asking who was on shift or stakeout to guard her mother.

I should have been the one making our guests comfortable and asking those questions, but I was too busy wracking my brain for why the Order would wait to cast such powerful spells as the ones in our spell book.

Jake spoke first. "The lead with the Order was a major breakthrough."

"Don't get their hopes up," Blake said to him. "The social network on the Order's official website doesn't list everyone. Min Park wasn't on it because he quit lickety-split, and some higher-up members get certain privileges."

"It's still further than we would have gotten in two days following French organized crime syndicates." Jake gave Blake the look I imagine fathers give their sons to remind them of something they'd been scolded for, and I realized Blake was still covering for me. Jake might have known I was investigating privately, but if he'd known I'd tampered with evidence... Well, Jake just might have found it in himself to be meaner.

"The Order is exclusive," Blake said. "They're superstitious but not any less macho."

"So?" I said. "Would they break into Aunt Astrid's home, attack her, even kill her chef, just because she did tarot card readings and tea leaf readings? Why not start killing in Sedona? Or Glastonbury, on the other side of the pond?"

"That's what we're trying to say," Jake said. "Mrs. Colette Lanier had a reputation in her town for giving astrology readings, up until her death from cyanide-poisoned biscuits."

"That were star-shaped," Blake scoffed. "It's just the sort of message the Order would send. Those cowards!"

Jake nodded. "The Order has a worldwide network. Maybe it wasn't Ted's dad who crossed the wrong people, but his mom."

Bea and I looked at each other. I knew we were both thinking the same thing. She and I have had to hide that we were witches all our lives. Aunt Astrid let it slip a little for harmless fun, and someone broke into her home and attacked her. Mrs. Lanier was poisoned to death, and we don't even know if she was a real witch. But the Order was allowed to have an online social network. It wasn't fair.

"New legacy," Blake said ponderously. "New blood, new people, new initiative, new mode of operations... and judging from their lodges—which have gone into disrepair since my old man's time—not as many resources to cover up their criminal ventures. You can only pull strings to get someone out of jail from outside of jail."

"We've got security on high alert both around the

perimeter of this house and around your mother's hospital room," Jake assured his wife.

Bea said, "I still want to stay with her. Maybe my being there would help."

I knew it would help Astrid. I was just afraid of what it would do to Bea. "Take Marshmallow with you," I said to her.

Jake looked doubtful. "I don't think having a cat in the hospital room would be very hygienic—"

"But Mom loves Marshmallow," Bea said.

I said, "She needs the drip removed and a vet's checkup, too. Aunt Astrid wanted to have him groomed the day of the fire, but she was too tired."

"If he's groomed first, it should be fine," Blake added. "Besides, what's a hospital but a vet for people? And you never hear at a vet's that it's not hygienic to have people running around."

I wouldn't have put it that way, and maybe Jake was already convinced, but in any case, after that, Jake and Bea left with Marshmallow.

Blake saw them off then turned to ask me what I'd been hiding from him. I knew he would. He'd prepared me without knowing it.

I interrupted, "Have you logged into your account on the Order's website?"

He looked at me with surprise.

"Really? Had nobody in the police department thought of that?"

Rejoining the Brotherhood

The Wonder Falls Police Department outsourced its computer savvy to Winnifred Hansen, whose image matched the wholesomeness of her name. She made video tutorials for quilting and knitting that Aunt Astrid loved. I hadn't known she'd also coded and designed the websites for every major business in Wonder Falls. She knew a lot more about computers than that too, if you can believe it.

Blake and I met the middle-aged Mrs. Hansen at her house to tell her our plan. For someone on the cutting edge of technology, she wasn't much for getting straight to business. She made Blake and me coffee and suggested that the Brew-Ha-Ha be made into an Internet café.

"Forget the small-town charm of Old Wonder Falls," she told me. "I haven't seen the sun in days, and I'm just fine."

Blake faked a cough to tell me to be cautious.

Winnifred caught it instantly. "Hey," she said, "I'm helping your investigation, aren't I?" She grinned mischievously. "So, if some whippersnapper with an entrepreneurial spirit and a lousy attitude finds her website under"—the next part was lost in a whirlwind of jargon that I doubt even Bea would have been able to decipher—"and it's allegedly by me, then what are you going to do?"

"We've got laws against that," Blake objected. "I would not recommend it."

I understood the first part, or I thought I did—Darla. I'm not the only one in town who doesn't take to Darla Castellan.

"I understand that the lady in question has that effect on people," I told Mrs. Hansen sympathetically. Of course, I'd never done magic to ruin Darla's life, and hacking might as well be something like magic done by nonwitches. I felt a little guilty, egging on Mrs. Hansen to use her skills against someone else, so I added, "She'd be more occupied by her divorce proceedings, I've heard."

"Oh," Mrs. Hansen said. "I've been divorced a few times. It's a hassle, I can tell you. I'll go easy on her from now on, then. Goodness knows there's been worse than her in town, lately."

That prompted us to remind her of the Order, and she led us into her den, where her computer was. After that, Blake simply had to sit down and type.

After he'd logged in, Mrs. Hansen nudged him aside and set about browsing. She observed, "Well, Detective Samberg, if you were afraid of stalkers, I can tell you not to worry. The permissions on your account say 'sour grapes' to me!"

I asked, "What does that mean? Is Blake's account no good?"

"Not entirely. I have more access now than I've had for hours, but everything important is encrypted. Of course it is. Whether I try to figure out which members of this site might be in Wonder Falls or who else in Wonder Falls might be on this site..." Mrs. Hansen shrugged. "I only have two hands."

Blake sighed, but not with relief. He said, "I know what would make this easier. Excuse me, Mrs. Hansen..."

Blake went to a chat box and typed, "Moved to Wonder Falls. Done some thinking. Time to rejoin the brotherhood."

"Are you sure about this?" I asked Blake.

Blake shook his head.

I took his hand. "Then don't do it."

"But there are innocent people being attacked," Blake murmured.

I drew myself up. "You shouldn't be one of them. I don't want you to be one of them!"

Mrs. Hansen scoffed, reached over, and pressed the Enter key.

"Mrs. Hansen!" I shrieked.

"Oh, spare me. Samberg knew what would make this easier. He was right."

Blake stared at the screen in mute horror, so I spoke up. "You're out of line! Those are very dangerous people!"

"You think that was out of line? Honey, you haven't seen

anything yet." Winnifred typed a string of numbers I didn't recognize, followed by the words, "Message me."

Blake found his voice too late. After Mrs. Hansen put that message through, he said, "That's my cell-phone number."

"Consider it a burner." Mrs. Hansen looked him over and said sarcastically, "Oh, I'm sorry, I didn't realize you had such a full address book and active social life."

Blake's phone rang. He leaped up and backed away as if a dog were attacking him. He wriggled his phone out of his pocket and threw it in the air.

I caught it. "Calm down, Blake! I'll answer it. They'll think it's a wrong number and hang up."

"No!" Blake said. "They'll hunt you down for that alone. Give it back to me. I'll play along with them until we can get them behind bars."

I lobbed the phone back at him. He caught it, steeled himself, and then crumpled. "I can't. I can't do it."

I wrenched the phone from him and actually looked at the screen that time. "Oh, it's just Jake." I answered the phone. "Hi, Ja—"

"There's been another fire," Jake said. "Meet me at 78 Whitewater Street, corner of Black Lake Bank. It's in Old Wonder Falls."

"That's Nadia LaChance's place!" I said.

"Cath?"

I tossed the phone to Blake, who caught it and said, "Yeah, I'm on the move. Mrs. Hansen?"

Mrs. Hansen had begun typing furiously. "See yourselves

out. Lock the door behind you. I'll call Chief Talbot if anything comes up, and you're welcome for the coffee."

On the way out, Blake asked me, "Who's Nadia LaChance?"

"At the insurance office yesterday morning—you couldn't have missed her," I said to him. "She's the closest Wonder Falls town ever came to having a Goth girl, so she stuck with that fashion all the way through her twenties. The Order's really scraping the barrel, aren't they? If they're targeting anybody who looks the slightest bit like they believe in magic, should we be guarding the kindergarten next?"

"It must be more than that," Blake said. "Cath, what aren't you saying?"

"She hates my guts. She has ever since..."—well, scratch that theory—"yesterday, after the fire. Umm..." What else was there to say? "She has a live-in girlfriend, so this could be a hate crime. She has an artistic Bohemian twin sister."

Blake took all that in. "Maybe she and her twin dress up like each other to trick people, and one of them is evil."

"Now *that's* scraping the barrel!"

Another Attack

When Blake and I arrived, I was horrified at catching sight of Treacle on the second-story balcony of Nadia's house.

"I found the smell! What I smelled yesterday!" Treacle thought to me. *"She's still inside!"* Treacle sent me an image of the interior of the house.

"Treacle, get out of there!" I thought.

"She fed me treats! She always does! When she didn't this time, I knew it was because of these other people who came downstairs and went away. They left the door open, so I went upstairs and found her like this. They started this fire. Maybe she saw their faces!"

Out in front, the fire brigade seemed to be having some problems with the nearest hydrant. Reuben Connors was almost laughing. "Let it burn out! It'll be fine."

Blake was just looking in the direction I was—he didn't

know what Treacle had told me. "He's a smart cat," Blake said. "He'll find his own way out. Cath?"

I glowered at Reuben, looked back at the balcony, steeled myself, and—despite Blake's protests—ran into the burning building.

The smoke and ash stung my eyes, and the heat was like an oven. I pulled the front of my shirt over my nose and mouth so I could breathe and ran through the fire as quickly as I could. Flames won't burn unless you actually touch them for more than three seconds, but they were growing, and I was surprised by how quickly I ran out of air because the smoke was so thick. I felt I was drowning without any water.

When I got to the bedroom, I was squinting so hard I had to close my eyes and just feel around for the body. The image Treacle had sent me helped, but at that moment, I wondered if I'd gotten myself into real trouble.

I felt a leg then an arm. No time to check whether she'd broken any bones or bled out anywhere—I couldn't see a thing.

I hauled the slackened body up and heard something drop, like a phone—maybe she had called the fire brigade herself. Then I half dragged, half carried Nadia to the balcony. On my back, she shifted. Good. She was still alive.

I took a huge, gasping inhalation of open air. It wasn't exactly fresh because it was still tainted by enough ash and smoke to make me cough.

The long ladder from the fire truck reached the balcony. Treacle hopped onto the roof, took a running start, and leaped. He landed safely in the sprawling branches of a nearby maple tree and scurried the rest of the way down.

NADIA HAD REGAINED consciousness by the time we reached the ground again. The rescue left parts of my skin feeling as though I had awful sunburn, and even though I was glad I could breathe again, few smells are fouler than singed hair.

Nadia shook off the firefighters who tried to get her onto a gurney and into the ambulance or even to give her a blanket. She walked toward me. "They say you ran in to save me while the place was on fire," she said. "I guess you're not so bad after all."

I guess you're not so bad after all? I gave her a disdainful blink. "Gosh, Nadia, can you hold a grudge or something?" I had to remember she might have stolen the book.

"Hey," Nadia chuckled, "I'm not like your cousin. I'm not made of hugs, you know?"

"Nadia!" Ruby elbowed her way past Fire Chief Gillian and tottered over to throw her arms around Nadia. "You should have gone shopping with Darla and me! This never would have happened."

"I have no regrets," Nadia said flatly. "She spent the night here to talk about nothing but herself. We're too old for slumber parties, and a few seconds was always too much Darla for me."

"Nobody actually lives in this part of Old Wonder Falls

anymore," I said. "The whole block could have gone up in flames before someone other than Nadia phoned the fire brigade. Great thing you got this place insured, huh?"

Ruby grumbled, "Processing takes a while, at least in Sutherland's hands. But I'm so glad you're safe!" She hugged Nadia again. The smell of artificial jasmine cut through the smell of burnt hair. She pulled away enough to ask, "You shouldn't have called if that meant it left you smothered almost to death!"

Nadia said, "Those jerks broke my cell phone! I wasn't about to wander around alone looking for a phone booth."

I asked her, "Did you see who might have done this, then?"

"Yeah!" Nadia said. "They weren't from around here. I clawed this one guy's stocking off his head, and I didn't hit my head or anything."

"I'll go and get you a lineup, then." I edged away and wandered the crowd.

Treacle found me.

"That," I told Treacle, *"was very reckless of you."*

"We're closer to the truth!" Treacle objected.

"We're too far from anything that makes sense!" I thought back to the beginning—Ted Lanier had been given a concussion and the Brew-Ha-Ha set on fire in predawn morning. Aunt Astrid was given a concussion in her own home—but no fire—and the attack had happened in the early evening. Nadia LaChance, in her own home, had no concussion, and the attack had taken place at noon. If there was a group of agents

from the Order doing this, then maybe they were working in shifts.

I needed Blake.

"Blake!" I called out to the crowd, but I couldn't find him. I picked Treacle up. "Blake! Samberg!"

One of the police cars had its driver's window rolled down. When the police radio on the dashboard started its static sound, I picked it up.

Jake was saying, "Samberg, please copy!"

So it was Blake's car.

"The fire's done," I told Jake. "It was definitely the Order's doing, but Nadia's alive—able and willing to identify them. Did you try Blake's phone? I can't find him either."

"His cell's busy. We're the only people he knows!"

My heart sank. "We're not the only people who know his number, though."

Human Sacrifice

The guys spent the rest of the afternoon getting Nadia's statement. I left Treacle with Peanut Butter at my place and went to the hospital. Aunt Astrid still hadn't woken up. I told Bea about that morning.

Bea was aghast. "But the Order has the book! The real one! Why bother attacking people who have nothing to do with it?"

I wondered for a moment. "Well, you did say that a lot of the spells needed a human sacrifice. Can you tell me more about them?"

"These spells were written in the medieval age. They took into account if the moon was void or what planet ruled the hour of the spell."

"That sounds complicated!"

"If none of the members of the Order were like us, basically born into magic and having to feel out for the right conditions and walk in the other worlds—they might want to do it by the book." Bea thought about it some more. "They could capture a human sacrifice to have ready, but Nadia wasn't captured, was she?"

"No. It's a good thing she wasn't concussed before they tried to burn her alive." I thought about it. "Actually, I think that makes the Order real sadists."

Bea nodded. "To save nonwitches from the horrible reality of magic, the old Greenstones always, always made sure that the sacrifice came from somebody within the coven."

"Do you think somebody would volunteer to be a human sacrifice?"

"If everybody else in the coven treated it like some great honor, then I wouldn't be surprised. But the way the book was written, it had to be the life of a sister."

"Or," I said, "a brother." I began to panic. "They wouldn't know how much bloodlines have to do with it, would they? They'd only see 'sisterhood' and think 'brotherhood' would be better. They lured Blake away. They captured him. They're going to kill him!"

Bea stood up. "If that spell succeeds, this might be the least of our worries. If it fails—say they don't have magic or something—then they'll try again, and we need to warn Min."

I nodded, relieved that my panic finally had a direction. "I'll call Min. You call Jake."

I tried Mrs. Park's number first. She told me that Min had gotten used to the bachelor's lifestyle, so he had rented an inn room of his own. She couldn't hide how relieved she was that I hadn't joined him.

I couldn't help but break down and cry. "My beloved aunt, who's been like a mother to me, was attacked last night! A gang of thugs won't quit terrorizing my family and our friends!"

"Cath, I'm so sorry," Mrs Park said. "I didn't know about Astrid."

"I should have warned you all," I told her. "You've been friends of my family, too. You've got to stay safe, all right? I mean it. Try to get Min to stay over with you until the culprits are behind bars."

"All right."

When I hung up the phone, Bea looked bleak.

"We're too late," she said to me. "Jake says that Blake called the police station. They recorded the call. You're not going to like what he said."

A Failsafe

I bribed one of the nurses to take care of Marshmallow, and Bea and I left the hospital room for the police station.

Chief Talbot greeted us as we came in through the door. "Miss Greenstone, Mrs. Williams."

"Is Detective Samberg safe, then?" I said, confused. "Bea only said on the way that he called for me. Why didn't he call me directly? What did Jake mean by us being 'too late'?"

"Come with me."

The Wonder Falls police force, along with Nadia, was clustered around a recorder to listen in on a call.

"Only four voices in the background," Nadia said. "I can remember each and every one of them."

"Right," Jake said. "Ready to play it back again?"

Nadia gave me a pitying look. Bea put her arm around my shoulder.

Jake started the recording.

"I'm calling to say that I've found the real power in this town." The voice was Blake's, but the words couldn't have been. "It's me. My birthright. The way was mapped by my father, and I walk it with my brothers!"

Three voices in the background whooped and roared in encouragement.

"We are beyond the reach of the law, and come midnight tonight, we'll be the rulers and not the subjects of nature itself."

Another voice shouted, "Help me!"

Bea and I both gasped.

"That's Min," I said.

Blake's voice continued, "Tell Cath that I knew she was holding out on me. If this pathetic little wimp—"

"Pipsqueak!" said a voice in the background.

"Reuben," Nadia said with grim certainty, identifying the voice.

"—is her idea of a worthwhile partner, then I give up. He's not the prince, doll! He's the damsel. Would you tell her that for me? Would you tell Cath?"

Jake's voice answered on the recording: "You can tell her yourself. I'll bring her in. Just give me an hour."

"An hour? Yeah. We'll be waiting."

"Man, no." That was Reuben's voice. "They'll figure out where we are by then."

"That's hard to do when we're moving! Back down, underling." Blake replied to Jake, "Half an hour. It can't be hard to hurry. This is a small town. There. That's the end of it. Move."

"Not again!" Min's voice sounded muffled.

Reuben's voice objected, "I'm serious, bro. You might be some hotshot legacy member of the Order, but we're not going to wait on your ex-girlfriend! We've gone too far waiting for this. If you think you can just come in here—" A scuffling noise was heard, then the line went dead.

I breathed a sigh of relief. "All right. Blake's bought us time."

"Wait, what?" Nadia said to me. She sat upright, a confused expression on her face. "Do you even speak English? Your beau's a traitor and a nutcase!"

"He called the police station when he could have called me," I said. "Blake knew to get the message out to the greatest number of people with the best skills to cover the most ground. They're on the move, right? But did you hear any vehicles, any footsteps?"

Jake answered, "No."

I nodded. "When Blake told the others to get a move on, Min said, 'Not again!' because Reuben had done this to him before! He put Min in a burlap sack and sent him downriver."

"And," Bea added, lying, "from what Blake told us of the Order's rites of black magic..."

I completed the sentence, "Min Park is to be their human sacrifice. There's a ritual they're going to try to do, to gain control over the forces of nature. 'Come midnight tonight, we'll be the rulers and not the subjects of nature itself.'

What's the grandest display of natural beauty and power that's closest to this town? The falls!"

"We have until midnight," Bea said. "The traditional sort of rituals that Blake told us about are very particular about it being done at a particular time."

"All right!" Chief Talbot said. "Let's get a move on!"

Bea caught up with Jake first. "Remember what I told you about not getting shot or killed."

He kissed her, broke away, and strapped on his holster and gun.

I sidled up to Bea. "The spell could work," I said. "Our police force won't be prepared for it. They think the Order are deluded and the magic isn't real. Even Blake still thinks so."

Bea nodded. "We have to get there first and stop the ritual. Keep the secret."

"This is about more than keeping the secret," I told her. "This is about not waking the Maid of the Mist. The other world of magic can't cross over into this place." I added regretfully, "And you can't come with me."

"What? No." Bea turned to face me. "Cath, your mother tried to stop something from crossing over. She tried to do that all on her own, and that killed her. That was just using the common magic that every witch knows to guard the boundaries between the nonwitch world and the other. This is trying to stop a big spell."

"I'm not going to stop something from crossing over," I said, "I'm going to stop a bunch of jerks from calling it over.

The police will do the rest. Everybody knows that I'm a loose cannon and impulsive."

"I'll just say that you dragged me into it, that I went along to try to curb your heroism!"

"Then we won't have a failsafe! You've got to take Aunt Astrid and the cats and head for high ground in some sturdy building. If I fail to stop the Order, something horrible is going to happen."

"But you..." Bea's sad, panicked eyes looked from me to her husband. "And Jake..."

"I'll do my best," I said to her. "But if my best isn't good enough, then you're our last hope to get that book back. That means you have to live. I'm sorry that we can't warn Jake."

I walked over to Chief Talbot. "Is there anything else I can do to help?"

He answered, "You've done plenty. We could use more people on the ground, though, so maybe you can take a message to the investigators at your Aunt Astrid's place?" He hollered to another officer, "Boone! Call everyone back from Min's room at the inn."

I followed Boone and his partner out of the police station, planning to visit Min's room at the inn on my own.

A Visit to the Inn

I thought that if Min had kept the necklace just because he thought it looked neat, then he'd have kept something I would be able to use, too.

When I was sure the police had been called away for a search of the area around the falls, I sneaked into the inn room.

I stole a black hooded robe from Min's luggage, which I pulled on over my clothes, and in the inside pocket of the robe, I hid Blake's father's journal.

On the way out, the sky rumbled, making me look up to see the storm clouds heading our way.

I avoided the police by sending out a mental call for every cat to either stay and help or head for the hills. The ones that chose to stay volunteered to be distractions or warnings.

That's how I made my way through the town and then

through the woods and then to a simple boat tied to a pier by the lake. I boarded the boat and untied it.

When the clouds rolled past the moon, I got out the journal and flipped through the pages even though a spell had caught my eye already. "If found, please return," I recited. "This prized possession's tether burn."

In my mind's eye, invisible to any nonwitches, a perfect line of bright magic shot from the journal over to where Blake would be. I tucked the journal into the robe's inside pocket again, took up the oar I'd found in the boat, and paddled as fast as I could in the direction of the magic.

Midnight—the witching hour—approached.

The Witching Hour

Bea returned to the hospital with Peanut Butter and Treacle at her heels.

The nurse I'd bribed on the way out tried to stop her. "Really, three cats! Mrs. Williams, that's too much! You can tell Miss Greenstone to keep her money and whatever favors she made up—"

"Actually, I can't," Bea said. "Don't worry. We're leaving."

Everybody in town knew Bea as the nice one, the sweet one. Her terseness surprised the young nurse into silence.

In Astrid's hospital room, Marshmallow sat upright and stretched when Bea entered.

"Ready?" Bea asked the cats. Awkwardly, she added. "I won't know if you are, because I'm not Cath. I don't speak Cat. I don't even know if you speak Human. But I need you to make magic—all three of you, not just Marshmallow. Can you do that?"

Peanut Butter meowed and jumped onto Aunt Astrid's hospital bed, followed by Treacle.

"I'll take that as a yes." Bea intoned, "Blood calls to blood, spirit to soul. This healer commands it: make my mother whole!"

A blast of magic rippled from the hospital bed.

Bea almost fainted with the effort. She steadied herself on the bar beside the hospital bed and looked toward her mother.

Astrid groaned. Beneath her eyelids, something moved.

"Mom!" Bea exclaimed.

Astrid was barely strong enough and alert enough to form words. "Don't... take the book..."

Bea flinched. "Yeah... about that..."

Astrid opened her eyes and looked at Bea worriedly. "Where's Cath?"

"She's out there doing her best with some crazy Cath plan that only Cath could think up, let alone go through with," Bea told her mother. "You and I need to get out of her way and out of the way of everybody who might be in Cath's way."

"What's she planning? What's she done?" Astrid groaned, struggling to sit upright in the bed.

Later, I realized Aunt Astrid wasn't talking about me at that point.

"That will be a great thing to discuss," Bea told her, "at the Parks' place uphill."

"First, I need to tell the police who attacked me."

"We already know. The Order, wasn't it?"

"What order?"

"Strange men led by Reuben Connors? Or did he shake off his henchmen and rob our home all on his own?"

Astrid shook her head.

THE THREAD of magic led me to a yacht floating between two of the three falls. A searchlight mounted on its mast swept back and forth across the turbulent waters. I let my borrowed boat float into it and heard two unfamiliar voices call out above the roar of the nearby falls.

"Let me talk to him!" Blake shouted. "This is Legacy business."

I pulled the hood of the cloak further over my face, and I held the journal up and out into the searchlight.

"See?" Blake said. "Dexter, stand over at the starboard side. Felix, stand over at the port side. Look smart, both of you. We're welcoming a grand master."

I tried to stand and move in as grand and masterly a way as possible as I tied the stolen boat to the yacht and stepped off it, up the ladder, and onto the deck.

Blake was there to greet me in a black hooded robe of his own.

"Cath, what are you doing?" Blake hissed.

"I had to make sure that Min was all right. Please say you still have your gun!"

"That thug, Reuben Connors... he took it. He's below

deck with Min right now, so you can be sure that Mr. Park is not all right. What's taking backup so long?"

"Maybe if you signaled with your handy searchlight!"

"I can't signal without these two mooks knowing that I'm signaling."

"Well, there's two of us, and there's two of them now, isn't there?"

One of the mooks piped up, "I don't like all these strange people showing up and claiming to be from the Order."

Blake rolled his eyes. "Silence, underling!"

"No, Felix has got a point," said the other mook, who must have been Dexter. "If anybody should be talking to the grand master, it's Reuben."

I told Blake, "We'll catch them off their guard. I'll take Dexter."

Blake turned to the two mooks. "The grand master would meet with this accomplished brother! Fetch him!"

As Felix made his way below deck, I pocketed the journal, strode toward Dexter, pulled his hood down, and shoved him overboard. The element of surprise—and the adrenaline rush—made up for how much bigger he was than me. He yelled much more loudly than I'd expected as he tumbled and splashed into the water.

I lowered my hood, shrugged off the robe, and handed Blake the journal. "That's bound to draw attention."

"I'll keep the other two distracted," Blake said. "Can you climb the mast?"

"Like a cat!"

"Good. Signal with the searchlight. Go!"

As I climbed, Felix and Reuben came up from belowdecks.

"What did you do, Samberg?"

Blake met his gaze and set his jaw. "Dexter and I got into a scuffle. I wanted to see how dexterous he really was. As it turns out, not awfully."

"Felix says that a grand master of the Order came on board."

Blake laughed. "Why'd you go and tell the boss a foolish thing like that? You know he wanted to have some uninterrupted time with Park."

From the searchlight, I saw a glint of metal as Reuben drew his gun.

A shot sounded.

"No!" I screamed.

Another shot sounded, and the searchlight shattered into darkness.

Reuben's voice taunted, "Here, kitty, kitty, kitty. I've got your boyfriend. Both of them! I've got your book! So you'd better come on out."

A cloud shifted so the light of the full moon washed the deck.

I climbed down and stood behind the unlucky Felix, who'd been shot in the head. "Why did you do this?" I asked Reuben, trying to keep the tremor out of my voice. Min was crumpled on the ground.

"I wanted uninterrupted fun time with Min Park and Cath

Greenstone and..." Reuben turned to look at Blake. "Actually, you can go." He sighted down the barrel at Blake.

"Don't you dare!" I shouted.

Reuben laughed. "Oh, come on! I don't want you ganging up on me. I'm just one person, and there's three of you. Bullies!"

I looked at Min, whom Reuben was grasping by the collar of his shirt. Min had ropes around his wrists and ankles and a gag over his mouth.

I said, "You were always the bully, Reuben Connors."

"Oh, yeah?" Reuben yanked Min's gag down. "Hey, Min, buddy. Why don't you tell Cath Greenstone what you said about me?"

"I say a lot of things about you," Min admitted.

"When we met up as brothers of the Order. Can you remember?"

Min shook his head.

Reuben said, "Min said that the Order obviously wasn't as elite and exclusive as they advertised, just because I was in it. How about that? My family called me a bad seed. I traveled around, tried to find the good in me, made friends in the Order... and this chink, who's got everything handed to him on a silver platter, says that I'm just dirt."

"You made life in this town awful for Min!" I shouted. "You make it awful for your sister. You've made it awful for me and my family for the past three days!"

"Welcome to the real world!" Reuben retorted. "The people who win are the ones who take power and keep it from everybody else. Don't act nice and pretend that you don't know it. Isn't that what the book is about?" With a nudge of his gun in my direction, I looked down and realized that Felix had been holding the Greenstone spell book.

"Pick it up," Reuben ordered. "The grand master of the Order gave me a talk, you know. Exactly what Min said—they wanted better than me. I said that I was the only one who could get them exactly what the Order really needed."

Blake spoke up. "What was that?"

"Real magic." Sharply, Reuben said to me, "Didn't I tell you to pick up that book?"

"If you shoot me," I said, "you'll be short one person to say the incantation, and I'm the only one here who's a natural-born witch."

"Cath?" Blake looked confusedly at me.

"Right." Reuben turned the gun on Blake. "Like all the Greenstones. Three people in a coven. Three cats. Three waterfalls. Three people to say the spell. If one backs out, every single one of us on this boat dies. I have the gun, remember?"

I glowered at him.

"Of course!" Reuben laughed, remembering. "Min's going to die either way. You don't care so much for your life, and you're the type who would take me down with you and tell yourself it's worth it. But if you do as I say, then Blake just might live."

"If I do as you say," I argued, "no one lives. You're in over your head! The forces of nature never answer to someone who doesn't respect them!"

Reuben scoffed and nudged Min. "Women! That's what killed Ted in the end, you know. A treacherous woman."

Blake cleared his throat. "I think it was a big, burly thug who broke his head open and burned him up."

"Yeah, it was," I said to Reuben. "What on earth are you talking about? If you hate women so much, then I should be the sacrifice," I told Reuben. "I'll be the one sure to die instead of Min."

Reuben considered it for a moment. Then his phone alarm went off. He shut it off. "Ten minutes to midnight. How long does it take for a sacrifice to die from drowning?" He hauled Min up by the collar, dragging Min's back against the yacht's railing. "Because I don't do eleventh-hour changes in plans."

"Don't do this, Reuben!" I shouted as Min struggled against him.

Sarcastically, Reuben said, "Oh, okay. If you say so." He scoffed and shoved Min overboard. Over the roar of the falls, I heard the splash.

I saw a loop of rope hanging on the railing of the yacht, where nothing had been before, and knew that Min had managed to tie it while Reuben and I were talking. Still, there'd been a splash. Min was underwater, tied up so he couldn't swim, and I couldn't pull him up. I reached my mind out to any animals in the area, but the roar of the churning waters and my own screams drowned out my attempts.

Reuben aimed the gun at Blake. "Stand beside Cath. Turn to the Wakening Waterfalls ritual and start reading! Now!"

I pulled the spell book from Felix's hands and flipped through the pages quickly. Blake sidled up beside me, and I traced my index finger below the words so he could follow. Blake caught on with the repetition—and, unfortunately, so did Reuben.

Our voices joined in a chorus, and I hoped Min was managing to stay afloat somehow. Without his life, the three of us could say the words until dawn but the spell wouldn't work.

However, the water began to glow.

I let my voice keep on chanting on autopilot to catch sight of Blake's expression. He looked at the water, too, disbelieving.

The other world had crossed over.

Tragically, that could be possible only if Min had drowned to death.

Tears fell from my eyes as a pillar of light exploded from the center of the lake into the sky. The book dropped from my hands. The spell was complete.

"Cath, are you seeing this?" Blake wondered.

"Bravo, Cath!" Reuben said to me. "It's too bad we'll have to share this power among the three of us, work in harmony or something. Can you imagine working in harmony with him?" Reuben gestured at Blake. "Actually," Reuben said, "now that it's done, why don't I kill the both of you and just do whatever I want with this portal of power? That's not *my* holy book, after all."

"It would kill you," I told him.

"Oh, Cath. I've found out so many of your precious secrets. Do you want to know one of mine?"

"Taking in that much power would kill you," I told him again with certainty. "And the Maid of the Mist will flood the town and kill everyone in it. She only speaks to the Greenstones in her dreams, in our dreams. Even that's too much for us. You do not want to wake her up!"

To that, Reuben replied, "I don't care. For once, I did something great." He aimed his gun at me.

Blake pushed me aside, and the shot missed.

"Go!" Blake shouted, "Get back to the boat and get out of here!"

Didn't he know a magic spell in action when he saw it? The town was doomed. This yacht was doomed. That tiny wooden boat that I had stolen didn't stand a chance.

I could only think of one thing to do.

I pushed myself up and half ran, half stumbled across the deck and jumped over the railing into the churning water.

My hands grasped at the rope between Min and the yacht railing, burning with friction as I fell still holding it, and then it snapped. I kicked as hard as I could to keep my head above water, my hands pulling at the rope until it became taut. I pulled until Min's drenched body came up to mine.

The glowing water of the lake moved like an ocean in a storm. The magic hit me as if I was trapped in a burning house—exactly how I'd felt while rescuing Nadia that morning, only a thousand times worse. I swam toward the bobbing wooden boat, pulling Min along.

Another gunshot sounded in the air. Reuben didn't have any other targets but Blake. With the tumultuous water, could he have missed?

As Blake told me later, Reuben didn't miss. Blake didn't believe in magic, and he'd only followed my lead with Reuben's gun aimed at his head, but he had taken part in the ritual of Waking the Waterfall. For a moment, he had magic, and the journal with the protection spell on it had stopped what would have been a fatal bullet.

When the movement of the waves made the yacht lurch, Reuben missed his next shot by a hair, and the bullet only grazed Blake.

Meanwhile, I'd reached the smaller boat, still lashed to the yacht. I kicked and jumped, reaching for the side of the wooden boat with one hand, still hanging onto Min with the other. I caught the boat's side and it tipped, filling with glowing magic water. I pushed the edge beneath me and, choking, hauled Min into the boat with me.

I rolled Min onto his back, as flat as I could manage inside the boat, and pushed down on his chest as hard as I could for a moment then released it. Again. I imitated his heartbeat.

"Min, you are not going this way!" I shouted at him. "Not because of me or my family secrets! And definitely not because of Reuben Connors!"

I leaned over Min's face, pinched his nose, covered his mouth with mine, and breathed into his lungs.

I drew a fist back and punched Min in the chest.

The lake went dark.

Min coughed and sputtered, then turned aside and vomited water. He pushed against the bottom of the boat with the heel of one hand and sat up, almost panting with panic. "Cath!" he gasped. "You saved me!"

I was so happy he was still alive that I kissed him.

"Stay here," I told Min, climbing up the yacht's ladder again as the waves calmed down. "I've got to take care of Reuben and Blake."

Blake shut the handcuffs with a snap. Reuben was now cuffed to the yacht railing.

"Blake!" I shouted, seeing the deck drenched with blood. The moonlight made the red fluid look black.

"You have the right to an attorney..." Blake persisted faintly. I shoved him a safe distance away from Reuben.

"Blake, you're bleeding really badly."

Blake stumbled, almost fainting. I put both my hands over his wound, trying to staunch the bleeding. "Hang on! Hang on, please! Stay with me. Jake and Talbot and everybody—they're on their way." They couldn't have missed that giant magical pillar of light, and they'd be curious about it.

"My heart's in your hands," Blake said faintly. "There are worse ways to die."

"You are not going to die," I told him. I knew it was a bad sign that Blake was getting so maudlin, though. "We saved the town. We saved Min! You don't do something like that and then just die. You just have to stay with me, all right? Blake?" He was looking at me, but his eyes seemed to glaze over. I called out to him again, "Blake!"

Reuben laughed, still struggling against the handcuffs and spewing threats that made no sense. My hands kept the pressure on Blake's wound until the police boats came.

One Loose End

Jake drove me home. I had some leftover pancakes for dinner, chewing ravenously as I called Bea to tell her the Order's devious plans had been thwarted. After that, I took a hot shower, slept without dreaming, and woke without Treacle.

With the Brew-Ha-Ha still closed, I didn't know what I would do. Still, I didn't feel like curling up in bed and replaying the horrors of the past three days in my mind. I also felt as though I was coming down with another case of magic burnout. It wasn't as awful as I'd anticipated after doing a spell as huge as Waking the Waterfall, but Min had given his life force—if only temporarily—and therefore did most of the magical heavy lifting.

Blake had said the ritual with me. I hoped the spell hadn't taken too much out of him, either. He would need his life force to, well, live.

I didn't know who to call first, so I decided I'd go to the animal shelter, make a donation, and thank some of the strays personally for all their help the night before. Maybe that would bring me back down to earth and clear my head.

The old man who ran the animal shelter, Murray Willis, turned out to be related to young Cody, from the insurance office. I found that out when I arrived to see a whole crew of news reporters filming an interview with Cody for a TV spot.

Old Murray was beaming with pride. As we doled out kibble into serving dishes, he chatted about how Cody had been studying bioluminescent flora and fauna in the Wonder Falls lake. "Glowing animals," Murray said, "too tiny to see just one. You can't even pet 'em! I never understood it."

I stroked a long-haired calico cat with a missing eye, and I said that understanding Cody's fascination was beyond me, as well.

"I would have wanted to be where you were last night, though."

I didn't know what to say to that. "Seriously, Mr. Willis?"

"Without the life-threatening hostage taking, o' course," Murray corrected himself. "But that bioluminescent pond weed made the falls glow brighter than a lightning storm. Think about that!"

"Oh, yeah," I said. "Nature's wonderful. Too bad people try to get in the way, right?"

"Folk like us and Cody just do our best," Murray replied. "And Samberg—is he out of the hospital yet?"

"I don't know. You know Blake? Detective Samberg?"

Murray nodded. "He's my most enthusiastic volunteer here at the animal shelter. It would be a pity if we lost him, and he hasn't even been a month in this town!"

The animal shelter didn't have a lot of volunteers. I decided to drop by more often, not just when I had to pick Treacle up again for wandering away.

At that moment, Bea called me on my cell. "Have brunch with us!" Bea said. "We're at the Parks' place."

"Still?"

"Of course we are. Mrs. Park wouldn't let us go off at—what, two or three in the morning? And with Mom just out of the hospital! Besides, Min's here, and"—Bea lowered her voice—"he's really eager to see you again."

I smiled. "That wasn't some overwhelming trauma, then?"

"You're his hero! He doesn't mind the broken ribs. Mrs. Park and Mom have been catching up."

At that, I gasped. "Aunt Astrid's alive! I mean, awake! Awake and talking!"

"Go," old Murray told me.

I hung up the phone. "Thanks, Mr. Willis!"

"Thank you!"

I ran out past Cody and the news crew and uphill to the Parks' home. The townsfolk had found a cover story for the giant magical display of the night before, and they found it all by themselves. Aunt Astrid had come back to us. The sun was shining. Things were looking up.

When I saw smoke rising from somewhere near the Parks'

front porch, I had a moment of panic, I admit, what with this town having had two suspicious fires in three days.

I only saw Mr. Park at the barbecue, though, which was surprising. He nodded a greeting and waved with the hand that wasn't flipping a burger with a spatula. I waved a greeting as I jogged toward him, noting the rest of the group gathered at a giant wicker porch table. Treacle was sharpening his claws on one of the table legs.

I was focused on stopping him, which was why I didn't see Min break away and come toward me. I jogged right into his cracked ribs.

"Oww!"

"Min! I'm so sorry!"

Min laughed and hugged me. "Worth it!"

We eventually broke apart, but we still couldn't quit grinning at each other. I craned my neck to look at the table. "What a crowd!"

Mrs. Park set down a tray of lemonade and beckoned me over as Bea followed up with a stack of paper plates and biodegradable plastic cutlery. I knew they were biodegradable because Aunt Astrid exclaimed at it, telling Mrs. Park, "You know me too well!"

Astrid really did look fully recovered. She turned back to chat with Jake.

"Detective Williams joined us only ten minutes ago. Other than him, our place was packed last night," Min said.

I watched as Jake nodded and waved goodbye at everyone.

He gave Peanut Butter a rub under the chin on his way toward us.

Min continued, "Bea brought her mom and all three cats up here to comfort my mom while I was... you know..."

"Our families have always been so close," I said, hoping he wouldn't say how weird and unlike Bea that action was. I also hoped that if Min didn't get a chance to say it, he wouldn't get a chance to really think it through and get suspicious about it.

"Mom wouldn't let me go back to the inn room where I got kidnapped." Min gave an embarrassed shrug. "So it was a bit crowded. We still missed you, though!"

I grabbed Min's hand. "The last three days might have been hell, and I know you don't have good memories of this town to begin with, but I swear, it's not usually like this. How long can you stay—so that we can catch up?"

"I can stay as long as it takes for us to get properly caught up." Min said, "Besides, not all my memories of this town are bad."

"Cath," Jake said to me.

"I guess you need a statement or a testimony or something?" I said to him.

"I'll go get my dad to put something on the grill for you," Min said by way of excusing himself. "We've got burgers, hot dogs, and sausages—oh, and Mom made her pork-sausage patty mixin's, so—"

"That last one! I want that! Two of them, please," I called to Min as he headed for the grill.

I walked Jake to the police car down the slope, afraid of

what he had to say. Aloud, I begged, "Tell me that Blake made it."

Jake said, "He's fine. It's not the first time he's survived a bullet to the heart, even. He told me so."

I sighed with relief.

"The doctors had to keep him sedated so he wouldn't try to work. Today! Can you believe that?"

"From Blake Samberg, I'm not surprised!" I laughed. "What's the Wonder Falls Police Department going to do with someone like that?"

Jake answered, "Well, lately I've been wondering what we'd do without him. His testimony, though... his and Mr. Park's..."

They'd both heard me admit to Reuben that I was a witch. "Reuben had me at gunpoint," I said to Jake. "He obviously believed that this old spell book, the prize of Aunt Astrid's collection, was real for some reason. But he had a gun on me! So I tried to play along."

"Blake believed that the three of you reading aloud from the book was what caused the lake to light up."

"Coincidence." I said, "I just came from the animal shelter. Cody was telling this news crew all about what happened last night—with the glowing, I mean. Of course, Cody wasn't at the standoff. Maybe when Blake's recovered a little more, he'll think more sensibly."

Jake persisted, "Min Park said that he had a vision of this goddess in the lake."

"Of course he would! He'd just had a near-death experience."

"Isn't his family Buddhist?"

I shrugged. "Last night was just confusing. By the way, when can we have that book back?"

"We have to hold it as evidence, unfortunately, until after the trial. It could be months before we can release it. It's obviously valuable to your family, but I've already bent too many rules. The chief has filed it as evidence with the justice of the peace. Someone would notice that it was gone. I'm sorry."

You don't even have the slightest hint of how sorry you should be! If that book falls into the wrong hands...

Almost as if he'd read my mind, Jake told me, "If there were a way I could get it back to you, you know I would. It's safer with your family."

I looked at Jake, startled. Bea couldn't have told him. But he'd figured something out. I told him, "It's just an old book."

"Really?" Jake said, in a tone of voice exactly between dismissive and challenging. Then he put the palm of his hand to his head. "Oh, would you look at that. You've been answering all my questions, and here I am without a notepad. We'll talk later, once you've thought through what happened last night. Right?"

I nodded.

"I'm off to follow up with Nadia LaChance," Jake said. "Reuben Connors and Dexter Edison haven't been cooperative."

"One goon got out alive, then?"

"Alive but behind bars. We don't have enough to implicate the entire Order, and Reuben Connors's alleged involvement with both fires... complicates things, especially in LaChance's case. But don't worry about the book."

Jake got into his car and drove away.

Not even three of Mrs. Park's pork-sausage patties, sandwiched in their respective English muffins, could get me to quit worrying about the book.

"Oh," I said when Min asked me what was wrong, "it's just that one of my aunt's most valuable pieces of a collection was stolen." He'd been showing me a slideshow of his trip to the south of Spain, and I think I might have confused an autopilot response to pictures of a bead shop with an autopilot response to the pictures of fountains that functioned somehow without modern pumping technology.

Aunt Astrid heard me and complained, "The police might as well have done the stealing if they don't give it back. Months, he said! Months!"

"Luckily," Bea added, "everyone who's deluded enough to think it's real is behind bars."

Min said, "Right!" sounding as though he meant it. "For today, for right now, everyone's safe. All's well in wonderful Wonder Falls."

Mr. Park said, "Show them the video of the Bali beach—the kites that were shaped like boats and look as though they're floating in the blue sky!"

So the records of Min's travels continued. Sunlight through the canopy of some African jungle. A performance of *A Midsummer Night's Dream* in some park in Australia, invaded by a swarm of giant bull ants. Beautiful stray cats in the Coliseum in Rome. A few more.

When it was done, I applauded. "It's great you got to see the whole world! Thanks so much for sharing it with us."

"Not that great," Min said. "You still take yourself with you, you know."

Bea said, "But you've changed! I mean..."

Mr. Park finished Bea's sentence, "You've grown. My boy's a man."

Mrs. Park disagreed. "He'll always be my baby."

I'd meant what I said about the rest of the world being great to see, especially through Min's perspective. His whole slideshow made me appreciate my own hometown that much more, though.

On the walk back to Aunt Astrid's place, Bea had a suggestion. "We should go camping."

We took turns carrying Marshmallow, as the old cat demanded. Peanut Butter didn't mind walking as long as he was with us. Treacle didn't mind wandering off and disappearing entirely.

But Treacle, with his scar, had been more loyal to me than any of the pudgy strays in Rome, with their unscratched coats, would have been. We didn't have playgrounds in Wonder Falls, but the kids could play safely in the meadows. Maybe one day I'd visit the mysterious jungles of darkest Africa or surf the magnificent and vivid tropical-blue waters of Balinese beaches, but I was in no hurry. We had enough mystery and magnificence in the waterfalls of my own little hometown.

"We haven't gone camping in years," Aunt Astrid said as we arrived at her place. She opened the door and went inside. "That would be lovely."

Bea set Marshmallow down on the sofa and followed her. Marshmallow scratched her ear with a hind paw and shook her head.

"So, when should we do it?" Bea asked.

I shut the door behind us and answered, "When this is all over."

Aunt Astrid nodded.

Bea looked from her mother to me, dismayed. "This isn't over? How can it not be over? Do you mean when we get our book back and can make sure that it's safe?"

"Yes. But also, I saw who attacked me," Aunt Astrid said. "It wasn't Reuben."

"Reuben Connors and that one guy aren't innocent in this whole thing," I said, as everything began to come together in my mind. "But there's one loose end that we have to tie up, and we can't involve the police." I paused. "Well, maybe Jake. I think he knows, but I think he doesn't want to know."

Aunt Astrid said, "I'll put the kettle on, and Cath can tell us all about what she's figured out."

Uninvited Guests

The three of us met Jake that evening at the Night Owl, where he sat across from the LaChance twins.

Bea approached them first. "Mind if I get my husband back?"

"We're through here. Don't worry," Jake said to Nadia.

Nadia, uncharacteristically, was nearly in tears.

Jake continued to comfort her. "Reuben Connors is not going to bother anybody in this town anymore."

"But if you don't have a solid case, he could walk!"

"Deal with that when it happens," I said to Nadia. "For now, have you got a place to stay?"

Naomi answered for her. "She's staying at my loft. I just had to drag an extra mattress out for the top bunk. I only got a bunk bed because I liked four posters with the curtain that goes all around it, but it's turned out to be useful."

Nadia said, "I would have taken the sofa."

"Oh, please, as if that would have helped!" At my confused expression, Naomi elaborated: "Ruby Connors thinks she's too good for either."

"That's not true," Nadia objected. "Ruby just had to attend to another one of Darla's attention-sucking vortex phases. I'm sure I've got friends who irritate her, too."

Nadia caught my eye for a moment and then looked away.

Bea asked Nadia, "Are you and Ruby breaking up?"

"No!" Nadia almost shouted. "Not over something like this. Especially not after yesterday!"

"We'll see," Naomi said in a singsong voice.

BEA SAT in the front passenger seat of the car as Jake drove. Aunt Astrid and I sat in the back with the Greenstone spell book between us. Jake had taken it from the evidence room.

Bea said, "You put a lot on the line for me and my family, Jake—"

"Don't mention it!" Jake said tersely, "Really, please—I love you, but... don't. Don't mention anything about this."

I expected Bea to look relieved, but she went quiet, her feelings quite hurt. I kept quiet, too. This was their marriage, and they'd have to figure it out themselves.

The police car pulled up to Darla Castellan's mansion, where Ruby Connors was supposed to be. We hid behind the bushes.

Jake rang the doorbell. From where I was hiding, with Bea beside me and Astrid with the Greenstone spell book on Bea's other side, I heard the door swing open and Darla ask what Jake wanted. There was a tremor to her usually steady, reedy voice.

Jake said, "Good evening. I was told Ruby Connors would be here. I just have some quick follow-up questions about yesterday's fire. They're sort of urgent."

Darla sighed and laughed. "Ruby! Detective Williams wants to talk to you!" She asked Jake, "Do you want to come in?"

"No," Jake said, "out here would be fine. I'm in a bit of a rush to get back to the station. I hope you don't mind. My interrogation with Nadia LaChance went on for longer than scheduled. She was upset."

"Look," Darla replied, "I might not have had my home invaded and burned down, but considering that nobody close to her just died, I think Nadia could be more respectful of people's time. Especially model members of the community such as yourself."

"It's no trouble."

Darla continued, "I mean *model* members of the community. You're quite the hunk, if I can say so. Like, you could be a model."

"You've said so before, ma'am, at which time I reminded you that I'm a married hunk."

I spared a glance at Bea, who was staring daggers at Darla.

Darla crooned, "Are you sure you don't want to come inside?"

At last, Ruby came to the door and followed Jake out to the courtyard. They passed by us without Ruby noticing.

"Now," I said, and the three of us started moving.

Darla had lingered too long in the doorway. Her face turned to outrage when she saw us approach, but Astrid opened the book. "You know what this can do? Just nod."

Darla nodded.

Bea said, "Unlike you or the Order, we actually know how to use it, so get back inside quietly."

"And we'll work something out," I added.

Aunt Astrid's expression softened. "I don't want revenge for attacking me, Darla. None of us want that. We just want some peace of mind."

With a resentful glance at our ruse—Jake was spinning his questions at Ruby in the courtyard, neither of them thinking to look over at us—Darla let us in.

A Collection of Little Bubbles

The entire inside of her house smelled like artificial jasmine.

"First," I said, "what did we do wrong? How did we let on that we were witches?"

Darla shrugged. "Weird things always happened around you—ever since we were kids. When I got wise to the fact that you had something real but impossible going on, I thought that I was just lucky in school that you didn't have the spells to—I don't know—make me vomit sewing needles that I didn't remember eating. Then I thought, no, if they can do that, then they're the lucky ones!"

Bea's expression was a mix of contempt and horror. "You have a morbid imagination, Darla Castellan!"

"Witches do that," Darla insisted. Mocking Bea's tone, she said, "You're not the only one who reads, Beatrix Greenstone!"

"It's just Bea. And I'm a Williams now, by the way, so watch how you talk to my husband!"

"Oh," Darla said, "*you* can watch how I talk to your husband if you don't watch yourself—nerd!"

I got between them. "All right! You wanted magic powers. You've got failed businesses, courtesy of Winnifred Hansen. A failing marriage. You thought that a magic spell would solve all your problems in life, and you knew that we had magic."

Darla nodded. "I also knew that you wouldn't tell me. Selfish!"

Aunt Astrid looked hurt. "I gave you a tarot reading about your love life. I told you what you needed to compromise with—"

Darla scoffed. "Oh, please! That so-called marriage was dead in the water. Besides, if you have magic and you still continue to pretend that you've got life so hard—then you're obviously wasting it."

I said, "You've got wiles. Ted fell for them." It wasn't a question. "Fatally." That must have been what Reuben meant by a treacherous woman.

"It was the only way I could get him to tell me anything. Ted knew real magic when he saw it," Darla answered as she sauntered over to an armchair. "But he was afraid of it because of his mother. Years ago, before we got together, Ted found the trapdoor. He thought he would remind your Aunt Astrid of it to make a wine cellar—"

"I remember that," Astrid said. "It broke my heart to stop a Frenchman from caring for his favorite wines..."

Darla waved a hand dismissively. "He didn't mind! He thought that he'd sneak some racks and bottles in anyway. But he found the book hidden in the fuse box, and he got all scared! That coward! It wasn't even real. But he wouldn't even tell me where your Aunt Astrid's cellar was. The Brew-Ha-Ha was the last place I'd think of looking. I thought it was in some secret cabin out in the woods." She paused. "Don't think I only used him. I liked the guy, all right? I'd surprise him on the way to work in the early morning. We could have carried on for a long while, I can tell you. I sometimes even forgot to pick his brain about you!"

Bea shook her head. "A torrid, star-crossed romance, I'm sure it was. What a tragedy it had to end!"

"And what," I asked Darla, "reminded you to pick his brain about us?"

Darla answered, "Four days ago, I met Ted as usual, early in the morning, before he started prepping the dough or whatever. That morning was different because I heard something in the restaurant area, where nobody was supposed to be."

The legacy journal that had belonged to Blake's father had a locator spell on it. The Order must have used something similar and sent someone to the café in search of the spell book.

"Which member of the Order found the book?" I asked.

"I don't know," Darla said. "He had a stocking over his head when he came out of the cellar. Ted grappled with him and told me to run. The thief had dropped the book first. I picked it up, and then I ran."

"Ted was fighting for his life! But you cared more about what you could get—the book!" Bea accused.

Darla rolled her eyes. "He was still alive when I saw myself out. And Ted had told me to run."

I imagined the necklace worn by a member of the Order getting ripped from his neck in the struggle. Ted could have pulled off the stocking too, revealing... Reuben? Dexter? Felix? It didn't matter.

"It was supposed to be a simple theft," I said, "but they'd run into a witness instead. They couldn't leave Ted alive, and without the book, they couldn't wipe his memory. So they killed him and set the place on fire to destroy the evidence. But the cellar kept the footprints. I also caught a whiff of your perfume."

"I feared for my life, in every sense of the word!" Darla exclaimed. "My love life, my business, my reputation in this town were all in jeopardy—and now there was this group of strangers prepared to murder! I needed magic, but all I had was the fake book!"

Astrid nodded. "You'd seen what these people were capable of and thought that you needed to step up your game. You came into my home, armed with a baton, and demanded the real book. I wouldn't give it to you."

Darla was vehement. "I had to take it, so I did!"

"But," Astrid said, "you didn't know what to do with it. You only knew that it was powerful."

"And," I added, "you might have suspected that these strangers you were up against had magic of their own."

"So you foisted it off on your best friend," Bea said, "probably your only friend—Ruby Connors."

"It must have been hard," I said, "to outgrow unhealthy friendships and break away when she didn't have a supportive family. Ruby would let you use her because she thinks that's what loyalty means. How much of all this did Ruby know about?"

"Nothing," Darla replied. "I come and go. Sometimes I leave things. I'd been staying overnight at Ruby's place a lot anyway since Darren served the divorce papers. Nadia hates it, but that book would be 'just another one of Darla's things.' I read a little, and I hid it under the floorboards of the guest bedroom. I didn't dare use the book yet, but I figured that if I kept it hidden and safe, it could be a point of negotiation if they came after me."

"But," I added, "you wouldn't be safe if you tried to keep the book safe with you."

"Obviously!" Darla scoffed. "But I'm not a bad person, especially not to my friends. I knew Ruby would be better off joining me on a shopping trip. Besides, I figured that Naomi would give them enough trouble if they tried anything, but she folded too quickly, and they got the book back anyway."

"Nadia," I corrected.

Darla drawled, "Yeah, yeah. They look the same."

"They look nothing alike!"

"They're twins!"

Bea was shaking her head disapprovingly. "I wish that I could see you sorrier about Ted," she told Darla, "but you're not the one who knocked him out and set him on fire. Afterward, though, you could have killed my mother! You could have gotten our friends killed! You're no better than the agents of the Order."

"Oh yeah?" Darla said. "They're in prison. I'm not. And you're not going to put me in prison, are you?"

Bea and I exchanged looks.

Astrid nodded. "We didn't bring Detective Williams here to arrest you, no. That would be too conspicuous."

Darla gave a laugh. "I knew it!"

Bea seethed with rage. "Is that seriously how you defend your unconscionable behavior? 'I didn't get caught, so it must not have been wrong'?"

"We all do what we have to." Darla leaned back. "And you have to deal with me."

I nodded. "You're absolutely right. We need the fake book back. We're going into hiding again, so we've got to swap the real one with something that can safely sit in the evidence room of the Wonder Falls Police Department."

"And," Aunt Astrid added, "show up on trial as Exhibit A or so-and-so alphabet letter."

I forced my voice to sound cajoling, even flattering. "It would be such a huge favor to us, Darla. You wouldn't believe—"

"How about this." Darla wasn't amused. "I'll give you the fake book. You give me the real one, which I don't know how to use, and you teach me magic. But I'll keep the book with me."

"Done," I answered.

Bea backed away in horror. "That's not possible! Magic comes from the soul, and you, Darla, don't have one!"

At that, Darla stood up. "Just try me! Yeah, come at me, copperhead."

Bea peered at her. "Have your insults matured at all since grade school?"

Aunt Astrid cleared her throat, drawing attention to herself. "The other book, if you please?"

As Darla stood and went over to the coffee table, Astrid handed me the real book—which I held open—and Bea turned to the right page.

Darla returned with the fake spell book, which Aunt Astrid received gently with a smile.

"All right," I said. "Now we teach you magic."

We used the only spell in the book that didn't call for something as cruel, criminal, and unsanitary as a human sacrifice—although the three of us who did the spell would suffer magic burnout for weeks. Good thing we wouldn't need our magic for a long time to come.

As the witch whose magic dealt most closely with the mind, I tuned into the otherworld and began to pick out Darla's memories. With the help of Aunt Astrid and Bea, I had the energy to make new ones for Darla. We made Darla forget that she'd ever believed in magic at all, let alone in our magic. She'd never become interested in Ted. She'd had nothing to do with the attack on Ruby's place.

Darla Castellan would get away with everything she had done because we took it away from her. Part of me wished she could have been taken to task instead, for Ted's sake, but beyond her mind, I could see her heart, which was entirely the wrong shape for accountability. She'd always been a bully.

In the otherworld, the memories were like a collection of little bubbles. The ones I removed faded into wisps, like foam under a waterfall.

The Beginning

We sneaked back into Jake's police car before he and Ruby parted ways—Bea in the front passenger seat, Aunt Astrid and I in the back, just like before—except we had two books between us.

I kept an ear out. When Darla opened her front door, she exclaimed, "Ruby! What brings you here?"

Ruby only remarked, "Married guys aren't my type. Or any guys, really."

Darla whined, "That's so hurtful of you to say! In case you forgot, it was Darren who cheated on me first."

"I didn't forget," Ruby told her. "But I know you still want to tell me all about it again. Of course I'll listen, but—"

Then the front door shut, and their voices became too distant and muffled to hear.

Jake revved the engine and drove us back home. He took the fake spell book back to the evidence room, and Aunt

Astrid took the real spell book somewhere even Bea and I didn't know.

BLAKE RECOVERED from his gunshot wound just in time to give his testimony in court. When testifying, both Blake and Min seemed to have decided for themselves that the glowing water was indeed a coincidence. My confession about the Greenstone magic heritage wasn't even mentioned, only referred to as "Cath tried to play along" or "Cath tried to talk sense into him."

The Order denied having any part in the incident, but even the coverage in a small town like Wonder Falls proved to be too much scandal for them to handle. The fraternity dissolved, and the jury sent Reuben Connors off to an asylum for the criminally insane. Dexter Edison would serve a sentence of eight years in prison.

Ted Lanier was laid to rest in Canadian soil. Min had offered to fund the memorial service in France, but considering how much Ted had wanted to escape his old life, Aunt Astrid arranged a small, quiet ceremony. I was surprised at the number of flowers laid on Ted's gravestone after that, considering Darla had completely forgotten him. Nobody else had expected her to remember.

We put a framed picture of Ted on a memorial wall in the new and improved Brew-Ha-Ha. Business slowed down due to the pastries from the Night Owl being unequal to Ted's and our being short-staffed in the front of the house. It leveled out fine in time, though. Any improvements we'd planned after rebuilding would just be a month or so later.

During what had always been the slowest time of the year for the Brew-Ha-Ha, we closed up for three days to go camping and fishing. We left the cats at the kennel even though Jake said that he wouldn't mind filling their dishes and cleaning their litter boxes. I didn't want him to follow an escaped Treacle into Greenstone Girls' Space, and the kennel seemed a more likely environment to keep the cats from wandering away.

As it turned out, though, there really was no stopping Treacle from going anywhere. He found our tents. So I let him have a jacket in my tent as a cat bed. I guess it would be a cat sleeping bag.

That night, Treacle woke me up again. He kept coming back to meow into my ear until I got up and followed him. It was a new moon's night, but my own magic let me tread unhindered through the forest. I could see with the sonic echolocation of the bats and find my way by starlight through the eyes of owls.

With my own human ears, though, I heard the rushing of the falls. I knew the way over the bridge.

That's where I met the Maid of the Mist. She stood on the bridge with me.

I know I saw her clearly, but I can't describe it now. My memory blurs in the strangest way, trying to remember if her dress was black or white.

"Well done," she said to me.

I gave a modest shrug. "I had help. I had my family—and Treacle, of course. I made new friends, too."

"That's all very important, and it wouldn't have happened if you hadn't played your part. It's been many generations since I've seen quite so much promise in a defender of this place, the falls between the worlds." She looked about my age, but my intuition told me I was in the presence of a being with years beyond wisdom.

"With all due respect, I can't make any promises. I should say that I appreciate you coming to meet me instead of speaking to me in a dream. This must be an honor of some kind, but I'm just sleepy. Unless this is a dream." I hugged myself, feeling chilled all of a sudden, and I rubbed my arms to warm them.

"Honor?" the Maid of the Mist echoed, sounding amused. "Necessity, maybe. You are a witch. You have bonds and duties. You will have more trials. Are you prepared?"

I took all that in and looked down at Treacle, who just looked back up at me. "Never," I replied. "I'm never prepared—but, you know, let me at 'em! When they happen, that is. For now, I think we all need to go back to sleep."

"True." With that, the Maid of the Mist dissolved. Treacle and I returned to the camp, where I first started writing all this out by flashlight.

I shouldn't be writing this down. I shouldn't have written it down. Those used to be the rules. I just feel as if I had to, though. Maybe it's because more is coming. The Maid of the

Mist said so. A witch's work is never done, and I used to dread it. Now I embrace it.

I've started writing so I can remember this better and maybe so the next generation of Greenstones can be better prepared—or at least know they're not alone, even if I'm long gone.

My name is Cath Greenstone, I'm a witch, and this was the beginning. This was only the beginning.

BOOK 2: PAWSITIVELY DEAD

The Anniversary

Death was a part of life. You didn't need to be a witch to know that. Witches might sometimes deal with it differently than non-witches, though it didn't seem so on the anniversary of my parents' death.

Before I left to visit them in the graveyard, my aunt Astrid and cousin Bea were varnishing the mezzanine in the newly rebuilt Brew-Ha-Ha, our family cafe.

Aunt Astrid was spry and clear-eyed at sixty-seven, always ready to roll up her sleeves and renovate. To people who didn't know her well, she was usually just an older woman with wispy swathes of blond-gray hair and loose tie-dyed dresses who always seemed to have a distant look in her eyes. Usually it was because she was remembering the future. Non-witches underestimated her; she was actually a lot sharper than she looked.

My cousin Bea approached the varnishing of the mezzanine more studiously, drawing from everything she'd ever read about primers and painting and architecture. She was the bookish sort and remembered everything she read. She was also beautiful, big-hearted, popular, and two years younger than me. I couldn't be jealous of her even if I tried. She wore her heart on her sleeve, and she healed everybody she touched. And I meant that literally. Healing was Bea's witch talent.

The Brew-Ha-Ha had been the most popular cafe in our hometown of Wonder Falls before the cafe had practically burned to a crisp. I was hanging a photo of our late baker on the wall behind the bar. Poor Ted. He had been tragically caught in the fires and passed away. He never knew his employers were three witches.

"Cath!" a familiar voice called my name.

That would be the elated voice of my childhood friend Min. He didn't know I was a witch either. Not many people did. Min and I had lost contact after he went out of town for college, and now that he was back, I was getting to know him again.

That day, he wore a brand-new T-shirt and jeans, looking a lot nicer than he used to in our childhood days. Probably because he'd sold his business and become obscenely wealthy. He was never a braggart about it though. He was even nice enough to come over and help take over my role in the renovation of the Brew-Ha-Ha while I had to step away for the morning.

"You look ready to work up a sweat," I said when he came

through the door. He gave me a light hug in greeting. "Thanks for coming in to help."

He peered through the bars of the mezzanine and waved hello at Bea and Aunt Astrid.

"Hey, Min!" Bea called.

Aunt Astrid added, "Just open the windows while you're down there, would you? Getting some air in here would help this all dry faster."

"Right." He made for the nearest window, stopped himself, and grinned at me, almost shyly. "Your hair's different. Nice, I mean. Not that it was bad the old way."

I'd had my dark ringlets straightened for the occasion—for two occasions, technically. "Samantha really wanted me to get it dyed or styled like, well, in her style."

"You went to Perry's Parlor just for a hair straightening?" Min laughed with incredulity.

Samantha Perry, a friend of one of Aunt Astrid's friends, had opened a hair salon in town. Samantha was almost fifty, but she was a real live wire and a rebel. I laughed with him. "I'm all for supporting small businesses in my hometown! My head just can't support a spiked green mohawk."

"That's what I want to do now. Support small businesses here." He quickly added, "I mean, not just because you mentioned it and I'm trying to copy your opinion or one-up you or anything like that."

I stopped myself from raising an eyebrow at his backpedaling. The Greenstones and the Parks had always been like family. Even if we hadn't seen each other in years, what was Min so nervous about?

He continued rambling. "I mean that supporting the locals is what I want to do, but I don't know. Putting my life to use is just something I've been thinking about since Tommy passed."

Thomas Thompson had graduated from Wonder Falls High the same year as Min and me. We didn't even know him well enough to call him Tommy, really, but he had become the pride of the town when the news network he worked for won a Michener Award. Then it turned out he won the award for an expose on the torture of prisoners of war under the Canadian Forces, and he became an embarrassment instead. That was, until he was caught in crossfire in some faraway war-torn desert and shot to death. From then on, he had been a hero.

"War correspondent is a dangerous job," I remarked.

Min nodded. "I don't mean I want to end up like Tommy. I just want to make a difference in our community, you know?"

I sighed. Our community. "I doubt anyone in this town would take too kindly to an investor, actually. They might view it as condescending. People here have a lot of pride."

I didn't really know why Min had even come back to Wonder Falls. If I hadn't been there to protect him, school life would have been unbearable, and even looking back at that time, we couldn't really call it happy. Min's father had impossibly high standards that Min could never quite meet, and Min's mother tended to be overbearing. He must have found a balance between the two though, and maybe he stayed in town just to be around his family. Family was the reason why I'd never left.

"I'm sure you'll think of something," I said then followed up with a reminder about the windows. "You know, it would be nice to have your problem, having the option of not working and doing whatever you want."

I put on my jacket, draped a black picnic blanket over one arm, and called my farewells to Bea and Aunt Astrid on my way out.

Death was a part of life, and life went on. When a mezzanine needed varnishing, we rolled up our sleeves and opened the windows to let out the fumes. We laughed about hairstyles and planned for a future where we could make our mark on the world and make it a better place to live. That day didn't have to be so full of doom just because it was my parents' death anniversary. But unfortunately, it was.

Graveyard Surprises

I walked down to the corner of Ebb and Eddy and considered that my shoes were formal but sensible enough to visit my parents' tombs. The sunshine shone pale yellow though the early morning air. I thought that I might as well take the path through the meadow to the graveyard.

That turned out to be a terrible idea. I wore all black and was sweltering by the time I was halfway down the path.

Wonder Falls didn't have a proper park. On one side of the path, children ran about, shouting in delight, playing hide-and-seek and other games, as their parents and guardians watched from picnic blankets or short boulders that served as seats. On the other side of the path, a Dalmatian strained against its leash as it snarled and barked at me. Gillian Hyllis, the local fire chief and the dog's owner, waved at me apologetically.

With my witch talent of communicating with animals, I joined my mind to the Dalmatian's and commanded it to quiet down. I sensed puzzlement in return, which translated in human to, "You smell like cat!"

Of course I did. My cat, Treacle, had helped me pick my outfit. That had been after taking him to the grooming salon, so at least my clothes didn't smell of alleyway or garbage or whatever cats got into when they insisted upon straying. Treacle was a black cat, so if any fallen hairs had stuck to my clothes, most humans wouldn't notice.

A lot of animals had senses keener than human senses, but if that dog—like a lot of dogs—couldn't be polite, then I ought to have just stuck to communicating with cats, as I usually did.

The unpaved meadow path sloped downhill and led into an abandoned orchard. The sprawling branches cast mottled shadows over the slope. A river stirred up a cool breeze as the water rushed to the distant falls somewhere over the horizon.

Our town was named for the falls, and my family had a bond with the Maid of the Mist that reached back for generations. How could I explain the Maid of the Mist? Some people were between worlds, and she was one of them.

The Greenstones were familiar with her, so we called her, as well as other people we could not explain to humans, our Familiar. The Maid of the Mist could take all manner of different forms, but something about being a witch meant that we recognized her every time. However, she didn't show up to me anymore, although she used to when I was a young girl, playing in forests and nature settings like where I was now.

I stayed a little longer in the orchard, looking for the right sort of wildflowers in the shade. I found them and walked on toward the graveyard, and on the other side of the stone bridge, I saw the St. Bernard dog by the river bank. It sank its giant paws into the shallows and lapped up the water. Part of a leash hung from its collar. It must have done what the Dalmatian had been doing, straining against the leash, but its leash must've been too weak or the dog too strong.

"Hey, there," I said. "Someone must be missing you. Come over here."

The dog looked up, startled, then backed away and whimpered. I hesitated going after the St. Bernard. I didn't want to mud wrestle with a dog the size of an adolescent bear all the way to the animal shelter. Instead, I used my powers, but when I tried to connect our minds, the dog did the magic-force equivalent of pushing me away. Then the dog bolted. Some animals were afraid of magic powers.

I took my phone out of my jacket pocket and called the Wonder Falls animal shelter. Old Murray, who ran the animal shelter, was out that day. His teenaged grandson, Cody, answered for him, so I told Cody about the St. Bernard on the loose.

Then I continued my walk to the graveyard from the meadow. The entrance was a waist-high, whitewashed wooden swinging door between two poles. The place was hidden, but everybody in town just knew where it was.

When I got to my parents' shared grave, a black cat with a star-shaped scar on his forehead sat before the tombstone, as if he were reading the names. Stella Greenstone. Gordon Greenstone.

The black cat's name was Treacle. My cat.

"Everyone's out walking their dog," I warned Treacle as I unfolded the picnic blanket. Treacle yawned and stretched over to sit with me.

None of the dogs in town had ever bothered him, but I knew he would appreciate the warning. Treacle was a street cat. He was clever. He could dodge dogs of any size, but then again, cats were smarter than dogs.

"Hi, Mom and Dad. I'm sorry I'm late," I said to the grave. "Mallows are hard to find when the meadow's crowded. It was nice to be out with everyone though."

I talked to my parents in my head after that. I didn't want anybody passing by to overhear the real story behind Ted's death or how we were rebuilding the cafe as fast as we could. But not too fast—we had to restrict our magic because we didn't want any townspeople wondering how we were getting it done in such a short amount of time. I also caught my parents up on other news, such as Thomas Thompson's recent death.

I wondered if witchcraft was really enough. We could protect people who weren't witches from evil beings and evil magic from other dimensions—other dimensions that only witches knew the ways of. But what could we do about the evil in this dimension, like wars? Unlike Ted, Thomas's death hadn't involved magic at all.

I sighed to my parents and stopped my train of thoughts, hoping I wasn't being too much of a downer. Treacle comforted me by putting his front paws on my knee. I stroked his head.

"I was orphaned," I said out loud. "Aunt Astrid was widowed. How do we protect ourselves from the pain of death?"

In any case, I blamed myself a little for my parents' deaths. They had, after all, been fighting the monster under my bed. A literal monster.

Aunt Astrid always tried to hammer into me that my mother was only doing her duty as a witch, protecting everybody in town from the evil thing masquerading as a child's imaginary monster. I didn't know enough to believe her though. Not until I found myself taking on the same duties. As witches, we had to do our best, but sometimes tragedies happened as a result of our jobs. I just had to do better, in whatever situation came my way, and hope for the best.

I thought, as I laid the mallow flowers on the grave, that I would be ready to do what needed to be done. That was what being a witch meant.

Then I noticed where the sun was in the sky, how bright its light was over the graveyard. The morning was going much faster than usual. I also realized that I'd forgotten to bring a packed lunch like I usually did on the anniversary.

I left Treacle on the blanket, conveying "I'll be right back" with my mind. I would swing by the delicatessen and grab something. I stood and fumbled through my jacket pockets, hoping I'd brought some cash, when something unusually magenta caught my eye beside the statue of an angel I was facing. The magenta was too glossy to be a bunch of wildflowers. It was human hair.

All of a sudden, even the sunshine felt cold.

"Excuse me," I called out, approaching the statue slowly. When I looked around the statue, I saw the body—the dress, the shoes. "Are you okay?" *Please be drunk. Please be sleeping, whoever you—*

The magenta hair turned into lime green where it fell on the ground and neon orange where it fell over her face. The neon orange hair over her nose and mouth wasn't moving with her breath. I stood still, holding my own breath, hoping I was mistaken, hoping she would breathe and blink and wake up.

"Samantha?"

I bent down to take a closer look at her face. Even though no one else in town would have that hair, I had to make sure. Unfortunately, it was Samantha.

I stepped back, slowly at first, then I stumbled a good distance away. I plunged my hand into the other pocket of my jacket and fumbled until I found my cell phone. Even with my hands beginning to shake, I turned my phone on and dialed the Wonder Falls police station.

"Wonder Falls Police," said a familiar voice on the other line.

"Blake!" I cried. "I'm at the graveyard. I saw Samantha lying here—Samantha Perry. I—I think she's dead!"

Blake maintained his professional cool. "We'll be right on over. Just calm down, and don't move anything."

I took a breath and choked on something that I smelled.

"Cath?" said Blake. "Are you all right?"

I answered with a cough. "Something reeks!"

I turned around, and I saw what must have caused the stench. It was a pile of bones, a skeleton essentially, with gray, brittle skin stretched over it. The lips had decayed enough that the skull seemed to grin at me. "Uh-oh."

"What is it?"

I said, "You might want to bring backup."

An Empty Casket

Blake and Jake arrived on the scene, and they had listened, bringing backup with them, along with the medical examiner. I met Detectives Blake Samberg, Jake Williams, and Marlene Strauss, the medical examiner, at the entrance and told them why I'd come there. Police Chief Talbot led the others to the area where I'd found the second body.

Blake patted an anxious Treacle as I described how I had seen Samantha's bright hair.

Jake asked, "And you haven't moved the body?"

"No," I said. "Didn't even touch it."

Blake asked, "And you didn't notice anything else unusual?"

"You mean, aside from the skeleton?" I asked.

"Did you see any other evidence?"

I looked around. What they saw was what I did. Then I

understood the intention behind his question and glowered at him.

"Well," Blake said, "you do steal evidence. You've done that."

"That was one time!" I said. "And what's important is that I didn't do anything like that this time. Cut me some slack, Samberg."

Jake interrupted with, "Blake, let's focus on the examination."

I watched Marlene examine Samantha's corpse until I felt queasy and had to turn away.

"Hmm," Marlene said, "all of this bruising is post-mortem. All of it."

I looked back, horrified, at the mottled gray and blue bruises on Samantha's arms, legs, and stomach. "I don't get it. Who would bruise her after she died? *How* did she die?"

I turned toward Jake and saw that the blood had drained from his face. Until recently, Bea's husband, Jake, didn't know our secret. He found out when he took on the case regarding Ted's death at the Brew-Ha-Ha.

Marlene looked up. "We'll need a more detailed autopsy. Cause of death might have been something like poison, but from what I can see so far, it wasn't physical trauma."

"Look at this—" Blake noted a strap of leather in Samantha's hand, frayed at the edge as if it had snapped. It was part of a dog's leash.

"Oh, poor thing," I whispered. At Blake's quizzical expression, I explained, "On the way here, over at the bridge, I saw this giant St. Bernard with a broken bit of leash on the collar..."

At that moment, Diane Davis, the newest member of the Wonder Falls police force, walked over. "We've found an open grave that the other body might have belonged to."

The three of us followed Diane to a crater in the ground, or more like a narrow tunnel. The tunnel's mouth was irregularly shaped and surrounded by loam and chunks of what might have been the grave marker.

Diane reported, "Boone took a look at the other body. Some parts were over fifty years old."

"Only some parts?" I asked.

Diane nodded. "A body that old shouldn't still have decomposing gristle on it."

"That's strange." Blake pointed at the grave. "And that's strange. If I were digging up a corpse, I would shovel the dirt out of the way. From how the earth is scattered evenly around it, the grave looks like it was broken from below."

I spared a glance at Jake, who, if possible, turned even paler.

"Maybe an explosive," Blake guessed. "Buried and remote-controlled. We ought to check for shrapnel in the ground. Once the coffin top was broken, a grave-robber only needed to fish for it, lift the bones out, without disturbing the earth... no fingerprints on the casket..."

Jake might know our secret now, but he didn't like to talk about it. Maybe it was his way of pretending that none of it was real. But as I watched him grow paler and paler, I could only guess that he had concluded that the skeleton had come alive with some dark magic and clawed its way out of the grave.

"I think I'll go pack up my blanket now." With another glance at Jake, I added, "I'll be with Astrid and Bea at the Brew-Ha-Ha."

"Good," Jake said faintly.

"When's it opening again?" Diane asked. "Coffee and sodas just fail as a pick-me-up compared to Astrid's herbal mixes."

"Renovations are almost done," I said.

But with these new revelations, the renovations might just have to wait a little longer.

Resurrection Spell

Aunt Astrid spotted me coming into the Brew-Ha-Ha. "Cath! You're back!"

"And you're early," Bea added. She craned her neck over the mezzanine railing and noticed the other guest. "Hello there, Treacle!"

"I *am* early." I sighed. "I found something awful at the graveyard."

Aunt Astrid set the paintbrushes to soak in their cleansers and sealed the tin buckets of varnish. She led Bea and me down the trapdoor behind the bar and into her nuclear bunker.

The last time I'd been in here, it had just been a dusty room with cement walls and a single flashlight. Now, it had been wallpapered and furnished with a low oval table and beanbag chairs, and she'd added some decent lights in paper-and-wire lampshades to make it seem more like a cozy secret place than a panic room. The trapdoor had been edged in something rubbery that made it difficult to close behind me.

"That's for soundproofing," Aunt Astrid said proudly when she saw me struggle with the door.

"Nice," I said.

"I stocked the mini-fridge," Bea said on her way down the stairs. "Everything here is being powered by the solar panels we put on the roof, but we also have a gas generator, although we should remember to change that every so often. Gasoline expires fast. Oh, and I opted for tatami over carpeting because of the way most carpeting catches mold spores and dust, but I did get a carpet-covered scratching post!"

Treacle made for the corner where the scratching post was and began to claw at it while the three of us settled down. I caught them up on what had happened.

Bea's first reaction was to shake her head sadly. "Poor Samantha!"

"Does she deserve so much of our pity though?" Aunt Astrid wondered.

"Mom!" Bea exclaimed, shocked. "Empathy isn't something that another human being has to deserve, especially when they've died."

"You're entitled to pity that she's dead," Aunt Astrid reassured her. "What I'm wondering is if she brought it on herself. We've had to deal with people trying to use magic for their own selfish reasons before, and we rescued them from taking on more than they could handle. Such arrogance can hurt and kill others in the process."

"It sounds to me like a resurrection spell gone wrong," Bea said. "But what if Samantha wasn't looking to be queen of the zombie armies?"

"You might be right," I said. "Samantha could have been the human sacrifice needed to resurrect another person."

"Even if Samantha Perry did it herself, with good intentions or ill intentions at heart," Aunt Astrid said, "we should find out *how* that much was accomplished and *why* it didn't work."

Bea nodded and asked me, "Who was it that came back to life? Maybe there's some connection between them."

"I don't know. The headstone was shattered. We'd better just let the officers investigate for now. If they find any evidence of a third person there, or put the headstone back together or something, you would know. Jake would tell you about it first, Bea."

Bea gave a sad laugh. "Oh, I don't know about that. Jake never wants to talk about magic with me."

"Poor man," Aunt Astrid said soothingly. "After last time, I'm sure it's just shock. Don't worry, Bea. He'll talk because he needs us to know."

"And we need him," I added.

Bea nodded again. "If or when it gets unbearable to pretend that Jake and I are normal and happy, like we used to be, well... can I please stay at either of your places?"

"In a heartbeat," I told her.

"As if you have to ask!" Aunt Astrid exclaimed.

I was convinced it would never come to that. At least, I

really hoped it wouldn't. We hugged it all out and went back to varnishing the mezzanine, this time with my help. Min had had to leave to help his family at their store.

Treacle also went off, wandering into town. I'd long since learned that there was no stopping him at the best of times.

Shelley Marina

I mulled over possibilities the whole day. When I got back home that evening, I took too long in the shower and came out to find that I'd missed over a dozen calls on my cell phone from Blake. Or Detective Samberg, as I should really be calling him. We were friends, sort of, except when I hated him.

I called him back. "What's so—"

He interrupted. "Shelley Marina, 1878 to 1958. Do you know her?"

I scrambled to understand who he meant. "That was the name and date on the tombstone that got blown up?"

"Yes. We put the pieces together. Only literally."

"How could—"

"We still have metaphorical pieces. The case is still unsolved."

"I think I got that, Blake. I don't know her. She died before I was born."

"Could you find out anything about her?"

I hoped so. I wouldn't let on that I was investigating though. "No offense, Blake, but that's your job and not mine."

He paused. "Have I said or done something recently to make you angry?"

Angry wasn't the word. "Look, I just came across something really awful today and..."

"Oh, really? What was it?"

Was the man being sarcastic or utterly clueless?

My expression couldn't show over the phone, but I was sure it conveyed equal parts confusion, outrage, and self-disdain. Why was I surprised? I should really have known Blake better by now. Although I really shouldn't call him that. He was Detective Samberg. And the things he said were just Detective Samberg being Detective Samberg.

I hung up. The man was so incapable of human empathy that it wasn't even funny.

BEA LAUGHED when I told her about my conversation with Blake the next morning. Seeing that I wasn't pleased, she covered her mouth with her hand to stifle the laughter.

"I think he's socially autistic," I said.

"Let's be more quiet," she whispered. "Aunt Astrid's in the

bunker, doing her thing to find, you know, tangents." We were in the restaurant area of the Brew-Ha-Ha.

Tangent was the word Bea and I had made up to refer to people who might be witches and not know it. Tangents could see into the other world and usually thought that they were hallucinating or, if they were old, getting senile. Tangents could even make things happen with magic, only they wouldn't know about the facts and history behind their magic because they wouldn't know that they were part of a lineage of witches and wizards.

"I thought the bunker was soundproof," I said. "Why do we have to be quiet?"

Bea shrugged and sifted through one of Aunt Astrid's dozens of notebooks on the floor, the contents handwritten. "We still don't want to be too loud and disturb whatever we might disturb."

Min whispered as he edged between us. "What's disturbing?"

I jumped and yelped in surprise.

"What?" Min asked. "It's just me! You never used to be so jumpy."

I almost answered that I wasn't so careful about my family's secret when we were teenagers. I'd still taken care, of course, because I knew it was important. Now that I was older, I knew just how much was at stake if our secret ever got out.

So instead, I answered, "Yesterday gave me a bad turn."

"Oh, yeah." Min flinched. "I heard about Samantha. When did this town get so dangerous?"

I thought that it was a crime, not a natural disaster, so it wasn't a matter of when. Somebody had made my town dangerous, and I was going to track them down. That was probably the attitude that Blake expected me to take the night before.

Bea explained to me, "Min thought that he'd help a little more today with the renovations, but Mom's got it in her head that she dreamed of Samantha Perry's death before, and if she could only remember the details, then the police could track down the culprit. I told Min that she's meditating right now."

The town knew Aunt Astrid as a fortune teller. It was strange. Humans believed in magical abilities up to a certain point. After that point, they found it entirely inconceivable and terrifying.

Aunt Astrid had a better memory of her visions of the future if they came to her when she was awake. She only wrote down the dreams that felt like they could come true, but she always forgot the dreams after writing them down.

"I'd help with going through the notebooks, but I can't read your aunt's handwriting," Min said.

"Neither can I," I lied, squinting at the pages. "And this is still Aunt Astrid's café, so she gets to direct how everything gets rebuilt. It's better to wait for her to get convinced that she's done all she could do." I shrugged. "Sorry, Min, I guess there's not much to do here after all."

"I could still hang around," Min said hopefully. "I don't really have any other friends in Wonder Falls, and I remember what you said, Cath, about nobody really wanting a white knight entrepreneur."

Bea and I exchanged glances. I liked having Min around, but he couldn't learn the Greenstone secret. It was hard enough for Bea and Jake, and they were already married.

"Actually," Bea said, getting up and moving over to the bar, where she'd left her bag. "It depends on the industry you're in. My friend, Naomi LaChance, manages this theater troupe—"

"The Curtains?" I asked.

Bea took a business card out of her purse pocket. "Here it is! Of course, The Curtains, Cath. Naomi doesn't run any other troupe for the local community theater."

"But they're terrible!" I exclaimed.

Bea pouted at me. "They do their best."

"They staged *Norma* for their autumn show last year," I said to Min. "I think only two people had had voice lessons and none for opera. Nobody in the audience understood Italian. I don't think that even was Italian—" I did want to keep the family secret, but sending him off to invest in a void of talent would be too harsh.

Min took that all in and came to entirely the wrong conclusion. His face broke into a smile. "It sounds like they need a lot of help!" He took the card from Bea.

I acknowledged, "They wouldn't turn down a patron, but it really shows that they've got contradictory artistic visions. Everybody has huge egos—"

"I can manage egos," Min said confidently.

"Naomi LaChance would be overseeing rehearsals right now," Bea said to him, pointing. "At the address on the card."

"Thanks!"

Nobody was listening to my warnings. Granted, I didn't even know what the Curtains would be up to this year. I hope it wouldn't be nearly as terrible.

"I'll be back soon," Min said.

Bea sighed. "Oh, take your time. This"—she waved at Aunt Astrid's dream diaries—"will definitely take a lot of ours."

Just as suddenly as he'd sidled up to us, Min was gone.

Bea and I sat on the floor around the notebooks and continued to sift through the text until the trapdoor behind the bar creaked open. Three cats came out. The first was Peanut Butter, Bea's dun-coated shorthair Abyssinian. Peanut Butter was usually high-strung and nervous. This time he was high-strung and excited. He rubbed against Bea and *miaowed* as she patted his head.

"Is that so?" I said aloud, catching Peanut Butter's meaning behind the *miaow*. "No luck?"

"Oh yes," Aunt Astrid said as she emerged from the bunker and shut the trapdoor behind her. "We've eliminated a lot of possibilities, but..."

"But no tangents then," Bea summed up as she stood and dusted herself off.

Aunt Astrid shook her head sadly. "Not a one."

"It's about time these kittens learn their magic," came another

thought from Aunt Astrid's cat, a longhaired white Maine Coon named Marshmallow. Marshmallow had been born looking like a grouchy grandmother, and at nine human years of age, she was finally beginning to act like one. *"But it wasn't a total waste."*

Aunt Astrid continued, "They would have Familiars in the other world, waiting to help train them."

I nodded.

"There are rules that tangents must follow," Aunt Astrid continued. "Firm rules. Even if they don't know them."

"I had no idea that the other world was so political," I said. "I thought that it was just strange and weird all the time."

"When it matters," Aunt Astrid said, "the Maid of the Mist can be very clear about what is allowed and what is not."

Peanut Butter sniffed at Aunt Astrid's notebooks and purred.

"He's worried about you and Jake," I translated. "Wow, Bea, how bad is it?"

"I don't know," Bea admitted. "Jake won't talk about it. He just said that he'll do what he can, and he trusts the Greenstones to do what we can."

Aunt Astrid gave Bea a comforting pat on the shoulder. "That sounds like a healthy boundary. Everyone needs that; we just forget it in a marriage."

"Boundaries? No, he's completely shut me out! Even Blake Samberg wants to talk more about the case to Cath."

I had a thought. "Shelley Marina was the resurrected. I

don't suppose we could do a séance or something to ask her about why she came back to life?"

"That's not a talent that any of us have," Bea pointed out. That didn't make it impossible, but that would make it difficult. We risked burning out on magical energy if we did something too far outside of our talents.

Aunt Astrid added, "If we relied on a ritual, the biggest help would be a waxing moon—and the moon was full last night."

Silence hung in the air as we processed that.

"If..." I began. "If whoever did this wants to try this resurrection spell again, and isn't even a natural witch or wizard, would they need the full moon again?"

Aunt Astrid considered that. "I'm not sure. Magic is more of an art than a science. Whoever's done this might have discovered a different way to do it than our way because, of course, we keep our ways secret."

"But I studied other ways to heal," Bea said. "There are all sorts of different ways to do spells for the same outcome. The moon really affects certain spells we do. I think it's likely it would be a factor in someone else's spells too."

"So we wait." I groaned in defeat and leaned back until I was lying on the floor. Treacle climbed up on my stomach and lay on it as if he were an Egyptian sphinx.

The Wake

A week and a half later, I attended Samantha Perry's memorial service. Judging by the turnout, she'd been popular among the townspeople, especially the young rebels, but Samantha didn't have family in town. She'd only moved to Wonder Falls three years ago. That made it hard for Jake's investigation.

I knew that because I saw and talked to Jake there. I also thought that he had some explaining to do in regards to Bea. I didn't want to start a fight at a funeral, but I was really bad at masking my annoyance.

As mourners milled about on the lawn in front of the church, I went up to Jake and said, "You're all in black. This isn't official duty then?"

"Yes and no," he answered. "Plainclothes should still be appropriate for the occasion."

"I thought Bea would be with you."

Jake looked surprised. "She couldn't come with me. She had..." He looked around at the mourners, as if to check that nobody was listening, then added in a low voice, "Some investigating to do with this case."

"It's so obvious what you're doing." I shook my head. "Jake, investigating this case is why I'm here. I checked the guest book, and nobody has the surname of Marina or Perry."

He cleared his throat and walked, signaling me to follow. I did.

Jake asked, "You tried to find a connection that way?"

"We're out of options on the magic investigation side. We really have no clue."

"Don't say that, please."

"But it's true."

"You can tell me the truth, just don't use the M-word."

I rolled my eyes.

Oblivious, Jake continued, "How can you be out of options and not have a clue? Don't you have—"

"The thing I'm not even supposed to say that we have?" I asked. "Does Bea have to talk around this, just like what we're doing now? Never mind answering that. I know the answer. The point is, it's more complicated than that, but we've done our best and turned up with nothing."

"You weren't going to find Marina on the guest book," Jake muttered. "If she had a daughter, Marina would have become a maiden name. In some places, the government still uses the mother's maiden name as a special evaluator for sensitive information."

"I know that," I said crossly.

"I thought you might, but I wasn't sure. Changing last names doesn't seem to be Greenstone tradition."

"It isn't."

"So did Bea get in trouble with your aunt when she wanted to become Bea Williams?"

"You could ask her yourself," I answered primly.

Jake's shoulders slumped. "Right."

I felt sorry enough for him that I added, "Aunt Astrid and I support Bea with everything, but the Greenstones have a legacy tied to the name. Bea gave that up for you."

"I don't want anything done for me," Jake grumbled. "I wish this was a part of her life that she could do with me, both of us together."

"Magic—"

"Ugh!"

"The thing," I said, "doesn't work like that, especially if you don't even want to use the word! It's usually bad news when people who aren't witches try to do the thing."

"Can we not use the W-word either?"

"I don't need to use the W-word if I turn you into a toad for being annoying and hurtful." I did not have the ability to do that, but Jake's expression looked cautious.

He said, "I'm not hurtful. I'm just overwhelmed by things too strange to handle."

"Welcome to the witch world. Peanut Butter thinks you're getting a divorce, and it's making him more anxious than usual. I share a heart and mind sometimes with animals, so that's been making me more anxious than usual. Also, Bea's been getting depressed, and I care. So should you! So I'm sorry that you're overwhelmed, but you can't honestly tell me that you're not also being hurtful." I realized that we were getting close to the low stone wall that was the other entrance to the graveyard. "Where are we going?"

"Blake found Samantha Perry's dog when we got here, and he ran into the woods after the dog. I'll call him to say that the wake's about to start." Jake got his phone out and dialed. He paused. "Why do we call it a wake?"

I assured him, "It has nothing to do with Samantha waking up after being dead." The poor dog had been without Samantha to take care of it for days, I thought.

"Blake," Jake spoke into his phone, "I'm with Cath Greenstone. We're waiting for you at the back entrance." He paused. "You took the dog to the animal shelter? All right." He ended the call. "It sounds like we have our first witness in custody."

I blinked. "I thought you were talking to Blake about a dog."

"Cath," Jake said, "I'm trying to be more open about this. Didn't you just say that you could talk to animals?"

The realization dawned on me. "I don't speak Dog very well, but it's worth a try."

Burger

Jake drove us to the animal shelter. The place was comprised of mostly chicken-wire enclosures with corrugated tin roofs where animals of the same species could run free. There was one tiny tiled room that served as a vet's office and was also where the mammals could be bathed. In the lobby was a long sofa of scratched-up, worn leather. I knew the place well, since I volunteered there a couple of times a month. Old Murray waited in the lobby with an unconscious Blake Samberg stretched out on the sofa.

"How did you get him to sleep?" Jake asked Old Murray.

Murray mustered up a sad smile. "I've had a lot of practice. You get as old as me, with friends who are as old as I am, and you've got to learn to handle them when their minds start going."

I peered at the gray half circles under Blake's eyes. I whispered, "Has he really not slept since Samantha's murder?"

"Of course he has," Jake whispered. "It would kill him otherwise. But every time he wakes up, Blake gets angry with himself for taking that time out of the case to sleep. He'll keep working until he faints. Then he technically sleeps, once he's fainted, but he has nightmares that he's solved the case, and the nightmares wake him up, and his epiphany makes no sense. He just won't accept that the Perry case could remain unsolved."

"He rambles a lot," Old Murray agreed. "He said the dog was evidence, but he couldn't take it to the police station because of conspirators."

"Conspirators? Blake must be paranoid..." I sighed then turned to Old Murray. "Can we see the dog that Blake brought in?"

Old Murray looked from me to Jake. "I told Cody to give the dog a bath." Murray looked worried. "Could the dog really have evidence on her? I kept the collar, if you want to look at it."

"I'll examine the collar," Jake said decisively.

"And I'll help Cody bathe the dog," I said. "I mean, she's a big dog."

As Old Murray wandered off to get the dog collar, Jake went with me to the tiled room. Old Murray had told me before that Blake volunteered frequently when there wasn't a case going on. I'd never run into Blake at the animal shelter though.

All of the veterinary equipment had been moved into the hall, on top of the stainless steel examiner's table. I knocked on the door to the tiled room and waved through the square window at Cody, who strained to reach over and turn off the faucet.

"Can I help?" I called through the window.

Cody looked me up and down—of course, I'd dressed for Samantha's memorial service, not for this—and said, "Nah, I'm fine. There isn't room."

The dog began to growl.

Jake asked, "Cath, what's happening?"

"I don't need to get in there to ask what's so wrong," I answered. "I can do it from here—"

That was a mistake. I reached out with my mind and got a single terrified and angry idea shot back at me. The dog lunged at the door, knocking Cody to the ground, its teeth bared in a snarl.

"Cody!" I shouted.

Jake threw himself between the door and me. His body slammed the door shut as the dog's muzzle tried to pry it open. "Cath, get out of here!"

I stood there, stunned.

"It's you!" Jake shouted. "Whatever you tried to do made the dog go wild! Just get out of here!"

I backed away and ran down the hall, out of the animal shelter, and into the driveway, where I caught my breath and tried to make sense of what had just happened. Jake followed a few minutes later, carrying the dog's collar. Old Murray and a limping, suds-covered Cody waved him farewell.

"We're not taking Blake with us?" I asked.

"He needs his rest," Jake answered. "Can you explain to me what just happened?"

I already knew some of the basics from experience and intuition. I would need to catch Jake up on that first. The truth was, I couldn't make complete sense of what had happened at the animal shelter. I took the collar, got in the car's front passenger seat, and Jake started driving. I saw from the tag that Samantha's dog was named Burger.

"It was like Burger was afraid of magic," I told Jake. "Most animals I talk to don't notice that what I'm doing is magic at all, because the mind and heart are part of instincts—senses that animals use all the time. They might be surprised that a human can talk to them the way that I do, but they don't think so much about it that they can't believe it while it's happening. That's a human thing. Some creatures, like fish or something, I can take over their minds completely because their minds are simple enough. People are too complicated, especially the ones that think about thinking. Domestic animals can be somewhere in between, and I guess Burger had a viewpoint that recognized magic and rejected it."

"Because Burger saw the magic happening," Jake concluded.

"It must have been the darkest magic, and it took Burger's only companion away from her. But it makes no sense! Aunt Astrid did a search for natural witches who didn't know that they were witches, and that turned up nothing. So that means that whatever happened to Samantha didn't come from a witch's talent. Burger shouldn't have recognized it as the same kind of magic."

"But it's both magic," Jake pointed out.

"There's a difference between music and noise, but both are sounds," I explained. "A ritual from a non-witch or wizard would have a specific feel. Magic that comes from a talent has a more natural feel, closer to reality."

"But it's all magic," Jake repeated. "It killed someone who's supposed to be alive, brought someone back to life who was supposed to be dead, and influenced a giant dog to attack you. Is there anything else I should know about how dangerous this is?"

There was a lot more to magic than what Jake knew, and they weren't all bad things. I wasn't in a mood to reassure him anymore though. "Magic killed my parents. It opened a portal to another dimension, and something unfriendly that had never been human came through. My dad was a non-witch who didn't stand a chance, and my mom was a witch who could only just manage to save me." That was all true, but I went on sarcastically. "Magic is barely a solution to the problems that we only have because of magic."

Jake drove on in silence and dropped me off at my house, where Treacle was waiting for once. I changed out of my black dress and into something more casual for the rest of the day, and I caught Treacle up on what I'd discovered.

Treacle had a lot of disdain for dogs and informed me that Marshmallow wanted the both of us to stay over at Aunt

Astrid's place. I gave Aunt Astrid a call, and she told me to come right on over.

Unfamiliars

"An animal afraid of your magic?" Aunt Astrid pondered that as she set the dining table for three. In the kitchen was enough macaroni and cheese—more like penne and fondue cheese with cayenne pepper—for five people. "Our whole lives dedicated to witchcraft, and we're still learning something new every day."

I gave a humorless laugh as I set down water dishes for Marshmallow and Treacle. "If you think that's bad, I should tell you that Jake learned more about magic today than he ever wanted to know. I wonder if whoever—whatever—tried to do the resurrection might not even have been a person."

I went to the kitchen to wash my hands. When I came back into the dining room, Aunt Astrid was still thinking about it.

"The Unfamiliar," she said, which was what we called the beings from the other worlds who weren't helpful.

That was also what we called beings that we hadn't decided would be helpful or unhelpful. When it came to Unfamiliars, we witches were kind of like kids who are taught not to talk to strangers. We just didn't know how dangerous an Unfamiliar could be, and the safest thing to do was to not have any association with them.

"The worst ones would know how to get past the notice of the Maid of the Mist," Astrid said. "They would be a pure expression of talent, enough to spook poor dear Burger. To do that kind of thing, they would need the vessel of a human."

I nodded. "Would an Unfamiliar really risk getting Samantha killed? Especially for a human that was definitely dead?"

"We would have noticed if Samantha was being used as a vessel."

That was true. Unfamiliars needed to familiarize themselves with their targets so that they could move from their world and into ours. Their attempts would be like hauntings, possessions—something that witches couldn't miss, even if the unfamiliar could get past great beings like the Maid of the Mist.

"Maybe this Unfamiliar made a grave mistake—literally," I suggested. "Maybe it did make Samantha its vessel but got her to do something that accidentally killed her. The Unfamiliar probably got kicked out of Samantha's body after that happened."

"We need to make sure of that before we relax and mourn the unlucky Samantha Perry," Aunt Astrid told me. "But I think of the timing and the act—it's too human. It was as if it were motivated."

"The Unfamiliar have motivations too, I'm sure," I said. "It's just that they never explain or express themselves properly."

"Understatement of a lifetime!" Aunt Astrid exclaimed.

"The Unfamiliars just aren't reasonable," I concluded.

Aunt Astrid set out the bottle of chilled white wine and said, "Won't you get the door?"

I had already made my way to the front door and turned the doorknob before I realized that there had been no knock, no doorbell ring. Bea stood at the doorstep with Peanut Butter in one arm and a trolley-bag in the other. She looked as if she'd been crying.

"Jake did not just kick my cousin and soul-sister out of her own home," I said, mostly to myself.

Bea shook her head and sniffled. "Jake said that he needed some time apart to think about things. I needed to leave. This is my home, with you and Mom and all of our cats."

I let her in, and we all dined on Bea's favorite comfort food and got slightly drunk on her favorite wine. Even though Bea insisted that Jake's need to take a breather was not my fault at all, I volunteered to make a run for the chocolates and DVD rentals Bea loved.

CHANGE IS another part of life. Life itself goes on, even when we feel like it shouldn't. Some things are so awful that the whole planet should stop and turn its face back to just notice. It never does, not even for witches.

I wanted to contact the spirit of Shelley Marina, but Aunt Astrid informed me that it would do no good, since Shelley was so old. Contacting Samantha Perry, Aunt Astrid was certain, wouldn't go well either, since Samantha would be too confused and upset this soon after death to be a good witness. Contacting the dead was no easy feat.

During the day, the three of us continued to work on the Brew-Ha-Ha. We moved in new tables and chairs, stocked up on new cups and glasses and saucers. While we were restocking, Min came back.

"The place looks great!" he said as he shook his umbrella dry and left it open on the patio. He stomped his shoes dry on the doormat.

Aunt Astrid laughed. "Welcome back. You've missed a lot."

"So have we, by the looks of it. You're back to wearing business suits, Min," I remarked.

"I'm a producer now, for the Curtains' next show. I wanted to personally issue my favorite family in town..." He gave a dramatic pause and drew a stack of cards from his pocket before finishing. "Their complimentary tickets!"

"Four of them," Bea observed, with a little smile that I knew was hiding a pang.

"For Jake, of course." In the silence that followed, Min's joy visibly wilted. "What did I say?"

"Excuse me," Bea said softly, heading behind the bar and into the bunker.

Even Aunt Astrid didn't know what to say.

"Nothing wrong, it was really thoughtful," I said to Min and flinched. "It's just that, as Aunt Astrid said, you've really missed a lot."

"What's wrong with Bea and Jake?" Min asked, sitting at one of our new tables.

I couldn't tell him the truth. "That's between them."

"We just support Bea emotionally through it all," Aunt Astrid agreed. "Want a cup of hot tea or coffee?"

"This might be hot chocolate weather," Min said hopefully.

"I'll get right to that," Aunt Astrid said with a smile and flicked her gaze from me to the table.

I sat down.

Min spoke first. "If you don't know what's going on between them, then why do you look like you blame yourself for it?"

"I've got resting guilt face. It doesn't mean anything," I lied.

"Cath!" Min exclaimed. "What happened to us?"

"Us?"

"You, me, and Bea. We were like the three Musketeers, except that we actually used muskets."

"Those were toys," I pointed out, but I understood what he was saying. "Bea and Jake have a problem that they don't even want to talk to each other about. If they don't catch each other up on everything after making one of the most binding commitments of adult life, then what chance does a cousin have?"

"Cousin and soul-sister," Min reminded me.

I'd use that phrase so many times for Bea and myself that it had become second nature.

"Marriage," I mused. "Apparently it's complicated."

"My parents never talked as much to each other as I've heard was recommended," Min remarked. "I don't know if that's an Asian thing or a generational thing."

"Aunt Astrid and Uncle Eagle Eye talked about everything, but it only made any sense to the two of them. Flower children, you know." I remembered them together better than Bea did because I'd been old enough to remember when my uncle passed away. "My parents didn't talk a lot, but then again, I was at that age when my mom was still all about just being my mom."

"All marriages are different," Min concluded. "A big decision like Jake's doesn't just come up because a third person said this or that thing. It must have been going on for a while, so don't blame yourself."

That was also right. It didn't make me feel much better though.

Aunt Astrid brought hot cocoa for the three of us.

"Jake's uninvited to the show until he realizes what a treasure Bea Greenstone is," Min said to us.

Aunt Astrid and I cheered with our voices, then we cheered with our mugs clinking against each other.

Topher

Bea was enthusiastic enough about the show to let herself forget about Min's well-intentioned fourth ticket. At Aunt Astrid's insistence, we dressed formally, despite Bea's laughing objection that it was only the Curtains.

My objection, once I looked through Aunt Astrid's bedroom window at the moon in the afternoon sky, was more grim. "We should be ready to get to the graveyard and fight zombies tonight, shouldn't we?"

"No, that's a gibbous moon," Aunt Astrid corrected without looking up. "The full moon is tomorrow."

"Already?" Bea gasped. "Well, it could be that nothing will happen."

"And that would mean that Samantha Perry died for no reason that we could find," I grumbled.

Aunt Astrid sighed. "That happens too."

A car horn sounded from the driveway. I looked down to see a limousine and a familiar figure in a blazer. The three of us tottered out into the driveway on our spindly high heels, wearing glittering shawls.

"What's this about?" I called to Blake where he leaned against the limousine door.

"Security detail," he replied gruffly.

The tinted window of the front seat rolled down, revealing Officer Diane Davis in the driver's seat. Diane blared the car horn again, waved, and said, "We'll protect you!"

Behind me, Bea exhaled heavily. Maybe she had been hoping to see Jake and Blake, the not-so dynamic duo.

"You look nice," I told Blake. "You should get sleep more often."

He cleared his throat and gave me a quick once-over. "You look... not so bad yourself."

This was the closest thing to a compliment I'll ever get from Blake. He opened the passenger door and ushered the three of us in.

Mrs. Park was waiting inside, and she and Aunt Astrid greeted one another warmly. Mrs. Park was almost two decades younger than Aunt Astrid, but she looked two decades older, especially that night, because of her nervousness.

"Mr. Park won't be joining us?" I wondered.

"Oh, no!" Mrs. Park exclaimed. "He thinks that the performing arts is a wasted career track and doesn't know why Min would invest in this show of all things."

Aunt Astrid clucked her tongue. "Min could invest in a wasted career track like this theater troupe four times a year for the rest of his life and still have enough for retirement. Isn't that right?"

"It is," Mrs. Park agreed. "And Min argued the same way. He should know his father by now, but I know he will be so disappointed when he sees that Mr. Park didn't change his mind."

"Well," I said wryly, "I've actually seen Mr. Park at a show staged by the Curtains, so he knows what Min's getting into."

"Don't be mean, Cath!" Bea exclaimed. "This is in honor of Tommy."

"The Curtains aren't without talent," I conceded. "It's just that they're so ambitious. Operas and ballets! Even their avant-garde stuff shows no concept of working within their limitations. I'm not even talking about the budget."

"I never met Thomas," Mrs. Park said. "Min looks up to him a lot now. It's funny."

I didn't think that was so strange. What I wondered was when Samantha would get anything grand done in her honor and what it would be. Then I wondered why Min would invite Blake. I thought they didn't get along.

We would soon find out.

BLAKE ESCORTED the four of us into the lobby of the Wonder Falls ballet theater, which had lush carpets and sparkling chandeliers. Most other audience members had opted for full-formal attire.

"You were right after all," Bea said to Aunt Astrid while craning her neck. "We aren't overdressed. Oh, look, there's Naomi up on the dais."

I peered in the direction Bea was pointing and saw that Min Park was standing with Naomi.

"Well, let's all go and say hi," I urged the other five.

Naomi squeaked with excitement when she saw Bea approaching. They gave each other a quick embrace and air kisses, then went to the side to chat. Min embraced his mother, nodded in greeting to Aunt Astrid, gave me a smile—and signaled at Blake to follow him.

"What was that about?" I asked nobody in particular.

"Security matters," Aunt Astrid guessed. "Maybe some of our less-than-model fellow townspeople haven't forgiven Tommy for that political article and are prepared to be less than constructive about it."

"That must be it," I said, completely convinced that it couldn't be it. "I'm just going to go make sure..."

I followed Blake and Min to an empty corridor, where of course I couldn't stay hidden until they made a turn. A set of double doors down the hall led to a function room, but I wouldn't be able to see or hear anything if I hid there. I ran forward as quietly as I could in heels but kept myself hidden behind the bend in the corridor. Blake was murmuring, and I heard, to my surprise, Old Murray's voice objecting.

"And here I thought you'd talk sense," Old Murray said to

Blake. "Here's Topher's ticket, right here. It's his ticket, but it was mailed to my address. Now are you going to show us to our seats?"

"But you didn't reserve or confirm a seat for yourself," Blake said.

"You saw all I've got to do, Blake! Do you really want to see how Topher gets without me? It'd be better to leave both of us out of this show if that were to happen."

Then Min spoke up. "Topher is Tommy's only family, that's all I knew. I didn't know that he—"

A fourth voice, doleful and trembling with age, yelled, "Alice! I know what you did to my Alice!"

"Wasn't lucid," Min finished.

Old Murray told Topher to be quiet.

After a pause, Old Murray spoke again. "So did we come all this way for nothing? Or did you mean what you wrote about being honored to have Thomas's family watch the show? I'm his family too, you know. Tommy was my grand-nephew. My sister Dolores was a Willis before she became a Thompson."

"Dolores!" Topher's voice spoke again. "Don't leave us like this! She's left us, Murray."

"I know," Old Murray said to him. "I've known a long time. It's been a long time, Topher, think."

Blake and Min walked back up to the corner.

"We can wait for the theater to fill up and just count Murray's seat as a complementary walk-in, if there's room," Min said to Blake.

"Right," Blake said, "I'll notify the ushers." There was static like a communicator coming to life. "Davis, do you copy?"

Had this all been about seating arrangements? As Blake spoke instructions into his communicator, I risked peeking around the corner and gasped through my nose at what I saw. There was definitely something, a ripple in the air, over Old Murray's balding head. It was probably an Unfamiliar!

"I don't know if you can understand me," Min said to Topher, "but thank you for coming. Thomas was such an inspiration to all of us."

Topher lunged—lurched, more like, but feebly—toward Min. "You've got so much nerve to say that, to show your face here!"

Min's expression was one of confusion and hurt.

"Sit down, Topher," Old Murray said calmly—and there it was again, that ripple in the air that hurt my eyes.

When Topher sank to the floor, his wispy gray-and-white hair falling all over his face, I thought the Unfamiliar had succeeded in controlling Topher too. I ducked back around the corner.

Min almost stammered but quickly recovered the poise that he'd learned in his time away from Wonder Falls. "I hope you don't mind waiting a little longer."

"Nah," Old Murray answered. "Although if you can get us any of those little sandwiches that they're passing around..."

"We'll do that."

Min's voice was too close. I tiptoed—in heels as high as

the ones I wore, there was no other choice—down the hall, slipped into the function room, and pressed my ear against the door so that maybe I could catch what they were talking about as they passed.

Min asked, "Was that enough to confirm your suspicions?"

"No," Blake replied. "I can't deny my suspicions either, but I want to."

"Maybe we should have brought Cath in this time."

"We didn't have to," Blake said. "She brought herself."

"She what?" Min exclaimed.

The door I wasn't leaning on opened, and Min and Blake peered into the function room.

"How did you know I was listening?" I asked Blake.

"I'm a detective," he replied coldly. "I notice things."

They walked in, and Blake shut the door behind them.

"Old Murray Willis is my prime suspect," Blake explained. "I don't know how, because none of the evidence adds up to anything that makes sense, but Old Murray acted suspiciously and lacks an alibi. He had Cody bathe Burger when I told him that the dog was evidence. What do you think?"

It was really too bad that I knew that the crime had been committed by an Unfamiliar possessing Old Murray, but I couldn't tell either of them. "You can't arrest Old Murray on a hunch."

Blake shrugged. "We can interrogate him. With lack of evidence, a confession will do."

"With the way you interrogate," Min said to Blake, "I

think that's too harsh. I would know, since you ripped me to pieces in that interrogation room."

"He did?" I asked Min. "When?"

"Doesn't matter now," Min muttered.

"You're still alive," Blake said. "Samantha Perry was brutalized and left for dead. No justice and no peace. For anybody."

"I'm a grown man, and I can take your interrogation methods," Min said. "Murray is the sole guardian of a minor—Cody. He's Topher's only friend. Topher lost his mind and is practically a hundred years old. This won't end well. Cath, am I wrong?"

"Unfortunately, no," I told him.

Blake's expression was usually a glower, so I didn't know how to describe the look he shot Min. He did say, sharply, "Cath and I spend at least one afternoon a week with Old Murray at the animal shelter. We know what good he's done. But if he's guilty of a murder in this town, we can't stand for it."

"I'm not telling either of you, or anybody, to stand for it," Min said, opening the door to the hall. "I just can't be around when you take any of your terrible options."

I sighed when the door swung shut behind Min. "Why did Topher Thompson accuse Min of doing something to Alice? Who's Alice?"

"Who knows? Topher knows, obviously, but good luck getting him to explain."

"Couldn't he get taken into custody too? I don't mean like an interrogation; he needs a doctor." I added to myself that

Topher also needed some expert witches to look him over and check to see that he didn't catch Unfamiliar spirits from his only friend.

"We'll do what we can." Blake was out the door before I could ask who he meant by "we."

The Curtains Rise

I thought that I would be a few minutes late for the show, but Naomi was still talking on the stage.

Bea whispered as I passed her, "You missed Min's eulogy for Tommy. Naomi had a shorter one because she started crying. She's introducing us about the show now."

Naomi continued, "This ballet was inspired by a German essayist, Heine, who traced the origins of the Wilis to Slavic and Austrian culture. The fantasy that they fulfill is common to humanity, whether that would be grief over the lost potential of a young life ended too soon or vengeance for deception."

"What are we watching again?" I whispered.

"*Giselle* is the name of the show," Aunt Astrid replied, "but personally, I'm watching those two old men up in the balcony seats."

I turned to look where Aunt Astrid had pointed. Sure enough, there was Old Murray and Topher.

Bea said to me, "One of them was very rude and loud when Min got onstage. I don't think he's well."

I cleared my throat discreetly. "Did either of you see anything... Unfamiliar about them?"

"Very," Aunt Astrid murmured.

Bea added, "Yes, but I don't know which one. It might be both."

"They'll be taken in at the end of the show, but I think I know which one of those men it's attached to. If they try anything before then..." I hoped that either Bea or Aunt Astrid would have a plan.

Their silence showed that they didn't, and Mrs. Park slipped into her seat beside Aunt Astrid just as the house lights dimmed.

I couldn't get too engrossed with the show, but it wasn't as bad as I'd thought it would be. None of the performers could dance ballet with the boneless grace of a performance-standard dancer, but the costumes were splendid—so money could sometimes buy entertainment-worthy quality. Nobody was trying to sing, at least.

I could relate to the protective mother of the frail and waiflike main character, and my favorite character was the princess huntress. They reminded me of Aunt Astrid, Bea, and myself. That was, until the title character got into a love triangle with two jerks, one who always lied and the other who told the truth—and it turned out the latter was worse, because that truth gave the main character a heart attack that killed her.

Then the house lights came on for the intermission between the first and second act. Old Murray and Topher didn't leave their seats during intermission, so neither did the three of us.

"I can't believe I didn't notice it at the animal shelter," I said, about Old Murray's Unfamiliar. "Burger didn't notice it either. I wonder if the Unfamiliar just wasn't around that day."

"Don't stop noticing it now," Aunt Astrid advised.

"Maybe we should," Bea suggested. "If it knows that we've noticed it, then it might try something. There are too many people here."

"Not right now," I whispered. "It's intermission."

Aunt Astrid shook her head. "They're too far away. There's no way to reach them from here with magic."

"If the abilities of the hosts are limited," Bea murmured, "the Unfamilars would be limited too."

I nodded. "Yes. They're already limited by human motivations and rules for performing spells under the full moon. The Unfamiliar would need to do a lot of work to get their host to do something improvised and magical. At least, I hope that's the case for these ones."

That had seemed to be the way it worked for the Unfamiliar that had haunted me and that had cost my parents their lives. The problem with the Unfamiliars was that we really would never know how they operated.

We had a tense evening, full of wary anticipation. It

occurred to me that the Unfamiliar could take action even today. The gibbous moon could be mistaken for full. What if the Unfamiliar or its host decided that it was close enough? Something had gone wrong with the first resurrection spell. The collateral damage of approximations didn't come off as too much of a bother for this Unfamiliar.

"I wish that we could just tell the Maid of the Mist," I said. "You would think that she'd want to know. Hasn't she interfered before for less important things?"

"Less important to us," Bea pointed out. "She might be Familiar, but she must have different priorities that we can't understand. We might be a mystery to her too."

"We can agree that Unfamiliars like this are bad though, right?"

"That's right," Aunt Astrid said firmly. "What to do about it is up to witches."

"Not right now, it isn't," I said ruefully, as the audience members returned and the house lights dimmed for the second act.

Mrs. Park returned with small dumplings on toothpicks for the three of us, which I was sure wasn't allowed, but she was the producer's mother. All the tension was making me hungry. I ate too fast and hiccupped most of the way through the second act.

The main character came back from the grave to face down the queen of the ghosts of women scorned, and in doing so, she rescued the people who had killed her—or one of them. The choreographer must have taken liberties with the original choreography, because I thought we had come to see a ballet. The final dance turned into a collective tap like Riverdance, followed by more modern street dancing.

"What am I even watching right now?" I mumbled, flabbergasted.

"Watch your manners around Tommy's family," Aunt Astrid said, only because Mrs. Park was sitting with us. She meant that I should keep watching Old Murray and Topher.

It was a good thing she pointed it out, because I saw Topher stand up and disappear through the curtain behind his balcony seat. Old Murray followed him.

"I've got to be rude and walk out on this," I said to Bea. "And I might need to run after someone. I won't take my shoes with me."

"I'll find a way to explain it to Min and Naomi," Bea said.

I shrugged and smiled at Mrs. Park's gaze of disapproval. She always thought that I was too harsh and judgmental. For now, that would be my cover story.

The Escape

As I made my way up the aisle, I tried to remember the spell to pull a host apart from an Unfamiliar. The process was often one long and exhausting fight. Being a witch wasn't like in the movies where they had unlimited power. If we used too much magic, we might get magic burnout, which was very depleting, and it might take days, weeks, or even months to recover.

As I'd mentioned, as a child, I had almost become a host for an Unfamiliar spirit. My mother tried to explain to me that I had the power to keep it away from myself, but I was too young and scared to really understand how. That was the easiest way to prevent becoming a host for an Unfamiliar though—and the best way. Maybe things would have gone differently if I'd done it on my own.

Maybe I could simply talk Old Murray into rejecting the Unfamiliar, but I doubted that would work. It hadn't work for me, and I'd already known the basics of magic and witchcraft. Talking someone through the Unfamiliar rejecting process left too much to chance, especially if they weren't witches.

So I had no other choice but to use magic. I could do a binding spell. The Unfamiliar wouldn't leave the host but simply be bound inside the host so it wouldn't do any harm. It sounded unpleasant, but what else could I do?

By the time I decided that, I was in the theater lobby. I caught Diane speaking into her communicator as she made her way up the grand staircase.

"Area clear," she finished then looked alarmed when I ran up to her.

"Not a chance," I told her. "Topher and Old Murray left the balcony seats a few seconds ago. Where would they be now?"

"The balcony leads straight to either the west wing or the east wing," Diane replied.

"Of course you've got backup watching both."

Diane shook her head. "Blake and I are doing a favor, private security just for tonight. Min told us to expect those two to make their way down here after the show, then Blake could read them their rights in private and take them in for questioning."

I groaned and started up the staircase. Diane followed me as I almost scolded, "Well, they're trying to dodge us by getting out earlier than that." When we reached the top of the grand staircase, I told Diane, "You and Blake block the east wing. I'll block the west, and we'll have them surrounded

—but if you find them first, don't do anything to threaten them. Just stall them until I meet with you."

There was no time to wait for her answer. I ran ahead to the west wing. Fortunately, that was where I found the both of them.

Murray was grappling Topher and saying, "I can't let you go out on your own and disappear again! Come back with me and just calm down!"

"Stop it!" I said as I fixed my gaze on the ripple over Murray's and Topher's heads. "You can't control him, Murray. You don't have the right. I'll give you one chance to leave him alone."

I concentrated on him to do my spell.

Murray raised his hand, palm toward me, and I was struck with a paralyzing fatigue. The Unfamiliar laughed. My knees buckled, and my field of vision darkened even though I tried desperately to remain standing and alert. In my panic, I thought I might have done the spell wrong.

But I sensed the Unfamiliar spirit's fading laughter. I used all of my strength to conjure a magic lasso. I made it wrap around the Unfamiliar again and again before tying a knot.

It had worked. For now. The spell could last a day, up to two or three, until I, or another witch, had to do it again. It took a lot of energy, and it wasn't sustainable for the long run.

Somewhere down the hall, footsteps sounded, followed by a scuffling sound. Murray made a grab for me as I began to faint.

A voice pulled my attention back to the world of the non-witches. "Step away from her! I'm telling you, I'm armed."

It was Blake. My vision focused, and I saw Old Murray looking confused and shocked.

Murray let me go. "What's going on here?"

Blake holstered his gun and drew a pair of handcuffs instead.

"I'm so sorry, Murray," I said as Blake snapped on the handcuffs.

Murray looked from his cuffed wrists, to Blake, to me, and back to his wrists. "What did I do wrong? I didn't do anything..."

He really hadn't, but there was no way to even try to tell non-witches what had really happened. Instead, I asked Blake, "Where's Topher?"

Blake nodded in the direction of farther down the hall. "I caught him as he was trying to run off and got him handcuffed. Diane will take care of him."

Diane trotted up behind him with her gun drawn. "Take care of what?" She saw us and holstered her gun.

Blake peered at her. "Wasn't there an old man in the hallway behind us?"

Diane paused. "Yes?"

Blake groaned with aggravation. "Diane! He was handcuffed and knocked out! Get back there and guard him like you were obviously supposed to!"

As Diane backed away apologetically, I raised an eyebrow at Blake.

"I can't wait until Jake clocks back in," Blake muttered.

"Handcuffed and knocked out? That's harsh, Blake. You could have given Topher a heart attack or a stroke." Old Murray, at least, was spry for his age, although I still felt sorry for him when he looked at us sadly. We took care of lost and injured animals together. We were friends.

Blake argued, "He attacked me first."

"He's over eighty years old! He couldn't have been too much of a threat."

As I said that, Diane jogged back into our hallway. She fidgeted a little and said apologetically, "The other old man got away. I went back and saw your extra handcuffs in the hall, so I tried to run him down—I guess he was faster than we gave him credit for."

"He was stronger too." Blake turned to Diane and said, "I think you should turn your resignation in to Chief Talbot."

Diane flinched. "That isn't fair, Samberg!"

I glared at Blake and touched Diane's shoulder. To Diane, I said, "Take us home first. Topher can't be all that difficult to find, right?" I looked at Blake, thinking that it would be on him to do it.

Normal

Diane drove us Greenstones and the Parks home.

"The first two-thirds, maybe, of the show wasn't all that bad," I admitted.

"If only Mr. Park had given the ballet a chance," Aunt Astrid said. "There's even a glowing review from Cath."

"Even if she did walk out." Bea chuckled.

Min talked about what had happened behind the scenes, the concepts that he enjoyed but didn't make it to the stage, and the battle of egos that I had warned him about.

We solved the mystery before the full moon, I thought. The town was safe again. I counted the binding spell on the Unfamiliar spirit as a victory, even if it is just for now.

There was still the question of how harsh the legal proceedings would be though. As uncompromising as Blake could be, I doubted that he would go too far in interrogating somebody who wasn't in their right mind and was so infirm of body. Maybe temporary insanity would be the best compromise between the truth and the consequences for Old Murray. I could only hope.

Bea was smiling again because she'd seen her friends. With some good old-fashioned family support, maybe she could figure something out with Jake.

Aunt Astrid and Mrs. Park had both been able to put on nice dresses and watch an entertaining show. Min had done something for the community like he wanted to.

We'd find Topher, or someone would, and we'd figure out a more reasonable explanation for his disappearance.

The Greenstones would finish renovating the Brew-Ha-Ha next week and have an opening party the day after.

Things were looking up.

SOMETIMES I WISHED I were normal. Then I remembered that not knowing about magic didn't stop it from ruining people's lives, and I realized that I was very lucky.

Then I forgot that and wished I were normal, because without magic, I'd have one less thing to think about on a crazy day.

The next morning got off to a running start. I received a call from the construction company's new accountant about a discrepancy in the amount billed for the Brew-Ha-Ha reparations. Something about the insurance, or the taxes, or the retainer fee—Bea usually did the numbers with that, so because the accountant was new and the filing was messy, I told them to call Bea. I gave them her house number, because it was the one I'd memorized. Then I realized only Jake lived there now. That wouldn't be so bad though. Jake was a good guy, and he would call Aunt Astrid to pass on the message, or even just give them Aunt Astrid's number instead.

Instead, I had my breakfast, got dressed, and received another call from the accountant about the Brew-Ha-Ha's internals manager no longer living at the number given.

"Is that what Jake is telling people?" I exclaimed, shocked and outraged. I might have called him some names, and I definitely hung up and stormed out.

On the walk to Bea and Jake's place—no, I thought with sarcastic fury, just Jake's place now—I checked my cell phone and found nine voice messages from Blake and two from Min. I'd expected the ones from Blake. Most of them were the increasingly improbable theories of a sleepless gumshoe, concerning Samantha Perry's murder. I wondered why he didn't just write them in his cop's notebook. I was more worried than flattered that he spent the entire night leaving me messages like that. The case was driving him nuts, and he didn't seem to have anyone else to turn to.

All right, maybe I was a little flattered—and a little frustrated, because I could never tell Blake anything close to the truth about these cases in Wonder Falls. The Greenstones had solved the Samantha Perry case, but we didn't have a cover story. An Unfamiliar took advantage of an aging man to stir up trouble in our physical world. How were we supposed to explain that? If not even Jake wanted to know, then Blake hadn't a hope.

According to Blake's messages, it had been Jake who convinced him to take up the security sideline at the show.

Blake's final message worried me the most. "No means, no motive, no evidence... this makes no sense. This makes no sense! This makes no sense! This makes no se—" He trailed off in wordless, muffled gargles of anguish. "Call me when you think of something."

Min's concerns were much simpler. His first message informed me that he wouldn't be available to help at the Brew-Ha-Ha because he had to talk something over with his dad. I winced. Min had always had a rocky relationship with his father. For Min's sake, I hoped that was water over the dam, but some family dramas never ended.

Min's second message informed me that he'd joined the search party to look for Topher.

The moment after I let all those messages play out, my phone buzzed to life with a call from Aunt Astrid.

"Honestly, Kitten Cath!" she exclaimed. "You have enough boy troubles of your own. You don't need to make more by interfering with Bea's."

I reached the corner of Rainfall and Riverfall and halted. Farther down Riverfall would take me to Jake's place, or I could turn the corner and head for Aunt Astrid's. Before making any decision, I needed to ask, "Aunt Astrid, how did you know that?" As far as I knew, Aunt Astrid could see the future, not the present.

Aunt Astrid answered, “Bea is helping me organize my dream journals. We’re only a fraction of the way through, but I read some of my entries, and they...” She paused as if thinking of how to describe it. “They reminded me of the future.”

“That might be helpful later, but don’t we have more mundane problems to worry about?” I told her about the construction company.

“One moment—”

I listened to her distant voice speaking to Bea.

When I could hear Aunt Astrid properly again, she said, “Oh, dear.”

I had mixed feelings then. Anger at Jake nagged my feet to run toward him. Worry nagged me to head for Aunt Astrid’s house. Guilt kept me frozen to the spot.

Aunt Astrid said, “Leave Jake alone. Bea needs her family.”

I bolted for Aunt Astrid’s house.

Enough is Enough

The first thing I noticed when I stepped in the door was that the cats were on the table in the anteroom. Marshmallow was curled up like a large fuzzy dumpling. Peanut Butter was belly up, mouth open and panting.

"Peanut Butter!" I exclaimed. "What happened?"

"I told him," Marshmallow thought at me. *"I showed him the other world, the one we all share, where Bea heals. I told him he couldn't make worries go away or else the first one Bea would have healed was him!"*

"And Peanut Butter tried anyway," I guessed and tickled the tawny cat's belly.

Our cats could sometimes work magic. Marshmallow was the best at it, because Peanut Butter and Treacle were both too young. They sometimes managed it, when they joined together or used the help of their humans. To heal a human all alone though, without even knowing how... *"How bad is his burnout?"*

Marshmallow assured me, "*Peanut Butter doesn't need to go to the cat hospital.*"

At that, Peanut Butter yowled. He sent me the thought, "*I'm fine! I want to try again to help Mommy. I need help.*"

"I'm not helping you," Marshmallow grumbled, shifting so that she curled up into a smaller ball.

I sensed Peanut Butter calling for Treacle.

"Treacle's not here then," I said. He tended to be most feral of the three of them. Marshmallow was like a crochety old lady, and Peanut Butter was a scaredy-cat.

If Treacle wasn't at my place when I left and he wasn't here, then I wasn't sure where he was, and I wasn't surprised. Treacle also tended to worry much less about what he couldn't understand. When I realized that, I tried to comfort Peanut Butter with the thought that what made Bea upset was a human problem that we could solve without magic. Bea just needed Jake to quit being such a jerk.

"Treacle doesn't worry about what he doesn't understand," Marshmallow repeated my thoughts to me. "*We should both give him a stern talking-to. He won't attend our magic lessons! He thinks they're boring and we can always depend on our humans to do it!"*

"The opposite problem you have with Peanut Butter then," I thought back.

"What am I going to do with these kittens? What are they going to do with themselves?" Marshmallow grumbled.

When I tried to pet Marshmallow between the ears, she lifted her head and nipped me.

Aunt Astrid was never as grouchy as Marshmallow could get. Bea could be sad but never seemed to reach the levels of desperation and anxiety that was Peanut Butter's personality. As I headed up the stairs to Bea's room, I thought about Treacle and decided to follow his example as a person of action... so to speak.

I knocked on the door to Bea's room, and Aunt Astrid let me in with a look of exacerbation. I saw Aunt Astrid's dream diaries stacked on one side of the room, forgotten, and I saw Bea lying belly-down on the bed as if she'd melted there. She lifted her head from the pillow, her eyes swollen as if she'd been crying.

"Enough is enough!" I announced. "Bea, I'm calling you a divorce lawyer!"

As Bea keened, "What? No!" I saw Aunt Astrid's expression shift from impressed to pretending to be shocked.

Aunt Astrid sat on the foot of Bea's bed. "Maybe I should have let you rip Jake a new one."

"Mom!" Bea exclaimed. "That's worse!"

"That," I declared, "is nothing. Maybe I said too much and scared Jake off from the Greenstones forever. But you know what? What I said was true. And what I said was... well, said!"

Bea looked confused.

"Because people are supposed to talk," I finished. "You and Jake are supposed to talk. He said he wanted space, time, peace, quiet—whatever. We should never have believed him!

When his wife who loves him so much—who he's supposed to love back—is in this much pain, and he doesn't even know because neither of you will say anything to each other? He gets what he wants, but what I think we all need is balance. That means you get right in front of him, right now, upset and noisy! He can have his peace when there's nothing to ignore!"

Aunt Astrid applauded as Bea looked from me to her and back to me in disbelief.

"Cath, I..." She sounded as if she was going to cry again.

Aunt Astrid and I looked at each other. I couldn't usually read the minds of other human beings, but when it came to family, some things went without saying. We pulled Bea out of bed and pushed her into the bathroom. I rummaged through her bags of clothing, looking for sharp and intimidating outfits that she would never wear. Aunt Astrid looked through Bea's computer for the transaction records between the Brew-Ha-Ha and the construction company.

Aunt Astrid remarked, "Paper records, I know how to deal with. I have an awful feeling that Bea left them at Jake's."

About a half hour later, Bea emerged from the bathroom and said with more confidence, "I am not coming at Jake with a divorce lawyer."

Aunt Astrid heaved a sigh of disappointment, but I knew she didn't hate Jake or not want him in the family. That day, I hated Jake and wanted him out of Bea's life, but Aunt Astrid wasn't as impulsive as I was. But Aunt Astrid had been staying with Bea, living with her like this, and the magic didn't let Aunt Astrid have so much as a peek at the final solution.

"It's too sudden, too much for him, let alone me," Bea continued. Still, she stood up a little straighter. "But you're right, Cath. I'll give him a chance on more even terms. I'm going to talk to him."

She wouldn't wear the outfit that I chose for her though. She would go visit Jake, in all honesty, as the Bea he knew and loved.

At the door, we saw her off.

I asked, "Are you sure you don't want us to come with you?"

"I'm sure that's what you want," Bea said, but she laughed.

Aunt Astrid cleared her throat. "Well, the matter Jake has with you is a little offensive to our entire family legacy."

Bea assured us, "I can handle him on my own. Fair is fair is one on one."

I could tell that Bea was nervous though. Luckily, right then, I felt something brush my ankle and saw Peanut Butter between us. He looked at her with large amber eyes and gave a weak *miaow*.

I urged Bea, "At least take Peanut Butter with you!"

"I will," Bea said, bending down to pick up Peanut Butter. With his front paws on her shoulder and his hind legs cradled in her arms, Bea nodded good-bye at the both of us and set off for Jake's place.

Aunt Astrid shut the door. The look on her face was one of anticipating doom.

"At least Bea won't be alone," I said. Jake couldn't possibly feel ganged up on by one person and her pet.

Aunt Astrid remarked, as her expression changed to one of exaggerated innocence, "And you'll be able to check up on her through Peanut Butter."

I would never admit to that ploy ever having crossed my mind.

Burger's Bite

Aunt Astrid and I sat down together to figure out what the problem was with the construction contractors' contract. I couldn't make heads or tails of it for the whole morning, although Aunt Astrid ultimately seemed to have figured out what had gone wrong. She made the call to their accountant while I made lunch: deli meat and cheese sandwiches, a giant garden salad, and some reheated crab-and-corn soup.

I let my mind wander to Treacle, letting our minds connect. "*I didn't leave food out for you,*" I reminded him. I used to do so, but that attracted other stray cats, and they tended to be rude or even violent to Treacle.

"That's all right," Treacle replied. "*I ate a field mouse on the way to the wire forest.*"

That would be all right if it had only been words, but when I join my mind with animals, they spoke in ideas and feelings...and the full imagery of experience. I flinched when I sensed the crunch of field mouse bones, the smell of its urine, and the fleas tickling Treacle's whiskers.

"*I wish you'd quit hunting wild things, Treacle. They could pass on worms in your gut that'll make you feel sick!*"

"Some human foods for cats are poisoned," Treacle reminded me.

That had been a freak outbreak of contaminated pet food in China. I'd read a news report about it and translated it for Treacle, who took it entirely the wrong way.

"Some human foods for humans are poisonous too," Treacle thought. "*Life is always going to be dangerous.*"

There was no convincing him otherwise. "*Marshmallow is grouchy that you don't take your magic lessons. Why did you go to the... wire forest?*" As I uncertainly repeated the thought back, I recognized the cracked concrete floor of the animal shelter—and the wire around the kennel area. Oh.

"Because," Treacle thought back at me triumphantly, "*I don't want to scare away our witness.*"

The reply made no sense to me.

Through Treacle's eyes, I saw the edges of worn blue jeans and sneakers. Treacle looked up and *miaowed* at a figure too tall for me to recognize, until it stopped and sat down. The air took on a ragged quality as the human covered his face with his hands.

Cody, I realized. Cody Willis was crying. Of course he was. Old Murray was his grandfather, and the only family he had left. Old Murray had been arrested for a crime that he didn't commit.

There was nothing I could do.

"Cody? Are you all right?" said a familiar voice.

Cody wiped his tears away and tried to laugh. "That's what I've been asking you, Mr. Samberg."

Blake approached them both and petted Treacle on the head. "I know Old Murray can't have done it."

"How can we make everyone else know it?" Cody asked. "You have to prove it. We can't even prove how anybody could do the crime in the first place!"

Treacle trotted purposefully down the hall and into the yard.

"A witness," I thought, *"you don't want to scare away... what does that have to do with Marshmallow's magic lessons?"* Then I remembered Burger. Samantha Perry's dog had been present when the crime took place, and she was afraid of magic. *"Treacle!"* I called urgently. *"Old Murray's been arrested! I feel sorry for Cody, but the mystery is solved. It's Old Murray, but it's not... the humans wouldn't understand."*

"You heard the other two humans talk," Treacle argued. *"They also know Murray didn't do it."*

"I saw the Unfamiliar attached to Old Murray. I saw it myself, with my witch eyes! What can we do?"

Treacle climbed the wire fence and walked at the top, balancing with his tail. *"What did the dog see? We never found out if it was the same sight. I'm curious."*

I tried to explain through my panic. *"There's a human saying about what curiosity always does to cats!"*

It was too late. Treacle had caught sight of Burger, alone in the kennel, lying down. Treacle gave a loud *miaow*. Burger perked an ear up but otherwise didn't move. Treacle jumped down and swaggered over to the giant, shaggy dog.

Burger whimpered, got up, and sent the thought, "*What do you want?*"

Treacle stretched and yawned. He approached Burger. "*I chased a mouse today. I caught it, then I let it go, then I caught it again. It was fun.*"

Burger waited for more.

"Maybe it's not as fun for the mouse. But maybe it is. I thought I'd see." With that, Treacle batted Burger on the nose with one paw.

Burger scoffed and lay back down. *"Leave me alone."*

Treacle didn't. "*I don't understand why everybody here is so miserable.*"

"My human is gone. We were such a small pack, just the two of us." Burger whimpered again. "*Of course I'm miserable. Cats can't understand. You're all so selfish.*"

"We're understanding each other now. How did that happen? You understand cats?" Treacle wondered.

Burger flicked an ear. "*When I was a puppy, our pack was three: the human, and me, and an old Siamese cat. I grew up knowing what a hiss meant.*"

"There are plenty of humans everywhere in this part of the moun-

tains," Treacle said. "*They like dogs too. If your human doesn't come back, I'm sure you'll find another.*"

"My human isn't coming back. Go away, cat." Burger began to growl.

Treacle didn't move. "*Tell me to go away again, but without the growl.*"

"Go away," Burger thought.

"How did you do that?" Treacle asked.

Burger sent a wave of confusion. "*I... we... just do...*"

"Was this so easy with your human?"

"No." Burger whimpered. *"It never needed to be! Why do you keep bothering me about my human?"*

"Because I want to tell you that not all humans have magic."

Burger stood straight up and growled. "*You are dangerous.*"

"Me? What about you! You're bigger!" Treacle fluffed up, tensing for a fight.

Burger lunged forward with a great bark. Treacle fled for the fence opposite the dog. My cat scrambled up that fence, almost losing his footing when Burger crashed her body into it. But Treacle landed on the other side.

"I saw your magic human!" Burger barked furiously. "*I saw the magic that was not human! They worked together to kill my human!"*

"Cath wasn't even at the cemetery that night!" Treacle argued. His fluffy fur flattened again, and he licked his paw to wash his face. "*Talk sense, dog.*"

Finally, Burger gave his testimony. Samantha had walked Burger around that night. The cemetery was just another part of the park-meadow to her, though she wouldn't let Burger pee on the gravestones. She could be respectful of the dead, but she was never afraid.

That night, Samantha should have been afraid. Burger had sensed a chill in the air, like the sky was being torn up. He bit on his leash and tried to lead Samantha away, but Samantha was strict and stubborn, and she couldn't sense what was coming. He remembered her telling him, “We always walk this way, Burger! Come on, what’s wrong with you?”

The graveyard glowed with moonlight. Burger couldn’t see as well as a cat could, but Samantha should have seen... if she’d only thought to look... if she could only believe...

A human was floating in the air toward them. The lower half, at least, seemed like a human. The upper half looked as if it were made out of smoke. The smoke spoke. *This is the one. Kill her and raise the dead.*

Burger didn’t know what to make of the smoke, but he lunged at the floating leg and got his teeth in. The floating body waved its hand, and a gust of some kind of force threw Burger against a mausoleum, snapping the leash. Samantha fainted, or seemed to.

Then a tombstone shattered, the earth opened up, and the bones of Shelley Marina emerged from them and lurched toward Samantha. The bones grew gristle at every step.

“Ooh...” the syllable came from the half-formed throat of the ghoulish apparition. “Noo... die... let... me... die...”

The bones collapsed beside Samantha Perry’s body and struck her before getting up and trying to continue on.

Samantha Perry was already dead. Blake had said that the bruises were post-mortem.

"I was afraid of this thing that I never saw before! Humans aren't supposed to fly!" Burger barked. *"I was afraid! So I ran, and I went back later in the morning to find my human was dead! I should have protected her!"*

"Treacle!" Blake called. It seemed that he'd gone out to see what all the noise was about. Blake scooped up Treacle in his arms and carried the cat away.

I thought about what Burger had shown Treacle—us. *"The full moon and the Unfamiliar made Old Murray fly. That explains the lack of footprints. The Unfamiliar..."*

"Was it the same one?" Treacle asked me.

It was indeed the same Unfamiliar that I'd encountered and sent away from Old Murray at the theater. I was certain of it, even more now that I'd seen it through Burger's eyes. Well, through Treacle's mind's eyes looking through Burger's eyes. *"Just come home to me and Astrid, Treacle. This was a risk."*

Treacle would never admit that he was wrong. *"Burger bit the human part."*

"There was no human part. It's a whole human and a whole Unfamiliar squished together. So what if Burger managed to bite him?" I wondered, without really wondering.

Blake set down a saucer of milk for Treacle, who began to lap it up. Treacle wondered, *"Did Old Murray have a bite on his leg?"*

"What's the latest with Peanut Butter then?"

Aunt Astrid's voice pulled me back to reality. I'd been in a trance while my mind followed Treacle to the animal shelter.

"That was Treacle," I said. "The Unfamiliar that I saw at the theater was the same as the one that Samantha Perry's dog witnessed. If Old Murray has a month-old bite mark on his leg, then we can confirm that Old Murray was haunted by this Unfamiliar spirit."

Aunt Astrid took a bite of a sandwich and nodded thoughtfully. "Treacle is trying to help the case. Be a dear and reheat the soup. I think it's gone tepid again."

"I don't think cats can understand how complicated humans make things!" I set the microwave to heat the soup again. "This is all well and good to know, but none of it would be admissible as evidence in court. We certainly can't tell Blake—Detective Samberg—"

"Or any other investigators," Aunt Astrid added.

"Yeah." Why had I singled out Blake? I pushed the thought aside and continued. "I'll bet Old Murray's Unfamiliar would have healed his leg anyway."

I poured the soup into two bowls. Aunt Astrid carried her bowl of soup and the plate with all of the sandwiches to the table. I carried my bowl of soup and the giant bowl of salad.

We ate for a while, then Aunt Astrid said, "Not necessarily."

It had been long enough that I'd forgotten what she would be talking about. "Not necessarily to what?"

"The Unfamiliar healing the physical injury of their host.

Most Unfamiliar spirits never had human bodies and wouldn't know to do that."

I remembered watching an old movie about a little girl who was haunted by what the Greenstones would call an Unfamiliar. In a famous scary scene, it forced her to turn her head so that her face looked behind her, like an owl... not a human. A human body couldn't survive that. She should have had broken her neck at that moment. But if an Unfamiliar wasn't familiar with a human body, then...

I shuddered in horror. That little girl in the movie could have been me.

"Of course," Aunt Astrid added, "it depends on what the motive is."

I munched on a lettuce leaf. "Now I'm confused. You told me that the Unfamiliars don't understand basic survival. How can we possibly understand what their motives are then?"

"Motive is a mental thing. Many other motives are much more in the realm of the other world than in the realm of the body. Remember Queen Myrtha?"

She was talking about the ballet, the queen of the ghosts. All of the ghosts were women who'd killed themselves out of unrequited love, or because they'd married somebody who'd cheated on them, or something.

"Imagine Queen Myrtha as Unfamiliar," Aunt Astrid continued. "She wants something from our world, and she's crossing lines and boundaries to take it. Nobody can know why. *But* the only method she knows to get whatever she wants depends on tempting all those other poor girls with the promise of getting what they want."

"Vengeance. The Wilis were the ghosts of women scorned." I remembered reading something like that on the ballet program. "When Giselle forgave those two jerks, Queen Myrtha didn't have any power anymore."

"Exactly." Aunt Astrid murmured into her soup, "If only it could be that simple."

"It can be simpler," I said. "Tell Queen Myrtha to get back in line. That's what witches do. That's what we did. Simple! Done!"

"Your mother would be proud of you." Aunt Astrid beamed. She added, "So I hope that you don't take personally that she would also be suspicious that this was so easy."

I took a piece of bread and used it to sop up the bottom of my soup bowl. "Aunt Astrid... whose motives was my Unfamiliar using? Mine?"

Aunt Astrid hesitated. "If you're not sure—and you were the only one of us who was actually there, who was actually being bothered by the Unfamiliar—we may never know."

My mother would be suspicious of getting rid of an Unfamiliar so easily because she gave her life for it. I steeled myself against that thought. We could know. There was a way.

I needed to know.

"It's full moon tonight," I said. "What about we finally try that séance?"

The Walking Dead

After the sun set, the moon was a perfectly round smudge of chalky paleness in a dusky blue sky. Aunt Astrid and I sat on my black picnic blanket in front of my parents' graves.

"I know, I know," I said to the gravestones. "I'm early." I turned to Aunt Astrid. "This suddenly got awkward."

"What do you mean?"

"I mean..." I tried to form the words. "Every year, for fifteen years, I've come here to talk to them. I took for granted that they were listening. Now... I don't know. I'm going to talk to them, and I know they're going to hear me, and if I'm lucky, they're going to talk back. That changes things."

Aunt Astrid phrased it better. "Your attitude toward death before was more normal and comfortable for you."

The other world, the one where all the magic was, also

seemed to be the afterlife. It was difficult to explore, and witches could only guess what it was like. The séance itself might not work because it was too soon, like with Samantha Perry. It might not work because it was too late, like with Shelley Marina. Just because somebody was dead didn't mean that they weren't not busy. At least, that was the explanation I'd received when I was thirteen and tried to conduct a séance. It might have been more because my magic talent wasn't that strong yet, or at least not strong enough in the direction of necromancy.

Death, even to witches, remained a mystery. Grieving remained a process.

"We can just sit here then," Aunt Astrid said. "It's a lovely afternoon in a lovely graveyard."

So we sat and waited. Eventually, I wondered aloud, "I wonder how Bea's talk with Jake went."

Aunt Astrid waved dismissively. "I'm sure she'll tell us."

"Eventually. Later. I'm wondering how Bea's doing now."

I nudged Peanut Butter with my mind. His anxieties covered me like a wave. Jake's hand waved toward Peanut Butter's face, making Peanut Butter jump back from where he sat on the table. It wasn't a table I recognized from Bea's place.

Jake demanded, "How do we know we're not under surveillance right now?"

Bea cried, "Cath doesn't do that!"

"You know with your magic?"

"That's not possible! Even if it were, I'd trust them!"

"Well, it's impossible for me. I can't live like that..."

There was a shout from outside the room—not any room in Jake's house, I realized. They were at the police station.

"What was that?" Bea stood and went over to the door.

I pulled my mind back to the graveyard, where I sat beside Aunt Astrid. "Oh, no. They're fighting."

Aunt Astrid sighed. "Better than not speaking to each other."

We sat for a little longer.

I said, "They were fighting about whether I would spy on them through Peanut Butter."

"You'd never!" Aunt Astrid said as if on reflex. Immediately, more humbly, she corrected, "You just did. But you'd never after this."

Suddenly, I stood. Aunt Astrid took my cue and stood with me. She moved off the picnic blanket, stepping smartly.

"I want to go home," I said as I bent over and folded up the blanket. "Wait for Bea there with all her favorite chocolates."

"And a divorce lawyer," Aunt Astrid added. She glanced behind her, startled, and said, "Can I help—"

I glanced up, afraid of how much the bystander had heard. Someone was approaching us slowly, step by lurching step. By the dress, I figured that it was a woman. The dress was faded and stained with dirt, but I'd seen it before. I didn't recognize her face, but it wasn't one I would forget if I'd ever seen it in town.

The skin was taut as a drum over her bones. Her eyes were

closed, and I wondered if she was some wandering homeless lady, starved and maybe blind... we never see them for too long in Wonder Falls. There was even a search party for Topher, who didn't have a family anymore.

She reeked something awful. I clapped a hand over my nose and mouth in reflex. She smelled awful, yet familiar.

"Cath," Aunt Astrid warned, pulling at my arm. She wrinkled her nose and coughed a little too.

I recognized the smell then. It was the same smell around the body of Shelley Marina. This woman was walking and dead.

"Let's run!" I said.

Another Resurrection

Peanut Butter caught me up later on what had happened at the police station. Somebody was screaming. Bea left the room to see where the screaming was coming from, and Peanut Butter followed her. It wasn't exactly logical. Peanut Butter was afraid of everything but would rather stay by his mommy and daddy and be less afraid. Even though his mommy and daddy were going toward the strange new danger.

Together, Bea and Jake rushed through the aisles between the police officers' desks.

They met Police Chief Talbot, who shouted over his shoulder at Diane, "Put that down and stop dialing! I said that we have a direct line!"

"Direct line to what?" Jake asked. "Who was shouting?"

"Our prime suspect in the Perry case, of course," Talbot

answered. “Murray Willis. Looks like a heart attack in the interrogation—hey!”

Bea ran toward the interrogation room despite Chief Talbot’s objection. She ran past Diane, who spoke into the phone that had a direct line to the hospital, “Hi, this is Officer Diane Davis, requesting an ambulance at the Wonder Falls police department. Please hurry!”

“Where’s your wife going?” Talbot asked Jake.

“I’ll get her,” Jake said to the police chief.

When he caught up to Bea, she had her face and hands pressed to the glass window of the interrogation room. “That’s not a heart attack. It’s something else. I can see it! I need to get in there—I need to help him!”

Jake didn’t hesitate. He rapped his knuckles against the door until Jason, one of the other officers, unlocked it for him.

Jason swung open the door but said, “Jake, we can’t have random civilians passing by and—even if she is your wife—”

“She knows how to resuscitate him,” Jake said as Bea bolted in.

Jason frowned as she passed. “So do I, and that’s what I was doing. But did you”—he turned to Jake—“stop me just now so that she could...” He turned back to Bea, who was on her knees beside Old Murray. Her eyes were closed and she was waving a hand over Old Murray’s unconscious body. “Do nothing? She’s not doing CPR. That is not CPR.”

“I’ll take it from here then,” Jake assured him then locked

him out. Jake knelt at Old Murray's other side. "What does it look like?"

"A heart attack," Bea said decisively. "But only because that's where the knot is."

"The knot?"

"Where Cath put the Unfamiliar. A binding spell. She can't get rid of the thing, only tie it up so it won't do any more damage to the host. The knot is still there, but the Unfamiliar is gone."

BACK AT THE GRAVEYARD, Aunt Astrid and I outran the smell. It wasn't difficult to outrun a corpse, which walked so slowly.

"How do we kill it?" I asked.

Aunt Astrid raised an eyebrow. "Ruthless! She hasn't done anything to us, other than come near when she smells bad."

"She's supposed to be dead," I argued. "If this body is anything like Shelley Marina, killing her would be a mercy. But this is impossible!"

"Saying that this is impossible obviously won't stop it from happening," Aunt Astrid said.

"I know her," I said, "but I don't want to wait until she grows back completely. Where's her gravestone? Can we walk around to take a look?"

We could, and we did, jogging over the turf in the afternoon sunlight. The corpse turned slowly when it heard us and inched toward the grave she'd left. On the gravestone, it said—

"Dolores Thompson. 1946 to 2009. Thompson! I thought I knew that dress." I turned to Aunt Astrid. "It belonged to Tommy's grandmother!"

"She was buried in it." Aunt Astrid nodded. "I wasn't at the funeral, but I heard when she passed away. Breast cancer."

"She was only sixty-three," I said gloomily. I hadn't been at Tommy's grandmother's funeral either.

A death rattle sounded behind us, like, "Taaa...mmm..."

"I think," I said, as I covered my nose and mouth with my sleeve, "she's calling for Tommy. How do we tell her?"

Aunt Astrid stepped between myself and Dolores and declared, "You can join him in the grave!"

"But how?" I wondered. "The bones are moving with some magic force, must be, because the muscles haven't even all grown back. That magic is borrowed by an Unfamiliar, but the only one I've seen in this town recently is bound to Old Murray. I tied it all up myself. Shelley Marina grew back her gristle because Samantha Perry died. Whose life force is Dolores taking to even walk toward us?"

Bloodline

"That made no sense to me," Jake said to Bea.

"It doesn't have to," Bea said distractedly. "I'm just thinking aloud. Look, there's a magic knot in his chest. It's slowly draining him of energy, maybe even his life. I'm going to untie it, and if the Unfamiliar is in there anyway... Jake, you run. Do you understand?"

"No," Jake answered. Then he said tensely, "I'm not going to leave you if this unleashes some demon from another dimension either."

Peanut Butter wandered in and *miaowed* plaintively. He'd been diligent with Marshmallow's magic lessons. He saw Bea's hand in the other world, struggling against the knot and forcing it to loosen.

"Almost there," Bea breathed.

Jake didn't see anything, but he kept quiet.

"They can't break," Bea realized. "The bond between Old

Murray and... they share a bloodline." She opened her eyes then opened her otherworldly eyes with a new clarity.

AT THAT MOMENT, Dolores Thompson collapsed into a heap of bones in front of Aunt Astrid and myself.

"What just happened?" I said.

Astrid peered at the air around Dolores's unmoving corpse. "Not a single Unfamiliar to be seen."

"Blake is going to lose sleep over this," I muttered. "We've got to get her back into her coffin before anybody sees."

"CATCH ME," Bea said to Jake, back at the police station. "I'm going to faint."

"Why are you going to faint?" Jake asked.

She answered as she put both of her hands over Old Murray's chest. "The drain on Old Murray's life isn't happening anymore, but it did happen."

Peanut Butter put his paws over Bea's hands and *miaowed* anxiously.

Jake tried again to make sense of Bea's rambles about magic. "He needs his life restored... and it's coming from you?" His expression quickly changed from confusion to apprehension.

"It won't kill me," Bea assured him and Peanut Butter. "But it's taking a lot out of—"

Then she fainted. Jake caught her.

BY THE TIME afternoon had turned into evening, Aunt Astrid and I were patting flat the pieces of turf atop Dolores Thompson's grave. I'd had to break into the groundskeeper's tool shed to steal two shovels.

"More than one Unfamiliar in town," I offered. "At least one witch without training. Another secret society, with a book of magic, who sin against nature."

"Wrath of ancient gods," Aunt Astrid added. "Curses that the dead shall walk the earth, outnumber the living, and eat our brains."

"Maybe we can try to ask the Maid of the Mist if this is just something that happens once a month in Wonder Falls for maybe so-and-so number of months every three hundred years or something."

"It would have been in the Greenstone family record."

Aunt Astrid and I went back to the tool shed to return the shovels.

"I think I know how Blake feels now," I remarked. "If he were only in the know, I could leave him voice messages in the wee hours of the morning, containing the increasingly improbable theories of witches."

"Let's start with what we do know then," Aunt Astrid said.

"Try to keep it as simple as possible." Aunt Astrid's phone rang. She took it out of her pocket, and I dusted off my hands as she reacted to the call. "Hello? What happened? Oh, dear."

When she hung up, I said, "The simplest explanation would be that I'm just not very good at binding Unfamiliars."

"We'll ask Bea about that," Aunt Astrid said to me. "That was Jake. He says that she undid your binding on Old Murray. They're both in the hospital."

JAKE HADN'T TOLD us how bad it was, so Aunt Astrid and I rushed to the hospital, expecting the worst. We found him and Bea in the hospital lobby. Bea leaned against Jake's shoulder, looking exhausted. He was laughing about something as Aunt Astrid and I approached, and eventually Bea gave a tired chuckle as well.

I said to them, "I'm glad to see that you both patched things up."

"Bea was telling me about burnout," Jake explained. He must have meant magic burnout, which happened when a witch used too much magic.

"And you're all right with that?" I asked, still sounding suspicious.

"It's not that different from keeping her comfortable during that time of the month," Jake said.

Then it was Aunt Astrid's turn to look suspicious. "And you're all right with that?"

Jake and Bea laughed together, in their own world.

Aunt Astrid and I looked at each other, and I knew that we were both thinking the same thing. It couldn't have been this easy. We looked at Jake until he remembered that we had arrived and that we both were waiting for more of an explanation.

Bea said, "Old Murray's in aftercare for cardiac arrest. I came in with low blood pressure."

Aunt Astrid sat beside Jake and asked, "And what's the real story?"

I sat beside Bea, and they caught us up on what happened.

Jake finished with, "I've been a coward. These are things I thought I couldn't understand even if you explained them to me. All I've known since the visit to the animal shelter was that this was dangerous. Bea showed me today that magic also heals."

I gave Jake an exasperated expression. "That was obvious."

"All right," Jake said, "I'm sorry that it took the danger of losing Bea today to get me to wake up to the fact that I don't want to spend any more time apart than we have to."

I thought, sarcastically, that we were so lucky to have life-threatening situations come up like this to save marriages... that shouldn't have been so rocky in the first place, if anybody was willing to communicate.

To test Jake, I said, "You won't have a problem then with the fact that the Greenstones never stay dead, but as witches, we rise from the graves to sustain our eternal youth by drinking blood."

Jake didn't miss a beat. "Nobody's perfect. Considering that blood is the private property of their owners until donated, however, I would be duty-bound to arrest your ancestors if not all transactions are conducted above board."

Bea chuckled.

"What?" Jake said. "I was serious. Was Cath joking? I thought she was explaining more about the Greenstone legacy—"

Bea hushed her husband with a kiss. Aunt Astrid gave them a satisfied smile.

"Anyway," I continued, "at this point, even if we Greenstones explained everything that we knew to each other about the past month, we wouldn't understand it."

Aunt Astrid and I told them about what had happened at the graveyard earlier that afternoon.

When we'd finished, Bea said, "It does make sense now. Dolores Thompson was the one taking Murray Willis's life force."

"No, wait," I said, "Burger witnessed Samantha Perry's death, which was instant. The Unfamiliar was making Old Murray fly around at that time too. It was there, and it was powerful."

Aunt Astrid finished, "Dolores Thompson's life force was slow because of Murray's age. We saw no Unfamiliars at the graveyard. Did you see one at the police station, Bea? Even when you loosed the binding?"

Bea shook her head.

Jake cleared his throat then made an effort to ask, casually, "So you managed to get Burger's, umm... testimony?"

I nodded. "Burger gave Old Murray a nasty bite."

Bea blurted, "No, he didn't."

The three of us looked at her.

"I heal people, remember?" Bea said. "I have an intuition for injury. I would have noticed a month-old bite mark while I was healing Old Murray."

I asked, "Even if the Unfamiliar had healed him?"

"I would have noticed traces of Unfamiliar interference too," Bea said with certainty.

Jake said, "And you mentioned something about bloodline?"

"Hey," I realized, "Old Murray and Dolores Thompson are related, right?"

At that, Aunt Astrid said, "It would explain the connection between them. Not so much with Samantha Perry and Shelley Marina."

"That's why!" I realized. "For all the Unfamiliar's power, the night that Samantha Perry died... if Shelley Marina wasn't drawing life force from the same genetic pool, then the resurrection would fizzle out on its own. If they did share a bloodline, however..."

"You're saying," Jake said, leaning forward, "that Dolores Thompson could have come back to full life and health."

"And Old Murray would have died," Bea said.

Aunt Astrid said, "But then the Unfamiliar wouldn't have a

host. They usually latch on to just one person. Crossing from their world into ours is difficult for them."

"Unless," I said, "some people already have a close enough bond for the Unfamiliar to move between. The Unfamiliar could have moved straight to Dolores Thompson."

Bea scratched her head, thought about it, and sighed. "I just don't feel like Old Murray was involved at all in the magical sense, not until this afternoon."

We sat around in silence for a while, lost in our thoughts.

Then I wondered, "Where's Peanut Butter?"

Jake answered, "I called Blake and Cody Willis over from the animal shelter. They arrived before you, and I left Blake to babysit Peanut Butter."

Bea beamed. "Peanut Butter's our baby."

"You know," Jake said, with a tone of mock suspicion, "he doesn't look anything like me..."

"Oh, don't even joke," I said.

But Bea laughed and snuggled against him again. They'd hardly heard me.

I put my face in my hands and released a groan of aggravation. "I don't know what to do with everything that's been happening."

Aunt Astrid reached over Jake and Bea to give me a comforting pat on the knee. "We won't have our next clue until next month."

I groaned again, even though I knew that Aunt Astrid meant that to be comforting.

"I'm hungry," Bea said.

Jake stood. "I'll get Peanut Butter, then we can head home for dinner." He turned to Aunt Astrid and me. "Both of you are welcome to join us, of course."

Aunt Astrid nodded. "I'd love to."

"I'll pass," I told him. I waved good-bye and walked away.

Night Jog

For dinner, I ordered a five-cheese pizza. It was still early in the evening when it came, only slightly later when I'd finished half of it, and properly nighttime by the time I felt I'd digested it. Since I felt guilty about binging like that, I decided to go for a jog around the neighborhood.

Sometimes I resented living in this town. In general, nobody liked to be singled out for gossip, but everybody liked to have a target to gossip about. They would say it was because they cared, and that was easy to believe when almost everybody knew each other. I was always wary about that though. How could anybody really know each other?

On the upside, as I said, nobody liked to be singled out for gossip. That kept most people's behavior in line. The Wonder Falls police department had nothing to do most days. It was usually a crime-free town, but that didn't mean it didn't have mysteries.

It was a chilly night. As my jog went on, I panted out white wreaths of mist. With each step kicking off the pavement, I imagined the momentum taking me one step closer to the solution.

"Cath!" Min's voice called behind me.

I jogged in place then turned around. "Hi, Min. I can't stop. I've got to keep my heart rate up."

He was dressed for jogging too. "I'll race you to the falls," he said as he jogged alongside me.

"Through the woods? I didn't bring my flashlight though." As we turned beyond the glow of the streetlamps though, I saw that Min's sneakers had lights at the toes. "So," I panted, as we jogged over the meadow, "did you find Topher?"

"Nuh-uh," Min replied. He had joined the search party that morning. "I'm still getting to know this town again, so I'm not that much help."

"Wish I could have joined," I said, "but, you know, family comes first. We didn't even catch up on rebuilding the Brew-Ha-Ha today."

"Is Blake part of the family again?"

I did a double take. "What, who? Him? Why would Blake be part of the family?"

"Bea's husband," Min corrected himself. "Jake. Blake. Blah, names."

I laughed. "It is kind of cute that they're partners and they rhyme. It sounds like a TV show, but to answer your question, apparently yes—Jake is part of the family again."

If Bea felt as though everything was all right in her marriage again, then I would support her.

We jogged through the meadow, down the slope, and into the woods.

"It must be good to have a family," Min remarked.

"Must be?" I gave him a playful shove. "Min, you have a family!"

"Don't I know it," Min exclaimed flatly. "I just feel bad for Topher, somewhere out there all alone."

Bea was usually the one who had intuitions about people. Min had kept things from me before that almost cost him his life.

I peered at him suspiciously. "It's not just that, is it? What's wrong with your dad?"

"Nothing!" Min told me. He jogged ahead, over the bridge.

I jogged faster to catch up. "Why didn't your dad join us at the show?"

"He never was a social butterfly."

"Was that the reason?" I pressed.

"I'll race you down the riverbank when the moon comes out!"

"If I win the race to the falls, you have to tell me."

Min stopped.

"Oh, come on!" I whined, jogging to turn around.

"I don't know what's going on with my dad," Min

confessed. "That's why I need to find Topher."

"What, to distract yourself from your own problems?" I couldn't believe it. "Is that where your newfound sense of philanthropy is coming from after all?"

Min looked hurt. "Cath, it's nothing like that! You couldn't be further from the truth."

"Enlighten me then!"

During the day, the river waters were clear in the sunlight, never muddy, not even after a storm. Now the full moon cast its white light over the same rivers, and the waves and eddies made oily black shapes like ink. I wondered what could be hiding in those waters.

The moment that thought crossed my mind, something surfaced.

"Get back!" I called to Min.

It wasn't something coming out of the water, I realized, but someone. That someone lurched onto the banks.

"It told me you'd be here!" a familiar old man's voice rambled. "It told me to wait, but then it told me to wait, but I'm not waiting another moonshine." He lifted an emaciated hand to point at Min. "You're next..."

The figure stepped into the moonlight. It was Topher.

"Min," I said, "did you bring your cell phone?"

He nodded. "I'll call the cops."

"The hospital," I corrected. "The old man must be freezing!"

As Min made the call, I hauled Topher up on land. One of his trouser legs caught on a nearby reed. As I untangled it, I saw the fading bite mark on his leg. There was no denying it now. If it wasn't Old Murray, then Topher had been the Unfamiliar's host all along.

"What did it tell you?" I demanded.

"You fool!" an ethereal voice hissed somewhere about him. "*I told you, not with the witch with him!*"

"And the Maid of the Mist so nearby," I added. "Do you think you won't lose if we fight it out right now? I'll call my Familiar, who will call my cousin and my aunt, and they'll bring their Familiars—then you won't stand a chance! We're both at full power at this moon phase. Let's fly around and blast magic fireworks at each other. Even if Min sees it, nobody would believe him." It was a boast. I couldn't fly on full moon nights, not even with a broomstick.

Then the Unfamiliar presence did something unexpected. *Mercy,* it begged.

"You came into my hometown and threatened my people," I said to it. "One of them is dead. Then you attacked me. How dare you even ask! How dare you!"

Mercy for you as well, it said slyly. *I can never win, that is true. But what will you lose so that I lose? Your binding was a mercy.*

"And that didn't work," I told it. "I won't try that again."

Will you do what your mother did? Not even for a child but for the sake of one not long for this world anyway. Give your life, and the life of the one with you, and the life of this body which I hold—all to ensure that I never come back here again. Will you?

"Yes." I stepped back and reached my mind out to the moonlight—

Motives! it shouted desperately. *The other witch said! The other witch thought! At the dance! There is another way. Why would you not take it?*

"Why would you suggest that? Why are you trying to help me?"

It replied, *You are a cat with a mouse. You will play with your prey. You want to find another way. I have a chance if you have a chance.*

"I shouldn't make deals with your kind. They never work the way we think."

Then came a voice like a rainstorm. "I am bound to this cause, that you understand this arrangement completely."

I looked around even though I sensed that the voice didn't come through my ears. I saw the Maid of the Mist flowing toward us from the shaded bridge. In the moonlight, she looked like a sigh of breath in the cold night, wreaths of fog floating in the shape of a woman. She moved like a ghost but with more life and purpose.

"The choice is yours, Cath Greenstone," she said. "Seal this door with the blood of all those the moonlight touches, or risk this Unfamiliar tipping the balance between my world and yours—for a hope that all may live."

"You're the Maid of the Mist," I said resentfully. "You could seal the door without bloodshed. Don't you have that power?"

She shook her head slowly. "We keep the balance. We follow our laws."

This all really was up to me then.

"You have to keep the balance," the Maid of the Mist said to me. "Find a way."

"And if I don't, will you step in?"

"Find a way," she repeated. "This thing has no power until the next full moon. You have to get Topher to release the Unfamiliar until then."

When I blinked, she was gone.

Topher curled up in a ball and trembled. "Why isn't it working? Where's Dolly?"

Min Park approached me. "Cath, we're in the middle of the meadows, so I can't give the paramedics a street address..."

"Tell them to meet us at the corner of Ebb and Eddy," I told him. "Old Mr. Thompson can make it there without a stretcher if he has our help. Isn't that right, Topher?"

Mournfully, Topher said to me, "You've got yourself a deal!"

I knew that he hadn't understood a single word I'd said to him.

"Was someone else here with us?" Min asked as Topher laid an arm over one of my shoulders. Min himself got under Topher's other arm. "I thought I saw someone, but then I didn't. She looked familiar..."

Topher answered happily, "Oh, yes, my Alice is a beauty. Come to help your old man, Tommy?"

"Yeah," I said, "there are a lot of people with us, here in Topher's head."

The Unfamiliar gave a sinister chuckle.

A Dungeon for the Insane

Topher's body had sustained no permanent injuries from wandering around. He lacked sleep and, ironically, hydration. He had no frostbite. He was obviously demented, so by morning, the attending doctors agreed to move him to a padded room below the ground level of the hospital.

Min and I went to visit him.

"Like a dungeon," Min said gloomily. "A dungeon for the insane."

At least it was clean, and the orderlies didn't look completely soulless, but I didn't like it either—and not only because I predicted that I'd be spending some days there, interrogating Topher and the Unfamiliar.

The floor had fluorescent lights everywhere. I think that was the worst part of rooms without natural light. I wondered if Wonder Falls had hidden away many other mentally ill people there.

"Don't we have an old folks' home in this town?" Min wondered.

"We do. I don't think they can help him as much there."

Min tried to stifle a yawn.

"I'm getting you home," I said. It had been a long night. "Where is home for you, by the way?"

"With my parents," he grumbled.

Min had the money to buy a house anywhere in Wonder Falls. A mansion, even, one designed to his tastes and built with the best materials. He'd stayed at a hotel when he first came back—and from that hotel room, he'd been kidnapped, terrorized, and almost killed. Since then, Mrs. Park wouldn't let him sleep anywhere that wasn't under her watchful eye.

At that moment, Min's cell phone beeped. He read the text message with bleary eyes. "It's my dad. I told him we found Topher and that I was waiting at the hospital... he's upstairs, ready to take me home."

"That's a bit much," I exclaimed.

Mr. Park had been cold and distant while Min was growing up, and that actually wasn't all that bad because Mr. Park was cold and distant to everybody. To come by for the sole purpose of hauling Min away was unlike him. Then again, if I'd learned anything from what had happened between Bea and Jake, it was that I should stay out of other people's relationships.

We had a long pause until he said, "I'll tell him not to and be right back."

"Take your time." In hindsight, I realized that Min had been waiting for me to offer to go upstairs with him. But I didn't offer, and maybe he'd thought it would be too emasculating or something if he asked.

Eventually, a nurse rolled in a wheelchair with Topher in it.

He looked directly at me. "You witch."

"Yes," I said, "this witch. It's going to be just you and me now." To the nurse, I asked, "What's his room number?"

"B2-9." She gave me a look when I walked alongside the wheelchair. She must have expected me to stay outside the room. "Are you family?"

"I brought him here," I explained. "My friend called the ambulance. He doesn't really have a family."

Topher shook his head. "Dolly. She's back."

The nurse frowned. "He's really not lucid."

"That's why we're rolling him in here, isn't it?" I sounded too callous. That wouldn't get anything done.

Topher insisted, "Dolly's back!"

I explained to the nurse, "Dolores Thompson was his wife's name. Dolly for short, you see?" I was guessing, but I guessed pretty well. "She passed away years ago." I continued, affecting a casual carelessness, "I think she was also the sister of Topher's best friend—Murray Willis. He's in the heart ward of this very same hospital, in recovery. I heard he was put in here just yesterday afternoon."

The nurse relaxed. Topher, on the other hand, whimpered protests against what he now knew that I knew.

"So you're the closest thing he has to family right now," the nurse said as we stopped at the door.

I shook my head modestly. "I'm just doing what I can to help." To Topher, I said, "I'll visit as often as I can." To the nurse, I asked, "Are there visiting hours?"

She pushed the wheelchair into the room, and I helped her lift Topher out of the wheelchair and onto a padded gurney. "There must be, but nobody ever visits, so we've all forgotten. You won't be allowed in the room after this." The door shut behind us with a muffled thump. The nurse rolled back the wheelchair and gestured toward the door. "You see, no door handle on the inside. It can only be opened from the outside." She pushed a panel in the padded wall beside the door, and it sprung open to reveal a single push-button, which she pushed. "We're really understaffed, so we can't have anyone just waiting on you for as long as you would visit."

An orderly came by to open the door.

Topher cried more loudly.

To the nurse, I said, "Could I just stay a little longer? I'll calm him down and say good-bye."

The nurse nodded to the orderly and said, "She's all right. We'll come back in ten." Then they both left.

"I'm sorry for everything that's happened to you in your whole life," I said to Topher. "I'm also sorry for what's going to happen, which will actually be my fault."

I needed to get Topher to talk. I hated what I was about to do, even more that I told myself that I had to do it. I hated that I got into situations where I had to be so awful.

Mr. Park

I belted his wrists with the straps on either side of the bed. His expression seemed apprehensive, but he didn't have the presence of mind to resist me.

I barred my arm against the defenseless old man's throat and told him, "You don't have a family. If I crushed your neck right now so that you couldn't breathe, nobody would miss you."

Topher's old eyes met mine fearfully.

"I'd do it if it would stop you from killing people! Why Samantha? Why Old Murray? What are you trying to do? Tell me!"

"Tommy," he said tremulously. "Not Alice. Can't with Alice. Bring them back."

"How?" I demanded. "What did it promise you?"

"It showed me that it could!" he wailed. "It showed me how! Your man..."

My man? I backed away. "Do you mean Min? Min Park? He's a friend."

He shook his head.

"Why him?" I asked. "Why any of these people?"

He continued to shake his head.

I put my hand against his throat and shouted, "Answer me! Why are you so fixated on Min Park?"

The door slammed open. Mr. Park stood in the doorway, and he looked at me with an expression that I'd never seen on his face. He was afraid. But he told me in a stern and commanding voice, "Leave him alone. Step back."

He wasn't afraid of me. He wasn't even afraid for me.

I stepped back as Min jogged up behind his father.

"Cath," Min said, "what are you doing?"

"She was going to kill this poor old man!" Mr. Park declared.

"That's a lie!" More of a mistake really. Unfortunately, it was an easy mistake to make. It was true, though, that I wasn't going to kill Topher—not on purpose. I was only threatening him. I knew that wouldn't have sounded better.

Mr. Park demanded, "What are you doing in this room then?"

I shot back, "What are you doing opening the door to this room? You're not an orderly. That's not allowed."

"Tell the orderly! I will tell them what I saw."

The nurse strode up to us and hissed, "What's going on? You're being very noisy and upsetting the patients."

Mr. Park and I glared at each other. Then Mr. Park told

the nurse what he'd seen me doing. I didn't know how to win that argument, and I didn't feel like I could. With the look on the nurse's face—shock, then betrayal, then contempt—I wouldn't even try.

Min looked from me to his father, not sure what was going on. "This is crazy. I'm leaving."

"You should all leave," the nurse said.

I WALKED from the hospital to the Brew-Ha-Ha. I staggered, more like, because I was sleepy and miserable. Long walks usually gave me time to think, but with every step, I could only think about how I'd ruined everything. I wondered if the nurse would file a police complaint.

Bea and Aunt Astrid were already there. They could tell instantly that something had gone horribly wrong, and they ushered me into the cellar of the Brew-Ha-Ha. I flopped onto two of the three beanbag chairs and begged them to leave me alone. So they did. Aunt Astrid shut off the lights.

My eyes burned with sleepiness, but my worries wouldn't let me drift off to a peaceful rest. I was heartbroken by the possibility that the awful things I'd said and done to Topher would all have been for nothing.

When I did sleep, I didn't dream.

I woke to Bea flicking on the lights. I was lying on the tatami mat—I must have rolled off the beanbags while I was asleep. Treacle and Peanut Butter bounded down the staircase and rubbed against me while I sat up.

"Dinner!" Aunt Astrid announced as she descended the stairway with two plates. She set one on the table in front of me. "My attempt at Ted's vegan poutine recipe."

The smell made my mouth water and my stomach grumble. "Vegan poutine. This is real witchcraft."

Bea added, "If it turns out all right, we can add it to the menu."

It was all right, I supposed. I was too hungry to really critique the dish in more detail than "edible." On top of everything else, I was crying as I ate, tears that I didn't bother to wipe away, and I tried to chew and swallow between sobs.

Once I was done being a mess, I confessed to Aunt Astrid and Bea what had happened that left me such a mess: the evening jog with Min Park, finding out who the real host of the Unfamiliar was, the deal I'd made with the Maid of the Mist, and finally how I turned Topher into a ticking time bomb of otherworldly horror... and ensured that we could never again get near enough to defuse him.

I was sorry. I was so, so sorry.

Bea and Aunt Astrid moved to either side of me and gave me a hug.

Bea said, "I'm so sorry that you had to go through all that on your own!"

"You did your best," Aunt Astrid added. "And you did give us a month."

I sniffled. "Did Min Park come to help with the renovations?"

They told me that he hadn't. I guessed he was still mad.

Woodworking Artist

A waning gibbous moon shone over Wonder Falls.

Aunt Astrid booked an appointment at the Wonder Falls spa for all three of us, because, as she said, we'd have a long month ahead of us. Getting pampered was part of preparing for it. I had my objections, but Aunt Astrid silenced them with, "You're not allowed to run yourself into the ground like you did yesterday."

Bea was reluctant to go to the spa, but she brought Jake, who had no reluctance at all and was very enthusiastic about sauna massages. Chief Talbot had given Jake the day off so that Bea would quit coming to the station and fighting with Jake (or worse—so Talbot said—making up with Jake) in Talbot's office. To Talbot, Bea seemed to have interrupted a crisis in the police department, yet did not help, before promptly becoming dead weight herself... that also counted against her.

I remembered that Jake remarked, "Blake should be here. Talbot forced him to take a vacation too, but Blake's not taking it. He's still investigating."

We came out of the spa a little more relaxed. I particularly liked the massage, almost as much as Jake, and would definitely go back. The relaxation period didn't last long however.

The next day, we spent the afternoon in the cellar of the Brew-Ha-Ha, formulating plans. Bea would research Christopher Thompson's family records, because if Dolores Thompson's relation to Murray Willis was important, then maybe we could predict the next link. Jake would keep us informed of the goings-on in the Wonder Falls police department and their investigation. Aunt Astrid would rally all of our Familiars, which meant a lot of meditating with our cats. If the Unfamiliar had its way by the end of the month, she said, then we would have help.

I would build the digital database for all of Aunt Astrid's dream diaries. The reason for that was obvious to me, even though Aunt Astrid and Bea would never say it—I'd done enough damage.

A WANING HALF-MOON shone over Wonder Falls.

The Wonder Falls police department had insufficient evidence to build any sort of case against Old Murray.

Bea visited Old Murray in the hospital and confirmed that Dolores Thompson used to be Dolores Willis—Old Murray's sister. She listened with genuine interest to Old Murray's stories of when he and Topher were young, but he seemed to grow suspicious when Bea asked about the names of their great-grandparents.

Old Murray recovered enough to return to the animal shelter.

Bea then had the bright idea to contact Naomi LaChance. Under the pretense of writing a biography for Thomas Thompson, Bea tried to glean what Naomi knew. Naomi, we knew, was a good friend of Tommy's.

From those conversations, Bea learned that Tommy had been raised by his grandparents, Dolores Willis-Thompson and Topher Thompson. Tommy had never spoken to Naomi about his mother. Naomi confessed to taking Tommy's death as personally as she had for one very simple reason—she and Tommy had been secret high school sweethearts. Not even Bea had known.

In short, Bea found out nothing useful, although that nothingness did have edges, and the empty shape formed by those edges, once filled, could be useful.

A WIDE WANING crescent moon shone over Wonder Falls.

Jake and Blake teamed up once more. Jake told me afterward he'd had to contrive a reason to search Topher's residence so that he wouldn't be tempted to talk to Blake about magic. Jake used the excuse of helping his wife research the biography on Tommy, saying that Tommy's childhood home—Topher's house—would be a good start.

"That's a terrible use of our time as law enforcers," Blake had said, probably with the tactless bluntness he always had.

Jake had ignored him.

In Topher's cabin in the woods, Jake found the living room furniture all piled against the walls as if they'd been caught in a hurricane. The middle of the living room was clear of furniture, and the floorboards had burn marks of perfect circles and sinister-looking glyphs.

Blake walked around, examining the scene. He told Jake that the burn marks on the floor gave him the creeps because they reminded him of the Order, a group of magicians that had targeted Blake. Blake thought the Order were crazy to believe in magic, and thankfully he still thought that, but he'd seen the way that those without magic talents tried to use the forces of the other world anyway. Geometry like that was one way.

Jake tried to move one of the tables that had been shoved against the wall. It had met the wall with enough force to splinter two of the legs, but it was solid teakwood. Jake had to strain to move it an inch, and Topher was old.

Blake became bored and impatient very quickly. He complained that they should continue to look for a murderer in town, the one who had killed Samantha Perry. Jake couldn't tell him that they'd found the killer. So they both left.

After Jake told us Greenstones what he'd found, we went to the Thompson residence to erase the burns on the floor.

Looking at them gave me a headache. The symbols galvanized the air with meaning: *Take a life this night.*

I had no doubt that Topher had been in that very room, letting the power of the Unfamiliar burn the wood, and the magic had moved the life force of Old Murray into his dearly departed Dolly.

"This way would have saved him from more dog bites," I remarked, over the sound of the sanding belt that Bea pressed down upon the panels.

Aunt Astrid nodded. "It could be learning. That is a dangerous Unfamiliar. Our advantage is usually that they don't know entirely know how our world works."

I sighed. "This thing needs to be stopped. We better be ready."

I didn't add that we didn't know yet how to stop it.

Trumpson

A slim waning crescent moon shone over Wonder Falls.

Bea and I went to do some grocery shopping at the Park family's supermarket. We were pulling out the shopping carts when Mrs. Park approached us.

I was happy to see her, and I said as much before asking, "Is Min here?" More apprehensively, I asked. "Is Mr. Park here?"

"No," Mrs. Park answered. "You shouldn't be here either. Please leave."

Bea sounded shocked. "Mrs. Park! What have we done?"

"Not you," she said to Bea.

"Oh, thanks!" I said, sarcastically. "That's really nice, with all that's happening."

Mrs. Park gave me a look of misery. "Who have you told what Topher told you?"

"He didn't tell me anything!" I whined. Then I straightened up. "Mrs. Park, what do you think he told me?"

The same fearful look that Mr. Park had had at the asylum showed on Mrs. Park's face then.

"If it worries you this much, you can trust me!" I said.

"What if I don't?" Mrs. Park challenged. "Will you handcuff me to the balcony railings and choke me almost to death?"

I flinched. "I've learned that... that's not going to help."

Mrs. Park set her jaw. "You're not the kind little girl that I baked cookies for anymore, who didn't need to be told not to shout and hit people. And this is not your concern."

I objected, "This is my concern, especially if my family is banned from shopping at your store."

"Get out, or I will call the police!"

"Mrs. Park, I don't know what you're so insecure about, but please do not talk to my cousin like that!" Bea grabbed my arm and led me away. "Come on, we'll shop at the farmer's market with Mom. Vegan, gluten-free, organic everything."

"Nooo!" I lunged away from her and collapsed in front of Mrs. Park, grasping at the hem of her apron. "Don't let her take me to that place, Mrs. Park!"

Bea pouted. "It's not that bad! Jake loves the meatloaf I make from the farmer's vegan ground beef!"

Both Mrs. Park and I gave Bea a look of confusion.

"From vegan cows," Bea explained. "The cows are vegan. It's a joke Mom and I... look, never mind! What's all this even about?"

"You really don't know?" Mrs. Park said to Bea, then she looked at me and her expression softened—more than softened but melted, or seemed to because she began to cry. She let out a sniffling sob, pulled her apron hem out of my clutches, and tottered away.

Bea sighed. "That could have gone better. Are you all right, Cath?"

I stood slowly, gathering my thoughts. "Topher's Alice." I turned to Bea. "Topher kept picking on Min for what he 'did to my Alice,' but of course we didn't know any Alice Thompson in school."

Bea shook her head. "Topher's demented."

"No, demented means that you forget. What if he's remembering too much instead? We know that Dolly's real and Tommy's real. We should look for Alice."

THE MOON DID NOT SHINE over Wonder Falls. It had blanketed itself completely in the earth's shadow.

As driven as Blake Samberg could be about an unsolved case, he could be easily distracted by petty crimes. Everyone at the Wonder Falls police department understood when Jake, who was supposed to be Blake's partner, threw his hands up in surrender and walked away—just to leave Blake to it. Jake used that time to search the Wonder Falls census. Bea spent her days at the library, searching the obituaries of the Wonder Falls newspaper.

I finished making the database of Aunt Astrid's dreams and thought that I would check up on the animals at the shelter.

WHEN I ARRIVED, Blake, Cody, and Old Murray were putting pet carriers into a van out front.

Cody saw me first and called, "Miss Greenstone! Good time to volunteer today!"

He didn't hate me then, for scaring Burger or getting his grandfather arrested. That was a nice change. I waved as I approached them. "How are you holding up, Murray?"

"Cath," Old Murray nodded, "it's been a while. I don't remember what happened at the show. I'm afraid my mind's going."

"You're looking well today," I offered, trying to comfort him. When he didn't look comforted, I added, "I can take care of myself. You've just got to find somebody to take care of you."

Cody piped up, "Hi!"

"Naw," Old Murray said. "You can't live your life for me, Cody. You've got your own to live. The old folks' home ain't so bad—"

Blake scoffed. "The Wonder Falls old folks' home is worse than most prisons." He moved to the front of the van, opened the passenger side door, and whistled. Burger bounded over and hopped into the passenger seat.

"I meant the idea," Old Murray muttered.

"Is that where you're taking all the animals?" I asked. "To the old folks' home? I'm confused."

Blake buckled the seat belt over Burger. The dog nudged Blake's forehead with his nose, making Blake flinch and back away.

"It was the Park boy's idea," Old Murray said. "Pets that nobody wants meet with people that nobody wants."

"Come with us," Cody said to me. "We could use an extra hand."

I spent the drive there talking with the animals. Most of them didn't want to share their lives with humans. They weren't hostile to the idea, because the Willises didn't include any animals that they knew were wilder than Treacle. Still, the animals didn't want human company so much as trustworthy company at all. Even among animals, that sort of company was more difficult to come by. Burger spent all of his life being looked after by a human. He might have needed human company and attention, but he didn't want one—because what if nobody really could replace Samantha?

We arrived at the old folks' home. From the outside, it looked charming, all red brick walls covered in ivy and an arch over the gate with wrought-iron letters that spelled HELL IN. We unloaded the crates, brought them into the courtyard with great care, and waited. Cody and Murray went inside.

I turned to Blake. "It's good that you're taking time away from the case to volunteer like this."

He looked at me so suspiciously that I almost laughed.

"I'm just saying!" I said. "Justice is very important, don't get me wrong, but when there's something wrong in the world that doesn't have a perpetrator, then it's too easy to forget about the victims. It's great to help this way, don't you agree?"

"No," he said. "This is the key to the case."

I sighed. "Okay, Blake, I take it all back. This was a bad idea, and you need more sleep."

"Didn't you read the sign on the way in?" Blake pointed toward the entrance.

I shrugged and read it aloud. "'Hell In.' Not a cheerful name for this place."

"Why are you only reading the letters that are still there?"

"Because," I answered slowly, "it's what's there?"

"Read the letters that rusted at the edges and fell off," Blake said. "Look! It's so obvious!"

"Obvious? I didn't study forensics in Boston."

"It says THE SHELLEY MARINA FOUNDATION," Blake said.

"Shelley Marina..." I gasped. "The name on the gravestone! The other body I found!" As quickly as it peaked, the feeling of epiphany plummeted to apathy. "So?"

"She was a philanthropist, just like Min Park," Blake said. "Some loophole in inheritance laws meant that her daughter, Rosemary, couldn't inherit after she married Basil Trumpson. Their ashes were scattered over the falls. The grave robber must have thought that the family treasure was buried with Shelley. We have a motive. Now I just have to find the means..."

Out the corner of my eye, I saw Min Park emerge from the home.

"Who did you say Rosemary Marina married?" I asked Blake.

"Basil Trumpson."

Then the idea hit me like a lightning bolt. "You mean Thompson. Basil Thompson. I remember that name in my research. Basil and Rosemary Thompson were cremated. They're the missing link!"

"Thompson must've looked like Trumpson in the old record books. They're ancient and falling apart." Blake shrugged. "Either way, I'm a genius."

I hugged him and said, gleeful again with epiphany, "No, you're not! The grave robbery attempt is the worst idea you've ever spoken out loud to me, and I've heard hundreds by now! You should get more sleep!"

"Now my feelings hurt." Blake frowned. "You're wrong. I won't sleep until I prove it."

I pulled away from him and ran toward the gate, calling behind me, "Then tell the Willises I had a family emergency! Say hello to Min for me!"

Next in Line

A slim waxing crescent moon shone over Wonder Falls.

In the cellar of the Brew-Ha-Ha, Aunt Astrid, Bea, Jake, and I met to compare notes. I'd bought a large whiteboard and was struggling to open a pack of markers.

"We found Alice," Jake said.

Bea pulled out a photocopy of a newspaper obituary. "Topher and Dolly's daughter. Tommy's mother. Died in childbirth at the age of sixteen."

Jake added, "Of course she was unmarried. The identity of Tommy's father remains a mystery though."

I said, "People around here must've known who she was. I suppose we could've easily asked around."

"Hmm," Astrid said, looking as though she was trying to remember Alice. "I didn't know the Thompsons well then.

Maybe I saw her around and I just didn't pay attention. I certainly didn't hear about her death."

"They probably didn't want to announce it," I said. "Kept it hush-hush. She did give birth out of wedlock. To Topher and Dolores, that must've been scandalous."

"We think she'll be the next to rise from her grave," Bea finished.

Aunt Astrid pondered that. "That's Topher's motive, isn't it? He doesn't want to be alone anymore, having outlived his whole family."

"He's not so careful about not outliving his friends," I said sadly, remembering Old Murray. That wasn't fair of me to say though. The Unfamiliar had made Topher desperate. At last, I got the markers out of their package and got one uncapped. "Let's go over what we know." I scribbled a word on the whiteboard, near the top: Resurrection. "That's what this Unfamiliar always does, because that's what Topher wants to do. The cost for a life is a life. Two full moons ago, for Shelley Marina"—I wrote her name under Resurrection then drew a sideways arrow —"the cost was Samantha." I wrote Samantha Perry next to the arrow. Beside that, I drew an equal sign and the word FAILED.

"They had no blood relation," Bea said. "In a town this small, it's unlikely to not have any blood relation. Samantha was a fairly new resident and didn't grow up here at all."

"The sacrifice for a resurrection," Jake offered, "won't be a random unlucky person again."

I nodded. "They'll still be awfully unlucky, but whoever it

is will be more carefully chosen. Not only that, but who is resurrected will be carefully chosen." Shelley Marina's only descendant was Rosemary Marina. Below the previous line, I drew a question mark and the names Rosemary Marina Thompson and Basil Thompson. "Rosemary and Basil were cremated and their ashes scattered over the falls. Why didn't we have ash golems wandering around town in the last full moon?"

Bea riffled through Jake's report. "No living relations on the Marina side still reside in Wonder Falls. Rosemary Marina's father was apparently an Italian celebrity who never set foot in the Americas, or so Shelley said. The townsfolk believed her. Rosemary grew up in unstigmatized illegitimacy."

"In this town?" The disbelief in my tone made the question rhetorical. "Now I'm really sorry to have missed the good old days!"

Aunt Astrid suggested, "It might be because the ashes were washed outside of the Wonder Falls boundaries."

Bea explained to Jake, "The Maid of the Mist claimed the land on which this town was built. Anything beyond that boundary that comes in gets checked or interfered with by the Familiars, same as anything from inside the boundary going out. Anything within is the responsibility of witches to police."

"Then why don't the Familiars stop the Unfamiliars before the Unfamiliars do anything?" Jake wondered.

We all had our own answers that we said at almost the same time.

"Familiars and Unfamiliars are only our words for them," I said. "We don't know which one they are until they do something good or bad, and even then we don't know until the next time they decide to do anything."

"Most magic, whether those are magic spells or magic beings, must follow the rules of space and time," Bea said, "or else it couldn't exist and affect itself here. The Unfamiliar transcend those."

"The Familiars are scared of this one," Aunt Astrid said. "I've gone all over. If worse comes to worst, they won't help us. They really feel that they can't."

"All right. So... the rules of this magic spell are that you can't resurrect your parents or ancestors, but only your descendants?" Jake asked.

"That's a good question. We do know that it resurrects siblings." I drew another moon and the name Dolores Willis Thompson, an arrow, Murray Willis, an equal sign, and the word INTERRUPTED.

Aunt Astrid stood and pointed at the names of the resurrected. "Shelley Marina was first; Dolores Thompson was second. Why this order? Was Topher more eager to have his grandmother back in his life than his wife?"

We thought about it.

"No," I decided. "The boundary of Wonder Falls again. The fact that spells have to follow the rules of time if they're going to have an effect on the temporal world... the Unfamiliar started with resurrecting the oldest body that still remained in town. Topher and the Unfamiliar didn't trade Samantha's life for Tommy's, even though Topher must have missed Tommy more than Shelley."

"So," Bea concluded, "after Dolores, the next to rise would be Alice Thompson. She wasn't cremated, and she was the next generation."

Jake asked, "If Alice Thompson is the next to be resurrected, would the victim be Murray Willis again?"

I quickly scribbled a family tree then changed marker colors to highlight the connection between Murray Willis and Alice Thompson.

RESURRECTED	SACRIFICE	RESULT
Shelley Marina	**Samantha Perry**	= **FAILED** (no blood relation)
mother of		
Rosemary Marina married to Basil Thompson NOT resurrected - both cremated		
mother of		
Dolores Willis Thompson	**Murray Willis**	= **INTERRUPTED** (blood relation - siblings)
mother of		
Alice Thompson	**Murray Willis again??**	

"That's possible," Aunt Astrid remarked.

"But it's usually not possible because the sacrificial human didn't survive," Bea added. "And therefore ran out of life force to sacrifice."

"We have a new Plan A then," I said. "We protect Old Murray."

Jake frowned. "What was the old Plan A?"

I sighed. "To convince Topher not to keep using the power of the Unfamiliar."

Unfamiliars confused people. They fed desperations, obfuscated other options, and all the while could only work with what the hosts gave them. Give them nothing—so simple, yet it always proved impossible.

LATER THAT NIGHT, after I'd gone home and gone to bed, I stared at the moon through my window from where I was tucked in and trying to sleep.

Renovations at the Brew-Ha-Ha were complete. With Aunt Astrid doing the baking and cooking—and some of the brewing and mixing—we'd still be understaffed. I'd submitted an ad to the Wonder Falls newspaper. Over the next week, hopefully, there would be applicants to vet and interviews to process.

We didn't have time for that. The moon shone through my window to remind me that we were running out of time.

Treacle had curled up on top of the quilt, over my stomach. He stretched a paw out to try to calm me down.

"No. I feel like we're missing something," I told him. The

feeling nagged at me. "We Greenstones have generations of records to study about the way magic works. This Unfamiliar works by trial and error. As Aunt Astrid said, it learns. It's learning its limits. What if the decisions we've decided they're most likely to make turn out to not be the decisions they actually do make?"

"Life is full of surprises," Treacle told me.

"Life is full of fatality," I said.

Treacle yawned. "*We can only do what we do.*"

And what did any of this have to do with Min Park and his family?

A wide waxing crescent moon shone over Wonder Falls.

Lost

For the next couple of days, I went about my daily routine feeling as if I'd left my wallet somewhere or forgotten to turn off the iron in the house. Nothing regarding Samantha's murder, the unnatural exhumation of not just one but two of the local residents of Wonder Falls Cemetery, the close call Old Murray had escaped thanks to Bea, or the weird behavior of the Park family seemed to fit together.

No matter how hard I tried, I couldn't help but worry it all like an annoying hangnail. It didn't help that while I was waiting at the animal shelter for Min, Blake showed up. He yanked the door open and stopped for a second, looking at me.

"What are you doing here?" he snapped, sounding a lot like the dogs in the back kennel as they demanded their food.

"I'm waiting on Min. And good morning to you, too."

Blake looked at me then at his watch as if to confirm it was morning. The sun was coming up in the east like usual. I wasn't trying to pull a fast one on him.

He nodded and pulled Dixie cup from the side of the water cooler across from the waiting room seat I was sitting in. After filling the cup with water, Blake tossed it back quickly. He looked tired. Another sleepless night for him too, I thought.

"I don't get this." He flopped down in the seat next to me. "I have turned this thing over and over in my mind a million times. Nothing has clicked, fallen into place, revealed itself, or even seemed to give me a nudge in the right direction. I've never had a case go cold and..." He stared into the space in front of him.

As much as I hated to admit it, I knew how he felt. "I've been trying to put the whole thing out of my mind so maybe I could look at it later with a fresh perspective, you know?"

"That's easy for you to do. You work at the coffee shop," he said, not even looking at me.

I let out a loud sigh, reminding myself Blake was no monument to social graces. Someday he was going to really push the wrong button, and I would not be responsible for my actions. Until then, I focused on the sound of the dogs barking. It was breakfast time. Cody was entering the kennel with their dog food and a watering can of fresh water. All the furry four-legged beasts were happy to see him.

Before Blake arrived to spread his cheer, I'd tried to talk with Burger again for a little more information. He wouldn't say a word, at least not to me. The pack mentality was nearly impossible to crack through, so even if he had told the other dogs something about his human or that night, they weren't talking to me either.

When Cody appeared again, the bag of dog food in his hand was visibly lighter. No sounds but happy crunching came from the kennel. Cody walked into the waiting room with us and set down the bag.

"So what is Min meeting you here for?" he asked in his usually awkward way, shifting from left foot to right then back again, looking at the ground before letting his eyes meet ours.

"Well, he was thinking of making a little investment in your animal shelter," I said.

"Do we need that? I mean, I think Old Murray and I are doing pretty well on our own, right? Would he be working here too, then?"

I saw Cody was a little nervous about a stranger coming in and up-turning the apple cart. He was comfortable with Old Murray. They were close, and I could understand how a kid like him would prefer things not change.

"He just wants to help, you know, if you guys need more room or repairs. He's looking to give assistance."

"Will he be my new boss?"

"Oh, no. Nothing like that. He'd invest some of his money, but you and Old Murray would still manage the place like you have been."

Cody's face visibly relaxed. That made me relax. Until I saw Blake's face twisted in a scowl of deep thought. He aggravated me by just sitting there. I was about to say something rude to him when my phone rang and cut me off. It was Min.

"Hey, Min. Where are you?"

"You won't believe this, but I got lost."

"How do you get lost in Wonder Falls? You've just lived here your whole life." I couldn't help but tease him.

The truth was if you weren't from Wonder Falls, it was quite easy to get lost. Most towns were planned around a grid pattern with the majority of the streets running north, south, east, and west. Wonder Falls was designed like a snake pit with dozens of windy roads that changed name and direction without warning. One-way streets and dead ends could make a tourist feel as if they are trying to maneuver through a maze. Min had grown up here, but he had been gone for years, and a lot had changed since he was a teenager.

"Where are you now? I'll talk you through it."

"No, no. I've found something interesting." Min's voice was excited.

"Yeah? What is it?"

"The Wonder Falls Orphanage."

I swallowed hard and pursed my eyebrows. Blake looked at me as if he thought he saw a clue on my face. I turned my back to him. It was childish, but the truth was my conversation didn't include him.

"Orphanage? Where? Are you sure you're in Wonder Falls?" I asked. "Maybe you stumbled into unincorporated Frankfort. I didn't know there was an orphanage here. Is it even open?"

"Yes, it's open. There are no children here, if that's what you mean. But it's still open. You've got to see this place. It's exactly what I'm looking for."

"Well, give me the address, and I'll be right there."

Blake's head looked in my direction, but I didn't acknowledge him. Instead I stood and headed out the door to my car, giving Cody a wave and smile good-bye.

As I got the address from Min, I tried hard to remember it without writing it down, and I noticed a shadow following me. At first I thought I had to break out magic in full view of anyone who might be innocently walking by, but then I realized it was nothing magic could ever make go away. It was Blake.

I hung up with Min and stood at my car with my hand on the door handle. "Yes?" I snapped.

"I'm going with you," Blake said.

"What for?"

"Call it a hunch. A detective never ignores a hunch."

I rolled my eyes.

"You don't even know where I'm going."

"You said the orphanage."

"Yes, but I didn't say what orphanage or where. I could taking you on a wild goose chase to parts unknown," I said, hoping he'd reconsider.

"It's the Wonder Falls Orphanage on County Road 57 and Cline, right?" he said as if that was the hottest spot in town and everyone who was anyone knew about that orphanage.

The twinkle in his tired eyes also let me know he was enjoying this a little.

I opened the driver's door. "How did you know?"

"I'm a detective. It's my job to know things."

I could have sworn he was trying to tell me he knew a few things about yours truly as well. I gave him a scowl and got in behind the wheel. Leaning over, I unlocked the passenger side door, and Blake climbed in. I couldn't be sure because I wouldn't give him the satisfaction of looking in his direction, but I thought he was smiling.

House of Records

Much to my dismay, Blake knew exactly how to get to the orphanage, and it was set pretty far off the beaten path. The building wasn't surrounded by lush trees or wildflowers or even a forlorn playground, long rusted over from disuse. That was what I had envisioned when Min told me where he was. Nope. This place was in the rougher part of town that was full of buildings sporting plywood windows and address numbers sprayed on with black spray paint.

At that hour of the morning, the neighborhood wasn't bad, but I felt the residue of negativity from the night before. I caught sight of an alley cat skulking around the corner of a brick building. It had a few jagged edges to its ears as though it had been in its fair share of fights.

"I recognize that smell." The thought from the alley cat came

to me clearly. "*You are with that animal that likes to sneak around where he doesn't belong. I taught him a lesson once to stay out of this part of town. If he comes back, I'll do it again.*"

Treacle. This cat knew Treacle.

"*From the looks of things, there's plenty of food and space for all you strays. Why worry yourself over one more cat?*" I hoped my thoughts sounded confident even if I was worried. I'd never had a cat, stray or domestic, intrude on my thoughts so hard.

The feline watched me with slow and lazily blinking yellow eyes. "*You just make sure to tell him, or he'll look very different next time you see him. And it won't be just a scratch on his forehead.*"

I gasped.

"What is it?" Blake asked.

"Oh, nothing." I coughed quickly. "For a minute, I thought I saw a rat."

I looked at the cat once more but said nothing. I'd have a long talk with Treacle about the dangers of slumming, but I knew it wouldn't do any good. The streets were his home. That sounded like a bad rap lyric.

"Is this it?" I asked, looking at a very nondescript red brick building that looked more like an abandoned bank than a place that had, at one time, housed children with no parents.

"Yup. It is."

"You don't think there are still children in there, do you?" I asked, my heart ready to sink if he said yes.

"Not at all. This place hasn't been in operation for some time. But it doesn't seem to be completely deserted."

"What makes you say that?" I was afraid he was going to say he'd seen some ghostly apparition in a window or something equally creepy. Being a witch didn't make me feel any safer from those mysterious things that go bump in the night, and even with the sun shining, I felt a shiver run up my spine.

"There are half a dozen cars in the parking lot." Blake jerked his chin toward the right of the building.

For sure, in a small parking lot surrounded by a chain link fence were a handful of cars. One of those cars was Min's. It was hard to miss the silver Mercedes, especially in this neighborhood.

Then some movement at the front of the building caught my eye. When I looked, I saw Min waving to us near the front door. He looked excited as he thrust his hands into his pockets. He must've gotten there just before Blake. As happy as Min looked, I could tell he was wondering what Blake was doing with me.

"I just thought I'd tag along. I hope it isn't a problem." Blake said. His eyes seemed to be searching every door, window, sidewalk grate, car, and garbage can that fell into his line of vision. His eyes finally settled on Min.

It was obvious that after Min had been a suspect in the deadly explosion of the Brew-Ha-Ha that had killed our cook, he and Blake would never be anything more than civil to each other. I couldn't blame Min. Blake was a jerk and hadn't held back when he interrogated Min. Blake had stuck to the rules, used his bullying tactics, and seemed to have the strangest ability to make people feel nervous around him even if they didn't do anything.

But to his credit, he was dedicated and willing to turn every stone, even if it kept him up for days at a time. And sometimes, when the light hit him the right way, he looked handsome. But then he would open his mouth and ruin everything.

Min shook his head at Blake then focused on me. "Cath, I think this place is just what I was looking for. A diamond in the rough."

"Well, it's not an orphanage anymore, right?" I asked. "There aren't any children here?"

"No. The last child that was adopted at this facility went home with his new family back in the 1960s."

"So what is this place?"

"Well, it's become sort of the Wonder Falls house of records." He grinned again as we made our way up the steps, and Min held the door open for us.

As soon as I stepped inside, I was hit by a very familiar smell from my childhood. It was the smell of old carpet and paper. I had grown up when carbon copies were just starting to be replaced by Xerox, and my school had smelled like this place. Tons of paper and a swatch of carpet big enough to sit on for story time. It was a weird smell but one I never forgot. But on top of that, the air shifted. I couldn't quite put my finger on it, but I could tell something was there that wanted to be noticed.

Had I been with Aunt Astrid and Bea, I would have leaned in and asked if they felt it too. But looking at Blake, who acted as if his head was on a swivel so he could look in all directions, I leaned a little in the opposite direction and kept my interpretations to myself.

"House of records?" I asked, knowing I looked confused. Then I heard another loud voice.

"Good morning!"

It was an unfamiliar voice but a friendly one. Even Min jumped a little at the startling greeting. Blake stood still and stoic.

"My name is Riley. I'm the custodian of this building. Is there anything I can help you with? Needless to say we don't get many visitors, so this is a surprise." He smiled cheerfully, his fat cheeks pushing his eyes into the shape of crescent moons.

Min stepped up and introduced us all. In a quick couple of words, he asked to speak to the chief administrator.

"Well, Detective Samberg, is there a problem?" Riley looked intrigued, as if he were hoping there might be some kind of scandal in the making and, for a moment, forgot about Min and me.

"Not at all. It's really Mr. Park who is here to inquire about the building."

"Oh, I see." Riley noticeably deflated a little, but within a few seconds, his cheery demeanor was back. "That would be Madeline Molitor. She's down the hallway this way." Riley led us down a lonely corridor. Our footsteps echoed throughout the building. "Are you looking to buy?"

"Min is a local boy who's looking to do a little good in his hometown," I bragged, making Min's cheeks color a little as he smiled.

"Is that so? That's mighty nice of you," Riley said. "I don't know what you'd want with the old place. It's long been forgotten. A skeleton crew comes in to turn the lights on and off, chase the spiders away, and keep the records in order."

"What kind of records?" I asked.

"Well, there are the documents of every adoption of course. But the new City Hall building that was built in 1999 was constructed without an insulated basement, so all the town records from there were put into these file cabinets. You've got marriage licenses, death certificates, building permit requests, traffic tickets, building permits, property lines. You name it, the paperwork is probably here."

"Is that so?" I said, trying not to tip off Blake as to what I was thinking of doing there.

"Yup. One stray spark or lightning strike here, and almost one hundred years of documented history would be gone with the wind. No one would even know what they lost."

"Why don't they put everything in a computer? It takes no time at all to scan these kinds of things," Min said, obviously adding it to the growing list of possibilities in his head.

"Well, I think you'll have to talk to Miss Molitor about that." Riley gave us all a wink and opened an old wooden door that had Administration stenciled in black letters across the frosted glass.

Inside, four gray-haired old women looked up from their desks as if they hadn't seen anyone under the age of sixty... ever.

"Miss Molitor's office is back there," Riley said, pointing toward the back of the room. "Good morning, ladies."

They all gave him a variety of greetings from spunky to grumbly. Min took the bull by the horns and strolled confidently to the back of the room and rapped firmly on the door Riley had indicated. I followed Min as Blake left with Mr. Riley. I hoped Blake wouldn't go on snooping. I wanted to find out what was going on with the death and desecration as much as he did, but a selfish part of me wanted to solve the case without anyone else's help. If Blake had the same idea to snoop in the records, he might find the Thompson records before me. But he'd have to do it the old-fashioned way. If I got my chance, a little witchcraft might help the medicine go down.

"Come!" was the greeting that came from behind the door.

Min pulled the door open and allowed me to enter first. Miss Molitor was a tiny woman who looked over a hundred. Her hair was permed into tight little gray curls. She wore glasses with decorative gold frames and garish pink lipstick that I'd bet was super popular in the fifties, when she was a newlywed or just started working outside the home or something.

Min began speaking instantly and didn't stop until Madeline Molitor was smiling and patting his hand as she shared the excitement of his plans to help preserve this amazing building. Under any other circumstances, I would have been Min's cheerleader, but I was distracted by the idea that I could very well be sitting just a couple of feet from the documents that might crack the case wide open. So I showed my support another way, and that was by asking a question.

"As things stand now, Miss Molitor, are people able to come and review these records? Say, if they were writing a report or tracing a family tree?"

"Not likely. The majority of the documents are in rows and rows of metal filing cabinets in the basement. We only manage material from the last three years on the main floor."

She barely looked at me as she spoke. I could tell she wasn't very interested in what I was asking. She was much more interested in dealing with Min. Obviously she was from that older generation of women who, if given the choice, preferred to talk business with the man. Well, he was the one with the money, and I was the one trying to snoop, and since I wasn't going to get very far with Miss Molitor, I began searching for plan B. I found it almost instantly.

Blake came back with Riley. The two of them looked as though they'd had a nice long talk together. From his expression, I was pretty sure Blake didn't have the same idea of riffling through the records as I did. I let out a sigh over that.

"Well, I'm really grateful for your time, Miss Molitor," Min said.

"Please, call me Madeline. I hope to hear from you again soon, Mr. Park. You have some wonderful ideas. I'm not promising anything, but let's talk again soon," the old woman said.

Hatching a Plan

Back at the Brew-Ha-Ha, I enjoyed an iced green tea and a turkey sandwich that Bea threw together for me. I told her how we discovered the orphanage and how we paid it a little visit.

"So you spent the morning with Blake."

I nearly choked. "Gosh, Bea! It wasn't like that. I didn't even want him to, but he insisted on tagging along." I spoke with my mouth full of food, totally ignoring any etiquette in order to set the record straight. "Just because you and Jake are back being all lovey-dovey doesn't mean the rest of us are interested in catching that bug."

Bea smiled as a guilty blush rose to her cheeks. I was happy for her. This was how things should be.

"Hey, since you guys are all back on better footing, I have a favor to ask."

"Anything, sister. You know that."

I shrugged my shoulders up to my ears and squinted. "Well, maybe you should hear what it is first."

Bea looked at me with her right eyebrow arching high up on her forehead while she crossed her arms. Just then, Aunt Astrid entered from the back kitchen.

"Aunt Astrid, I'll need you too."

She looked a little startled as if she had been deep in thought. We made our way to the cellar to have a private conversation, and I revealed my genius idea.

"You're talking about breaking and entering," Bea said calmly. "I don't know how Jake would be able to help us with that."

"Actually, it would just be entering. I noticed a window on the first floor without a mesh screen or bars, and as luck would have it, the lock wasn't in place. All we'd need to do is get up to it and push," I said proudly, as if I had just recited the capitals of every state. But the looks I got from Bea and Aunt Astrid made it seem as if I had just recited the filthiest limerick ever penned.

"And where is this place located?" Aunt Astrid asked with slow, deliberate words.

I gave the address, and both women threw up their arms.

"Are you kidding?" and "You've lost your mind" came out of their mouths at the same time.

"That part of town is a demilitarized zone. Are you serious? Jake has told me about what kinds of things the beat cops over there have had to deal with. To say it isn't safe is an understatement." Bea put her hands on her hips. "I can't tell him anything about this. He'd hit the roof."

"So you're in?" I said, grinning slyly.

"I don't know. Mom?"

Aunt Astrid stared into space for a moment. Then, looking at me with twinkling eyes, she said, "Unfortunately, Cath is right to think we might find the answer there. And even if Blake had put two and two together and seen the importance of those records, he would get them by the book, and that could take days, if not weeks. Who else will get hurt in that amount of time?" She pulled the hem of her dress up as she ascended the cellar stairs back into the Brew-Ha-Ha. "Bea, you'll stay home. Cath and I will go."

"Wait. What?" Bea looked a little let down.

Aunt Astrid stopped climbing. "With you and Jake just getting things back on track, you don't need to steer yourself off a cliff by breaking the law with us. Besides, we'll need a connection inside the WFPD if we get pinched."

"You just used the word 'pinched' like the short guy in that one mob movie," I said, looking Aunt Astrid up and down.

"Be at my house at eleven thirty. We'll leave at midnight," she said and disappeared up the stairs.

Bea took my hand and looked at me sternly. "Be careful. And if Jake finds out... I'll deny I knew anything about it."

I chuckled a little as I squeezed her hand. But inside, my nerves were full of electricity.

THAT NIGHT, before I left to pick up Aunt Astrid, I had a long talk with Treacle. Actually, Treacle had a long talk with me. It seemed word got around in the feline world, just as it did in the human world.

"That just isn't a safe place for people to go," he said.

"I saw that. And I saw what kind of strays you're dealing with. That doesn't make me very happy either," I replied.

That wasn't what he wanted to hear, and he sat with his head and neck stretched up tall and his tail whipping back and forth. *"It isn't just that. Those places are everywhere. They have a sickness. Like a rabies. And sometimes you can catch something."*

"We aren't going to move there," I reassured him. *"We're going to get into that building and research the records then hurry up and come home. That's all."*

The only thing on Treacle that moved was his tail. He was not happy. Finally he stood, stretched, and trotted off toward the open bedroom window. Hopping up on the sill, he turned and looked at me. *"Be careful."*

"Yes, you too. Come back home tomorrow, and we'll have breakfast. Smoked salmon?"

He licked his whiskers but said nothing and was again out into the darkness. I looked at the clock and realized it was time to go. Aunt Astrid would be waiting.

Breaking and Entering

The idea of breaking into a government building and rummaging through some records had been enough to keep me flighty and distracted all day, but when I pulled up to the house, Astrid was asleep on her front porch swing, a pink, floral decorative pillow snugly wrapped in her arms. Waking her up was like poking a grizzly bear with a stick.

"Come on," I whispered, hoping no insomnia sufferer was watching us. "We've got to get moving."

Finally, after she gave some low grumbles and growls, her eyes flickered open and she smiled. "What are we waiting for?" She walked briskly down the front porch steps to my car and got in.

I hadn't seen her that excited and animated in quite some time.

We drove to the orphanage in relative silence. I knew

Aunt Astrid was mumbling a protection spell over us as we drove, and one of the perks was that every light turned green in our favor. But as the neighborhood began to turn, the sad, frumpy place I had seen in the morning transformed into a sinister maze of streets with jagged shadows and unseen eyes from pitch-black windows.

"Are you all right to do this?" I asked.

"Never better," she said, smiling.

"This... I don't get... is this something on your bucket list or something?" I asked. My head went back and forth between the road and Aunt Astrid. "To break a major law, commit a halfway serious offense before you pass into the great beyond? Because I'm starting to think you're enjoying this a little too much. Usually I'm the one taking unnecessary chances."

"I can't help it," Astrid said. "I find it exhilarating."

She laughed, and I shook my head. We drove for just a little longer until we came up to Cline Street.

"Well, my stomach is in knots, so let's get this over with. That's the building just up ahead. I think we should park a little bit away from the building, but that means if we get into any trouble, we'll have to run."

Suddenly, Aunt Astrid's face became serious. "There's a protection spell already on that building." She spoke in a quiet voice as if she didn't want the building to hear her. "And it isn't a friendly one."

I stopped the car about a block away and turned off the ignition. My chest got a lot tighter. Maybe I should have told

Blake my idea and waited the couple of weeks for a warrant. "Can we get through it?"

"Yes. It's been there for a while and is pretty thin and worn. But be prepared for a little nausea. It isn't a white protection spell."

Goose bumps rose on my arms, and I shivered. We got out of the car and looked around suspiciously. Cat burglars we were not. Laurel and Hardy... well, maybe.

"The open window is on the southwest side of the building," I whispered. "Just around that corner."

As soon as we set foot on the property line, I felt it, a shift in the air that made it smell a little like metal. We stuck to the shadows as we inched our way around the building.

"I didn't notice this during the day," I whispered.

"You wouldn't have. It is a nocturnal spell designed to protect..."

"The building?" I asked nervously.

"The contents of the building."

"So you think the records might have more information than we first thought?"

"I'm not sure it's protecting the records at all."

I swallowed hard. Finally, I saw the right window. With just a little elbow grease, it slid right up. Cigarette butts littered the sill and the ground outside the window. Someone was obviously too set in their ways to adhere to the strict no-smoking policies implemented in every government building.

I gave Aunt Astrid a boost, and she shimmied into the open window with such grace that if I didn't know her, I would have thought she had been doing it her whole life. She helped pull me up.

As I had predicted, the office was creepy and scary in the darkness. It was just an office with desks and files and not a whole lot more, yet I got the feeling that weird things roamed the halls at night.

"Where are the records?" she asked.

"Miss Molitor said they were in the basement."

"Let's go." Aunt Astrid pulled a small LED flashlight from her pocket. It cut through the darkness and illuminated millions of little dust particles swirling in the air.

We exited the office and tiptoed down the hallway, checking each door until we found one at the very end of the corridor that read STAIRS. With a deep breath, I pulled the door open. It squeaked terribly, echoing throughout the building.

"Hasn't been opened in a while, I guess," I said, trying to calm my nerves.

Aunt Astrid gasped. Her flashlight shined on nothing other than stairs, but she obviously felt something.

"Let's hurry," she said, making her way down the stairs one step at a time, carefully holding on to the railing.

At the bottom, there were two more doors. One read Boiler Room. The other said nothing. We entered the nameless door.

I barely noticed Aunt Astrid had been mumbling almost the entire time we came down the stairs. Finally I looked at her face in the eerie glow of the flashlight and saw her sorting through the layers of the past to hopefully zero in on what we were looking for.

"There." She pointed at an olive green filing cabinet with at least an inch of dust on top of it.

I walked up to it and pointed at the top drawer. She shook her head. The second drawer was also a no. Finally, Aunt Astrid indicated the bottom drawer. I sat on the dirty floor, yanked open the drawer with a metallic *clink, clank zzshronk*.

There it was. The file stood out as if it had been waiting for us to find it.

Thompson Family: 1808 – 2009

The file was thick with birth certificates and death certificates for dozens of obscure branches stretching out from their family tree. Names that were familiar in town but faces I just couldn't remember. One thing jumped out at me so suddenly, I felt as if I had been slapped.

"We have to get going," Aunt Astrid hissed urgently.

"I don't believe this." My mind couldn't focus. I was shaking and felt a chill run up my spine.

"Cath!" Her voice sounded scared. "We've got to go! Now!"

"Should I take the file?" I was tripping over my thoughts and didn't know what to do. It was like one of those dreams where I was struggling to run but my legs just wouldn't move.

"No! Put it back! Put everything back! We need to get out of this building now!"

Finally my head clicked, and I heard her loud and clear. Stuffing the folder back where it belonged, I shut the drawer and jumped to my feet. Just then, we froze. We heard noises. I quickly tiptoed next to my aunt and held her hand. We stood there for what felt like an eternity. I watched her face as she sorted through the dimensions of the future and past and everything else in between. Her grip became tighter until I wasn't sure if it was *our* present where we were hearing noises or something in another dimension trying to bust its way through to this one. It seemed to be all around us and even, I shuddered to think it, inside us, echoing in our heads.

"Let's go!" I pulled Aunt Astrid toward the stairs.

I thought I might have to help her get up the stairs, but to my surprise and relief, she shot up them like a bullet. We burst through the wooden door into the dark hallway and pressed our backs against the cold concrete wall. Both of us held our breath.

Something was pursuing us. Something big and diabolical was rattling the foundation of the building.

"It was down there with us," Aunt Astrid said in a terrified whisper. "I think it's coming up the stairs."

Reluctantly, I pressed my ear against the wood door. As sure as the stars were in the sky that night, I heard the footsteps. I heard the breathing. I heard the growling.

This time it was Aunt Astrid who grabbed my hand and pulled me back toward the office. Once inside it, we quickly shut the door and ran to the window that, thankfully, was still open.

While Aunt Astrid backed her way out onto the safety of the pavement, I felt my body shake with fear. This had to be how the men floating around the sunken USS *Indianapolis* felt while being rescued as sharks continued to attack them from below.

I wouldn't turn around. I wouldn't look at the office door for fear of what I might see. But I knew whatever it was had crawled up from the basement. It had moved up the stairs with slow, deliberate steps, and now it was making its way down the hall.

"Hurry," I urged my aunt. "Please."

She nodded and grunted as she swung her second leg over the sill and hopped down. Looking around quickly, she saw nothing and waved to me. "Come on, Cath. Hurry."

She didn't have to tell me twice. But against my better judgment, against my gut instinct, against my own will, I turned and looked at the wooden door with Administration stenciled across it.

A ghoulish face, distorted by the glass, grinned a sadistic grin at me as its red eyes burned into mine.

I dove out the window, slamming it shut behind me, and onto the hard pavement, where I scraped up my palms and tore a nice size hole in my favorite black jeans.

"Are you all right?" Aunt Astrid asked as she yanked me to my feet and pulled me toward the car. Had I broken a leg, she would have continued to drag me away from that place, all the while soothing and encouraging as she was doing. "It's okay. We're all right now. The car is just up ahead. Come on, honey. Let's keep going."

Once inside the car, I locked the doors, started the engine, and peeled out of there under the blurry gaze of a couple of men sharing a drink from a paper bag.

Only once I saw the cheery sight of Aunt Astrid's front porch did I let out a sigh. It seemed as if I might have been holding my breath for the entire drive.

"Can I..."

"Sleep overnight here?" Aunt Astrid finished my sentence. "Absolutely."

I sighed with relief. "Thanks."

We didn't say too much about what we had heard. I didn't tell Aunt Astrid about the face I had seen. I would wait until the sun came up and Bea was with us. The hustle and bustle of a normal day under a normal sun could chase away the shadows and boogeymen.

The Park Family Secret

"I stayed awake all night waiting for the phone to ring. I was sure I'd get a call from Jake telling me my mom and cousin had been picked up for breaking into a government building," Bea said, pouring hot tea into our cups the following morning in Aunt Astrid's kitchen.

"You have no idea," I said, wrapping my hands around the warm mug.

"Did you find out anything?"

Aunt Astrid sipped her tea and looked at me. I hadn't told her what I'd read in the documents on the Thompson family. I felt a little guilty even mentioning it. It was obviously something that was intended to stay buried.

"Yes," I said, looking back at Aunt Astrid.

"So? Don't keep me waiting." Bea's eyes bounced back and forth between us.

"There was something there. Something that knew *we* were there and wasn't very happy," Aunt Astrid said.

"What happened?"

Aunt Astrid told Bea in great detail what had happened while I had my back to her as I read the complete Thompson file. She saw people coming and going, heard conversations about the building and the files, and she also saw where the protection spell had come from.

"Topher?" Bea gasped, looking at me.

"This is the first I'm hearing about this too," I said, shaking my head in disbelief. When we had gotten back to Aunt Astrid's place, we were so shocked and exhausted that sleep overcame us almost instantly. Even if we had wanted to talk about what had happened, our minds just wouldn't allow it.

"I'm not sure why but..." Aunt Astrid shook her head and pulled an apple pie, with one slice missing, out of her refrigerator. With three graceful movements, she swept up three rose-decorated small plates, pulled three forks from the copper canister on the counter, and snagged the pie server from the cutlery drawer.

"Well, I'm not sure what to make of this, but from what I saw in the file, that may not be so hard to believe." I took another sip of tea as a heaping slice of apple pie made its way in front of me.

Pulling her chair up to the kitchen table, Aunt Astrid took a seat.

"There was a birth certificate in there. Well, there were

lots of them throughout the years and nothing strange, nothing out of order except..." I felt as though I was gossiping, and that was bad enough, but I saw no other way to help get this situation under control. "I saw Thomas Thompson born to mother Alice Thompson and father..."

Bea's back straightened, and her eyes widened.

"Lei Park. Min's father."

"What?" Bea and Aunt Astrid cried at once.

"Hey, I'm not saying it's true. I'm saying that that's what was on the birth certificate. But why would it be there if it wasn't true? I mean, the whole thing is really messed up, right?"

"Min's father was Tommy Thompson's father too?" Bea exclaimed. "How could that be?"

"Well, the certificate didn't go into details, but I'm guessing that when they were younger, Mr. Park and Miss Thompson had a fling that resulted in a child." I shoveled a huge scoop of apple pie into my mouth so I wouldn't have to say any more.

"Well, duh, that's what happened," Bea said. "But something like that would have gotten around. People would have heard about it. This is a small town, and gossip tumbles from mouths as easily as the water down the waterfall."

"That is a beautiful comparison," I said, giving Bea a wink.

"Thank you. But still, don't you think someone would have spoken about this before?"

"People can keep secrets if they choose to. It's just that so many people choose not to," Aunt Astrid said.

"If that's true, then it might explain why Topher seemed so agitated at the play," I said, thinking hard while cutting myself another piece of pie.

"What are you talking about?" Aunt Astrid asked.

"The play. You guys were in your seats when I was in the back with Min and Blake. Topher came galloping along with his britches in a bunch, calling Min all kinds of names. It makes a little more sense that he'd have some animosity toward the men in the Park family."

"But Topher was never rude to them before. He might be a bit on the eccentric side but never hurtful," Bea insisted and sipped her tea.

"Right, but now he's got an Unfamiliar attached to him, feeding him lies and pulling him down into that darkness where who knows what worms its way into his mind," I said. "Maybe thirty years ago, he did hate Lei Park or everyone in the Park family for this indiscretion but came to terms with it. If there was still just a sliver of resentment, that creature would find it and infect it until it became a consuming cancer."

"And all the while making it look like Old Murray was the problem." Aunt Astrid nodded. "All along, that Unfamiliar had its vise grip on Topher and—"

"Pointed out to Topher that someone in the Park family was a closer living relation to Alice than anyone else in town. If he gets his hands on Min, or preferably Lei Park, then raising the dead and giving life to the Unfamiliar will probably work." I swallowed hard as I thought about the face I'd seen staring back at me through the frosted glass at the orphanage.

"What?" Bea asked. "Your face just went pale."

I wasn't sure if I should say anything about it. Maybe I hadn't even seen it. Maybe I had just gotten wrapped up in the moment and my mind was playing tricks on me. Maybe it was a result of the old spell hanging over that place like webbing.

"When we were getting out of that building, I saw something," I said.

"The Unfamiliar," Aunt Astrid said as if she already knew.

I looked at her with wide eyes. "How did you know?"

"I caught a glimpse of it moving through time. It rips the fabric of the dimensions like it's going through paper."

"What was it doing hanging out at an old government building that practically no one ever visits?" Bea asked.

"That I don't know," Aunt Astrid said. "But I knew we stirred it up just a few minutes after I was shown where the files that might help us were. I just thought we could get out of there before it made it through to our dimension. I guess I was wrong."

I shivered. Even with the comfort of the sun and the protection of my family around me, I felt vulnerable, as if I was only wearing a towel and had to go slay a dragon.

"Does that mean the Unfamiliar sometimes detaches itself from Topher?" Bea asked, pushing her empty plate aside.

Aunt Astrid walked to her pantry and opened the door, revealing not just canned goods and baking supplies but three shelves filled with books. The one she retrieved was a small black leather-bound thing with fingerprints in flour on the cover. The pages inside were yellowed and almost transparent with age. She peeled them away from each other delicately, one at a time. "According to this..."

"What is that one? I don't think I've ever seen it," I said, peeking at the writing.

"This is sort of like the Cliff's Notes on Unfamiliars," Aunt Astrid said, her brow wrinkling over her nose. "It won't tell us how to get rid of the little bugger, but it will tell us its schedule."

I looked at Bea, who shook her head and shrugged.

"The Unfamiliar is strongest during the full moon, but last night was two nights *before* the full moon. It was weak, and Topher must have either pushed it out of his mind or was so exhausted when he fell asleep that it couldn't get through to him. We can assume it whispers to him incessantly, driving him crazy one word at a time."

"That poor man," Bea said. "He needs a healing spell, but it's no good to do one until the Unfamiliar is gone."

"So it came sniffing around for us. It knows we're here. It knows what we are. And it isn't scared." Aunt Astrid had barely touched her pie.

I finished my second slice of pie and washed it down with the remaining tea, which had gone lukewarm. "Well, it's going to be up to something tonight. My gut is telling me that we need to let the Parks know they're in danger."

"How are you going to do that?" Bea asked. "Do you

realize how crazy our story would sound? Not to mention how embarrassing for them? There's no easy way to address the issue."

"No, there isn't. You want to do it?" I asked, looking at Bea with puppy dog eyes.

She put her hands up in front of her and shook her head. "No way. I'm getting my own house in order before I butt in on anyone else. Besides, you're the one Min has eyes for. It would be better coming from someone he knows and cares for."

"Has eyes for?" I felt my cheeks flash hot pink. "What are you talking about?"

"Oh, nothing." Bea folded her arms across her chest and snickered.

Marshmallow jumped into Aunt Astrid's lap, hopped up on the table, and made herself comfortable there.

"Treacle was here this morning. He looked like he had gotten into a little scuffle," Marshmallow said to me.

"I'm sure he did," I said. *"Did he say where he had been or where he was going?"*

"He didn't want you to see him the way he looked, so I assume he was going to the shelter for a quick cleanup from Cody and Old Murray before you could see him."

"Oh, that little sneak. Thanks for the tip." I scratched Marshmallow behind the ears, starting her purr engine.

"Sure, but you didn't hear it from me."

Bea and Aunt Astrid didn't hear my conversation with Marshmallow, but I think they could tell something was up.

"I'm going to go get this thing with the Parks over with," I said. "It isn't something that needs to be put off any longer. Plus, if it is the full moon the night after tomorrow, we have to be prepared."

Again, I thought of that thing that had grinned at me. It suddenly wasn't as scary as what I had to tell the Parks. I thought what I needed to do was walk off the two slices of pie I had just eaten while I came up with a script that would prompt the Parks without revealing the whole story.

Leaving Aunt Astrid and Bea to discuss the plan for the evening, I drove to the animal shelter to pick up Treacle. I'd drop him off at home with a little food and a stern talking-to, then I'd head off to the Parks' house.

Monsters Under the Bed

The shelter was several healthy blocks away, and with the sun shining on my face and just a kiss of a breeze blowing through the trees and carrying the smell of mimosa, I was feeling better. I knew I still had a lot of work ahead of me in the next few hours, but I was beginning to feel like I could handle it. Come what may, I'd make it through, along with the other Greenstones.

But as I caught sight of the sign for the shelter, something inside me started to doubt my success. And not just success in talking with the Parks but everything. Suddenly the sun was covered by storm clouds and the flowers wilted. I knew it wasn't really happening, but it felt like it was, way deep down in my soul. Not realizing my pace had slowed down, I felt as though maybe I should turn around.

"Treacle is in there. At least, I think he is. I can't just leave him," I said, my steps getting smaller and smaller.

The thought of my cat made me square my shoulders and pick up my pace. If I got hurt, that was one thing. But if something thought of hurting my cat, well, that was just plain cruel. I wasn't about to leave Treacle just because of a few woogie-boogie feelings.

I tried to focus and call his name with my thoughts, but I couldn't get through. Something was blocking my thoughts. Now my steps really quickened, until I was almost running up the sidewalk to the front entrance. Before I could even get my hand on the front door handle, I heard yelling.

It sounded like a poker game gone bad. I instantly recognized Cody telling someone to just calm down. I heard a female voice saying she was sorry and didn't understand. It sounded like Naomi LaChance. She had been stopping in regularly to check on Topher while Cody worked at the shelter, probably because she still felt attached to Tommy.

A million thoughts went through my head as my hand touched the door handle, took hold, and pulled it open. I took two steps inside. Cody was saying he was sorry over and over. He and Naomi were cornered and looking at an old man, who had his back to me as I walked in.

"What's going on?" I asked, a little out of breath. I heard Treacle calling me from the back room. In my mind, I answered him, but he kept calling and talking too fast for me to understand what he was saying.

"Cath. Oh jeez, you might want to go and get Chief Talbot or Jake or someone to come over here right away." Cody's eyes looked at me then darted back to the old man who still had his back to me.

"Now, Topher, you need to just calm down. I don't know what your issue is, but we can help if you'll just relax a bit." Naomi's voice was barely any calmer than Cody's. She was visibly shaking.

"Topher, come on, man. You and me are friends. There's no need to get mad. I don't even know what I said. I just..." Cody stumbled over his words, his eyes wide and scared.

Topher was blocking the door and preventing me from getting any farther in the room. I looked at his hands and didn't see a weapon, but his fists were clenching and unclenching in a menacing and deliberate manner. There were papers and a broken potted plant on the floor, along with an overturned waiting room chair, and I saw a new crack in the plaster of the front reception desk.

"Hey, Topher," I said in a quiet voice. "It's me, Cath Greenstone. What's going on here?"

His head tilted a little in my direction as if he was listening, but he didn't turn around. Everyone stood still. Not a sound came from any of us until Topher spoke. Or at least the words came from his mouth. I don't think it was really him talking.

"I know you," he said. "I know you are still afraid of monsters under your bed."

The words struck me dumb, and before I could utter anything, the old man spun around to face me. It was Topher's body and face, but something was working just below the surface. My eyes blurred, as if I was viewing a photo taken in mid-movement or perhaps filtered through a frosted window.

The temperature in the room dropped at least twenty degrees, and I was paralyzed with fear. I wanted to run, but the thought of Treacle in his cage held me there. With Cody and Naomi just as scared as me, well, someone had to stand up to it.

"Under the bed," it hissed again.

The evil smile fell from his face, and the Unfamiliar looked at me seriously. Before I could call out a binding spell or even a simple hex to numb his legs, the old man rushed to me and pushed me into the wall, where my head snapped back and thudded against the fake wood paneling. Out the door he went. I didn't dare chase him.

"What was that all about?" Naomi asked. "He was as pleasant as punch all day until he started talking to you." She elbowed Cody, who looked at her apologetically.

He was just a kid compared to the rest of us. Compared to the Unfamiliar, he was just a baby who it could easily frighten.

"I don't know," Cody said, sitting on one of the waiting room chairs and running his hands over his short dark hair. His eyes looked worried as if he might be in trouble.

I rubbed the back of my own head and sat next to Cody. "What were you guys doing?" I tried to act as baffled as they were even though I knew the thing that was hiding there in the old man's body.

"I just brought him over to get a little fresh air," Naomi

said. "While Old Murray is still recovering and taking it easy, Topher doesn't have anyone, really, to look out for him except for Cody. So I've been stopping by his place. I asked if he wanted to take a walk and see Cody."

"And he was okay with that?" I asked, still trying to remain calm.

"Yeah. We walked here, and Cody brought him out a little cup of water and told him that he went to visit Old Murray," Naomi continued, still standing in the same spot as if she was afraid to move.

I put my hand on Cody's shoulder. "How's he doing?" I hoped Cody couldn't feel my nerves trembling.

"He's doing great. That's what I told Topher. I told him how good the old man was doing, thanks to Bea's alternative medicine and what the doctors did for him, then I said I saw Mr. Park, and it was like someone flipped a switch, right?" He looked at Naomi, who was nodding as she swept a couple of stray strands of long black hair away from her face and nervously tucked them into the bun she was wearing.

"Lei Park stopped by to see Old Murray?" I asked, hoping maybe I wouldn't have to pay a visit to the Parks' residence.

"No, no. I meant Min Park. He's a mister too, you know."

I nodded. That made more sense. Min was that kind of person.

"It just sent Topher off the deep end. He started knocking things over and yelling out all kinds of gibberish that made no sense. Then he was saying things like, 'If it doesn't work with him, I'll try you next. The both of you. The both of you.'" Cody looked at Naomi again.

"What is that, like, dementia? Could he be having a breakdown after living all those years by himself out in the woods?" Naomi asked, picking up some of the papers on the floor.

"Uh, yeah. Well, it could be." I couldn't tell them that it was more than likely not even Topher talking, but some really annoyed, really nasty demon with a yearning for a strong, young, previously deceased body to dress up in and roam the streets looking for more lives to ruin.

"I'll get you Treacle. He moseyed in this morning looking a little worn. I think he got into a fight." Cody slowly walked to the back door with the word CATS in thick black block letters with a silhouette of a cat underneath it.

He emerged carrying my big black cat, and I instantly saw the small clip out of his right ear.

"Oh, Treacle, what have you been getting into?" I said, scooping the cat into my arms and holding him tightly. He had been scared, and so had I. His motor started to run, and the purring felt comforting as he nuzzled into my neck. "If you could put this on my running tab?" I joked. It seemed as if I was always paying the shelter a fee for my cat. "Are you two going to be all right? Do you want me to send Chief Talbot over, you know, just for the heck of it?"

Cody and Naomi shook their heads.

"I'm going to see my grandpa again tonight. I'll ask him what he thinks we should do," Cody said.

"Good idea," I said.

All we needed was a few more hours, and we might be able to help Topher without police intervention. I hoped. But now I still had to get to the Parks. If just the mention of the Park name sent Topher off like that, only heaven knew what he would do if he actually got his hands on one of them.

Park House

Stepping foot into Min's parents' house was not only like stepping back in time to my teenage years but to an exotic and mysterious place. Beautiful Korean paintings graced the walls. The furniture was sparse but elegantly arranged. Lush green plants grew from baskets and pots placed all over the house, giving the atmosphere a natural, organic feel. Family photos of Min growing up were scattered around in abundance.

At the front door was a row of shoes, including a pair of size nine black ballet flats that were mine. It was customary in Asian homes to take off your shoes even before closing the door. The home was a sanctuary. It was a peaceful place for contemplation and meditation. Usually. But not today.

Mrs. Park seemed civil, while Mr. Park was cold and standoffish as usual. I tried not to take it personally. I told them why I'd come. It seemed they knew exactly what I was talking about when I said I'd come to warn them about Topher's behavior while pretending I knew nothing about why he might be acting that way. I thought I'd pulled it off fairly convincingly, but the Parks still seemed to assume I knew something.

It wasn't long before they started arguing. As I looked at them, Mr. Park particularly, I thought about Tommy. He hadn't looked much like Mr. Park, except for the black hair and tan skin. He must've taken after his mother. I supposed if anyone were to look closely, he could have seemed a bit Asian, but mostly, he seemed Hispanic.

"What are you trying to say?" Mrs. Park yelled at her husband, who stood straight and defiantly in their living room.

I had shrunk back into the chair I was sitting in in the kitchen, trying to figure out how to get to the front door and slip out unnoticed.

"You heard the girl," Mr. Park said in a low voice through clenched teeth. "This trouble has come back to us and now—"

"To us? This was not my trouble. You brought this with you, and now we have to explain to the whole world—"

They went on arguing for several more minutes.

"I really just think he's chosen you guys to fixate on." I'd explained how he had exploded at the theater and at the mere mention of Min's name. "I hate to say it, but you guys have a nice business in town, and everyone knows you. You know how Topher is. If we didn't grow up with him around, we'd think he was just a string of dynamite short of being the Unabomber, living up there alone in the woods and keeping so much to himself. Yeah, it's just one of those things." I tried to act naïve, but when Mrs. Park's eyes filled with tears, I knew they knew what this was about. I was pretty sure they knew I knew.

"You know what this is about, don't you?" she'd asked her husband.

"No," was all Mr. Park had said at first. But he couldn't look at his wife. Instead, he held his head up high and looked past her out the window.

That must have been something he had done before, because Mrs. Park pounced. "Yes, you do. A problem of the past has finally risen to the surface. There will be no rest until you face this shame."

"I do not need the council of a woman!" Mr. Park had barked. He got angrier and angrier by the minute. "The past cannot be changed!"

"That's true, but you can make amends. You never did that with me or with Min. You let Min think he wasn't good enough when it was you who had the indiscretion."

My whole body had heated up with embarrassment. What was I doing, sitting there with a tiny cup of tea that Mrs. Park had poured for me over fifteen minutes earlier? Had they forgotten I was sitting there? Didn't they want to know what to do next?

Apparently not, because they'd continued their argument,

and I learned a little bit more about the whole situation than I really cared to know.

"What can I do now? The mother is dead," Mr. Park growled.

"Her name was Alice. You are not so cruel you have forgotten the name of the mother of your first son? Your first son, Thomas, who is also dead, not knowing his real father." Her voice was loud, and if no one in the town knew about this, there was a good chance a couple of them might know now. "You never talk to me about this. You say it happened like it was nothing. Like I was to accept it and just move on. Forgive and forget. But all this time, you never make things right. So how can I make it right? How can I clean up your mess? And when you see his name in the paper, you say nothing? You shed no tears. You don't go to the funeral? You don't mourn him?"

Those words made Mr. Park lower his head and close his eyes. "I do mourn him. You don't know this burden I have carried."

His voice was low, and I thought for a moment I would cry myself.

Mrs. Park walked up to her husband and stood directly in front of him, forcing him to make eye contact with her. For a second, I thought she was going to crack him across the face. But she didn't. She stood there strong and straight.

"How can you say that when I have carried it with you?" she asked.

"A woman's burden is not the same as a man's. There is more to this than you can possibly understand."

Mrs. Park folded her arms across her chest. "Then maybe you need to talk to Topher. Man to man. And you both can mourn and finally lay to rest this mess that you caused."

"I wouldn't suggest doing that," I said, putting my hands up and instantly regretting opening my mouth. They glared at me like I was some kind of interloper, which, at that moment, I was. "I'm not trying to get into your business. Really, I'm not. But going to talk to Topher right now may just be, well, too dangerous. You may end up doing more harm than good."

"You are not part of this family," Mr. Park said calmly but with bitterness. "I don't need advice from you."

Mrs. Park seemed to agree with her husband and looked at me with anger and hurt in her eyes. All I could think of was what Min would think of all this. What would he think of me bringing this into his family's home?

I nodded and stood, hearing the bones in my knees crack with relief. I had been sitting so stone still, they had locked up a little. "I'm sorry. But please don't go talk to Topher. He's not well. Give it a couple of days, or weeks even."

I could tell by their faces they were getting angrier by the second, and their silence was making me nervous. Images of Mrs. Park physically tossing me out of her home to land square on my keister flashed through my mind, so I made my way quickly to the front door.

They resumed their argument in Korean. I felt bad for them and for myself. Had I done the right thing by warning them? Yes. Yes, I had. They had to know that Topher wasn't stable right now.

But no matter how much I tried to comfort myself, I still felt as though I'd done way more harm than good. I wanted to call Min right away and maybe give him a heads-up about everything that had gone on, but I could only imagine what Mr. and Mrs. Park would say if I told Min about the relationship between his father and Alice Thompson.

I decided to try something new and kept my mouth shut.

I made my way back to Aunt Astrid's house. When I got there, Bea had left for the Brew-Ha-Ha and Aunt Astrid was searching around for a couple of books we needed to study to prepare for the full moon in two days.

"There is nothing you can do now, Cath. What's done is done," she said, searching through her library, which was spread throughout almost every room in her home.

"You sound like you aren't happy I went to them."

"Your intentions were good. I know they were. But this is a sticky topic. It might have been better if you'd gone over your plan with Bea and me."

I picked at my thumbnail. I didn't think anyone could make me feel worse than the Parks had, but I was wrong. Aunt Astrid was right. I should have talked it out a little more, especially after I'd seen the shape Topher was in at the animal shelter. That reminded me of something I was reluctant to talk to anyone about. When I mentioned it to Aunt Astrid, she looked at me with a frightened expression.

"He mentioned monsters under your bed?" she said, her hand to her chest and her voice quieter.

I nodded.

She quickly turned back to her books and pulled an old-looking gray tome off the shelf. When she blew on it, a few specks of dust flew off, and she hustled to another shelf across the room. She ran her index finger along the spines until an "a-ha" let me know she'd found the book she was looking for.

"Sit down," she said to me without emotion.

I sat in the corner of her soft, flower-patterned couch and looked at her. Aunt Astrid's eyes scanned around deliberately, as if she was pushing her gaze through the various dimensions that only she could see. She opened the gray book and read aloud.

When Aunt Astrid read a spell, it sounded like a song. The words were like a poem and brought a slight swirl to the air, like a gentle breeze. I felt calm settle over me. Then her voice became quieter and the words indistinguishable as she muttered them. Her hand rested gently on my head, and I felt the tingly sensation of magic float over and through me. The whole ritual took less than a minute, but I immediately felt different.

"What was that for?" I asked.

"It's just a little protection spell. That Unfamiliar looked at you. He saw your face, even if it was just through the frosted glass of that door. Today he got a good look at you. Not just your face but inside your soul. He knows more than he should. I don't know how that can be."

I didn't like how her face looked and how she wouldn't meet my gaze.

"So this spell will protect me?" I asked.

"It will make it a little hard for him to read your thoughts, but it isn't permanent nor is it foolproof. And for a short time, you may not be able to talk to the cats."

My eyes filled with tears, but I nodded my understanding.

"I'm sorry, honey, but it's the only way," Aunt Astrid said.

I knew she felt bad, but I also got the feeling I was being punished just a little bit.

Protection Spell

The next two days were spent preparing for the full moon as if we were all cramming for finals. This was difficult as we'd reopened the Brew-Ha-Ha already. The whole town had missed us, and we were busier than ever. We took on more staff to handle the customers. We would've rejoiced in our grand reopening if it weren't for all of this Unfamiliar trouble.

Every night after closing down the Brew-Ha-Ha, we gathered in the cellar, and while sipping herb tea, we dog-eared pages, underlined passages, made notes into the wee hours of the morning.

"Well, from everything we've read, it's pretty obvious the Parks will be the next target. They're the only family Topher has left, even if they don't acknowledge each other as such," Bea said. "Everything in these books regarding raising the dead confirms a familial tie is the strongest way raise the dead. No wonder it's never practiced. How morbid."

"Is anyone hungry?" I asked a little sheepishly.

"Really? You're thinking of food now?" Bea looked at me while Aunt Astrid chuckled in the corner.

"Come on. We have to open the Brew-Ha-Ha in what?" I looked at my watch. "Holy moly. Forty-five minutes. I don't know about you two, but I want something a little stronger than tea to drink and something with sugar to eat."

"I think Cath is right," Astrid said. "We'll need our strength tonight. We need to eat and get some rest."

We made our way up from the cellar. The bright morning light cascaded in through the big front windows, and coffee was quickly brewed. Every morning, Daisy's Garden, the local flower shop, left a fresh delivery of flowers by the front door. I scooped them up and deeply inhaled the wonderful smell of rosebuds with sprigs of baby's breath. After breaking up the bouquet, I filled the tiny bud vases that graced the counter and the couple of mismatched tables we'd acquired during the last village-wide garage sale.

A bit of movement out of my peripheral vision caught my attention. It was Treacle. He slinked in, setting off the tinkling bells over the door. He looked at me. I looked at him. I couldn't hear a thing.

Nearly bursting into tears, I scooped him up in my arms, stroking his black fur. "I'm sorry, buddy. I can't talk right now. Not until this whole mess is over with."

I rubbed his head and felt his purring motor. I don't know

if he understood me since we usually communicated telepathically. I hoped he did. I inspected his scratches from the other night. They appeared to be getting better, and for that, I was thankful. I set him on the counter, where he batted the baby's breath for a second then looked at me.

Aunt Astrid came up to the counter and skirted around it to sit at the nearest table. "Well, look who came to visit." She ran her hand over Treacle's back, making him arch his body happily.

"I can't hear him. I don't think there has ever been a time I didn't hear him talk to me."

Tilting her head to the left, Aunt Astrid smiled. "It won't last too much longer, honey. I promise. But it's better safe than sorry. You can explain to Treacle once this whole mess is over."

I nodded, my eyes still stinging as I tried to keep from crying like a baby. Then someone set off the bells over the door with a fierce push. It was Jake and Blake. Wiping my eyes, I straightened up and squared my shoulders.

"Good morning, boys. Coffee?" I said, sniffling as I smiled.

Blake looked at me as if I had turned green. He stepped a little closer and was about to say something when Jake made his announcement.

"No, Cath. We've got a problem."

Bea came up front from the kitchen. "Hi, honey." She leaned over the counter to greet Jake, who met her halfway for a kiss. "Something wrong?"

"Topher's gone missing. Have you seen him?"

Bea, Aunt Astrid, and I looked at each other, and even Treacle stood up and nudged me with his head.

"No. We haven't." I said. "Are you sure? He's been known to roam around the woods and sometimes stake out a place to sit and think or meditate or whatever it is that he does by himself."

"No, he's missing. Cody has been taking care of him since Old Murray is recovering, and he said he never came back after their altercation and he hasn't touched his medicine today or yesterday."

"Oh no. Poor Topher," Aunt Astrid said.

"That's not the only problem," Jake added. "Have any of you seen Mr. Lei Park recently?"

My heart sank down to my stomach. "I saw him the day before yesterday."

Blake gave me a once-over. The look he gave me made me think he might be worried that I had been crying about something related to his case, but that quickly went away as he shifted into facts-just-the-facts mode. He pulled out his little notebook and pen.

"Where did you see him?" he asked, his voice hard and all business.

"I... was... at their house."

"What time was that?"

I rolled my eyes. "It was in the morning."

"What did you go there for? Did you have something to do with the argument he had with his wife?"

My heart that had sunk to my stomach tightened up and

pounded in my ears. I knew I looked guilty of something. "Why?"

"Mrs. Park said you were there when they were having a fight. Do you know what it was about?"

I knew Blake was studying my body language, my eye movement, my tone, but I couldn't tell him the truth. I couldn't tell him about Alice Thompson. Not only would the Parks never forgive me, but I'd never forgive myself. "I did kind of arrive as something was heating up, but I was looking for Min. I only stayed for about fifteen minutes, maybe half an hour tops, then I left." It wasn't a complete lie. It was just maybe half the truth.

Blake nodded as he scribbled his notes. Then he looked at Jake as if to say he didn't think I was telling the truth, the whole truth, and nothing but the truth, so help me God.

When the two detectives left, they didn't have much more than they had started with. Jake gave Bea a wink as if to let her know he might pick her brain a little later when no one else was around. The truth was none of us knew where Topher or Mr. Park could be. Even Treacle was on edge as he nudged me and forced his head underneath my hand. He must have sensed something was wrong and wanted a little extra attention.

"Where do you think they could be?" Bea asked, looking from me to Aunt Astrid.

I shrugged, but Aunt Astrid had a very calm expression. Her chin was raised, and she looked off as if she were staring out the windows.

"They may not be there now, but they will be there later," she said. "Where everything started. In the cemetery."

"Are you sure?" Bea asked, a shiver visibly running up her spine.

"Tonight is the full moon. If the Unfamiliar is going to take another shot at raising a corpse with Mr. Park's life force as the trade, he'll try to do that tonight."

"But we're ready for it, right?" I asked.

For some reason, I felt as if I might be the weakest link in this chain, and I had never felt that way before. Some of this unrest was my fault. If I hadn't interfered with Mr. Park's personal business, he might still be home or at the shop, without any idea Topher was harboring in his head a fugitive from another dimension that was encouraging acts of violence.

When Aunt Astrid didn't reply immediately, I shook where I stood.

"So how prepared are we?" Bea asked, placing her hand gently over mine.

"We need to unite our strength," Aunt Astrid said. "This is no ordinary Unfamiliar. In fact, it is a little too familiar for my liking."

"What does that mean?" Bea's eyes bounced back and forth between Aunt Astrid and me, and it was obvious that she had been left out of something. "You can't keep a secret from me. Not now. Not when so much is going on."

"The Unfamiliar knows about my mom," I said. "It knows

about the monster under my bed, and it seemed to be kind of happy about the whole situation."

Bea gasped and slapped her hand over her mouth. "Oh, Cath, what are we going to do? Maybe you shouldn't come tonight. Mom, does she have to come? Can we do this ourselves?"

"That's what I was thinking. Cath, you may have to sit this one out. Maybe you could continue a vigil to help keep the spell of protection over us. You could perform a cleansing ritual for the house to make sure nothing tries to sneak in the back door. You could—"

"Oh, no. I'm not sitting this out on the sidelines. You're both off your rockers if you think I'll do that. Even if you insisted I stay home, I'd just follow you without you noticing." I put my hands on my hips. "I've got to come. You can't shut me out. I feel like this one is partially my fault."

I understood where they were coming from, I really did, and I couldn't shake the feeling that maybe they were right. But like the idea of letting the Parks know they were in danger, I just had it set in my head that I had to go with them. I had to help shut this door and get Topher some peace while making sure he wasn't charged for the murder of Lei Park. The idea that I might be the cause of someone else losing their life was too much to ignore. It was bad enough my own parents had died trying to protect me. It was all my fault, my fault, my fault.

Wait. Where had that thought come from? I'd never felt like that before. Something was going on inside my head, and the only way I would get to the bottom of it was to go to the cemetery tonight.

"Please," I begged. "I think... I think something is wrong with me. I can't put my finger on it, but I can feel it. Aunt Astrid, I think something is trying to break through your protection spell. I can't tell you how or why. It's just a hunch. But I'm afraid it will stay around, picking at my brain, if I don't go with you tonight. Please don't leave me behind."

"Protection spell? Why do you have a protection spell?" Bea looked at me as if I had just informed her I had a slight case of the plague.

I shrugged and smiled awkwardly.

"The Unfamiliar. It's stronger than you thought. Could it be trying to wear Cath down?" Bea asked Aunt Astrid.

The older woman nodded.

We discussed what we were going to do, and the staff relieved us in the afternoon so we could get some rest. When it was finally eight o'clock, we closed the coffee shop for the night. Aunt Astrid and Bea had decided to meet at the cemetery entrance at eleven thirty. Neither of them had given me a solid affirmative that I was to go with them, so I was left alone at my apartment with instructions to start a vigil and wait for their phone call. Darkness was coming. And it knew my face.

Shadows

Being told to stay home when my "sisters" were going out to fight a battle on a spiritual level made me feel like I had gotten stood up for prom. I tried to keep the vigil. I had lit the candles in the order Aunt Astrid had instructed. I knew the words to say and at what time to say them. But my heart wasn't in it. Why couldn't I just recite them at the graveyard? Why couldn't I be there?

The minutes seemed to tick by five at a time, and before I knew it, it was already ten thirty. If I left now, I could make it to the meeting place just in time to meet Aunt Astrid and Bea. They wouldn't have any choice but to let me tag along. I decided to leave. Sure, my judgment hadn't been the best for the past two days, but unlike my experience with the Parks, I didn't feel this was the wrong thing to do. I felt it was exactly what I needed to do.

If I left right then and there, I'd make it to the cemetery

just in time. Without another thought, I blew out the candles, stepped into my shoes, threw a shawl around my shoulders, and left.

The street was quiet, amazingly quiet, as if it were in a bubble. No one in Wonder Falls was outside at that hour. Usually there were some kids strolling around past curfew or couples walking hand-in-hand along the dark streets, giggling and stealing kisses when the shadows made a quick pocket of discretion. But there was no one out tonight.

A couple of homes were illuminated by the flicker of their television sets. Others had quiet music coming through open windows. It was as if they all had been told, on a subconscious level, to stay inside. So for all intents and purposes, I was alone on the street.

Or maybe I wasn't.

As I neared the cemetery entrance, the streetlights flickered. Sometimes they surged as I passed; other times they winked out completely until I had made it a couple yards away, then they'd pop back on.

The shadows appeared to be taking on life of their own. Even my own shadow, which stretched out long and lean from my feet each time I passed under a lamp, seemed to have turned on me, pulling other shadows to it and getting darker and darker. I felt that if I stared at it, I might just fall into that darkness. But I kept moving. I recited the words Aunt Astrid had told me to. I couldn't tell if they were doing any good, but I didn't want to stop chanting them for fear things might just get worse if I did. For a second, I wondered what other girls did on their Thursday nights. How many enjoyed a stroll down ever-darkening sidewalks with shadows creeping up on them? Did they welcome the occasional demon expulsion, or was it just routine to them? My internal attempts at humor weren't working.

I felt my footsteps become quicker and clap softly along the pavement with each step. Finally, I was within view of the cemetery entrance, and I saw Bea and Aunt Astrid there. They were talking, probably making a plan before they went in. As I broke into a run, I tripped and tumbled over myself, scraping my knee.

"What in the world?" I mumbled, turning around to see nothing on the ground except shadows.

At least, I thought they were shadows. But they began to writhe around my ankle like snakes. When I tried to push myself up, I felt them tighten like rubber bands, digging into my skin. Something didn't want me getting to the cemetery.

Everything inside me jumped into panic mode. All I wanted was to scream for my family and see them come running. But I couldn't yell for help without the risk of drawing attention to us. How would we explain traipsing through the cemetery at this hour? The shadows were writhing and pulling me back into a bigger pool of darkness. My knees and hands were getting terribly scratched up. I thought of my mother. This wasn't much different from the way she got dragged under my bed, except I had seen the hands, or should I say claws, that held her.

Like a bolt of lightning, the words she had been saying that day shot out of my mouth. "*Plestipacidus cum leviora*."

In an instant, the shadowy snakes recoiled, wriggling and thrashing all over themselves until they became plain, flat shadows on the pavement again.

Needless to say, I was sort of struck dumb. I hadn't thought of those words in years. The memory of my mother's voice was like an old music box wrapped up in sheets of tissue paper and stuffed into a hope chest. It was a treasure that I couldn't bear to listen to. But as I pushed myself up off the sidewalk and hurried toward my family, I felt renewed.

Everything around me appeared to become sharper and more focused, but one nagging thought remained. Why hadn't the Unfamiliar pounced on me when it had the chance at the orphanage? Aunt Astrid had already slid out of the window when it appeared at the door, yet it made no attempt to enter. It would have gotten to me before I could shimmy out the window, but it didn't even try.

And when it was speaking through Topher at the animal shelter, it had a perfect opportunity to take me out or at least give me a jolt so strong, I'd be afraid to set foot outside my home for years. Instead, it just threw out a couple of insults and low blows and scurried away. Was it weak? Had it drained its strength? Was it just waiting for the full moon?

There was an answer there. The clarity I had felt was slipping away again. Cotton was filling my head, making it hard to think. This wasn't Aunt Astrid's protection spell. Something was trying to break through it.

I gritted my teeth and ran as fast as I could to the cemetery entrance just as Bea and Aunt Astrid disappeared among the trees and tombstones.

Normally the stone structures with names and dates of loved ones from Wonder Falls never caused me any apprehension. But as I slipped between them, trying to see in what direction the other two Greenstones had gone, I felt as if I was getting lost. Things started to swim and tilt a little around me. My legs felt as if they were weighted with cement blocks, and I just wanted to sit down and rest. The headstones became large and menacing and seemed to muscle me in the opposite direction of my family. When I opened my mouth to call out to them, nothing happened.

Before I fell to the ground, I stopped and tried to steady myself. I saw a small black shadow slinking up to me. It had brilliant green eyes that looked as if they were lit from behind. I recognized those eyes.

The Three Witches

"Treacle," I whispered.

The black alley cat jumped into my arms and purred and rubbed his head on my chin. As I stroked his black fur, I felt my head clearing. With a deep breath, I looked into his eyes as his thick black paw tapped my chin.

"I'm so sorry. I can't hear you. Aunt Astrid's spell. It should be over soon."

He gave a quiet meow, his jowls vibrating with excitement. He pushed out of my arms with his front and back legs, and landed in the thick grass. Looking over his shoulder, he obviously wanted me to follow him.

"Where are they, Treacle? Show me," I whispered.

With that, he trotted toward the southeastern part of the cemetery.

The cemetery had about four acres of pristine land. It was

a good distance away from the street, and a visitor would require a map to locate any particular grave. The tombstones that had been erected in the southeastern section, where the ground was softer and the grass was still visible in the sections of sod that were rolled out like carpet, seemed brand new and polished compared to some. My parents were between the really old section, where the stones were simple rectangles with worn, barely legible names, and these new, elegant eternal resting markers.

Thankfully, there weren't many new tombstones in these four acres. But one, flanked on both sides by two of the beautiful old oaks that grew majestically throughout the property, had been recently tended to. The dirt had barely had a chance to settle when it had been so disrespectfully disturbed.

I saw Aunt Astrid and Bea crouching behind a large tombstone with the name Smith chiseled across its face. They were watching with disgust as the man who used to be harmless Topher laughed and taunted the gravesite of Thomas Thompson while kicking and poking Lei Park's unconscious body.

I ran up to them and felt their positive energy start to chase away my vertigo. But they didn't seem all that happy to see me.

"Cath, what are you doing here?" Bea whispered angrily, grabbing my wrist and yanking me down into the shadow behind the tombstone. "You were supposed to stay home and continue the vigil."

"Yes, I know. But I couldn't—"

"Catherine, I am telling you right now to leave. Your cousin and I can handle this."

Aunt Astrid was either furious with me or the shadows made her look more angry than she actually was. I preferred to think it was the latter.

"I know you can. But I think this thing wants me to stay away. I think it might be scared of something about me. It had two perfectly good chances to get me out of the picture, yet it didn't. Why?" I held each of their hands. "You can't tell me you don't feel a little stronger now that we are all together. Right?"

Topher stopped what he was doing and glared in our direction. His lips peeled back from his teeth, and he looked nothing like the gentle hermit we knew. We were looking at a devil.

Aunt Astrid looked at Topher then back at me. Squeezing my hand, she nodded. With a fearlessness I had never seen, she marched up to Topher until she stood only about ten feet in front of him.

"You will cease your actions here, monster of the darkest dimension. Leave this place of peace and slither back down the hole you dared creep out of!" she said.

Topher's body convulsed, and his eyes rolled to the back of his head. Words came out of his gaping mouth in a voice that was not his. "Get back, old woman. Witch! While you still have a chance to live out your next few years in ignorant bliss. This host has summoned me. He has allowed me in. *You* slither back."

"The Maid of the Mist and the Creator of the universe condemn you back to the darkness you came from!" Bea stood and joined Aunt Astrid. Her voice was confident and strong, but her body shook as the thing inside Topher sneered and laughed at her.

Whatever it was residing inside Topher was wreaking havoc on his body. His hands were dirty and looked to be bleeding. I assumed he had used his hands to dig up poor Tommy's grave. His face was contorted into a painfully unnatural grimace, and I heard the Unfamiliar grinding and gnashing Topher's teeth, which were already in pretty bad shape after years of avoiding the dentist chair. His skin was scratched as if he had tried to get relief from hives or mosquito bites, and in some places, his skin was scratched open and bleeding a little.

It continued to laugh then spoke quickly. "You can't stop me, witch!" It leered and pointed dirty, bloody hands at them. "Don't you know what he's done? Don't you know he's invited me in?" It laughed in a freakish, almost childlike tone. "This creature summoned me. I'll do his bidding, and in return, I get his soul."

Just as I was about to join Aunt Astrid and Bea in the expulsion ceremony, with one wave of his mangled and dirty hand, the spirit in Topher brought down a huge branch from one of the thick old oaks. The branch didn't land right on them, but as she lunged out of the way, Bea's foot got pinned beneath it. She let out a cry of pain, and the Unfamiliar cried out in a mocking sort of way.

As I sat there watching, I was paralyzed with fear. What if I had been wrong? What if I should have stayed home and done what my family wanted me to? I could have totally screwed everything up by coming to the cemetery. And what did I do when the tree branch fell and Aunt Astrid lost her balance and Bea cried out in pain? I stayed right where I was. I was frozen in place. Tears filled my eyes as I thought that this was exactly how I had reacted when my mother was in trouble. I was so scared.

The Unfamiliar chanted in weird languages that I was sure were a lot older than me and Wonder Falls and maybe even the earth itself. Mr. Park wailed. His eyes were still closed, but he cried out in anguish as the words the Unfamiliar was saying began to separate Mr. Park's life force from his body.

Revenge

Treacle jumped onto the tombstone I was crouching behind, and he hissed at me. Never in his life had he done that. The protection spell Aunt Astrid had slapped on me must have been extra-strength, because I was still unable to communicate with any of the cats. I didn't know what Treacle was saying, but he looked at me then at the Unfamiliar. It was clear if I wasn't going to do something, *he* would. My pet cat, which had gotten into scrapes with the alley cats, was braver than me at that moment. He turned away from me and made himself known to the horrible spirit inside Topher just as I stood from my hiding place.

For a second, everything fell silent. Bea and Aunt Astrid didn't make a sound. The demon in Topher stopped and stared. The wind ceased to blow, and I swore even the crickets held their breath. My pulse was pounding in my ears. The thing was ugly, yet I stared at it.

Finally Topher let out a cry, stretching his human mouth long and wide. It wasn't the demon making that noise; it was Topher. He was still in there and in terrible pain. I could feel it. I looked at Bea, who was crying. She felt it too. She felt the suffering that the Unfamiliar was inflicting on this harmless old man more than any of us could.

Then it laughed. "So you didn't listen to your instinct and decided to come. I knew you would. Your mother said you would. She said you would." The Unfamiliar stared at me.

Aunt Astrid helped Bea pull her foot free and get to her feet.

It was trying to rattle me by talking about my mother, but I took a deep breath, held it, and walked up to the girls. I tried to look brave, but something told me I wouldn't be winning any Oscars for my performance.

Aunt Astrid and Bea took turns commanding the demon. They shouted spells and demands, but nothing was getting through. It was as if it had its own protection spell that we couldn't break through.

"It's Topher," I mumbled, my eyes widening with surprise.

The Unfamiliar began to chant its poisonous incantation. I stepped closer and looked at its dead white eyes and dirty, scratched hands and face.

"Topher! I know you're in there! I know why you did this!" I shouted over the Unfamiliar's gurgling, diabolical gibberish. "I know what you're feeling. I wanted revenge too."

The words stopped. The white eyes looked at me, and the mouth, although still moving, was no longer making noise.

The real Topher was listening, and I was sure the Unfamiliar was afraid of me. It hadn't wanted me there because I had the power to get through to Topher.

"I did, Topher. I wanted revenge. Why did my mother and father have to die? What did I do that was so bad I should be left alone? I didn't even get to say good-bye." My eyes filled with tears. I couldn't help it. "I didn't get to say 'I love you' one more time. Yes, I wanted revenge."

"Revenge," Topher hissed.

"And I thought about all the people who were mean to me. The people who were cruel and nasty, yet still they had both of their parents. Maybe I should be cruel and nasty too, right? Maybe that was what the world needed. Maybe if I just called for some help, I'd get it. It didn't matter who from. Then I could have revenge. And once I got revenge, Topher, what would I have left?"

Topher shook his head like a dog after it gets out of a sudsy bath. His expression was confused and almost embarrassed.

"I wouldn't have anything left. I wouldn't have my parents any more than you'd get Tommy back. I wouldn't get even with those mean girls any more than you'll even the score with Mr. Park. You don't want to do this, Topher. Death is a part of life. It's the part that makes us cherish our memories."

"No. No. No," the Unfamiliar hissed.

"It's the part that makes us value each day. To try to

reverse the natural course of life is to hand ourselves over to the evil one. You're just sad, Topher. It's okay. It's okay to be sad and angry. But if you don't fight it, you'll feel a part of you die slowly every day as hatred consumes you. Please." I clenched my fists and stood up straight. "Fight it!"

"No. No. No," it hissed. "No. No. No." Its voice was quick, and it took three fast steps toward me.

I flinched a little but recovered and stood my ground. I looked into its eyes as a thin string of drool dripped out of the corner of its slackened jaw. For a flash, Topher's gentle old eyes appeared.

"I see you, Topher. Don't let it win. Tell it to go. Tell it to leave!"

Just as quickly, his eyes became strange again. It threw its head back and cried a pitiful, painful howl.

"Leave me." The words sounded as if they were being choked out.

My heart broke for the old man. The hatred I felt for this evil spirit was palpable. It fed off the emotions of humans who were beyond sad, beyond hopeless. I wanted to take Topher's hands and hold them, but I didn't dare.

"Leave me alone!" Again Topher spoke, his voice slightly stronger.

I could only imagine the pain he was going through. Removing the Unfamiliar was like pulling one of those spiny, prickly weeds out by the roots. Their tentacles wove through the dirt, spreading out until they consumed everything around them. Nothing but sheer will would get them loose.

Right now, that was what Topher was doing. He was pulling this weed from his soul, and it was hurting him for it.

"Leave me alone! Leave me alone! Now! Now!"

Suddenly he stopped. For a minute, I thought he was dead on his feet. I stared at his eyes, which had snapped shut. I looked for his chest to rise and fall with breath. Any twitch of his hands or face. But there was nothing. He just stood stone still.

"I'm afraid!" Topher cried to me. "I'm afraid." He whimpered as tears dragged dirt down his cheeks.

"You should be," I spat back, recognizing the trick of the Unfamiliar.

Taking one step back, I reached out my hands. Bea took one, and Aunt Astrid took the other. Like pulling a bent, twisted, rusty nail from a board, we recited the expulsion chant. The Unfamiliar contorted poor Topher as it tried to stay inside him. It scratched at his body and made him fall to the ground, writhing like a maggot in hot sun. But we didn't stop. We chanted until our throats were scratchy and our palms sweaty from holding on to each other.

Finally, the Unfamiliar couldn't take any more. Topher tossed his head back violently, and the Unfamiliar flew from his mouth until it became a long black serpent hovering over him in the air. Its eyes were a sickly orange color with black pupils, and it rolled its tongue around its face like a lizard licks its own eyeballs. It screamed.

"Gamodan! Ex! Enfinitu!" Aunt Astrid cried. "You will cease your actions here, monster of the darkest dimension! Leave

this place of peace and slither back down the hole you dared creep out of!"

In its true state, the Unfamiliar crinkled up as if it were being burned. Folding around and over itself, it became smaller and smaller until it was the size of a golf ball. With a loud clap like a door slamming and the sound of glass shattering, it was over.

Topher fell to the ground, crying. Bea rushed to his side, and he looked at her with red eyes and wet with tears.

"I didn't get a chance to tell him how proud I was of him," he mumbled. "I just wanted one minute, just one more minute to tell him that."

Bea put her arms around the old man.

To him, it was just a hug, an opportunity to literally cry on someone's shoulder. To her, it was a chance to see some of his ailments caused by his grief. The Unfamiliar had filled his mind with so many whispers that it was probably clouded over like an extra membrane had developed around it. His heart was already grief stricken, but the guilt the Unfamiliar had poured onto him pierced his heart like thousands of tiny thorns. While Bea spoke gently, soothing his worries, she worked diligently to pull away the fibrous remains of the Unfamiliar's brain haze and pull the barbs from his heart one at a time. With each passing minute, he became more peaceful until he fell asleep with Bea's arm around him.

"What about Mr. Park?" Bea asked, jerking her head in his direction.

"He's still out cold. I think they're both sleeping," Aunt Astrid said.

Bea nodded in relief. Non-witches recuperated from encounters with the supernatural by shutting down. In the morning, what they'd seen, heard, felt could be easily waved away as part of some lucid dream. Us Greenstones, on the other hand, would feel as if we had drunk moonshine straight from a homemade pressure cooker still, and that would stick with us for a couple of days.

Image Ruined

I called Jake to tell him that we had found Mr. Park and Topher. He and Blake arrived with an ambulance ready to take both men to the hospital.

Blake marched right up to me even though Aunt Astrid and Bea were both standing just a couple feet from me. "How did you know they were here?"

"I, uh, didn't know they were here, Detective. As you know, my parents are buried in this cemetery, and I wanted to visit."

"In the middle of the night?"

"I couldn't sleep."

"We decided to come together," Aunt Astrid interrupted. "I also wanted to say hi to my late husband when Cath couldn't sleep, so we decided to make it a family outing."

"With Bea?"

"She's very supportive," Aunt Astrid said. "We heard Mr.

Park trying to get Topher to leave his grandson's grave and go home. Mr. Park was telling him how worried Cody was, but Topher was just inconsolable. By the time we could see what was going on, Mr. Park tried to lead Topher away, but the old man jerked his hand away. When he did, Mr. Park lost his balance, and down he went. Hit his head. Topher just crumpled... from grief, I'd guess. You ever lose someone close to you, Detective?"

So it wasn't the greatest story ever told. As I watched Blake's eyes, I was positive if he didn't slap cuffs on all three of us, he would string us up in straitjackets. But he didn't do either.

After he finished writing everything, he went over to Bea, who was sitting on the SMITH tombstone that just a short while ago we were all hiding behind. She was cradling her foot, and her toes had swollen to two times their original size. Jake knelt in front of her, talking to her quietly as Blake approached.

"Is that what happened?" Blake asked firmly.

Nothing makes you feel like a liar more than having someone check your story right in front of you.

"Yes, Blake. It is," Bea said gently.

Without another word, he nodded, folded up his notebook, stuffed it into his shirt pocket, and looked at me. I wasn't sure why his eyes roamed up and down my body, but I felt a blush rush over me. Placing one hand on my hip, I gave him my best *what now* look.

He didn't say a word but turned back to Jake and Bea.

"Better get that looked at." He pointed at poor Bea's gigantic foot. "How did it happen?"

"I was running to help and tripped over poor Mrs. Marconi over there." Bea pointed at one of the flat rectangular tombstones. One edge peeked up over the grass just high enough to cause a person not looking to trip.

And what did Blake do after she said that? Did he turn to Aunt Astrid or me and ask if that were true? Did he study her up and down as if she were some kind of lying machine? Nope. He just nodded and gave me another once-over.

"We're going to the hospital," Jake said, sweeping all one hundred twenty pounds of Bea into his arms. Slowly he made his way between the graves, and I heard Bea giggling just a little as he spoke to her.

"Can I give you ladies a lift home?" Blake asked, looking more at Aunt Astrid than me.

"Absolutely not—"

"That would be nice of you, Detective," Aunt Astrid said. "It has been a long night, and I just don't feel like walking anymore."

She slipped her arm through his, and I saw him ruffle just a little at being touched. He didn't dare say anything to Aunt Astrid though, who began asking him a dozen questions about his job.

I thought about Topher and hoped that Mr. Park would have enough of a magic hangover that our story would sound like what really happened. An argument. A tussle. No attempts at raising another corpse. No minion of Hades taking over an old man's body. The whole thing was nothing but a simple misunderstanding and bad footing.

Blake let Aunt Astrid sit in the front of the car where his partner usually sat. I sat in the back where the doors locked and couldn't be opened from the inside. I felt like a teenager embarrassed of everything and anything. Within a few minutes, we were in front of Aunt Astrid's place. Blake opened the back door, and I climbed out as Aunt Astrid made her way up her front porch steps.

"I'd be happy to take you to your apartment. It's on the way to the station," he said in that annoying just-the-facts manner. Even when he said he was happy, it always ended up sounding sarcastic. I never knew what he was really feeling.

"Uh, no. I'm going to sleep here. Truth is, I probably won't be able to sleep much after all that."

Blake nodded again as he looked at the pavement. "So you go to the cemetery at night on full moons. Why?"

I couldn't believe it. He was still digging. I had to make my lie a good one.

"I told you—I couldn't sleep. But the truth is, I don't like people to see me get emotional. No one except family. Even though my parents have been gone for a good while, it still hurts. I just don't want anyone to see me like that. So I go at night, and Aunt Astrid and Bea come with so no one will bother me. Strength in numbers, you know."

"Yes, I do." He looked at me. His eyes were intense, and in the dark, with just the full moon shining on one side of his face and Aunt Astrid's warm yellow porch light lighting up the other side, I thought for a second he looked downright handsome. “Well, I’ll be in touch. There might be a few more questions.”

I rolled my eyes. “Don’t worry,” I said as I stepped around him to follow my aunt into her home. “I won’t plan on taking any long trips across the border any time soon.”

What was I thinking? Handsome... maybe. But then he opened his mouth and spoke. Whole image ruined.

Don't Mess with Texas

The next morning, Bea hobbled into the Brew-Ha-Ha on crutches with a cast on her foot, signed with a big heart with arrows going through it and Jake's name written in big letters inside it.

"I can't believe it," I said as she hopped behind the counter next to me. "You make a plaster cast look fashionable. How do you do it?"

Bea let out a sarcastic chuckle and bumped me with her hip.

My eyes searched her face. "Did you tell Jake what really happened?"

"I did."

"And?"

"And he said he'd convince Blake to leave Samantha Perry's death unsolved," she said.

"I think that might be kind of hard. Blake was grilling me

last night after he dropped us off at Aunt Astrid's house. He's like a dog with a bone."

"Oh, he dropped you off, did he?" Bea pulled a stack of napkins from behind the counter and stuffed them in one of the silver boxes along the counter.

I scrunched my eyebrows together. "What?"

"He kept checking in the rearview mirror as if he thought she might fall out of the car," Aunt Astrid added as she placed a pecan pie on the pretty wire display on the counter.

"I don't know what you two are talking about."

They both giggled like schoolgirls, and I couldn't tell what for. If Blake had been looking at me, it was because he didn't believe what any of us had told him and was plotting how to catch us.

"Aren't either one of you worried that he's going to keep snooping around until he finds something? Something about *us*?" I said.

"Well, if he does, he won't have anything from last night to help his case. I conjured a mirroring spell over that part of the cemetery. The other dimensions that cross over that area will bounce off each other, making it all look smooth and undisturbed. He won't be able to find so much as a footprint. Not even his own."

I took a deep breath. I was happy to hear that. Treacle jumped on my lap and purred.

"It's all right," I told him. *"I can hear you now."*

Being unable to talk to me had been strange for him, and

he became a little more affectionate now. I think a part of him didn't take our communication for granted anymore.

Treacle's wounds were fading. It turned out he'd gotten into a fight at the old orphanage. He'd been snooping around and ran into that nasty street cat who seemed to be the gatekeeper. Treacle found out from the street cat that the Unfamiliar was bigger and badder, but he couldn't tell me when I had the protection spell on. I rubbed his ears.

Min's smiley face peeked in underneath the open sign that hung on the front door. He knocked gently on the glass. Smiling, I waved him in.

"Oh, and number two makes an appearance," Bea teased, making Aunt Astrid laugh.

"You two can shut up now," I grumbled as Min opened the door and strolled up to the counter.

"Hello, ladies," he said with a smile.

"Good morning. You sure are in a good mood," I said, bumping Bea intentionally with my hip. "Considering..." Considering that his missing father had gone to the hospital last night.

"I'm just glad we found my dad," Min said, understanding what I meant. "And that he's safe. He's going to be fine."

"That's great," Bea said.

"That's not all," Min said. "I have amazing news."

"Oh, then wait." I grabbed one of the many eclectic coffee mugs we had lined up underneath the counter. The one I grabbed said "Mother, put the tea on." I'd never quite understood it, but it seemed to fit in in our odd little shop. I filled it with hot water and picked out an Earl Gray tea bag that I dropped in the steaming water.

Min wrapped his hands around the cup and took the seat across from me. "I'm reforming the Wonder Falls nursing home. I just got through talking with the director. We drew up the paperwork right then and there. I'm now on the board of directors, which consists of the librarian, a guy from the post office, and David Wayne of the law firm Wayne, Van Driska, and Associates."

"Is that good?"

"It's great! And not only am I on the board of directors, but my father has offered to provide some goods from his store every month at no charge."

My face screwed up in a confused grimace, but Min shook his head as if he was in as much shock as I was.

"I know what you're thinking," he said. "But after I went with my mother to see him in the hospital last night, it was like we met a different man. All he would say was that he and Topher had a talk. That was it. Him and that hermit."

I looked at Bea and Aunt Astrid, who shrugged and went back to wiping off the small tables at the front of the coffee shop.

"Did he say what they talked about?" I asked carefully.

"No. But I did hear him speaking in Korean to my mother. He usually only does that when he's mad, but I could tell by his tone he wasn't mad. It was hard to hear him since I wasn't in the same room, but I caught the gist of it. He was saying something about being sorry and how things would be different. But after my mother left, her cheeks glowed."

I couldn't help but feel happy for Min. It was nice that whatever Mr. Park remembered about last night wouldn't be an issue for us. I could only guess that he and Topher had resolved to put the past behind them. It must've been painful, carrying that secret for all those years. I wondered how Mr. Park could bear to see Thomas in this town, but maybe Topher didn't allow them to see each other. Mr. Park would have had to respect Topher's wishes.

"And, as if that isn't great enough," Min said.

"There's more?"

"Yes."

"Well, in that case." I grabbed a cup for myself. It had the flag of Texas on one side and the words "Don't mess with Texas" written in a rope on the other. After pouring in some hot water, I dropped in a tea bag for myself.

"Topher," Min said.

I felt my heart jump in my throat. "What about him?"

"Well, he and Cody and I talked in the hospital too. My father has agreed to sponsor him. As soon as he's released, he'll move into his new apartment at the Wonder Falls Retirement Community."

"Oh, Min, what a nice gesture."

"You know, it's the least I could do for the man who talked my father into changing."

I smiled broadly. "This really is amazing."

I was glad the past few months were behind us. The Unfamiliar was gone for now, and it was still a mystery. Did it know the Unfamiliar under my bed? Would it ever come back? We would have to see. But for now, I wanted to enjoy a moment of peace in my hometown.

"I know. I tell you, Cath, I can't believe how things have turned out. You just never know how life is going to twist and turn and..."

Min talked with me through the morning rush, and I was happy to listen. It was almost as if the Unfamiliar had been just a tiny detail mixed in with all of the miracles that seemed to pop up like new buds after a long winter.

BOOK 3: CAT-ASTROPHIC SPELLS

Soothsayers

Soothsayers were not very common among us witches, sort of like redheads with gray eyes. But they might as well have been as common as the name Smith with the way they were portrayed in books and movies. Crystal balls, tea leaves, chicken bones, and a dozen other weird trinkets covered every surface in our homes so we could see the future, which was always filled with tall, dark strangers and long journeys. Right? Not really. In reality, depending on the augur, fortune-telling was either a rare blessing or a curse.

For Aunt Astrid, on the day Levi Cummings came into the café for his reading, it wasn't just a curse. It was a nightmare.

"Go on, honey. It will be fun," Sarah Cummings said to her husband Levi that early Saturday morning. It was the first time Aunt Astrid was doing her Tarot readings in the newly refurbished café.

Aunt Astrid's ability to see the future often made her look as if she were daydreaming or concentrating on a complex puzzle. The fact that she dressed in flowy, colorful, ultra-feminine dresses, wore her graying hair in loose piles on top of her head or a long braid down her back, and smelled of clove made her even more exotic to the locals. Many of them saw her on a monthly basis to get their readings.

However, Levi was not only a newcomer but a skeptic. "Sarah, you know I'm not into this stuff." He rolled his eyes and dropped the newspaper he was reading to take a cautious sip of coffee.

"Just do it for me," Sarah urged. "I'm telling you, you'll be shocked by what she tells you. I just know it."

My cousin Bea was engrossed in the directions for the new cappuccino maker. "This doesn't seem too difficult," she mused.

I usually left that kind of detailed project to her because reading instructions, following steps in a specific order, and doing things by the book—well, those just weren't my style. Had the installation of the new, state-of-the-art cappuccino maker been left up to me, people would have been getting cups full of steaming hot froth and coffee grounds.

Bea's eyes sparkled with excitement. "So, let's crank this baby up and see what happens."

She snapped on the machine, pulled an espresso shot, and began to steam some milk. I watched, fascinated, as Bea tugged a few levers, pressed a few more buttons, and let the machine growl and gurgle its response. She placed the cup underneath the left spigot, and the foam bubbled out in a perfect peak on top of the cup.

"Here you go." She handed the cup to me.

I smelled the sweetened coffee, raised the cup to my lips, and sipped. "Wow. That tastes good."

She flashed her pretty smile. "You like?" Bea wasn't just my cousin; at two years my junior, she was also my best friend and soul sister.

I nodded as I took another sip.

"Good. Then we can add cappuccino back on the menu. Even though people really should be drinking more tea."

As a healing witch, Bea was very much into the healing power of healthy diets. That gift was also a blessing and a curse. Since Bea was a hugger by nature, no one ever suspected when she was curing their ailments with a touch. Her actions just came across as a pretty girl being friendly. Had someone paid attention, he would notice that when Bea said hello with a hug or pat, he would leave with a little more spring in his step. But she always lost a little bit of herself in the process. The transfer of energy gave the recipient a nice boost.

"I'm waiting for the day we add double cheeseburgers to the menu." I didn't look up from my cup as I set it on the counter.

"That reminds me. We are almost out of kale for the Green Fiend salads."

A shiver ran down my spine. *Kale.* How did that vegetable ever catch on? I grimaced. "I'll add it to the shopping list."

I looked up at the Cummings. Levi was still reading the paper.

Sarah nervously glanced over her shoulder at Aunt Astrid then muttered to her husband, "Well, I booked a ten o'clock session with her, and it's now three minutes after. If you don't want to do it, you need to tell her so she doesn't waste her time waiting. We can go ahead and get to that sports store you like for those thingies for your tennis racket."

Sarah looked down at her fingernails as if they held something fascinating then focused her attention out the window, avoiding her husband's face altogether.

Levi peeked at her over his newspaper and grinned. "Oh, all right. I'm going, I'm going." He folded up the paper and stood.

Sarah's face instantly lit up. "Really, Levi. Get ready to be amazed."

"Yeah, yeah." He kissed his wife on the top of her head on his way to the back of the café.

The new Brew-Ha-Ha had a nice long counter that I liked to work behind because it gave me a view of everyone coming and going. It was made of beautiful dark wood that Aunt Astrid and Bea had sanded and stained themselves. There were a dozen cozy wooden tables with mismatched wooden chairs scattered throughout the comfy dining area. The walls were painted a deep red, and we had splurged on vintage pictures of romantic old castles against vivid green landscapes and fluffy cats lounging on thick, plush pillows.

We could have been a cliché and had stereotypical pointy-hat-wearing, broom-toting, cauldron-stirring sages placed around, but we didn't want to advertise. No one in town knew we were witches. They thought Aunt Astrid might have been a medium, but I often heard people comment that she wasn't as good as the woman from New Jersey who contacted the dead on television.

And that was just fine with us. Witches have never been all that well-received throughout history. My thought was: *if it ain't broke, don't fix it*. It was better to keep our family secret exactly that... secret.

The kitchen was around the counter to the right. Our new baker, Kevin, was busy making something from Aunt Astrid's recipe box that smelled delicious.

To the left, a single booth was recessed into the wall to look like one of those romantic alcoves at fancy restaurants that were reserved for couples who wanted to be out in public yet secluded. The small area was painted a golden yellow and had sheer navy curtains draping either side of the threshold.

Aunt Astrid did her fortune telling in the alcove. She didn't have a crystal ball or anything. She would just have her guest sit down across from her and hold her hands. Then she would talk with them and let the images and hints of the future come to her.

"Have fun, Levi," I said as he passed.

Bea took the opportunity to sit with Sarah and chitchat

for a few minutes.

I scanned the dining area. A dude with long hair, glasses, and ear buds dangling from his ears stared at his laptop, his head bobbing to some beat only he could hear. An older man with wrinkled skin was reading a good, old-fashioned book with a steaming hot mug of coffee next to him. Two college-aged girls talked as fast as birds chirping at sunrise.

I took a deep breath and stretched, then nearly jumped out of my skin when I turned to find Levi standing at the end of the counter and looking pale and sweaty. "Are you all right?" I asked.

He nodded slightly but didn't look at me. He slowly walked up to Sarah, who had her back to him.

Bea looked over Sarah's head, and the words stopped in her mouth. "Levi?"

Sarah turned around in her seat. Her face instantly transformed into a mask of worry. "Honey?"

"I think I need to get home," Levi said quietly.

Sarah stood and placed her hand on his arm. "You look like you've seen a ghost. Do you want to sit down?" Her eyes darted to mine then Bea's. "For heaven's sake, what did she tell you?"

He shook his head. "No, Sarah. It wasn't the fortune. I just suddenly feel out of sorts."

I quickly poured a glass of water and whisked around the counter. "Take a load off, Levi. Here." I held out the glass. "Drink this."

"Yes, Levi. Please sit down," Bea added. I could tell she

wanted to place her hand on him to see what exactly was the matter.

But he flinched away from her, and she missed her opportunity. "No. Sarah, get me home." His voice was soft.

Suddenly, I remembered Aunt Astrid. I turned, and in a few long strides, I was back at the cozy alcove, looking at my aunt, who was shaking her head and chewing her lip thoughtfully.

"Aunt Astrid, are you okay? My gosh, Levi Cummings looks like you clobbered him over the head with news worse than cancer. He doesn't have cancer, right? Oh, please tell me it's not cancer."

"It's not cancer. In fact, I didn't get a chance to tell him anything. He told me."

I looked back at the dining room and saw Bea on her way toward me. "How about you? Did you get a chance to diagnose him?" I asked.

She shook her head and looked at her mother. "Are you okay?" She slipped into the booth and placed her hand on her mom's arm.

"I'm completely fine. Except..."

"Except what?" I shifted from my right foot to my left.

Aunt Astrid took a deep breath and looked around the back area of the café, past me, past Bea, and into a realm we couldn't see. Her lips drew down, and her eyebrows inched closer together while her eyes squinted. She swallowed hard then looked at us.

"Someone is being murdered, now, this very minute."

419

"What?" I asked skeptically.

"Why would you say that, Mom?" Bea asked.

"Levi told me," Aunt Astrid explained. "Well, it wasn't Levi. I doubt Levi has any idea that he said anything. I'll bet he thinks he was just struck by some unexplainable migraine, nothing more." Still, her eyes wandered.

"Wait. Are you telling me that Levi Cummings, the guy who sells carpet, channeled some spiritual informant and gave you a tip on a murder? Did he say who? Should we call the police?"

"Hold on, Cath. Mom, what exactly happened?"

With a forlorn look on her face, Aunt Astrid told us her story.

Before Levi had even decided to come back and have his fortune told, Aunt Astrid could sense something had accompanied him into the café because of a shift in the air. It was as if a breeze gently blowing a spiral spider web had moved the dimensions she could see. She sat very still, waiting for whatever was causing the ripples to show itself.

"Hi," he said pleasantly. "I'm—"

"Levi. I know." Aunt Astrid smiled. Apparently, that gave Levi a bit of a start, so she added, "Your wife made the appointment for you."

"Oh, yes, she did. She thought I'd enjoy it." Tentatively, he scooted into the booth.

Aunt Astrid stretched out her hands, and as soon as his skin touched hers, everything changed.

Levi's eyes rolled over white. His body went rigid, and he held onto Aunt Astrid's wrists with a tight grip. He opened his mouth as if he expected a doctor to place a tongue depressor inside and ask him to say "ahh," then froze.

The words that came out of him were not from his own vocal cords. They weren't even from a person. They were from somewhere else. And there had been many of them.

Aunt Astrid shook her head at us. "But I could hear each one as clear as my own voice right now."

"What did they say?" I asked, not sure I really wanted to know.

"'She's killing him, you know. She's killing him because he told her no. He's dying right now. And she'll get away with it, too.'"

"Did you ask him who?" Bea asked.

"Yes, but it was too late. Levi's eyes snapped back to

normal. He closed his mouth, began to sweat, rubbed his head, then just said sorry and excused himself. I didn't dare tell him he had been channeling."

"Right," I said.

"Maybe it isn't true," Bea said. "I mean, we have no name, no location. This could have been a transmission he tapped into from another part of the country, or the world even. Maybe it was a delayed inter-dimensional echo, something that happened a decade ago that just bounced off the café walls today."

"No," Aunt Astrid said. "This happened here and now. I am sure of it. Before Levi even sat down, I saw the waves. Something was pushing its way through the layers of astral plains to get to us, here, at this moment, in this place. I'll bet we'll hear of a murder in town before the day is over."

"So what do we do?" I asked. "Just wait around?"

"What would you suggest?" Aunt Astrid asked, leaning back into the soft padding of the booth. "We can't very well go door to door. And I wouldn't advise calling the police. The last thing we want to do is draw attention to ourselves. Not to mention cause any unnecessary worry for Jake. If he knew we knew something about this..." Aunt Astrid and I looked at Bea. "Well, it could cause unnecessary problems."

Bea nodded. Jake, Bea's husband, was a detective for the Wonder Falls police department. He had just started coming around to the fact that he was married to a witch, his mother-in-law was a witch, and her cousin was a witch. That was a lot for any man to take in, and we didn't want to rush him.

I untied my apron and folded it neatly, getting ready to make my getaway and start snooping around. "You're right. Maybe Treacle has heard something?"

Treacle was my cat. He was a beautiful black cat that roamed the streets like a lion, proud and dangerous if need be. We communicated by telepathy, which was my gift, and I saw no downside to it.

"Have you seen him this morning?" Bea asked.

I shook my head. "He slipped out two nights ago. I'd have heard if he was in any trouble. I'll call him while I go for a walk. Think this whole thing through a little bit."

"Okay," Aunt Astrid said. I could tell she was mulling over the whole incident.

Bea was also a little preoccupied as she scooted out of the booth and took my hand. She pulled me to the front of the café. "Tell Marshmallow not to mention anything to Peanut Butter. He'd just worry, okay?" Bea said, wringing her hands.

Marshmallow was Aunt Astrid's fluffy white cat. She used to belong to a magician, and she was the most powerful of all of our cats. Peanut Butter was Bea's young, brown cat.

"Of course. I'll be back before the lunch crowd."

WALKING THROUGH THE NEIGHBORHOOD, I called out to Treacle in my mind, focusing on the animal shelter Old Murray Willis ran. Treacle usually turned up there. I got no response. For a second, I felt a twinge of worry.

Under normal circumstances, I wouldn't give it a second thought. Treacle was a wanderer, like the hobos who rode the rails during the Depression. I could say with a country twang the highway was his home. Yet the idea of something pushing its way through the dimensions to get us a message freaked me out just a little. I would have been better able to focus if I knew my favorite feline was okay.

Then, I saw a familiar sight. The siren of Jake's unmarked squad car beeped at me in salutation. It was just my luck he had his partner with him, Blake Samberg. Jake and Blake, the detective duo.

Blake was a serious, no-nonsense, by-the-book, just-the-facts-ma'am kind of detective, and he had little time for anything else. On his days off, he probably did nothing but sit around watching old film noir movies and practice brooding in front of the mirror.

I walked up to the car as it swerved to the curb. Bending over, I leaned through the window.

"Hey, Cath." Jake's smile looked a little tired.

"Hi, Jake. What are you two guys up to?" I looked around again, searching for Treacle.

"Responding to a 419," Blake said, barely looking up from his notepad.

"Care to translate for Mr. Manners over there, Jake?" I jerked my chin in Blake's direction, but he didn't give me the courtesy of looking up to see my eye rolling or my smirking. He just kept looking at his notes.

"A 419 is a dead body," Jake said.

I hoped my expression didn't give me away. Judging by Jake's response, he didn't notice I was just a little more than interested.

"My gosh," I murmured. "Not a good way to start the day for you guys." I swallowed. "Was it natural causes?"

"We don't know yet. The place was neat, but there were a few bits of weirdness, and the body had no signs of outside trauma. Actually"—Jake patted my arm—"I shouldn't be telling you this. You'll have nightmares."

"I'm two years older than your wife. Nothing scares me, except maybe that mug over there." I nodded in Blake's direction. He still didn't look up, but his pen stopped moving.

Jake chuckled. "So what's got you out and about? You got the day off?"

"No. I just took my break early to see if I could find Treacle. He's on the loose again. I haven't seen him in two days." My voice was casual, but I couldn't help the slight tremor in it. I hoped I hadn't sounded too interested in all the gory details of the 419.

"That big old alley cat will be back. He knows where the food is. That's usually what brings the drifters back home. It's easier than chasing mice and working for a meal."

Nodding, I looked over the top of the car anxiously—not to find Treacle, but because I wanted to get back to the café and tell Aunt Astrid and Bea about the new information I'd learned. Except Jake didn't say it was a murder. He'd just said it was a dead body.

"You're probably right. I should get back to the café,

anyway. We've got inventory to do. We need more flour and kale, and I think I'm going to get extra chocolates from Sweetie's across town. You know that Marvin makes the greatest toffee you've ever tasted. The stuff won't stay in the display for—"

"I hate to say it, Cath," Blake interrupted. "But you won't be getting any more chocolates from Marvin. He was our 419."

My mouth fell open. "You're kidding."

Just as I was about to press them for more information, the police radio crackled to life. A female dispatcher called for any unit in the vicinity to report to something going on a couple of blocks away.

"Sorry, Cath," Jake said. "We gotta run. Tell Bea I'll call her later."

I nodded and stepped away from the car. It quickly pulled away as Blake placed the red bulb on his side of the roof.

Hurrying back to the café, I continued to call Treacle in my mind, but I wasn't shouting as loudly as I should have been. I was distracted. Jake had said there were no marks on Marvin. Maybe the poor guy just had a heart attack. But what had Jake meant by there being weird things around Marvin's house?

I hustled back to the café for the lunchtime rush. I grabbed my apron and hopped behind the counter. I thought I was going to explode with my news.

"Have I got to talk to *you*," I said to Bea in between running the register and making out the list of necessities we needed at the counter. Kevin was very particular about the ingredients he used for Aunt Astrid's recipes, so thankfully, I was able to stay clear of the massive pantry in the back.

"Oh, yeah?" she asked, looking intrigued. "Can't wait."

We worked together like two parts of the same machine in an effort to get everyone fed and taken care of. The clock ticked, and every minute seemed to creep by at a snail's pace. Finally, around two o'clock, the café was empty enough that I could corral Aunt Astrid and Bea together out of earshot of the remaining customers. I told them everything Jake had said.

"I don't believe it," Bea said. "Marvin was a nice man, and I'll tell you what, I don't recall him having any kind of heart trouble. In fact, aside from a bit of a spare tire and bifocals, the guy was in good shape both physically and spiritually. Still a little sadness over his wife passing away a few years back, but nothing out of the ordinary. Nothing that would kill him."

"Now, girls, just because Jake happened to mention this doesn't mean it is *our* murder," Aunt Astrid said. "It could just be an unfortunate coincidence."

I looked around at the few remaining customers. "Aunt Astrid, you might not want to say the words 'our murder' too loudly. People might overhear and get the wrong idea, you know?"

No one really seemed to be paying any attention to us. I thanked Kevin for that. His cooking was mesmerizing, and the aromas filled the entire café with warm waves of deliciousness. Murder or no murder, I was going to get a slice of the German chocolate cake he was baking before the day was over.

"Well, if you both can hang on until tonight, Cath, you've given me a perfect excuse to bring it up to Jake. I'll see what I can find out," Bea said.

Aunt Astrid handed each of us a rag. "Until then, we should just go on with things as normal."

Taking the hint, we began to wipe down the tables. I thought it was hard waiting to tell them what Jake had told me. It was even harder waiting for Jake to get home and Bea to find out the rest of the story.

The rest of the day dragged, and staring at the phone after I got home didn't help. Bea finally called at a little after nine o'clock. I took the phone out to my backyard. The air was cool, and the cicadas sang a haunting tune. After I answered, Bea told me I needed to get to the café right away.

Sweetie's

The café was dark when I got there. I knocked on the glass door, and within a few seconds, Bea hustled up from the basement. She flipped the bolt then yanked open the door.

"Thank goodness you're here. Come on." Taking my hand, she pulled me into the shadowy restaurant and around the counter to the concrete basement steps. The little bunker was sort of like our clubhouse, where we could meet and talk freely about... well, in this case, murder.

Aunt Astrid handed me a cup of tea she'd heated on her little hotplate. Bea could barely contain herself, and I saw she had a cup of tea she hadn't even touched. For her to let an all-natural herbal remedy sit untouched meant she must have something big on her mind.

"When Jake came home, I just casually mentioned that you'd said you ran into him. I thought I was going to have to do a lot of tip-toeing around the topic, but as it turned out, he was ready to talk."

I took a seat on the soft imitation Oriental rug that covered the concrete floor, folding my legs underneath me. "What did he say?" I carefully set my teacup down in front of me. It wouldn't be long before the tea became cold. I was so shocked, I didn't sip a drop as she told me everything.

The call had come into the Wonder Falls Police Station almost the minute after Levi had left the Brew-Ha-Ha Café. A frantic woman screamed and cried into the phone that she had found her father on the floor of his home, and he was not responding.

When the paramedics arrived, they found Brit Clegg near hysterics next to her father Marvin Clegg who lay in the middle of the living room floor. From what the EMTs could see, the first level of the house was torn apart. It hadn't just been ransacked by a junkie looking for drugs or money. The place looked violated, purposefully vandalized.

Some pictures had been ripped in half while others remained untouched. The seat cushions looked as though they had been clawed open. Weird graffiti was scribbled on the walls with both marker and spray paint. A grimace on the dead man's face made it obvious he'd been in great pain or fear when he died. The paramedics had estimated he'd been dead for a couple of hours.

"Jake said it broke his heart to see the ambulance drivers wheel that sheet-covered body out of the house with the daughter still sobbing on the floor. She kept crying 'Daddy, oh

Daddy,'" Bea said. "It took him almost twenty minutes to get her to stand and step out onto the porch for questioning."

"Did he think she had something to do with it?" I cleared my throat as I pushed the image of my own mother out of my mind. Days went by in which I didn't consciously think of her on that terrible night. But as sure as the sun rose in the east, I would see those giant monster hands pulling her underneath my bed and hear her voice at least once every day. I'd be back on top of my bed in my pink nightgown, eleven years old, screaming for help that didn't come in time. I assumed my mother was dead. Whatever it was she'd fought off had wanted me, and I was pretty sure it wasn't to play dolls. Instead, it took my mom, and I was left all alone.

Sure, I had Bea and Aunt Astrid, and I loved them with all my heart. They were my family. They believed my story about a monster under the bed dragging my mother away. But no matter who you were, when your parents passed, you'd prefer they simply fell asleep peacefully in the house where you grew up, surrounded by family and friends. Anything other than that was... unnatural. And all too real.

My eye stung as a single tear tried to surface, but I blinked it back.

Bea's voice shifted from factual to sympathetic. "Jake said they weren't ruling anything out. They were going to wait a couple of days and call her back into the station. He was going to let Blake question her."

I finally took a sip of my tea and cringed a little at the ice-cold flavor of "green." "Well, that ought to scare a confession out of her. Was it for money?"

Aunt Astrid looked down at me from the soft, green chair she had moved into the basement for herself. "Aren't you being a little judgmental?"

I defiantly sipped more of the cold tea. "I don't know. Am I? Levi did say *she,* didn't he? And the chocolate business was making a pretty penny, right? I mean, I know what they were charging us for a couple dozen boxes of chocolate-covered toffee. They certainly couldn't have been starving."

Aunt Astrid looked past me to the highlights and shadows only she could see. "It doesn't look good for the girl, but something is telling me it isn't that easy. I can't put my finger on it."

"Well, they guessed the cause of death was a heart attack. A real bad one," Bea said. "But they'll know for sure after the autopsy."

"So I guess we just wait and see. We might be able to sit this one out and let the cops handle it. Let Blake work his own special brand of magic." I chuckled at my own clever play on words.

"I wish we could. But Jake gave me this." Bea took a crumpled piece of paper from her front blouse pocket and handed it to Aunt Astrid, who gasped.

"What?" I mumbled, narrowing my eyes. "What is it?" Aunt Astrid handed me the paper, and it was my turn to gasp. "I know what these are. Not all of them, but I know what some of them are. Where did Jake get these?"

She swallowed hard. "He said they were all over the walls. He quickly drew them as best he could because he thought I might know what they meant. He couldn't very well get us the crime scene photos."

Scrawled in thin, blue ballpoint lines were bizarre symbols and letters from a long forgotten alphabet. The markings were crude, and some weren't even correct, making nonsensical commands if translated literally.

"This is... it looks like a third-grader did this," I said. "Am I looking at this right? A cessation summons?"

Bea shrugged. "Taking Jake's artistic abilities into account, I thought that same thing myself."

"Are we sure he drew them right? If you don't know this stuff and leave out a line here or there, it looks close enough, to a non-witch. But to us witches, it can read totally different."

"I asked him, and he said he drew them exactly the way they were."

Aunt Astrid chewed her bottom lip thoughtfully. "The problem with this assumption is that we are reading this with witches' eyes and a little bit of information the police do not know... Levi's tip. Those scrawlings could be a summons, or they could be a random act of vandalism. The difference between the two is negligible."

"I hate to say this," Bea said. "But I need to see the body."

"Did you ask Jake?" I was surprised Bea was even making such a suggestion. It was a little on the morbid side for her.

"I didn't." She bit her lower lip. "I know the body is at the coroner's office right now."

Aunt Astrid looked seriously at Bea. "Are you sure you want to see it? You and Jake have been working so hard on things together. You don't want to start with any secrets again, do you?"

"No, but... I have a feeling in my gut," Bea said.

"You could blame me," I offered. "Lord knows it wouldn't be the first time I got you in trouble."

Bea chuckled. "I couldn't do that."

"Sure you could."

Aunt Astrid stood and began to sift through a small stack of books she'd brought from her house. "You guys are talking like walking into the coroner's office at this hour of the night is the easy part. Even if Jake knew about it, he can't just take you in there to see a body."

"I don't know, Mom. Something isn't right with those symbols that Jake wrote down. If he or Blake gets any closer and we do nothing, it could turn out badly."

Picking up what looked like a child's cardboard book, Aunt Astrid cleared her throat. "I might be able to help. But the sooner we get this over with, the better." She studied the thick pages without looking at us. "We have some time. Levi gave us that. This hasn't made the news yet, so any traces of a cessation summons, or of any witchcraft, may still be left behind."

"Unless we are dealing with a *diabolist*." A shiver ran up my spine.

"You don't really think it could be that?" Bea asked, shaking her head. "Do you?"

When Aunt Astrid didn't say "Oh, no. Stop being silly," I wished I hadn't mentioned it.

"Let's get our facts straight before we start guessing. Bea, do you have any idea how you might get into the coroner's office?" I would follow my family to the ends of the earth, but the idea of seeing a dead body brought back memories of the ones haphazardly exhumed at the cemetery not so long ago.

Poor Marvin. Instead of thinking of his wonderful candies, I would be waiting for his eyes to pop open, for him to pull himself clumsily off the table and stagger toward us, arms outstretched, gurgling horrifically.

"Well, what do you say?" Bea asked, looking at me.

"To what?"

"To going to the coroner's office and causing a distraction?"

"What?"

"I thought I could pretend to bring Jake a late-night snack."

"Is Jake going to be there?"

"No. He's at the station. I already know that."

"If he's not there, then why would you bring him a snack?"

"When they say he isn't there, I'll just ask to use the bathroom, slip into the autopsy room, and get a quick peek."

"And what am I supposed to do?"

"Keep the guard talking. Flirt, or ask a lot of questions."

Bea was smiling and nodding. "Dazzle whoever it is with your sparkling personality."

I rolled my eyes. "Fine. I'm in. It'll give me a chance to keep an eye out for Treacle, too."

"He still hasn't come home?" Aunt Astrid's voice was a little worried.

I shook my head.

"He's a smart cat. He'll be back," she soothed.

I hoped she was right. Even though he had disappeared for longer periods of time before, I was starting to worry.

Bea reached down, took my hands, and hoisted me up. "Grab a paper bag on your way up, and I'll grab some snacks."

"For what?" I asked.

"We can't say we're bringing Jake a snack and not have a snack."

I slapped my head. I was glad Bea was taking the lead because my mind didn't seem to be in it. Thoughts of Treacle distracted me. I didn't want to admit how worried I was, and my unease was affecting my concentration.

I confided my fears to Bea. "I just have a different feeling this time, Bea. Usually, I can call to Treacle and get a couple of clicks or squeaks to let me know he's heard me and is okay. This time, it's like shouting into a cave and hearing my own voice echo back to me."

"Did he tell you anything when he left?"

"No. He just wanted out for the night like usual."

Bea gently patted my back. "We'll keep an eye out for him. I'm sure he's okay."

As we slipped out the front door of the café, we didn't see a soul on our side of the street. Across the way, a boy rode his bike in wobbly patterns then began pumping his legs faster as he sped away. Down the block, we heard a couple talking as they climbed into a car. The chirp-chirp of the car doors being unlocked echoed down the street, followed by the car doors slamming as the couple got in and drove off.

"Are you scared?" I asked Bea.

"I'll be a lot more scared if I don't find out what we're dealing with."

"I hope they don't close down Sweetie's. Where would we get our chocolates?"

Bea rolled her eyes at me. "Really? You're worried about the chocolates?"

"I'm not trying to be disrespectful. It's just that those were some darn good chocolates."

"They were."

"Do you think there's an angle there? Someone after the business?"

"That's what Jake was saying. But he didn't elaborate very much."

At this time of night, the streets were quiet. We drove to the coroner's office in a little over five minutes. The building was a friendly-looking place. Considering most people went there under painful circumstances, the city did its best to give it a positive and peaceful appearance.

I especially liked the colorful flowers flanking each side of the entrance. I could never get anything to grow like that. I had two cacti in my kitchen window that reached about four inches in height then decided that was enough.

Quickly, we went over our plan.

"Got it?" Bea asked, her eyes serious.

"Yeah, I guess. Let's do it."

A Grump

Bea and I walked up to the building, and the automatic sliding glass doors swooshed open. We probably looked like a couple of kooks strolling in there, and I made a mental note of the cameras recording us. We hadn't thought of those.

Closing my eyes, I mumbled a vision spell that might, just might, cause a temporary camera malfunction long enough to keep us out of view. It was sort of like pulling a little extra electricity from the air into one concentrated spot.

Bea glanced at me, and I knew she could smell it. The act of the vision spell gave off a slight odor as if a storm were coming. That smell would probably be what the front desk clerk would remember, too.

"Can I help you ladies?" the man at the reception desk asked. He was wearing the uniform of Wonder Falls' finest, and the name on the desk plate read Stephen Ferdeck. His name was familiar, but I couldn't place him.

"Hi, Officer. I'm Bea Williams, Detective Jake Williams's wife. Is he here?"

Officer Ferdeck looked at us as if we had suddenly turned green. "No, Mrs. Williams. He isn't here. He's at the station. Do you want me to ring him there?" His eyes shifted back and forth from me to Bea suspiciously.

"Oh no, I'm sorry. He had mentioned something he had to deal with today, and it seemed to bother him, so I brought him a little treat to keep his spirits up."

Again, Officer Ferdeck didn't budge an inch.

"Well, we're sorry to bother you. I hate to ask this, but... would it be possible to use the ladies' room? I should have gone before I left. You were right, Cath." She looked at me then rolled her eyes back at the officer. "Too much green tea." She giggled uncomfortably.

"Sure," Officer Ferdeck said. "Restrooms are right over there." He nodded toward the restrooms behind us. They were nowhere near the autopsy room.

I cocked my right hip and folded my arms across my chest. "Yeah, you should have gone at the café, Bea."

Bea shrugged. Just as we turned toward the restroom, a car pulled up in front of the building. The high beams poured through the glass, and Bea cleared her throat. We had both seen the familiar unmarked vehicle a million times. The lights shut off, and the car door slammed.

Blake Samberg came through the sliding doors. Then *he*

looked at us suspiciously. I don't think a plan had ever gone more wrong. "Evening, Stephen," he grumbled in his typical brooding voice. "Bea? Cath? What brings you two here?"

"Is Jake with you?" Bea asked, her voice masking her nervousness. She was a much better actor than me. I'd have liked to tell the detective to mind his own business, even though I knew I had "guilty of something" written all over my face.

"No, Bea. He's wrapping up some paperwork at the office. Do you need him?"

"No, no. I must have heard him wrong and thought he was going to be here tonight. I brought him a little treat from the café." Bea stepped up to Blake and in a hushed voice said, "I heard about the man you brought in today. I'm so sorry."

Blake, whose features never changed when he spoke to me, seemed to soften slightly. "Yeah. It was disturbing. It looked like some kind of witchcraft, hoodoo-voodoo nonsense in that house. I'm actually here to pick up some of the paperwork on that very case."

"Witchcraft?" I asked as my eyes darted from Bea to Blake. "Do you have any knowledge of that? I mean, any formal training or anything that would make you think that? It's kind of jumping the gun, don't you think?" I couldn't help myself. The words just came out. So many misconceptions existed about witches and witchcraft. I sometimes had a hard time controlling my tongue.

"No, I don't. But thankfully, it won't be hard to find out. It was a very rough scene, as I'm sure Jake mentioned." He blew me off as if I were an annoying fly to be swatted away.

"No, he didn't go into detail. He usually doesn't." Bea glared at me. "Blake, I'm wondering if I can ask a very big favor?" She placed her hand gently on Blake's shoulder and turned him away from Stephen and me.

They whispered to each other then Blake nodded. He walked over to Stephen and said something quietly so I couldn't hear. Apparently, I was being left out of this particular game of telephone. I was annoyed.

Stephen reached underneath his desk and pressed a button. The doors leading to the autopsy room opened.

"Where you going?" I asked Bea innocently.

"I'll be right back," she said in a quiet voice. I looked at Blake, who was staring at me oddly. I couldn't say how it was odd, just that it was. I wondered what Bea had said to him.

Stephen looked at me as Bea and Blake headed toward the autopsy room. A few awkward moments passed, and I walked a couple of paces back and forth, trying to casually escape the gaze of Stephen, whose name was familiar even though I couldn't place his face.

He kept staring at me.

"So, what's your problem?" I asked. "You've been looking at me like you've seen my face up at the post office. What's the matter?"

"You're Cath Greenstone, aren't you?"

"Yes, I am. Have we met before?"

"Not formally. But I know *of* you."

My eyebrows shot up. Did I have some kind of torrid reputation I was blissfully unaware of?

"And truthfully, I don't like you," he said. The statement from a stranger felt like a punch in the gut.

"You don't like me? You don't even know me!"

"Oh, I know you. You were never nice in high school, and from the looks of things, you are still a grade-A grump." His body never moved. He didn't shift in his seat. Only his lips moved as he spoke, and his eyes followed me.

Raising my hand to my chest, I couldn't contain my awkward giggle. "High school? A grump?"

"Well, another word comes to mind, but out of respect for my deceased mother, I won't say it... but it rhymes with ditch."

For a second, I thought this mystery man from my youth knew my secret until I realized there was a word that might fit the bill besides witch. I felt a little stupid. "Can you tell me what I did? I'm not trying to be rude or anything. It's just that high school was a long time ago. I didn't have a very good go of it myself."

Stephen took a deep breath then looked up at me. "You ran for class president our sophomore year."

"Yeah, and I lost... by a lot."

"If you hadn't run, there would have only been two candidates—me against Paula Lipinski."

"So what? I was doing it just to see what would happen. I didn't expect to really win. I just wanted to conduct a social experiment of sorts. Have a little fun stirring things up."

"You were like the Ralph Nader of our sophomore class. Because of you, I lost the election. Who knows how much differently my life would have turned out if it weren't for you?"

I stood there in shock. A high school election has bothered this guy all this time? Was he just sitting around hoping someday I'd stroll into the coroner's office so he could give me a hard time? "Stephen Ferdeck for President: Not Your Mama's Candidate." That was his slogan. The memory came rushing back to me, and I smiled. "You had the best slogan!"

He looked at me oddly. "What are you talking about?"

"'Not Your Mama's Candidate'? That was you, right?"

He thought for a moment, then his eyes brightened.

"It was more creative than mine." I rolled my eyes. "'Cath Greenstone: Why Not?'"

I laughed. My high school days were not fun. I ran for class president my sophomore year on a dare from my best friend Min. If it weren't for him, high school would have been unbearable. As Stephen Ferdeck had said, who knew how much differently my life would have turned out if it weren't for Min. But the memory of our slogans sneaked up on me, and I had to laugh.

Stephen was also beginning to laugh. "I had forgotten that."

"Yeah, you were so caught up in me throwing a wrench into your candidacy, you forgot the best part of your campaign. What did Paula Lipinski use? See, I don't even remember. I had totally forgotten about her until you brought her up."

A smile started to form on Officer Stephen Ferdeck's face. I couldn't help but smile back.

"Officer Ferdeck, I'm sorry. If you have been holding that in all these years and feel I ruined your future, I am truly sorry. You look to be doing pretty good from where I'm standing right now."

"I do love my job," he said reluctantly.

"Well, let me make it up to you." I folded my arms over my chest and pretended to think hard. "Do you know the Brew-Ha-Ha Café across town?"

He thought for a moment then nodded. "That place burned down, didn't it?"

"Oh, yeah." It was common knowledge the café had experienced a bad fire.

"I didn't realize it had reopened."

Nodding, I shifted from one foot to the other. "Well, I own the café with Bea and my Aunt Astrid. How about you come in and visit? We can reminisce about high school, and lunch and coffee will be on me. We just hired a fantastic new baker, and he makes everything from scratch."

He smiled and blinked. "I'm vegan. Does that make a difference?"

I rolled my eyes. "Seriously? Well, no, it doesn't make a difference. Bea is very educated when it comes to feeding the body and soul, so I'm pretty confident we can accommodate."

He stuck out his hand to shake. I walked up and obliged.

"Thanks, Cath. I'm sorry I called you grumpy, and... you know."

"Hey, I've been called worse. I can't say you're that far off the mark."

Just then, Bea emerged from the autopsy room with Blake following her. They were talking in hushed voices, and when I looked at Bea's pale face, I instantly became worried.

"Thank you, Detective. I am grateful," she said, shaking Blake's hand. She took a wobbly step toward me and slipped her arm through mine, gently urging me toward the front sliding doors.

"What is the matter with you?" I asked urgently. "Are you all right?"

"Just get me to the car. We've got to get home."

Exploding Heart

I waved to Officer Ferdeck and gave Blake a slightly concerned look. He knew something but wasn't telling me. And I knew something but wasn't telling him. We were both looking down the same scary tunnel.

Bea held onto me tightly as we walked to her car.

"So? What did you find out?" My voice echoed off the three cars in the parking lot, the garbage dumpster, and the brick walls of the coroner's office. We were totally alone, but I worried someone might overhear us.

"It was a mess in there, Cath." We climbed into the car. Bea sat behind the wheel and took a couple of deep breaths. "I barely touched the body. When I walked in, I could see the metaphysical residue from what had happened to him all over. It was thick and black, and there were globs of...stuff...so thick, it was piling on the floor. Even though it was only me who could see it, I swear Blake knew something was there. He stood back from the table, like he was afraid he might get some of it on him."

I took a deep breath. "Maybe he's just squeamish around carcasses. I can't say I don't know how that feels," I said quietly, as if dismissing Blake's behavior could somehow change what Bea had seen.

"No. He was onto something. I could tell he could feel it."

I cleared my throat and looked through the windshield at the bushes in front of us. A thick, soft, piney type of foliage bordered the small parking lot. For a second, I half expected to see something peeking back at me from the pitch-black shadows. But there was nothing.

"And Cath, that isn't even the worst part." Bea turned her head and looked at me with tears in her eyes. "He didn't just die of a heart attack."

"What did he die of?"

"His heart exploded inside his chest."

I was speechless. What do you say to that kind of news? "So, the cessation summons?"

"Oh, it's definitely a witch doing this. This was a pitiful attempt at a cessation summons. But whoever did this, he or she isn't very good. They made a mess of everything."

I had never seen Bea so upset. She was squeezing and kneading the steering wheel as she spoke. "Obviously they didn't expect anyone in Wonder Falls to be privy to the realm of spells and magic." Bea wiped away the tear that had snuck down her cheek.

"Well, was there any kind of clue or tip to point us in the

right direction? Marvin knew a lot of people. I mean, his candy was shipped all over the country. What if he crossed someone who lives in New York or Florida, and we are all the way over here? How could we ever hope to narrow down the search, let alone catch them?"

Bea slowly shook her head. "It's not a local person, but they are located here now. Inside all the mystical goo and filth that they left all over the body, I sensed a transference spell. I couldn't pinpoint the location without giving Blake something unnatural to contemplate telling Jake, so I did what I could with what I was given to work with. It came from somewhere on the west side."

"Well, that is better than nothing, right? Even though the west side is a couple miles in all directions."

Bea started the car and put it in reverse. "Don't be so negative. We need to talk to my mom."

We arrived at Aunt Astrid's house a few minutes past ten. After letting ourselves in, we found her sitting cross-legged on the floor surrounded by towers of books. And of course, Marshmallow was sprawled across an open book, her tail waving lazily at us when we walked in.

Bea took center stage and repeated to her mom what she had told me: the gross residue, the amateurish technique, the transference spell directing us to the west side, plus Jake's discreet information regarding the weird writing on the walls.

"Yeah, what about all that stuff?" I had to ask how it got all over the walls. Why would a witch make a man's heart explode in his chest from a distance yet take the risk of being seen at the crime scene and leaving crucial evidence? It didn't make any sense.

Sounds like trouble, Marshmallow said to me telepathically, looking up and licking her paw as I scratched the top of her head.

"I'll bet if we were to go back to that house, all those sketches and symbols would be gone," Aunt Astrid said. "You said this was done from a distance. I believe that. And those images were just an attempt to scare the victim. They emerged from the wall as they were uttered by the witch. But I'll bet they're gone now. This person, who is so magically sloppy and careless, decided to show off a little to Marvin. 'Look at what I can do. I can scare you. I can cause you pain. I can kill you. I am in charge.'"

I was still worried about narrowing down the search. "So you don't think this was like a loan-shark arrangement gone bad, or a union dispute or something?"

"Not at all," Aunt Astrid said. "That wouldn't make sense. I don't think loan sharks deal in witchcraft. And as far as I've heard, the Teamsters don't have a clause allowing for heart explosions in their contracts."

Laughing a little, I could see Aunt Astrid's point.

"No." Her eyes narrowed. "This was personal. Whoever did this wanted to make sure Marvin took notice of them immediately. My guess is that he didn't move fast enough for them."

"Well, we know it's magic. We know it is an amateur trying to do what I'd call 'big girl magic.' And this person killed Marvin intentionally. Who would have a motive like that?" I thought out loud.

Bea scratched the side of her head. "He didn't have any business partners. He grew Sweetie's with his own hands, so I don't think it was over the business."

"His wife died years ago," Aunt Astrid said.

"Yeah, I remember," Bea said. "It was the only time he ever closed his doors for so long. I think he was out for two weeks. He had that black wreath on the door and that pretty note to the customers about her going home and the angels and such. It breaks my heart to think of it now."

I nodded. I sadly remembered that, too. "I think it's safe to say it was no jaded wife or her 'other man.'"

Aunt Astrid shook her head, agreeing with me. Then her eyes widened as they did when she had an idea. "He has children, right? A daughter, at least. Anyone being left out of a will or looking to inherit the business? People in desperate situations resort to desperate means."

"What about disgruntled employees?" Bea offered.

Suddenly, I slapped my hand to my forehead. "I hate to say this." I rubbed the back of my neck.

"What? You're hungry again?" Bea looked at me with a smirk.

"What? No." I bumped her with my elbow. "Darla."

Arch Nemesis

"What would Darla have to do with Marvin?" Aunt Astrid asked.

Darla Castellan was my arch-nemesis in high school. She had decided our sophomore year that her proverbial claws needed continual sharpening, and I was to be the instrument used to keep them pointy and dangerous.

Like a young Clark Kent, I had powers no one would let me use. Unlike Clark Kent, who could run and had super strength, I possessed the ability to afflict Darla with warts. I could have caused her to have a paralyzing fear of pencils, or I could have made the grass and trees pull and yank at her as she walked by. But I never did. Instead, I had to take her abuse.

Darla was wealthy and beautiful and spoiled rotten. The boys loved her, but most of the girls were scared of her wrath.

After seeing how she treated me, they were too afraid to stand up to her.

As if that power weren't enough, she thought she could dive into Greenwood history and master the art of witchcraft, too. Her selfish actions resulted not only in the Brew-Ha-Ha going up in flames but also in the death of our previous baker, Ted. She didn't kill him outright, but she could have saved him if she'd had even a shred of conscience.

"Darla worked for Marvin back when she was in college," I said.

"But that was several years ago. What would she be mad at from then that she'd remember now? *And* seek revenge?" Bea asked.

"Well, first Darla got fired from that job. I had heard around the neighborhood that she wasn't just rude to customers, but that she had a real aversion to doing any kind of actual work. I mean, look at her." I raised my hands with my palms up. "Is it any wonder she married money?"

"Then divorced it," Bea said smugly.

"Then got half of everything and is looking for the next lucky Mr. Castellan," Aunt Astrid added.

"I also heard she was blackballed after that because Marvin wasn't going to lie for her and give her any kind of reference," I said. "Plus, she's so dumb, half the town knew she had been working there, having seen her with their own eyes and experiencing her radiant personality. She wasn't going to get a job in this town anywhere." I was unable to contain my glee while repeating the story. I knew gossip was bad, but this gossip was the truth.

"Where did you hear all this?" Bea asked.

"From none other than Ruby Connors."

Both Bea's and Aunt Astrid's eyes got as wide as saucers.

Ruby Connors was Darla's lackey all through high school and still was. I thought Ruby liked the attention that trickled off of Darla and sometimes splashed on her. But if I got Ruby alone, she couldn't help herself. She'd spill the beans on her own mother if it made her the center of attention for a few seconds without the model-perfect Darla.

"Still." Aunt Astrid shook her head skeptically. "That was several years ago. She's moved on, don't you think?"

It was my turn to shake my head. "Have you ever known Darla to move on after someone did her wrong?" I folded my arms over my chest as if I had just cracked the case wide open.

"But this is magic, Cath. We got the book back from her. We watched you erase her memories and even helped put new ones in their place. You don't think that we missed something? That her memories somehow grew back and she's trying to hone her craft again, do you?" Bea asked nervously.

"I don't know." I shrugged. "But she's as logical a first step as anyone else at this point."

"If she is up to her old tricks again, she'll be covered in residual magic," Aunt Astrid said. "Based on the description you gave of the coroner's office, she wouldn't be able to shake that off of her for a couple of days. We just need to get a look at her to tell."

I shivered at the thought of being anywhere near that woman. "Yeah, okay. How are we going to do that? Heaven knows she would be suspicious if I suddenly showed up at her door."

"I know," Bea said. "I'll call her and tell her she's won a free lunch at the café. We pulled her business card from the bowl."

"We don't have a bowl of business cards," Aunt Astrid pointed out.

"Doesn't matter. She doesn't know that because she goes to the Night Owl Café. We can just say someone must have dropped it in for her. Whatever. It'll get her there. She won't turn down a free lunch *and* an opportunity to gloat."

I nodded and smiled. "Nice one, cuz. I like your thinking. And I like how you're going to wait on her and do all the talking while I hang out in the kitchen until she leaves."

"Fine. Leave me to face the Gorgon alone," Bea joked then yawned loudly.

"It's late, girls. We need to get some rest. All of us. If it's Darla, we're going to have a heck of a mess on our hands. The better prepared we are, the better off we'll be. So rest up, and I'd suggest we all wear a protection spell tomorrow just in case."

We all agreed. Bea and I left Aunt Astrid's, and I walked Bea to her car.

"Hey, before you go, I have a question." I linked my arm

through Bea's. "What did you say to Blake that got him to take you back to see the body? Did you put a spell on him or something?"

"Of course not." Bea smirked at me.

"Well, what did you do? Because had *I* asked, he would have had me on the ground, slapped in handcuffs, dragged to the backseat of the squad car, and on my way to the station before I could say hocus-pocus."

"That is because I can attract flies with sugar, and you are still trying to do it with vinegar." She slipped her arm gently out of mine and quickly climbed behind the wheel of her car.

I gave her a blank stare. "Okay. Be sure to use some of that sugar on your favorite person, Darla. Yup! Lots and lots of sugar!" I yelled as her car pulled away.

I turned and started to walk in the direction of my house when I froze. For a second, I thought I had heard Treacle. I strained to listen and held my breath. I called to him in my mind then waited. Nothing.

Did I imagine it? Was it just wishful thinking? I don't know, but as I made my way home, I walked almost on tiptoe, breathing slowly and trying hard to hear past all the quiet.

Magic Residue

The next day, Bea called Darla to inform her she'd won the weekly business card drawing. In addition to a free gourmet lunch created by the new baker, Kevin, the drawing entitled her to a homemade dessert, an herbal tea infused with fresh fruit, and a small hot coffee the next time she came in.

"That means she's going to come in one more time after this." I wrinkled my nose.

"Afraid so," Bea said. "Unless, of course, we find her guilty of death by witchcraft, and then, well, justice will have to prevail."

"Now if that doesn't give me mixed emotions about this whole situation, I don't know what does." I put my hand on my hip. "When is she coming in?"

Just then, the front door jingled, and I instinctively looked up. There she was.

"Hi, Darla," Bea said in an overly sugary sweet tone. "Congratulations."

Pulling her long, black hair behind her and letting out a deep breath, Darla reciprocated with a quick smile that squinted her eyes into tiny slits for a split second then snapped back to her normal grimace.

She looked around the Brew-Ha-Ha. "I haven't seen the place since it was a smoldering mess. I didn't realize it, but the Night Owl has the most fantastic soups. I've been eating there at least once a week. I tell everyone I know they have to taste it to believe. Best food in town if you ask me."

I was about ready to tell her to drag her sorry behind back to the Night Owl, but I remembered Bea's reason for getting her to the café in the first place. I tried to peek in Bea's direction but couldn't tell if she had seen anything on Darla or not.

"Well, we really hope you enjoy your lunch," Bea said sweetly.

Darla jingled her bracelets, several gold, sparkly things that I'm sure cost a small fortune, and pushed them away from her watch with perfectly manicured nails. "Yes, well, I'm meeting with my accountant this afternoon, so if we could hurry things up, that would be great."

"Just give me a second to get it all together for you." Bea turned and swiveled around the counter and into the kitchen.

Letting out a deep sigh, Darla looked me up and down. Within a split second, I was transported back to my sophomore year in high school, feeling awkward and out of place. I had to remind myself that we were in my café, my family was right there, and Darla couldn't bully me like she used to. But still, old wounds ran deep.

"Um, Cath?"

I snapped out of my trance and turned toward the kitchen to see Bea peeking around the corner.

Aunt Astrid had taken her usual seat at the small table for two at the end of the counter. She was filling sugar holders, folding paper napkins, and watching Darla as inconspicuously as possible.

When I looked at Bea, she mouthed, "*It's not her.*"

I nodded and bit my lower lip. I was glad Darla didn't have the telltale residue of magic spells on her since we knew from our last experience with her that she wasn't very capable. Magic requires patience and common sense. And if you're going to do it right, magic requires that you have a heart to guide your decisions. As far as I could tell, Darla didn't have a heart.

Aunt Astrid went back to filling the sugar holders and nodded slowly. I could tell she was thinking about what we should do next.

Darla looked around the café, and her eyes homed in on the only man sitting by himself. I'd seen him in the café before. He was a nice-looking guy in his early thirties, with light brown hair going gray at his temples, and an athletic build. He was just Darla's type—male.

Darla took a seat at the tiny table next to him. After

crossing her long legs, only a few minutes passed before the man struck up a conversation with her.

Aunt Astrid watched discreetly with mild amusement. I wasn't as discreet and openly stared at Darla. Something inside of me hoped to see a sign of shiftiness or deceit on her face that might give her away. Maybe I could catch something Bea missed.

Unfortunately, all I saw was the same girl from high school who always got whatever she wanted. I don't know how long I stared at her, but she caught me and gave me a look, tilting her head with the attitude of a Hollywood prima donna.

I rolled my eyes and went back to wiping down the counter.

"You sure you got nothing?" I asked, turning my back to the counter and leaning against it. "Not a sliver, not a shred, nothing that we could use to lock her up for a couple of days?"

"Give me just a second." Bea quietly scooted past me with a fantastic-smelling veggie sandwich and a tall glass of our homemade iced tea with raspberries. She also handed Darla a fork and knife wrapped in a napkin, and I saw their fingers touch. When Bea turned around, she shook her head. "Other than a slight case of constipation, she's clean."

"Well, that's something." I felt a little satisfaction.

"Of course, after she eats my healthy, complementary lunch, that won't be a problem for her either." Bea frowned at me. "Sorry, Cath. I should have given her something with beans in it. I wasn't thinking."

"I know you would have, Bea. Thanks."

By early afternoon, I was busy helping Kevin in the back with inventory when Aunt Astrid called my name. "Cath, someone here to see you!"

Toffees

As I came around the corner, I saw that Darla was still there. Her new friend had pulled up a chair and made himself comfortable at her table, leaning in to talk.

"Cath." I turned to see my best friend Min Park.

"Hey!" I suddenly felt happy and confident.

Min and I had met in high school and had been glued at the hip until we graduated. Min had recently moved back to Wonder Falls a retired millionaire, and I could honestly say nothing had changed in him. He was still the sweetest guy I'd ever known.

I gave him a big hug. "What brings you in here at this hour? Let me guess. It's the people." I jerked my head to the right, making Min turn toward Darla who was obviously trying her hardest to look as though she weren't paying attention to us.

Min's fortune never made a difference to me. Whether he'd come back rich or poor wasn't the issue. I was just thrilled he'd come back to Wonder Falls.

Darla, on the other hand, hated the fact he'd come back to town a multimillionaire. Not only was he the richest resident in ten counties, but he had no interest in Darla, and that was what bothered her the most.

His disinterest in her wasn't just because she was mean to me for sport or because of idle gossip or teenage teasing. Her affiliation with Ruby Connors was why Min would never have anything to do with Darla.

Ruby Connors's big brother tormented Min. One horrible moonlit night, Ruby's brother stuffed Min in a sack and dumped him in the river. It took some fancy maneuvering on my part and a deal with the Lady in the Lake to rescue him. He almost died that night. But that is a story for another time.

Darla turned to stare at me. I knew it was killing her that Min and I were still such good friends, and that he had heaps of money.

Of course, I liked Min before he made his fortune. Rich or poor never made a difference to me, which was probably part of the reason Min and I were such good friends and the reason why Darla and I would probably always be mortal enemies.

The sweetest thing about his success was that without trying, Min had achieved the most divine retribution against the bullies he'd had to deal with. He was happy, healthy, and just happened to be rich.

"Can I get some of that chocolate you guys have? The little toffees?" In all the years I'd known Min, he'd never had a huge sweet tooth. A man after Bea's own heart, he liked fruit and maybe, if he were splurging, a little honey as sweetener. But he usually came in for green tea and not much else.

"Of course you can." I pulled out one of our delicate little bags with The Brew-Ha-Ha written in antique script across it. "But eat them slow. We won't be getting anymore of this quality for a while."

"Really? Why is that?" he asked.

Darla had shifted in her seat and was trying to hear what I was saying. I turned my back to her and slipped my arm through Min's to pull him down closer to me so I could talk semi-privately. "Marvin the chocolatier at Sweetie's is dead. Died of a heart attack just yesterday morning." I released Min's arm and folded the top of the little bag over then added a gold sticker to hold it shut.

"You're kidding," Min said in a hushed voice.

I shook my head as I handed him the candy. When he reached for his wallet, I waved my hand.

"On the house, as always. And no, I'm not kidding. You didn't hear anything about it?" I probed a little.

Min didn't know about my bewitching family history, and I preferred to keep it that way. If our friendship were to ever progress in a more intimate direction, I'd fess up, but at that moment, I was just your average woman asking about the latest town gossip.

"No. Nothing at all." He looked down at me with shock on his face. "I have been spending a lot of time at the nursing home. I haven't had a lot of time to even see my parents, let alone get the scoop on what's happening with the locals."

"You're right. You have been very busy. I haven't seen your bright face around here as much. Is everything going okay with the Wonder Falls Retirement Community? Are they liking their new Chairman of the Board?"

One of Min's goals when he returned to Wonder Falls was to give back to the community. He chose to start volunteering at the old folks' home. Maybe it was his Asian heritage that made him feel more indebted to the older members of our community since it was part of his tradition, or maybe it was just that he had a kind heart. Either way, he was helping, which was ultimately what he wanted to do.

"Oh, I think they are liking me fine." His cheeks reddened as he looked down at his shoes and smiled.

"Min? Are you...blushing?" I bumped him with my hip. "Something is up. Tell me now before I have to resort to violence."

Finally sitting on a stool at the counter, Min made himself comfortable and ordered tea. I hopped around the other side of the counter, propped my head up on my hands and waited.

"Her name is Amalia."

My jaw dropped. A girl?

"She's a nurse at the Home. She's been there for over two years but had worked the graveyard shift..."

"Not a good term to use in regard to the 'old folks' home.'" I used air quotes to emphasize my point. Any talk of graves, tombstones, or death should be avoided at all cost for fear of bad jokes ensuing.

"Right?" Min chuckled a little. "When her schedule changed due to one of our older nurses retiring, I got the chance to meet her."

I smiled. "I see." Was I happy about this? I don't know. It was the first time Min had ever mentioned a girl—no, a nurse. A woman. It was the first time he'd ever mentioned a woman to me. I had to admit I was feeling a little weird.

"You'd like her, Cath. I know you would."

"I'm...sure that I would, Min. I'm really happy for you. You'll have to bring her into the café sometime."

Just then, Darla stood, making a spectacle of herself by flipping her hair and giggling at something her new boy toy had said. He was already grabbing her purse to carry for her, and they both scooted out of the café. How did she train them so fast?

"She didn't even say if she liked the meal," Aunt Astrid scoffed, shaking her head in disgust as she finished the last of her napkin folding.

"Well, she did everything but lick the plate clean," Bea said, holding up the plate, which looked as if no food had even been served on it. "She didn't stay for her dessert."

"She couldn't, remember? She had a very important

meeting with her accountant," I said, not holding back the sarcasm.

"It's about time someone made her handle her own finances. We all know she's been mooching off these poor men long enough." Aunt Astrid slowly stood and stretched her bones. The lunch rush was over.

"She'll be back, you know, to collect on that. It's just an excuse for her to come in and do a little snooping. She's so obvious." I didn't try to hide my feelings, yet I felt a pinch of irony since we lured her there to do the exact same thing.

"Your feelings for her haven't changed," Min said sympathetically.

"It would take divine intervention to make me even consider changing my opinion of Darla. Sometimes, high school brings out the jerk in people, but when they remain that way years later, then you know the problem is them. If I never saw her again, it would be too soon."

Min patted my hand. "She's like that because she's jealous of you, you know."

"Of course she is. I have this good-looking guy that I call my best friend. Who could blame her?"

Min smiled broadly and puffed out his chest. "So, you started to tell me about the chocolatier before. Tell me what happened." He cupped his hand under his chin and leaned forward. I scooted a little closer, and it felt as though we were back in high school discussing our secrets and stories at one of the lunch tables.

I never would have imagined that at any time our secrets

and stories would involve a dead chocolatier...and a new girlfriend. I certainly wasn't prepared for there to be a connection between the two.

Cat Attack

Another day had gone by without a word from Treacle. I was beside myself with worry and couldn't relax. Even when I was sitting, my nerves were stretching and pulling inside of my skin.

Finally, I decided I couldn't just sit around and wait for him anymore. I had to go out on my own and see if I could find a furry associate of his who could give me a tip or point me in a new direction.

The funny thing about being able to talk to cats is that I have to alter my mind to think like they do. It was easier than learning Chinese but harder than talking to yourself inside your own head.

Thinking like Treacle was going to take me in a myriad of directions I had never even imagined. Most cats loved to prowl at night, so I waited until the sun went down. Cats were connected to the supernatural, so they left a sort of footprint when they were out stalking about. It was how they could find their way back home so easily.

Unlike dogs that got lost and couldn't find their way back home, cats left a very light trail of energetic breadcrumbs they could pick up on. Even the smallest traces could linger for a long while, especially if it hadn't rained. And lucky for me, it hadn't.

With hope in my heart and tears in my eyes, I began my search. A small thread of Treacle's energy caught my attention, and I followed its glowing color from my house, through the streets, through a park, until finally it disappeared near the industrial area of Wonder Falls.

Deep in the industrial neighborhood was a building Aunt Astrid and I had broken into not long ago. At that time, the place housed a demon of sorts. The building was important because a feline had been there who had remembered Treacle. That puss even had a concrete opinion of me, so if I could find him, he might be helpful.

But I was having trouble finding anything that slinked on four legs. Usually, they sensed me as if I were one of them. They would come to inspect who was in their neighborhood. I got very nervous all of a sudden. Where had they all gone?

I continued at my casual pace. A few people were sitting on their stoops or hanging around on the corners, and they paid no attention to me.

I wasn't drawing attention to myself, and I had conjured up a camouflage spell before I left. I wasn't totally invisible, but I took on the appearance of what the gazer expected to see. In one instance, I might look like an old lady, and in another instance, I was just a young man making his way home. But the cats could see me as I was if any of them peeked out from their hiding places.

Finally, after a few more blocks, I caught sight of a calico peering from behind a dumpster. Her ears were flat back as she stared at me, her eyes glinting pale yellow against the darkness.

You look scared down there. I'm not going to hurt you, I said in my mind. I was speaking slow and clear, but the cat looked at me as if I were a junkyard dog. *I just want to ask you...*

The cat let out a hiss and darted off. She didn't say a word, but I could tell she was terrified of something. Whatever it was must have looked or acted like me... like a person. My blood was beginning to boil as I thought of someone terrorizing these cats.

Another black-and-white tuxedo cat slunk along the ledge of an old, run-down apartment building. A television light glowed through one of the apartment windows.

"Hey! You look like you see a lot of things going on around here," I called to the cat, again making my thoughts clear and calm. *"I was wondering..."*

In a split second, the cat arched its back, its fur stiffened, and it gave me a deep, guttural growl. My eyebrows shot up to my hairline. This had never happened before. Never.

As I watched the cat slink back underneath a raised window and into the apartment with the glowing television, I stopped for a moment to think.

During the days when witches and suspected witches were being burned at the stake, family stories and legends always mentioned how cats seemed to be aware before anyone else. In their simple minds, they knew a storm was coming, and they took shelter. Was that what was happening? Was a storm coming?

I kept walking. My camouflage spell was holding up, and I was weaving in and out of the neighborhoods with very little attention being paid to me.

Then I saw a familiar face. A large gray four-legged beastie glared at me the same as he'd done the last time I was in this part of town.

He was perched on a tall stack of skids at an alley entrance. I would never forget that cat's face, with his scarred mug and dirty, gray fur. He knew Treacle and didn't like him. He obviously picked up Treacle's scent on me and decided he didn't like me either.

"I know you," I said to him. He watched me with wild, wide eyes. "*You told me I didn't belong in this neighborhood and neither did the black cat I took care of. Do you remember?"* I stood perfectly still. I could see the muscles rippling underneath his fur as they tensed. *"I'm not going to hurt you. I was just wondering if you saw that black cat of mine. You know the one.*"

He still didn't respond.

"What is wrong with all of you?" I mumbled out loud.

Finally, the big alley cat stood up. His fur was on edge, and his back arched as his unblinking eyes bore into mine. *"I've seen that one. Five nights ago.*"

"Five nights ago? Where did he go?" I pointed up and down the street. *"What direction?"*

"He was lost in his mind. He walked in circles and mumbled and made his way through the buildings. He wouldn't fight. Couldn't fight and rushed past all of us. Something has him. He won't be back."

Tears filled my eyes. *"What? What has him? What are you talking about?"*

"There is a badness here. It's here! And it'll get you, too! You talking humans can't be trusted."

"Why would you say that? Wait." His words struck me. *"What other human is talking to you?"*

Call me territorial, but as far as I knew, being able to communicate with cats was a rare and special gift. If someone else had that same talent, I sure the heck wanted to know who it was and why, since that person had come to town, all the cats were more high-strung than ever before.

Like the crack of a whip, the cat leapt at me. His claws were out, and one sharp nail gouged my neck, leaving a long trail of torn skin that instantly began to bleed in a thin line. He pushed off my body and bound down the street, slinking underneath a parked car and into the shadows.

"What in the world?" I said out loud. I was crying openly. I had never had a cat attack me. Dogs, bats, even a raccoon may have tried to take a swipe at me before but never a cat.

The feline's words were of no comfort either. Treacle was in that neighborhood five days ago? He walked in circles? The only thing that came to mind was a word I didn't want to say. A horror worse than any other talking human for my poor, beautiful cat, and if it were true, it would be all my fault.

I took a few steps, not knowing what direction to go. I thought back to the last time I saw Treacle and wished I could go back to that moment. If I would have kept him in the house, maybe he wouldn't be lost and possibly hurt. I was used to letting him go and picking him up at the animal shelter or seeing him weave in through the back door of the café. I had taken him for granted.

Rabies.

No, I wasn't ready to say the word or even think it. That horrible disease eats an animal up slowly and painfully from the inside, starting with its mind. Hadn't Treacle had his shots? I know I'd gotten them for him at the shelter. I know I had.

Hadn't I?

Rabies. No, there had to be another explanation. Treacle would have come home if he'd been attacked that badly. I would have seen a wound or a bite or something. No, something more sinister was at play.

I was near hysterics. Treacle may not have had rabies, but something was hurting him. Something was keeping him from me, and I needed to find out what it was and make sure it never harmed him or any other cat again.

My heart was broken, and I felt very tired. It was as though a weight had been added to my shoulders and ankles. I needed to get home so I could rest and figure out what to do next.

That big alley cat may not have been telling the truth. But that thought was no comfort.

As I made my way back home, I recalled taking Treacle to the vet for his shots. Wonder Falls had a lot of bats, raccoons, squirrels, and other things that could have gotten a hold of him at any time. I didn't take chances because I knew how much he loved to roam.

But even if he didn't have rabies, what if he had some other disease? What if he had gotten into a fight with something bigger and meaner than he was? What if he was hurt and wondering where I was? I felt my heart crack into pieces. I had to find him, no matter what.

Enchantment Spell

The next day, I showed up at the Brew-Ha-Ha half an hour before we opened, and I must have looked a dozen shades of pitiful.

"Cath? What's the matter?" Bea asked, her eyes wide with concern. "Mom! It's Cath!" She poured me a glass of water as I took a seat at the counter.

"I'm okay. I just didn't get much sleep last night."

"Cath, Bea, what's the matter?" My aunt came from the kitchen where she probably had been helping Kevin. She wiped her hands on her apron, and her look of annoyance was quickly replaced with concern. "My heaven's, Cath. What happened?"

I swallowed hard. "Treacle hasn't come back." Both women looked at each other then back at me. "I went out last night looking for him. I didn't find him. None of the cats were talking. They're terrified of something. And one of them... " I took a drink of water to clear my throat and tried to hold back the tears. "One of them managed to tell me they saw him, and he was not acting right. He said Treacle was lost in his mind and mumbling. But that was five days ago. Where could he be?" I lost my composure and began crying like a baby.

Losing my parents was sad, and I missed them terribly. But a pet was different. Most people thought pets relied on us to take care of and protect them. I thought we relied on our pets to protect our hearts. The world could be a scary and lonely place. The animals we kept prevented that world from becoming too much to bear.

"Has Marshmallow been acting any differently?" Bea asked her mother. "Peanut Butter is still so young that I can't tell when he is onto something or when he's just chasing a shadow."

Aunt Astrid thought for a moment then shook her head. "But you have to remember that my house, like yours, is protected with an enchantment spell. Our cats don't leave the houses. But your cat is a roamer, Cath, and only the threshold spell will protect him if he's inside the house." Aunt Astrid made sure we all had some kind of protection on our homes. "Plus, Treacle has been a roamer since he was a kitten. There is nothing you could have done to keep him inside if he wanted to go outside. You know that."

I nodded and wiped my nose with a napkin.

Aunt Astrid pursed her eyebrows and stared at the floor. She nodded and then shook her head as if responding to someone else. She mumbled a few words under her breath before looking up at Bea and me. "I think this has something to do with Marvin."

I cleared my throat noisily. "What? Why do you think that?"

Aunt Astrid walked around the counter and sat on the stool next to me. She folded her hands on the counter and continued to stare down. It looked as though she was studying the grains of the dark wood.

"We have some pretty good proof that this witch is not very good at what she does. She or he likes to call themselves a witch more than they care to know the history, the theories, the proper procedures. They like the image and care not for the substance."

"What does that have to do with Treacle?" Bea asked.

"He's a black cat. Black cats are the most magical. I think he's hiding from this wanna-be witch. If what you're saying about all the other cats is true, he may be hiding, too."

"But what about what the gray alley cat said about him not being right in the head and stuff?" I hoped Aunt Astrid might have an answer to dowse the flames of nervousness in my belly.

"His solid black coat makes him very attractive to anyone dabbling in the occult. If they are dabbling and doing it all wrong, as we think this witch is, Treacle could be getting hit the hardest."

"That is, if he isn't..."

Bea reached across the counter and squeezed my hands.

She had wet eyes, too. "Don't say it, Cath. Just don't. Treacle might be in bad shape, but he's still alive. That gray kitty would have told you otherwise, especially since he made it clear he didn't like you very much."

Someone suddenly knocked on the glass door. All of us looked to see the faces of a couple of regulars and some new patrons waiting for us to open the café.

"Oh, geez!" Aunt Astrid yipped, hopping off the stool and running to the door. "Sorry, folks! Just a little family business to tend to. Come on in. Glad you're here. Free fortune-telling today for the first five customers. That will make things better, no?"

I hopped off the stool and hurried behind the counter to help Bea. It was a beautiful morning. I couldn't help but think it was the calm before the storm. My body moved mechanically as I served our regulars and smiled, saying "good morning" and "have a nice day." My mind was in a million places at once, yet I couldn't cling to a single thought. It was frustrating.

"I'll be right back," I said to Bea. She patted my shoulder and nodded. I walked to the ladies' room at the back of the café, needing a minute to myself. I ran my hands under the cold water and looked in the mirror. My eyes were red and tired. I'd been up all night, and it was starting to catch up with me. Just as I decided to ask for a personal day, I heard a quiet knock on the door.

"I'll be out in a second," I called through the door.

"Honey, Min is here," Aunt Astrid said politely.

"Oh, okay."

"He's, uh... not alone."

I dried my hands on my pants and opened the door. "Really?"

She nodded and walked back to the front of the café. I smoothed my hair back and imagined who Min was with. It had to be a girl, or Aunt Astrid wouldn't have said anything. Of course, today had to be the day I met Min's new girlfriend.

A Lead

Truth be told, I was thankful for the distraction. After spending almost the entire night worrying about Treacle, I needed something else to focus on.

I walked around the kitchen to the front of the café and saw Min standing next to a petite young lady. She had curly, auburn hair, wide eyes, and freckles over the bridge of her nose. Min was talking with Bea, and the young lady was also contributing to the conversation, laughing and nodding at whatever Bea was saying.

Aunt Astrid tugged on my sleeve from her regular seat. "You all right?"

"I'll be fine. I know I'll find Treacle. He's around somewhere and..."

"I meant about this." She jerked her chin in Min's direction.

"What? Oh my gosh." I hoped my reply was convincing. "Of course. Are you serious?"

Aunt Astrid's right eyebrow arched, and she gave me a sideways look.

I rolled my eyes at her and walked up to Min with my shoulders back and my chin held high.

When he turned and saw me, he smiled. "Cath!" he stooped down to give me a hug.

I hugged him back, and for a moment, I felt a little superior to the woman. I didn't want to feel that way, but it crept up inside me like an aggressive vine that wrapped itself around my heart.

For years, it had been Min and me against the world. When he left to make his fortune, I didn't worry about what he was doing or who he was with, and when he came back, we picked up right where we left off. You can only do that with a rare friend. I had been spoiled.

For so long, Min had been my shoulder to cry on, my pillar of strength, my confidant. But he'd found a cute woman who was going to share her secrets and her dreams with him and, who knew, maybe even more than that.

Min pulled away first, and I followed suit. I didn't want to come across as one of those women who were clingy and needy, even if all I wanted to do was cling to Min because I needed his help to find Treacle. I stood back and waited for the bomb of disappointment and annoyance to go off between his girlfriend and me.

"Cath, this is Amalia. Amalia, this is my best friend in the whole world, Cath Greenstone," Min said.

The woman walked around the table and gave me a gentle, heartfelt hug. Some people may have thought it was a little forward to hug someone upon first meeting them, but with the way I was feeling at the moment, I really appreciated it.

"I am so glad to meet you," she said in a clear and kind voice. "Min has told me so much about you that I feel like I've known you my whole life." She pulled back and smiled pleasantly.

"Don't believe him. He likes to elaborate and lie," I said, making Amalia laugh. "Please, guys, have a seat. Let me get you something to drink. Coffee, tea, lemonade or a water or..."

"I'd love a tea," Amalia said. "I just got off work and don't want anything too strong to keep me up. I'll need a nap for sure."

"I'll get them," Min offered. "You ladies can talk behind my back for a few minutes."

I looked awkwardly at Amalia, who didn't seem to be uncomfortable or nervous at all.

"It must have been a full moon or something last night because several of the residents had me running my tail off from the minute I got there to when I checked out this morning." Amalia rolled her eyes. "First, Mr. Lessing said he heard scratching on the walls. The residents are allowed to have small pets, and Mr. Lucio's cat got out of his room and was finally cornered in the recreational center after knocking over half a dozen potted plants. Mrs. Toon said there was a person outside digging at the corner of the building. The best one was Mr. Cavanaugh who said he needed a sponge bath because Marilyn Monroe was planning on paying him a visit."

I smiled, and a little laugh rattled out of my chest.

"If Mr. Cavanaugh had his way, he'd have a sponge bath every hour."

I felt my heart get a little lighter. "That's funny."

"Don't get me wrong. I love working at the Home. The job can be hard at times, but I love the stories around all the residents. Sometimes, one or two of them just decide they want to cause a little drama. It's like high school."

She was charming. I hated to admit it, but I felt a possible friendship tugging at my thoughts. The corners of my mouth would not stay down. I smiled, and it felt good.

"I'm sorry I'm so talky." She patted my hand quickly. "I get this way when I'm tired."

"Would you like a chamomile tea? My cousin adds a little lavender-infused honey, and even though I'm not a tea drinker, I have to say it's really soothing."

Amalia stared at me with her mouth open. "That sounds like heaven. Yes. Yes, I would like that. Thank you. Please."

I laughed again and waved for Bea to make her special tea for Amalia. We chatted a little more until Min sat down with us. Then I really got an earful.

"So the man who made those delicious toffees passed away? Min was telling me about it." Amalia wrapped her hands around the sides of her warm mug of tea. I was glad she wasn't hanging on Min. They sat close to each other, but they weren't all touchy-feely like new couples sometimes were.

"Yeah. It was a heart attack, we heard," I said.

"That was Marvin Clegg, right?" Amalia asked, squinting her eyes a little.

"Yeah, it was," I said.

"That's really bizarre because just a few weeks ago, I'd say maybe two weeks ago, his daughter, Brit Clegg, had come in inquiring about a place for him at the home."

My heart leapt. "Really. Gosh, that's weird. Was she nice?"

Amalia took a sip of her tea and rolled her eyes. "Oh my gosh. This *is* soothing. Holy moly. Yes, she was very nice. But now that you mention it..."

I held my breath and leaned in.

"She was a little vague about some of the questions we routinely ask, and then she had some strange questions for us." She took another sip. "I remember wondering what kind of daughter asks if female visitors other than her can come to her father's room and stay overnight?"

"That is weird," I said. "What else did she say?"

"Well, she asked if there were cameras, and she asked if her father could burn candles and incense in his room."

"Well, maybe she was just concerned with security, and maybe her dad liked incense. My late Uncle Karl had a dog that died, and he kept a picture of it with a little votive candle burning all the time. Maybe he had something like that going on. His wife did pass away several years ago."

"Maybe." Amalia shrugged and took another sip of her tea.

"The weirdest thing was that she wanted to know all these things but said her father didn't know she was inquiring. She said she didn't know when he'd be ready to move in, just that it would be soon."

"And now he's dead," I said thoughtfully.

"I know. It's so sad. If only she could have gotten him in there sooner, he'd have had medical attention as soon as it happened. He might still be alive today."

Not with an exploded heart, I thought. "Was his daughter living here?"

"Yeah, that was another strange thing. When I asked her for her home address and a phone number where we could contact her, she gave the address to a rental located in, well, not a very good part of town. Do you know where all those warehouses and random mills are located? Apparently she's living over there. Wishing Well Court trailer park. Frankly, I wasn't sure how she was going to pay for her father's room, but many people find ways when they need to."

I thought of my adventure to find Treacle. His trail had gone cold just as I was roaming through that area. Whatever was there was affecting the cats, too. This was the biggest break I could have hoped for.

Amalia let out a big yawn. "I'm so sorry to be yawning. It isn't the company, really, but I am beat. I think it's your cousin's tea. It's like sipping a down pillow and comforter."

Min and I laughed. "I better take you home," Min said. "Tonight, we're going to the Music Box to catch *Casablanca* on the big screen. Cath, do you want to come with?"

"Say yes," Amalia said. "You'll have fun. I've seen that movie at least a dozen times, and I just can't see it enough. When the French start singing their national anthem over the Germans'... I get goose bumps talking about it."

I would have loved to go, but the wheels in my head were spinning.

"You know, thank you so much for inviting me, but I can't. I've got plans with my aunt and Bea that have to do with family stuff. Boring but necessary, you know."

"I do." She yawned again.

"Let's make plans to do something together soon," Min said, beaming with a happiness I knew was because Amalia and I had hit it off.

I smiled back. I couldn't tell him, but meeting Amalia was more wonderful than he could ever know. Not only had she given us a lead on the real cause of Marvin's death, but she'd also given us a lead suspect. And quite possibly, she may have given me a tip to where Treacle might be. If there was a witch in that area, she might have *my* black cat.

Even after the terrible night I'd had, I felt rejuvenated and couldn't wait to tell Bea and Aunt Astrid what I'd found out. All I needed was Brit Clegg's address.

After I told them, we agreed not to talk about our new discovery at work. Once the doors were locked and the CLOSED sign hung in the door, we met at Aunt Astrid's for a nightcap.

Wishing Well

"The Wishing Well Trailer Park is huge, and it goes way back into the woods," Bea said. "Those trailers are secluded for a reason. It's not exactly the kind of place you want to go around asking questions."

"Why would Marvin's daughter be staying there when he had a successful business and a nice house in an affluent part of town?" Aunt Astrid asked. "That doesn't make any sense."

"Maybe they didn't get along," I said. Neither my aunt nor Bea said anything. "I'm going to go and do some looking around." I felt the strong gust of a second wind coming over my tired body.

Bea put her hands on her hips. "Cath, Wishing Well isn't a safe place. You shouldn't go by yourself. You shouldn't go at all. Look, if we wait until tomorrow after we've slept on it, we'll be better prepared to come up with a plan. But for you to just go snooping around is crazy. Besides, you don't know what Marvin's daughter looks like, and there are hundreds of trailers in there. What are you going to do, knock on their doors?"

"No, I'm not going to knock on their doors. I just want to get a look at things. See what we're dealing with. Maybe see if I can pick up a vibe or two."

Aunt Astrid took my hands in hers across the book-covered dining room table and closed her eyes. "It's no use, Bea. You know how your cousin is once she gets a bee in her bonnet." Astrid mumbled a few words I could barely make out, and I knew she was putting a protection spell over me. Letting go of my hands, she gave me a wink.

"*You're not going alone*," I heard a familiar voice say. "*I'm going with you.*" It was Marshmallow. She rubbed her head against my calf.

I looked down at her and smiled. "*Thank you, but whatever is going on doesn't seem to be cat-friendly. I couldn't bear it if something happened to you* and *Treacle.*"

"*That is exactly why you're taking me*," she insisted. A curt meow was all Aunt Astrid and Bea heard. "*You're taking me with you.*" She laid her paws on my foot, and I felt the tiny prick of her claws starting to come out.

Letting out a deep sigh, I interrupted Bea and Aunt Astrid, who were still talking about the weird alignment of the facts we had so far. "It seems I won't be going alone after all." Marshmallow jumped up on the table.

Just then, Peanut Butter scurried around the corner in a panic. He was still young compared to Treacle and Marshmallow. He loved to visit Marshmallow when Bea brought her along. Peanut Butter would stalk, pounce, swat, and dart from room to room with just the slightest, if any, provocation. Marshmallow would watch him with dreamy and disinterested eyes.

"*You can't go,*" Peanut Butter cried. "*Who'll take care of me?*"

Marshmallow peered over the table and meowed back. "*I have to. We have to find Treacle. I can help. He'd do it for us.*"

"*Then I'm going with you,*" Peanut Butter said in almost a hiss.

"*No,*" I said firmly in my mind. "*You are too young. I don't like the idea of taking Marshmallow. I'm not taking you along, too.*"

"*I'll be all alone,*" Peanut Butter cried sadly.

"*I'll be back. With Treacle.*"

"*Promise?*"

Marshmallow looked at me. She was acting brave, but I could see fear in her eyes. She was a house cat. Rarely did she go outdoors unless a bird, mouse, or cricket was within a few feet of the door.

"*I promise,*" I said.

Marshmallow purred and rubbed her head under my hand.

"It looks like I'll have this furry companion to help me," I said out loud.

"Oh no, Cath, I don't think so," Aunt Astrid said, scratching Marshmallow behind the ears. Then Marshmallow did something I'd never seen her do before—she swatted Aunt Astrid's hand away and bared her teeth. She didn't hiss, and I don't know if her claws were out, but Marshmallow let her mistress know she meant business.

"Sorry, Mom. Looks like you don't have much of a say in it," Bea said, her eyes wide with surprise.

"I promise we'll be careful," I said. "I won't let her out of my sight." But in the back of my mind, I was worried. I remembered how all the other cats behaved near that part of town. I also knew Marshmallow wasn't like Treacle. She didn't have experience roaming the streets, slipping along inside shadows, or making quick decisions to get away from danger. Still, she insisted, and she'd never asked to help before. Even though she loved her human family, the love of her lifelong feline friend was entirely different. She wasn't going to leave Treacle out there if she could help it.

I placed her gently in her travel box, loaded her into my car, and headed to the Wishing Well Trailer Park. I left Aunt Astrid's house feeling as though I were about to solve the mystery in a matter of hours. I'd have proof, a motive, and be able to tip off Jake and Blake in an anonymous phone call, giving them credit for arresting the woman who killed Marvin... his own daughter. The thought of it made me sad.

I'd give anything to see my parents again, and Marvin's daughter was so selfish that she thought her father's life was something to be thrown away like a toy she no longer had use for. On top of everything else, she may have kidnapped Treacle, thinking a black cat would improve her half-baked attempts at witchcraft. Nothing was going to stop me from finding her trailer even if I had to knock on every door.

Finding Treacle

The sign for the Wishing Well Trailer Park was an old, faded piece of plywood cut into the shape of a wishing well. The peeling red letters appeared to have been partially scratched off so if you looked at the sign a certain way, the only defined letters were the "h," "ell," and Trailer Park.

I ignored the chill running up my spine as I drove past the entrance to the Wishing Well in search of someplace to park where no one would notice us. I saw a used car lot about a quarter of a mile down the road and an office building that looked like it had once been a Pizza Hut.

I decided to park in the used car lot. Thankfully, the cars in the lot looked a lot like mine. They were old, a little rusty, and not very glamorous. The only difference was that my car didn't have the $2500 OBO or 87,000 miles written in soap on the windows. But I didn't plan on staying around long enough for anyone to notice my car.

"You doing okay?" I asked Marshmallow. She didn't purr as I lifted her from her box. I felt her nails instinctively come out when I held her to my chest.

"I'm okay," she said quietly in her head.

"Do you want to walk, or should I carry you?"

"I'll walk. It's all right."

Gently, I set her down. For a moment, she stood perfectly still. Her body was low to the ground as she looked around, and for a moment, I thought she was going to bolt. *"There is something here, but it isn't what you think it is. I can feel it."* She stared into the dark woods separating the trailer park from the used car lot.

"What do you see?" I asked, looking into the darkness.

"I see fear."

As if shaking like a leaf and second-guessing my idea to visit the trailer park weren't bad enough, my companion then said all she could see was fear. I didn't even want to know what that looked like.

Marshmallow walked ahead of me. I knew if she heard anything, she'd stop, yet I held my breath and listened for any unusual sounds—footsteps, groaning, weird whispers, and anything else I'd seen in a horror movie. I desperately hoped I didn't hear the rev of a chainsaw.

Okay, I was being silly. Thankfully, the ground was even. It wasn't full of dips and mounds, and there weren't tons of fallen trees and sticker bushes. Most of the trees were thin and relatively young by tree standards. I grabbed onto them as I walked. The darkness was thick, and I used the trees to maintain my balance. Touching nature always grounded me. Trees were real. I didn't feel magic or spells yet.

After a few more paces, Marshmallow and I saw a faint, green-tinted fluorescent light in the distance. Squinting, I could see a few trailers in its weakly illuminated circle.

"We're almost there," I said. Marshmallow gave me a quiet meow as a response.

I looked behind us and could no longer see the lights of the used car dealership. It was as if the whole world had dropped into some black place. If a tree fell in the woods, and no one was around, did it make noise? If you couldn't see the lights, was the dealership still there? If Marshmallow and I had to run back, would we eventually see the lights, or would we keep running and running in darkness?

I shook my head and focused on the lights before us. The trailers were nothing like the trailers at the front of the Wishing Well that faced the road. Those trailers had roots in a way. The people who lived in the front trailers had flowerbeds and even cement stairs leading up to their homes. I'd seen a tool shed or two and a few gazing balls. Statues of St. Francis, wind chimes, and sun catchers made the place look homey and attractive. A person driving by might think the homes didn't fit the stereotype of a trailer park. They looked clean, pretty, and proper. But when someone got to the back of the park where we were, he would see where reality lived.

Three trailers were huddled together under the sickly green lights. The trailers looked like members of the same gang, all of them beat up with dents and scratches. Two of the three trailers were most likely breaking the rules as they were supported by cinder blocks and what looked like plastic milk crates. Lit up from the inside, the windows displayed either dirty curtains drawn tightly shut, a trash bag, or thick towels preventing anyone from seeing in or out.

"This isn't where we want to be," Marshmallow said, stopping in front of me. She raised her head, her whiskers twitching wildly, then crouched back down on her belly. *"But we aren't far. Something is up ahead."*

I looked where Marshmallow was looking. More trailers were lit by sickly green light. The lampposts were in just as bad a shape as the rest were.

Staying within the safety and confines of the trees, we skirted along the perimeter. The pitiful light from the trailer park cast menacing shadows all around us, but I was able to see, which made me calmer. It was a big park, and I began to think it was a bad idea to go snooping around.

But this wasn't really snooping, right? I wasn't peeking in windows or listening to conversations. That was snooping. I was just... exploring, trying to map out the lay of the land so I could snoop around later.

"There. Up ahead. Do you see that glow?" Marshallow asked.

I looked and squinted but saw nothing.

"It's coming from the middle of that row," Marshmallow said. *"We've got to go in there."*

I looked around, listening and scanning the shadows for any kind of movement, any hint that someone was watching us. But there was nothing.

"Stick to the shadows, and lead the way," I said, watching Marshmallow morph from the lounging butterball of purring fur to a svelte predator on a mission.

We quietly and carefully slunk along the sides of the trailers, moving in between generators and storage pods until we got to where Marshmallow had seen the glow. I saw no glow. I only saw a dark trailer. It wasn't menacing like the three at the ass-end of the park, but it wasn't a showpiece like the ones at the entrance either.

It was simple—a white trailer, no wind chimes, no decorations on the lawn, wooden steps leading to the entrance. As I stood in the shadows, I realized I was starting to feel ill, as if something I had eaten was fussing deep in my gut. I swallowed hard and tried to shove it away.

"That's the house that's glowing?" I managed to say to Marshmallow but got no response. I assumed she was busy studying the terrain. Perhaps something else had caught her eye. I took a step closer to the trailer and again felt a wave of nausea settle over me. My skin was becoming cold and hot at the same time. I shivered, but I was also sweating. I couldn't imagine what I could have eaten that would hit me like that.

After a few deep breaths, I began to feel better. I took a few steps closer to the plain, little trailer in the middle of the park.

A bunch of mason jars set on the steps leading to the front

door. As I looked closer, I could see they had something in them. The jars held a yellow liquid and some odds and ends I couldn't make out. I counted eight jars on the steps, and to my surprise, they were in the windows, too.

I tried to inch a little closer but stopped cold. I gripped the side of the trailer behind which Marshmallow and I were hiding. *"Something is wrong with me,"* I said in my mind but still got no response. *"Marshmallow, what are you..."*

She was staring straight at me. We couldn't communicate. She couldn't hear me, and I couldn't hear her, yet we were right next to each other.

This wasn't right. My stomach was doing flips, and I was beginning to shake. Goose bumps had risen all over my arms and shoulders. I was about to scoop up the cat and head back to the woods when I stopped and held my breath.

Headlights. And they were coming this way. I flattened myself against the aluminum siding and tried to shrink into the shadows. If the car turned right, its lights would flash across us, and we'd be seen. If it turned left, we'd be okay. Closer and closer it came. Just then, lights popped on in the trailer, and I saw a familiar face in the window.

"Treacle!" I said in a hushed, sickly voice. Could he see us? Did he know we were there? I tried calling to him in my mind, but everything bounced back to me. What was going on?

Thankfully, the approaching car veered to the left and pulled into the gravel driveway of our plain, little trailer. A short woman, who I guessed to be in her early twenties, stepped out from the driver's side.

She wore jeans and a baggy shirt and carried a grocery bag. Gingerly, she stepped around the jars on her steps. Then she bent down and removed something from the threshold of her door. Rattling her keys, she unlocked the door, stepped inside, sprinkled something over the top step, replaced whatever had been in front of her door, then shut it quietly. From where we were, we heard several locks slip into place.

I wouldn't be able to kick in the door to get my cat. Even if I wanted to, I was in no condition to do it. My stomach was rolling up and over itself, and as I took a step closer to see what she had put in front of the door, I almost lost my balance.

It's a broom. A broom?

I noticed a gap in the curtain by the tiny window next to the door. I squinted and tried to see in, inching my way closer and closer to the front steps. I tried to see what was in the jars, too. A tiny light outside the door helped me to see.

Looking into the jars, I saw what appeared to be hair. It was repulsive. I knew I was too close and at any minute, I was sure I'd throw up, alerting not just the cat thief but the neighboring trailers as well. Finally, I couldn't take it anymore. With Marshmallow in my arms, I trudged back toward the trees. With every step, I started to feel better.

"Cath! Cath!" Marshmallow was screaming, clinging to my shirt. *"Why won't you answer me? I'm right here!"*

"Marshmallow! I couldn't hear you. Calm down. I can hear you now. Something was happening at that trailer."

"Did you see him? She has him! That person has..."

"Treacle. Yes. I saw him."

"Oh, how are we going to get him back?"

"I don't know. There's something going on at that place, but it wasn't a spell. At least, it wasn't any spell I've ever experienced. We've got to get Aunt Astrid and Bea. Maybe it's just something that affects me, you know, because Treacle is my cat. Maybe that's why I was getting sick. I don't know. But we need reinforcements for sure."

"Take me home. I don't want to be out here anymore." Marshmallow sounded pitiful. I snuggled her to me as we slowly made our way back to the used car lot and my car.

"You found Treacle, Marsh. I don't know what you saw that was glowing, but you saw it. I'd still be roaming around in there lost if it weren't for you. And Treacle is there."

"We have to come back to get him."

"Yes, we do."

"But how?"

I shook my head. The lights over the Pizza Hut-looking building guided us back.

"I don't know." I lowered Marshmallow back into her travel box. Before I even started the car, the cat was asleep. I wish I could do that.

That night, I tossed and turned. How was I going to get my cat back if the spell around that trailer made me feel like I had eaten a pail of dirt?

Witches' Vials

"Jars of liquid and hair? Oh, dear." Aunt Astrid looked off in the distance.

Bea poured some of her strong Oolong tea into the tiny flowered cup setting in front of me.

I waved my hand. "Even after getting a couple hours sleep last night, I don't think I can keep anything down. There is still a twinge of sour that I just don't want to tempt."

Aunt Astrid's house was almost directly centered between my house and Bea's house. Jake always worked odd hours, so he was pretty understanding that we were always together.

I wrapped my arms around my stomach and sat very still in my aunt's straight-backed dining room chair, trying desperately not to look at the Dutch apple pie she had within arm's reach.

"That poor girl," Aunt Astrid mumbled.

I didn't have to speak. Bea read my mind. "Poor girl? She

stole Treacle. She killed her father and is the kind of 'witch'"—Bea used air quotes to emphasize her disgust with our cat-napping nemesis—"that gives the rest of us a bad name. How can you say 'poor girl'?"

Sitting down calmly, Aunt Astrid pushed her long locks behind her and looked sternly at her daughter. "Sit down, Bea."

Taking a seat next to me, Bea looked at her mother curiously.

"What you saw, Cath, are what we call witches' vials. This girl is not a witch, but she's obviously very scared of one."

Aunt Astrid went on to explain that during the days when people would see witches around every corner sabotaging crops, causing diseases, and stealing children and husbands, the fearful would use witches' vials. The person fearful of the witch would fill the jar with urine, nail clippings, hair, sometimes a scrap of clothing, sometimes drops of blood, small pieces of skin like a hangnail or a scab, then seal it tight. The jars were then set near all the entrances, preventing witches from crossing the thresholds.

"There are various ways witches' vials can affect a witch. If Bea were to go there and try and get close, she might get lost and turned around. If I went there, it might make me forget who I am and what I was doing there in the first place. In your instance, it made you nauseated."

"Seriously nauseated. I'm still feeling it." I rubbed my belly. "I also couldn't talk to Marshmallow or Treacle for that matter."

"I believe it. It's like mountains in the way of using a cell phone," Aunt Astrid explained. "The signals you are used to get cut off. Nothing can pass. This little girl just put a big mountain in our way. She must have a very scary reason for doing so."

"But what about the broom?" Bea asked. "Cath said she put a broom down in front of the door. What does that mean?"

"This girl is no dummy. She has obviously done her research." Aunt Astrid started to slice herself a piece of pie, and I had to look away. I couldn't handle the sight of food yet. "When people thought there was a witch in their village, some of them would put their broomsticks across their thresholds at nighttime. Because witches were supposed to use these things to fly around on if they came across one lying on the floor, they were forced to count each bristle. By the time they actually counted them all, it was believed the sun would be on the rise, and the witch would be unable to complete her evil deeds."

"So, would that have happened to me? If I didn't get all shades of queasy, would I have been forced to count the bristles? That sounds crazy." I rubbed my head, feeling the sickness from my stomach traveling up the back of my neck. A headache was quickly approaching.

"I'm afraid so," Aunt Astrid said, taking a big bite of pie.

"And I'd have had no control? How can that be? I mean, what if this girl decides to render us powerless by throwing brooms at us, and we're compelled to count every bristle?" I was getting angry. First, the woman had my cat, which was bad enough. Then she put out witches' vials and thousand-bristled broomsticks to compel us to count, and she is the poor girl? I was starting to wonder if someone had put a hex on Aunt Astrid.

"More importantly, how are we going to get to this girl?" Bea asked. "We obviously need to talk to her. A witch did that to Brit Clegg's father, but Brit isn't the witch. So who is?"

"Well, we can't get to her at her place. We might have to bring in the reserves." Aunt Astrid took another bite of pie. In four forkfuls, the dessert was almost gone. Where my aunt put it was anyone's guess because she still had quite a cute, soft figure for a woman her age.

We both looked at Bea, who rolled her eyes. "How am I going to nonchalantly tell Jake that Brit Clegg, the daughter of the man who died of one hell of a heart attack, has weird and quite offensive witches' vials all around her trailer home and also has Treacle?" She put her hands on her hips. "He'll hit the roof if he knows that we're sneaking up behind him on this case."

"I think we need to handle this the way we'd handle Darla Castellan." Aunt Astrid pushed herself up from her seat, reaching over to cut another piece of pie.

"You mean with a whip and a chair?" I asked as Aunt Astrid placed the plate in front of me. As soon as she did, my headache was gone, my neck relaxed, and my stomach grumbled with hunger. "How did you know?"

"It is also pretty common that the effects of witches' vials only last a couple of hours. Enough to keep us off our balance but not enough to keep us laid up for long. Besides, the color just came back into your cheeks." She gave me a wink that made me feel special.

I ate the pie and listened to Aunt Astrid's plan for getting Brit Clegg away from her home and someplace we could talk to her. "It's so simple, it has to work." I wiped my mouth after practically inhaling my dessert. I just needed a hamburger or something to wash it down.

"Bea, I think you should be the one to contact her. You have a natural way about you that sets people at ease," Aunt Astrid said.

I furrowed my brows after hearing this. "Wait a second. I can put people at ease. I am quite a people pleaser when it comes down to it."

Both women looked at me as if I were a baby babbling incoherent words into the middle of their adult discussion.

"No," was all Aunt Astrid said.

I shrugged, giving Bea a wink. The truth was I knew she was much more diplomatic and, well, just kinder than I ever was. I remembered my parents being good, loving people, but I didn't remember if either of them had a temper or what their limits were. I always had the feeling I developed my pattern of harsh, scratchy behavior after realizing how fate had cheated me.

808

After another slice of pie, some strong coffee, a bagel with cream cheese, and some leftover veggie chili, I was feeling much more like my regular self. Yet I couldn't shake the weird cottony feeling still in my head. It was as if a small corner existed in my mind in which the light couldn't penetrate. No matter how hard I reached and stretched inside my head, I couldn't get to that corner, but something was telling me I needed to see what was there.

I left Bea and Aunt Astrid alone to devise a plan in which Brit Clegg would bring me my cat. I couldn't help because my idea was to stomp over there, nauseated or not, and pound the door down. If she believed witches were so bad, I was more than happy to prove her right. She would be called some very nasty names and told to stay away from my cat and me. I'd also slam the door, if given the chance, and stomp away with a scowl on my face that she wouldn't soon forget. Yup! That would teach her.

Still, Treacle hadn't looked hurt or in pain. The worst thing for him was probably staying cooped up all day and night. If I knew my cat, he'd probably already introduced his claws to her upholstery and curtains. *Serves her right.* But if she didn't like witches, I hoped she wasn't going to take it out on Treacle. He couldn't help it that he was an exceptional black cat.

My eyes filled with tears. Treacle didn't see me last night, and I couldn't call to him. He hadn't even known I was there. What really bothered me was thinking that Treacle might think I wasn't looking for him. That thought broke my heart the most.

I made my way down Bryn Mawr Avenue and took a left onto First Street. There were dozens of little shops and restaurants to look into. The pedestrian traffic was bustling. I looked into the windows of the shops, thinking of nothing and everything at the same time. When I came to Standee's twenty-four-hour diner, I peeked in and saw two faces I knew.

I went inside and walked up to Jake and Blake, who sat at the counter sipping coffee. "Are you guys off duty? I promise I won't tell Bea and Aunt Astrid you're getting coffee and lunch at a place that's not the Brew-Ha-Ha."

"Hey, Cath. Want to join us? We're technically getting dinner then heading home. Had a wild morning." Jake was a handsome guy. Bea was very lucky because as pretty as he was on the outside, he was even more so on the inside. He was the big brother I never had.

"You know, I just ate at Aunt Astrid's." I patted my stomach. "So what kind of excitement did you guys have?"

"An 808 at the Walona Motel," Blake said after he took a sip of water. He was always so stiff.

"Okay, what is an 808, and what is the Walona Motel?"

"Disturbing the peace. The Walona Motel is over in the industrial part of town. It's on a side street just before you get on the expressway."

"The Walona Motel? I've never heard of it, but it sounds like a respite station for kings. What happened?"

"Apparently, two occupants of two separate rooms decided they didn't care to share the same air space with each other," Jake said as the waitress behind the counter served up big cheeseburgers in front of him and Blake. "A loud shouting match between a woman who was there by herself and another woman who was there with her husband. Nobody was drunk. No one had any priors. It just got loud. The woman and her husband said they'd be leaving, so there was no need for us to do anything."

"Well, that doesn't sound so bad," I said. "With the way the world is, it could have been a lot worse."

"Well, it was over and done with for me, but Blake here had a little more on his hands than just an ornery woman." Jake chuckled and nudged Blake with his elbow just before he took a big bite out of his burger.

"Really, was she looking for a stone ornament for her yard?" I asked, completely serious.

Blake looked at me then shook his head. "Some people in the world are just a little lonely. That's all."

"Or desperate," I mumbled. "Well, I gotta run. I'll tell Bea you're on your way home."

"Well, if you wait, I'll drop you wherever you're headed," Jake offered.

I shook my head. "No. I don't know if Bea told you, but Treacle hasn't come home for a few days." Technically, it was true, but I couldn't tell him any more than that, nor could I tell him anything about the mystery rolling around in my head like a silver pinball.

"That's the big black cat I see at the Brew-Ha-Ha, right?" Blake asked, looking at me oddly.

"Yeah, that's him. He's a prowler. He has all his claws, and he never likes being indoors for very long. But usually he's come back by now. I'm just strolling around, hoping maybe I'll see him." It wasn't a total lie but more like a lie of omission.

"Well, I usually take a ten-mile run at the end of the day to get centered," Blake said. "I'll keep an eye out on the south side of town for you." His eyes were serious, and there wasn't any of the cold hardness that was usually there.

"I'd appreciate that, Blake. Thank you."

"I lost a pet once. When I was a kid, we had an English bulldog named Buddy. We think someone stole him."

My heart just broke at the simple tragedy. He said it quickly, but I could tell it held a certain amount of weight in his heart. When I looked him in the eyes, he didn't look away. I saw the shadow of a memory there, then just as quickly, it was gone. He was back to Detective Blake Samberg and just the facts.

"How terrible." I put my hand over my heart.

For a moment, we looked at each other. He looked at me as if he were surprised I would say something so kind. I felt bad about that and wondered if he'd become a cop, and then detective, in order to help other people find their lost Buddies.

"Nothing worse." The right side of his mouth curled up in a sad grin.

"Right." I nodded. "Well, I better let you guys finish your lunches." I smiled at Jake and couldn't help feel my eyes drawn to Blake's. He was still looking at me a little more intently than usual. I don't know what was going on behind his eyes, but they were deeper than I had noticed before.

Brit

A couple of days had passed since Aunt Astrid and Bea put their plan into motion. It was a very simple idea, but we'd have no way of knowing if it worked until Brit Clegg showed up at the café.

"Did you offer her a free lunch, too?" I'd asked when they first told me they had sent her a letter.

"No," Bea said. "We told her the truth."

"What?" I hissed over the counter at the Brew-Ha-Ha.

As I looked to see if anyone had noticed my outburst, Bea took my hand. "I told her we were sorry what happened to her father. We were sorry she was afraid, but that we knew what she was afraid of and wanted to help."

"What about Treacle?"

"Of course. We told her we knew she had a cat that didn't belong to her, and unless she wanted the authorities involved, she'd bring the cat with her."

"And when is she supposed to arrive here?"

"Today. We told her we're open from seven in the morning until eight o'clock at night. We said we understand people have to work and that she probably had many details to tend to. We said we didn't want to inconvenience her, yet at the same time, we had to talk to her."

I took a deep breath. "Well, that sounds like you were real nice. I think she might come."

Bea shrugged and widened her eyes. It was a crap shoot, but what other choice did we have?

All day long, every time the bells over the door jingled their happy little tune, Aunt Astrid, Bea and I looked up to see if it was a woman carrying a cat box. Every time, we were disappointed.

It wasn't until we were serving our last evening customers at ten minutes before eight that the door opened and the frantic "meow, meow, meow" that had been so familiar to me snapped my head toward the door.

"Treacle!" I cried out loud. *"Treacle, are you all right?"* I called to him inside my head. *"Are you hurt at all? I missed you so much!"*

"Cath!" he meowed loudly. *"You won't believe what is happening! I was afraid I might never see you again!"*

"Hi. Hi. You must be Brit," I said quickly. As much as I wanted to be mad at this girl, looking in her eyes, I couldn't help but feel sorry for her. Her expression was a mixture of sadness, fear, and strength. No matter what had happened with her father, something else was going on that had her on edge and ready to fight.

She nodded and handed me the cardboard cat carrier. From the little air holes, a black paw kept sticking out, reaching and scratching for me. All anyone else could hear were wild and continual meows. I heard the relief and happiness coming from my beloved companion.

"Please, sit down," I said, looking at Bea and Aunt Astrid, who were coming around the counter.

"I can't stay," she said curtly. Her eyes bounced from Bea to Astrid to me and back again. She wasn't just nervous. She was also very, very scared.

"Brit Clegg? It's really nice to meet you. Thank you so much for coming," Bea said with her hand stretched out for Brit to shake.

The girl looked at Bea's dainty, pretty hand as if it were a claw and nervously took half a step backward.

"Honey, believe me when I tell you you are safe here," Bea said gently.

"Very safe, dear." Aunt Astrid stepped up with her hands folded neatly in front of her. "Your father was our friend. We did business with him. It was a sad day when we heard he had passed."

I studied Brit's face and could tell she was doing something I was familiar with. She was biting her tongue so she wouldn't cry. How many times had I done that when I was young, and a memory of my mother came vividly into view? When a smell or sound came out of nowhere and sent me whirling back to when I was a kid, I would ache inside even as an adult. Then I'd bite my tongue so I wouldn't cry.

The furry paw of my friend pushed through a space at the top of the box to touch my hand, and I took him to a table away from the ladies. I barely had the top open before Treacle leapt into my arms, rubbing his soft head under my chin and along my face as his claws poked into my shirt and pricked my skin. He acted as though he couldn't get close enough to me, and I hugged him back, kissing the top of his head, rocking him gently, and listening to his happy motor purring the whole while.

"I was so worried," I said in my mind, feeling tears in my eyes.

"I was so scared she was going to take me away. I couldn't talk to her. I didn't know why she had me. Then I thought I saw you, but I couldn't hear you. I was afraid."

Squeezing tighter, I held the big black ball of fur in my arms and stroked his head. *"You're going to have to lie low for a while, Treacle. Until we figure out what is going on, you're staying in the house. There are two other scaredy cats who've been worried to death over you."*

"I miss my friends."

"Well, be sure to thank Marshmallow. She was the one who found the trailer."

"How?" Treacle asked. *"How could she see it?"*

"She came with me on a whim. She could see an aura around the place that I would have never seen. You didn't see her when you peeked out the window?"

"I thought maybe the female was bringing you to me."

"Was she mean to you?"

"No. She was kind. But she is afraid of something, and that made me more afraid. And I think we should all be afraid."

I swallowed hard and looked at Brit Clegg as Aunt Astrid and Bea tried to talk to her.

Then Brit started to get loud. "I'm not staying," she said sternly. "I have to go."

"We just want to talk to you," Bea said, and I could tell she hoped to touch Brit's sleeve or hand. "You aren't in any trouble."

"Please," I said. "Let us put on some tea and fix you something to eat. We've got apple pie and some vegetarian chili and—"

"No." She looked at me sternly. "Don't let that cat out. Next time, it might not be me that gets a hold of him. Why you'd let a black cat roam around, I don't know. People don't like black cats."

I lowered Treacle back into the box. He lay down immediately, and I could tell he was exhausted.

"What do you mean?" I tried not to come across as scary or intimidating. "Treacle is a roamer. He's just a tomcat. He's been roaming the neighborhood since he was a kitten, and nothing—"

"If you love that cat"—her eyes filled with tears—"then you'll listen to me and keep him inside. Not everyone sees him the way you do." Brit grabbed the door and yanked.

"Wait!" Bea called after her. "Don't go. Please, we can help you. We know you're afraid of witches. We know there's one in Wonder Falls, and she's responsible for..." Bea couldn't bring herself to say the words. "We know she, or *he*, is responsible for what happened to your father."

Brit froze. Her body began to tremble. She looked over her shoulder at us. Tears soaked her cheeks. *"She,"* she hissed. Brit's eyes displayed the hatred she was feeling, and she clenched her teeth. "It's a she." She threw the door open and stomped out.

For a few seconds, none of us moved.

"Meow?" was the only noise that cut through the silence. I looked into the box and saw Treacle looking contentedly at me as I scratched his head. His green eyes blinked lazily, and his tail waved almost in slow motion.

"Well, that could have gone better," I said.

Witches Can Die Too

Two days had passed since Brit had returned Treacle.

The black cat seemed to be happy inside for the first time since he was a kitten. As soon as he settled in, and I knew he was home and safe, I asked Treacle what had happened.

He climbed onto my lap and stretched his arms to either side of my neck as I stroked his short black fur. He looked at me intently. *"I was across town. Something was buzzing around there,"* he told me in his mind.

"What do you mean?"

Treacle licked his nose. *"My usual felines would tell me what was going on, but I couldn't find anyone. They were all hiding. They wouldn't come out, but they peeked out from corners and shadows."*

"You didn't think maybe you should get out of there?"

"I saw the gray cat with the scar. I don't like him. We usually

fight. He seemed to know something, but he wouldn't tell me. He growled low at me as I approached him. Not his usual fighting growl but more like he was mad I was giving away his hiding place." Treacle's claws poked from soft paws as he continued his tale. *"I should have run. I should have hid like the other cats, but I didn't."*

"Oh, my poor boy," I soothed, rubbing his head behind his ears and stroking his back.

He continued his story. *"The next thing I knew, I couldn't see. Someone had covered me completely. I scratched and bit and tried to move. I screamed. I cried. But I was pulled off the ground. I was in something... a sack. I didn't have a lot of room, and I couldn't see anything. Nothing I did seemed to help. I was being carried away."*

The thought of Treacle being taken away against his will, violently, cruelly, and brought to a strange place, tore at my heart. My eyes filled with tears.

"When I was finally free of the confines, I was in a place like this," Treacle said, looking around our home.

"You were in her trailer."

"Her trailer, yes. She'd never had a cat there. She fed me and tried to pet me." Treacle scooted closer to me, so close his whiskers rubbed against my cheek as he nuzzled his head along my jaw. *"But she wasn't you."*

I scratched the back of his head and neck.

"I missed you, Cath."

"You have no idea how much I missed you, big kitty." I hugged him, letting my tears fall into his shiny black fur and disappear. *"You're home now and safe. And tomorrow, we'll go visit your*

friends Marshmallow and Peanut Butter. They've been so worried about you."

"I've missed them," he purred.

Treacle fell asleep next to me on the couch. I stretched out, putting my feet up and stuffing my favorite throw pillow behind my head. Every time I moved even slightly, it set off Treacle's purring mechanism, and he'd start buzzing happily, his eyes still closed.

I must have been more tired than I thought because I fell asleep within just a few minutes. I was so grateful Treacle was safe and sound. Brit may have been weird and scared, but she didn't hurt him. What had she wanted with him? She'd gone through a lot of trouble if all she wanted was a cat.

And I couldn't help but wonder what she meant when she said not to let that cat out because next time it might not be her who got a hold of him.

That thought rolled around in my head as I fell asleep, leading me to a terrible dream. Treacle was gone again because I'd simply left the door open, something I'd never do in the waking world. I intentionally left my home vulnerable and Aunt Astrid's, too. Marshmallow was also gone because I'd left a door open.

In the dream, I didn't tell anyone it was my own negligence that led to the animals' disappearance. I held the guilt inside and pretended nothing was wrong until something made its way into my home.

The strange creature in the dream was human-like. It had two arms, two legs, and a head, but it was shrouded in a black robe that was dirty and worn and appeared to have been buried or left in the elements for several seasons.

I couldn't be sure, but I think there were living things on it... small, ugly, writhing living things that fell onto my beige carpet along with bits of dirt and twigs. Bony, white hands were all I could see.

On the right hand was a gaudy, obscene ring with a black gemstone and a rhinestone pentagram. Had the horrific creature decided it needed a little bling to be truly terrifying so it bedazzled a cheap, imitation gemstone ring?

I stared at the ring on the monster's hand as it proceeded to crawl through my open bedroom window. It was pulling itself through in a grotesque manner that made me think of someone having a convulsion. I didn't try to stop it. I was paralyzed and could only watch as it pulled itself farther and farther into my home. Finally, it stopped its horrible jerking movements and looked at me.

Underneath its shroud was a ghostly pale face with empty, black sockets where the eyes should be. As I stared at its face, the thing laughed. It sounded like the voice of a classroom bully, a heartless child mocking another. And the voice was even more terrifying than the face because it was unnatural.

The whole thing was unnatural.

When I opened my mouth to scream, all I could hear was the hiss of a cat.

My eyes snapped open, and I felt my heart pounding. My skin was wet, and as I blinked, my familiar room came into focus. But the hissing sent my body into a spasm that jerked me clear off the couch and to my feet.

It was Treacle. He was in my bedroom. He stood stone still on the floor about two feet away from the bedroom window. Then I heard it. Scratching. In my head, I tried to remember if I had left the window open or closed the night before. I was pretty sure it was closed as I listened again.

I tiptoed to the bedroom door entrance and placed my hands on either side of the frame to steady myself. Luckily, the window was closed.

Treacle slowly arched his back. Every single strand of his jet black fur stood on edge, making him look as though he were at least ten pounds more cat than he actually was. Whatever was making those scratching noises was not supposed to be there.

The scratching was slow and long as if whoever or whatever was doing it was scraping its claw, fingers, talons, or something from the top of the window diagonally across to the opposite bottom corner.

Treacle's whiskers twitched, his eyes unblinking as a serious, mean growl came from deep inside his gut. The creature at the window was more than just a squirrel or chipmunk getting too close to Treacle's personal space. Whatever was outside was something dangerous.

"What is it, Trea?" I asked, carefully whispering with my thoughts.

"I don't know," he said, still growling. *"But it's out there, and it wants to be in here."*

We both stood perfectly still. I don't know about Treacle, but I held my breath, focusing intently on whether I could hear any other noise besides the scratching. I remembered the image from my nightmare that had snapped me awake, and I began to sweat.

It couldn't have been a premonition. I didn't have that gift. Aunt Astrid was the one who could see future possibilities, not me. My dream was probably just a collection of all the things that had been going on, right? There wasn't going to be some disgusting, eyeless form with maggots and worms on its clothes pushing through my bedroom window, right? And if there were, Aunt Astrid would have seen it already, right?

Well, she would if she were looking, but if she were distracted and looking in another direction, then who knows?

I let out my breath and felt winded. Just as I was about to take a step inside the room, Treacle bolted to the window. He was up and underneath the curtain within a split second, hissing, clawing, and scratching at the glass. Not wanting my precious pet to get hurt, I forced myself to move.

Throwing back the curtain, I watched as Treacle continued to scratch at the glass, growling and hissing. Then I looked up to where his eyes were focused and saw nothing.

Growing up in a witch's family instilled a few rules in my head that most kids probably wouldn't think twice about. One rule was that seeing wasn't always believing. Sometimes, we believed in things greater than ourselves, even though we may not have been able to see those things.

But as puny humans, we were terrified of things we couldn't see. All I could see was the little patch of green grass outside my bedroom window along with the nearby tree line.

I squinted into the foliage and saw nothing... no cluster of moving shadows outlining a human form, no eyes peering back at me, nothing. But Treacle was still going mad.

Leaning closer to the window, I pulled the curtains back to see if I was missing something.

BANG! BANG! BANG! BANG! Someone was pounding on my front door. The blows were so loud and hard that Treacle and I jumped a good foot into the air.

"Why is someone knocking like that? I have a doorbell," I said more to calm myself than to actually get an answer.

I looked at Treacle, who seemed to have calmed a little. He sniffed around the edges of the window, his eyes scanning the yard. Whatever had been out there was either gone or suddenly not so menacing. Treacle perched himself on the small ledge and stood as my sturdy and true lookout.

Tiptoeing to the front door, I had already made the decision not to answer it. No way was I was just going to pull the door open. I squatted down to see if I could make out the shadow of feet across the bottom threshold, then I stood and stretched my neck to see if a shadow could be seen pulling away from the peephole.

I saw nothing. I turned my head and listened. Then I heard a swish sound coming from beneath the door.

Treacle was at my side in an instant, hissing madly. Both of us stood there, stepping closer to see what was inching its way underneath the door.

"Should I rush the door and yank it open?" I asked out loud.

"No," Treacle said then made a dash for the bedroom again.

I swallowed hard and watched. It was paper. Just paper. A note was worming its way through the narrow slash of space between the door and my foyer floor. I'd never been so terrified as I was watching the scene unfold in front of me. It felt as if I were watching a film being run in reverse, in which rain fell upward, and people backed out of doors. Our brains were conditioned to recognize when something felt wrong.

I listened for Treacle and heard the *thump-thump* of his tail whipping on the floor as he sat studying something. I looked at the front door, half expecting it to explode inward or pulse as though it were alive. But it didn't. It remained a normal door.

"Stop being silly," I said to myself. "Whoever is dropping off notes is obviously more scared of you than you are of them."

That line of complete bologna made me feel a lot better. Sometimes, I impressed myself with my own words and how I could encourage myself. I walked up to the door, bent down, swiped up the note, and took several careful steps back, just in case.

My hands trembled. What I saw was shocking and obscene. Letters cut out of magazines formed a jagged message that looked as dangerous as the threat:

Stay away from Brit.
Witches can die, too.

The message was bad enough, but the handwritten scribbles at the bottom froze me to my core. Next to a cutout magazine picture of a black cat on a silver platter with its head separated from the body, someone had scrawled,

The cat will be mine.

Boiling Blood

Terror and anger filled me. I wasn't sure what emotion won out. I was terrified that someone knew we were looking into Marvin Clegg's death, and that the person was most likely the killer and a witch. The fact that the hag would threaten my cat made my blood boil.

Treacle snapped me out of my conflict. He was in the bedroom again, growling and scratching the glass.

"What? What is it?" I called to him.

"Outside! It's out there!"

Darting into the bedroom, I threw aside the curtains with more anger than I expected then stopped. It was a cat. I had never seen him around before. He was just sitting there, staring at us.

Normally, a cat would blink, a muscle would twitch, or its nostrils would flare as it picked up a scent. But I wasn't looking at a normal cat. The black-and-white tuxedo cat with intense green eyes *looked* like an average cat, but there was a hollowness in its eyes. Something else was there… something sinister.

I heard Treacle calling to it. He said he'd seen it before around the trailer park. The tuxedo cat would slink underneath trailers, around cars and garbage cans, and climb on top of mailboxes and makeshift fences so it could stare at Treacle when he was at Brit's. The cat never spoke to him, and it wasn't speaking to me either. It just sat there as if it were studying us.

"Treacle?"

"Yes?"

"Why did you say it's *out there?"*

"Because that's what it is. It's not a feline. It's an it.*"*

My body shook. I had the sneaking suspicion this creature could hear our thoughts and just chose not to speak.

I don't know how long Treacle and I stood there trying to stare down the creature in front of us, but the tuxedo cat seemed to become more and more menacing with each passing second.

The *ping, ping, ping* of my phone made the two of us jump. I ran into the front room, grabbed the phone quickly, and ran back to the bedroom to look out the window. It was gone.

"Where is it?" I asked Treacle, who had stayed in the bedroom.

"I don't know. I looked at you leaving the room, and when I looked back, it was gone."

I pulled the cord on the slatted blinds, letting them fall all the way to the floor then made sure the curtains were in place before answering the phone.

Bea was beside herself on the end of the line. "She threatened Jake!"

"What? Who did?" I suddenly forgot about our furry, glass-eyed visitor and sat on the edge of my bed.

"The witch. She threatened Jake. Said what happened to Marvin could easily happen to him if we didn't back off and leave Brit alone. She left a note under our front door."

My heart flipped over in my chest. "When did you get this note?" I already knew the answer.

"Just... now. Just a few seconds ago. Jake went running outside to see if he could catch the person, but there wasn't a soul in sight."

"Was there a cat around?"

Bea sniffled on the other end then I heard her stop as though she were thinking. "A cat? I don't know. Why?"

"I got a note, too. Just now. At this very moment. It said she was going to get Treacle."

Bea gasped on the other end and shouted to Jake, repeating what I had just told her. "Jake said you and Treacle need to get over here quick. He's going to go get my mom in the squad car."

"Make sure she brings Marshmallow. I don't think any of our companions are safe from this witch."

Just then, Treacle made such a loud crying noise that Bea

was able to hear it on the other end. “Cath, what’s going on over there?” Bea cried into the phone.

“Oh no.” I pressed the phone hard to my ear as the shade snapped all the way up to the ceiling, and the curtain fell to the floor. The black-and-white cat sat right in front of the glass staring inside at Treacle.

“What it sees, she knows!” Treacle hissed then snapped. He would have flown through the window and fought with everything he had if he were able. But I wasn’t going to give him the job of defending the house. That was my job.

I turned and stomped to the foyer with the phone still in my hand, grabbed an umbrella from the stand, and was about to yank open the door when I froze. “Bea?”

“Cath, what is it? Oh, talk to me. All I can hear is Treacle hissing and meowing.”

“I was about to open the door and chase this other cat away when something in me told me not to. It wants us separated. It wants my cat. Whatever this thing is wants my cat, and I don’t think it will let anything stand in its way.”

“Then you guys pack a bag and get over here.”

“Yes. Yes. We’re on our way, Bea. We’re leaving right now.”

“Okay. We’ll see you in a few minutes. If it takes any longer, I’m sending all of Wonder Falls P.D. to get you.”

“We’re already out the door.” I scooped up my keys and Treacle before I even hung up the phone.

Threats

I carried Treacle in my arms rather than a carrier. Just in case we met with any kind of trouble, I wanted him to be able to get away, to defend himself... just in case I wasn't able to. The thought sent a shiver down my back.

"I wouldn't leave you," he said. *"Not if you needed me."*

"I wouldn't leave you either, pretty kitty." I let out a deep breath. The closer I walked to Bea and Jake's place, the better I started to feel. I reached the front of their house just as Jake pulled in behind me. Aunt Astrid was in the front seat next to him holding Marshmallow.

Thank goodness she brought her cat, too. The whole family was underneath one roof, and I knew what kind of power we had together. I hoped the evil witch, wherever she was, got a good, long look at us. We weren't just a couple of teenagers dabbling in mischief.

"Hey, Cath," Jake said, getting out of the car.

I waved and walked over to help Aunt Astrid. Bea stood in the doorway, holding the door open for everyone. We set our cats down, and they quickly pranced into the door, where Peanut Butter was eagerly waiting for them.

Once we were all inside, Jake locked the door. He kissed Bea on the cheek and went upstairs.

"Where's he going?" I asked quietly.

"He's going to take a shower then go to work," Bea said. "Blake is stopping by to pick him up."

Bea looked at me oddly when she mentioned that Blake was coming by to pick up Jake, but she quickly busied herself with pouring water into a copper kettle.

I hadn't seen Blake since he spoke to me about losing his own pet. I looked at my reflection in the glass on the microwave door and smoothed my hair little.

"I think we have a real issue here, ladies." Aunt Astrid sat on a stool next to the long counter.

"Did you get a note, too?" I asked.

She nodded.

"What did it say?"

Aunt Astrid waved her hand. "Oh, not much different from you both. A lot of huff and puff. The problem is this witch thinks she knows what she's doing. She's careless and sloppy and yet has found a connection to the darkest elements that are working for her." Aunt Astrid pinched her lips together.

I helped myself to a bottle of water from Bea's fridge and

took a seat next to Aunt Astrid. "Have you told Jake any of this?" I asked carefully.

Bea and Jake had just recovered from some bumpy growing pains, and they both vowed not to keep secrets from each other anymore. Jake knew Bea was a witch, he knew she had a rare and beautiful gift of healing, and he knew witchcraft ran in her family. But I wasn't sure he was ready to know we suspected the death of Marvin Clegg to be murder, not just a heart attack.

"Yes. I told him about Levi, the morgue, and Brit and Treacle. He grumbled at first." Bea placed the kettle on the stove. "But he said as long as none of us were breaking the law, he wasn't worried. However, this note changes things." She folded her arms across her chest.

"Brit Clegg knows who this is, but she isn't going to tell us." I took a long drink from my water bottle. "At least not without some serious coaxing, and even then, I don't think she'd crack."

I looked over to the sitting area of the kitchen and saw Peanut Butter, Marshmallow, and Treacle lying close to each other, their eyes narrow slits, their breathing slow and calm, and their tails waving lazily. Peanut Butter kept touching Treacle with his paw every couple of minutes, wanting to make sure Treacle was still there. I could hear them talking. They were discussing the tuxedo cat that had been staring at Treacle through the window. Just the thought of that *thing* sent a shiver up my spine.

"Did Jake offer any advice?" Aunt Astrid asked. "A fresh set of eyes on this might be just what we need."

"Actually, his advice was that if Levi started all this, maybe he should be the one to handle it."

"I'm all for passing this off onto some unsuspecting schlub to deal with. Exploding hearts, death threats, cat-napping... count me out." I stood and went to look in Bea's cupboards for a snack.

"That isn't a bad idea," Aunt Astrid said, standing and grabbing her big purse from the floor where she'd dropped it.

The lovely, vintage carpetbag purse was similar to the one Mary Poppins had carried. And just like Mary Poppins, Aunt Astrid could pull dozens and dozens of oddly shaped items of all sizes out of her purse. Right then, she pulled out her all-purpose spell book. Doctors referred to the Merck Manual to look up lists of symptoms that helped them narrow down the cause of an ailment. Aunt Astrid could sort of do the same with her lofty tome.

"You're kidding, right?" I asked. "You're not going to hand this over to Levi. He doesn't even know he's a medium, let alone know how to do battle with a black witch who got her witchcraft degree off the back of a matchbook."

I shoveled some salt-free, gluten-free pretzels into my mouth then grimaced and spat them into the garbage. "Don't you have any real food?"

"There's one thing you're all missing," said Jake's deep voice from the hallway.

He was standing there dressed in a nice pair of dark gray

slacks and a white button-down shirt. He walked behind Bea, gave her a playful pinch on the butt as he passed, then opened the cupboard, reaching up where I couldn't see. "This person sent you all threats. She had to take the time to cut out the letters and glue them down."

He pulled out a bag of Doritos, full of salt and fat and all the things I loved, and handed them to me with a wink.

"So that proves she knows where we all live." Bea shook her head at Jake's stash.

"Right," Jake agreed. "So if she was so good at what she supposedly can do, making hearts explode and whatnot, why couldn't she have done it to you guys? It would have looked like nothing more than a freakish coincidence."

The doorbell chimed a happy little ding-dong, and Jake went to answer it.

"Check the peephole!" Bea yelled to him before he opened the door. He did just that then yelled back to us that it was all clear. After he opened the door, I heard him say hello to Blake.

When Blake came into the kitchen, he nodded at Aunt Astrid and Bea. Once again, I got the royal treatment... a judgmental once-over. I blinked in an attempt to hide how I rolled my eyes in annoyance then shoved a couple of Doritos into my mouth.

"Hello, Detective," Aunt Astrid said, closing her book and reaching her hand out to shake. "It's nice to see you again."

"You as well, Mrs. Greenstone. Looks like you're doing

some heavy reading there." He nodded at her spell book but didn't look very closely at it.

"Just a book of family recipes. Trying to help Cath learn how to cook." She smiled happily at the detective. I was shocked when I saw the right side of his mouth curl up a little.

"Well, good luck." He was probably completely unaware that his reply was totally obnoxious. Not that it mattered. His response made Bea and Aunt Astrid laugh.

"I know how to cook," I mumbled. Turning around, I tossed the Doritos bag back up on the shelf for Jake.

"You boys be careful out there tonight. Extra careful," Bea said, pulling on Jake's strong arm until he bent down far enough for her to kiss his cheek.

"Don't worry. We'll be fine." Both men left, talking about some sporting event or news story they'd heard as if tonight were no different from any other night.

Bea let out a big sigh and drummed her fingers on the counter. Finally, she turned on the stove, and within minutes, the teapot was whistling happily.

She had already prepared two cups, knowing I didn't drink tea, and poured the hot liquid over the little mesh bags. I hated to admit it, but it smelled wonderful... mint and lemon and something else I couldn't place. But I knew if I tasted the tea, it would be the same old hot water taste I always disliked.

"I don't understand how that man can be so calm when his life has been threatened. I'm a nervous wreck," Bea said.

Aunt Astrid patted her hand. "I cast a quick spell of

protection over him in the car on the way over. He just thought I had a sneezing fit. It should get him through tonight's work all right. I am still not convinced this person we're dealing with really knows what she's doing."

"So, what should we do?" I asked.

"Well, Jake is right." Aunt Astrid casually leafed through her book of spells. "If this woman knew her stuff, why didn't she just use her magic? Instead, she resorted to scare tactics and threatening letters. It doesn't quite make sense."

"So what are you looking for?" I asked, peeking over my aunt's shoulder as she flipped through her book.

"I don't know yet, but I think a little extra protection for us and our feline friends is definitely in order."

Aunt Astrid hopped off her stool, reached into her bag, and pulled out some sage, a book of matches, and a black lace fan. Conducting a smudging ritual was easy and very effective in keeping away the spiritual creepy crawlies. Similar to how hedge apples kept spiders away, smudging filled a place with positive barriers. The ritual ensured all the juicy goodness stayed inside, while the evil parasites were left to starve from lack of energy on the outside.

Aunt Astrid lit the sage, a candle for Bea, and one for me. We followed her through the house as she fanned the pleasant-smelling herb into every room, into every corner of the floors and ceilings, around every window and door, until finally, the whole house felt light and airy.

The cats continued their vigil of lying and stretching across the carpet, bounding from chair to chair, and taking short naps. Every once in a while, I would catch Treacle looking out the sliding glass door into the yard. His fur never rose, but I could tell staying cooped up inside was starting to get to him.

He was a roamer, an alley cat deep down, and he longed for the freedom that came with chasing down mice, climbing fences, investigating strange parts of town, and talking with other felines. Even the occasional fight was in his blood. Watching him look outside, hearing him take a deep breath then letting it out listlessly, broke my heart.

It was one thing for someone to go after people. We've been screwing up our own lives since man first began to walk upright and utter the word "no." But to go after an animal that only longed to do what it was created to do? A person who would do that was a certain kind of evil for which there were no words.

Levi

We had to find out who was behind all this. And as if those words had made a complete circle through the cosmos, we were all pleasantly surprised the next day to see Levi Cummings walk through the door of the café.

Aunt Astrid and I had spent the night at Bea's house. Jake preferred being at the station at night until early morning and apparently, so did Blake.

Bea had tried to tell me that Blake Samberg was really a very pleasant fellow. He was alone, no family to speak of, very intelligent, and not one to throw around his emotions as if he might need them for an emergency later. He liked to read and think about things very intently.

Bea and Jake had had him over for dinner a couple of times. It was a custom among those who worked in the police department to do that sort of thing to get to know one another. They were, in a way, responsible for each other, so spending time together helped develop that weird bond so many cops had. The bond often didn't just save their lives but their sanity as well.

Like a caravan of gypsies, Aunt Astrid, Bea, and I traveled to the café, leaving the cats at home all together. There was strength in numbers for us as well as for them. We had stayed up late talking and going over everything we knew to see if there was anything we'd missed.

Aunt Astrid tried to use the threats we'd each received to locate the person who sent them, to get a name, a face, or anything that might be helpful. But the psychic energy around the messages was so messy and disorganized, it was like trying to read poetry written by a five-year-old.

I talked with Treacle to see if he remembered anything from being at Brit's house that might help us. But there was nothing.

We felt like we'd hit a dead end, that is, until we saw Levi saunter in. Aunt Astrid was at his side almost immediately.

"Well, hello, Levi. How are you feeling?" she asked in her most innocent and disarming matronly voice.

"Hi, Mrs. Greenstone. I'm doing just fine." He smiled down at her.

"We were a little worried about you the last time you paid us a visit."

He shook his head, and seemed a little embarrassed. "It must have been something I ate. Not here, of course." He quickly tried to cover up his misstatement. "I mean, whatever it was just sort of snuck up on me. But I'll tell you what... after I got home, my head was clearer than it's ever been. Not sure if the two are related or not, but I'm feeling good."

"Well, that is good to hear. What can we get you?" Aunt Astrid asked.

"You know, I don't know what it is, but I have been trying to get here for the past couple of days, and my schedules and traffic and construction have all seemed to have been pointing me in another direction. I have had such a craving for your tea with the lavender-infused honey that I just said if I do nothing else today, I'm getting that tea."

Aunt Astrid hid the worry on her face. "Absolutely. Cath, would you get Levi a tea with honey while I sit and have a chat with him?"

"One specialty tea with special honey coming right up," I said, also aware of the game being played on Levi.

"The forces are working against him," Bea said. "He's been trying to get here, but something always prevented it. Here, give me that tea bag."

I handed Bea the little mesh baggie that smelled like apples, oranges, spice, mint, and some other soothing scents I didn't recognize. Bea pulled it open, and with a few waves of her hand, added some special guidance to the herbs so Levi would find his way safely to his next destination.

Aunt Astrid led Levi to the back table where she had first tried to perform her psychic reading on him. They sat back there for a little while. Bea and I didn't hear any shouting or arguing or anything. We assumed that was good.

About ten minutes passed. Levi's tea was steaming hot and ready. Finally, he came strolling up to the counter, looking as fit as a fiddle and quite in control of his faculties. He gave us both a cheery good-bye as he scooped up his tea and left the café.

"That was weird," I said. "Last time, he was nearly carried out on a stretcher. This time, he skips out of here like a guy who just won the lottery."

Bea swallowed hard and went back to check on her mother. Aunt Astrid had not followed Levi to the front of the store. I waited on a few customers. The rush hour was coming to an end, and still neither Bea nor Aunt Astrid had come to the front. Finally, there was a break in the customers, and I scooted back to the round table in the cubby to see my aunt pale and shaking.

"There's going to be another murder," Aunt Astrid said.

Spiritual Informant

Before Aunt Astrid could say anything else, we were called back to actually *work* at the café. A study group of about sixteen young people came in all at once. They each wanted something different, and they took up just about every seat in the café. Once they left, the lunchtime rush came in.

As soon as things started to slow down, Min and Amalia paid us a visit, which was a refreshing and much-needed break from all the talk of mediums and murder. After they left, our after-work and evening crowd came in a steady stream until finally we turned around the CLOSED sign and locked the door.

Before I could speak, I saw a strange movement outside the big window. I stepped a little closer and peered through the glass. I had to cup my hands around my eyes to cut down on the glare, then I saw a cat crossing the street. It froze for a second and looked my way. Then it darted into the shadows.

"*What it sees, she knows!*" I heard Treacle's warning in my head. I couldn't be sure it was the same tuxedo cat that had been at my house, but none of us were willing to take any chances. We all retreated to the safety of Bea's house.

"So, did Levi say who will get murdered?" I rocked slowly in the big swing on Bea's front porch. "Maybe give us directions to their house? Maybe tell us the name of the killer, too?"

Aunt Astrid sat in the wide-backed, wicker chair, staring into space but seeing something neither Bea nor I could. Bea stood across from me, leaning on the white banister that outlined her entire porch.

Aunt Astrid was obviously amazed by Levi's channeling ability, but she couldn't tell him about his particular gift. She didn't feel as if it were her place, plus it would open up the possibility that he could discover the true heritage of the Greenstone women. My aunt was not willing to risk our secret.

"It was as if someone had flipped a switch," she said, shaking her head in amazement. "He was completely unaware of the transition. It was seamless. One minute, he was smiling, plain old Levi Cummings, and the next..." She swallowed hard. "It just began. Whatever was communicating through him was just waiting, as though it knew it was in the spotlight."

She then described an experience I didn't think I'd ever

want to encounter. I certainly didn't want to sit across the table, face-to-face, with whatever had become our informant.

Levi had taken his seat, and the second Aunt Astrid reached out to pat his hand, he gasped. He sucked in a great gulp of air as if he were afraid he might not get another one, and his eyes rolled over white. The corners of his mouth contorted into a vicious grimace, and he leaned in close to Aunt Astrid.

He was so close, she could not only feel his hot breath in her face, but she could hear the echoes from the dimension in which the entity was poking through. She heard other sounds, too... clicks, buzzes, and whispers from unseen spirits that may have hoped to tell their own tales.

"It's going to happen again," Levi said—well, not Levi, but our spirit informant. "All those cars driving by, and no one sees. It will happen again."

"What will happen again?" Aunt Astrid asked.

Levi's body began to jerk back and forth just enough to be unsettling. Something laughed through Levi, but the laugh sounded more like a hiss.

"Death. It surrounds her. She summons it, and it will burst through like it did before. And she wants that cat!"

"Wait!" I said, interrupting the story. "He said that? He said this person wants Treacle? What for?" My eyes brimmed with tears. I had never worried about Treacle before. Letting him out to roam was part of our routine. It was innocent, and we trusted each other, but someone was trying to ruin that. Treacle would go crazy if I kept him inside all the time. How dare someone do that to us? How dare she.

When Aunt Astrid nodded, Bea quickly came to my side and slipped her arm around my shoulder. We listened to the rest of my aunt's story.

"I asked it *who*. I asked it to tell me who was going to die. Who was going to be put through this agony?" She brushed her hair from her face and looked out onto the darkening street, which was quiet and peaceful. "All it would say was that the daughter knows. And that she was going to suffer for it."

"She'll do it again," Levi had jeered. "She'll keep doing it. She doesn't know how to stop, and she won't even try."

"And that was the end of it. Levi's face became his soft, unassuming self, and his eyes were back seeing this world and not clouded by the other's visions. The poor boy asked me what I'd been talking about as his mind seemed to have just drifted off on its own for a second."

"So, when are we going to Brit's place?" Bea asked, standing from the swing and brushing off her pants.

"Yeah, I'm ready now if you ladies are." I pushed myself off the seat with a grunt. Bea always was the more ladylike of the two of us.

"I agree, Cath." Aunt Astrid smoothed out her gypsy-style skirt. She looked like a fortuneteller, exotic and mysterious. You'd never guess she could fling you across the room with the wave of her hand and a few chosen words if she absolutely had to.

"Mom, maybe you should sit this one out. It's going to be

a mess, I can just tell. From what Cath described and what I have seen so far, I have the feeling the psychic backwash is going to be darn near revolting. And—"

"I was thinking the same thing, Bea, honey, but about you."

"Me? What for? I can help."

"Of course you can, my dear. But the facts are that Cath knows how to get there, and I'm the only one here with the strength to combat those witches' vials. If she made them correctly, and from the sound of it, she has, then neither one of you would be strong enough to get past them. Plus,"—she stepped up to her daughter and cupped Bea's chin in her hand —"if anything happens to Jake, you have to be here, and the cats must also remain here."

"Won't you please take care of Treacle? Make sure he doesn't get out or that anyone gets a hold of him?" My gut felt tight when I asked Bea to do that for me. On one hand, I worried about Treacle. On the other hand, I worried about myself. Those witches' vials knocked me out, and I was not looking forward to encountering them again.

Skala

❧

With much trepidation, Aunt Astrid and I made our way to the trailer park, but this time, we drove through the main entrance.

We weren't there to skulk around in the shadows or sneak up on Brit. We were there to find out what we were dealing with. There was no time to play games.

The trailer park was dark, and crickets kept up their vigil in the nearby woods. Moths and June bugs circled lazily around the fluorescent lights, which gave off a queasy green light matching my complexion at the moment.

"I can feel it already." Aunt Astrid pointed in the direction I needed to follow. "This poor girl is terrified. I can sense it. The vials were put together very well. Why didn't she let us help her sooner?"

I remained quiet. The nausea and sweats were getting worse with each inch we rolled down the gravel drive. It felt as though a cold, clammy fog had seeped deep into my body, all the way to the bone, until even the slightest movement made me want to vomit.

"That's the place," I said, feeling dry heaves race up my throat. I pointed to the little trailer with all the bottles around it. The curtains were drawn, and the car I had seen Brit pull up in was parked next to it. The broom was also lying across the threshold.

"You wait here." Aunt Astrid, who normally maneuvered slowly and purposefully, picking her way through simultaneous dimensions, was walking quickly and nervously, like someone who was late for an appointment.

I nodded and kept my eyes open in little slits, hoping nothing would ambush us. I was in no condition to fight off a mosquito, let alone an attack from anyone.

If I closed my eyes, the entire world tipped over, flipping me violently around like a ping-pong ball on ocean waves. But when I opened my eyes, everything spun quickly, as if the Earth's rotation had sped up a thousand times its normal speed. If I even slightly turned my head, I was afraid I'd heave all over the inside of my car.

Looking around suspiciously, Aunt Astrid waved her arms. Within an instant, a floral-patterned sheet and a tattered pink towel flew like exotic birds from a neighbor's clothesline and gently landed over the vials on the stairs. The little jars set all around the trailer, but covering just those few made a big enough difference that I was at least able to open my eyes.

Without hesitation, Aunt Astrid picked up the broom and

tossed it over the stairs. The broom must have done something to her hand because I could see her shaking it and rubbing it against the back of her skirt as she knocked on the door with her other hand.

When the door opened, I could hear Brit yell. "Oh, no! Does she have her cat?"

My aunt tried to settle Brit down, but the girl shook off my aunt's gesture and continued to cuss and shout. "You've got ten seconds to get off my property before I call the police!"

I rolled my eyes. Our visit was not going well.

"No!" Brit said. As Aunt Astrid calmly talked to her in a low voice, I could hear her say "no" again. A "yes" that was much quieter. A "maybe." An "I don't think so."

Finally, I heard the mumbling of a halfway civil conversation. Aunt Astrid said something quiet to calm her down that I couldn't make out, and after a few seconds, Aunt Astrid waved for me to come up to the trailer.

I climbed out of the car, still feeling nauseated as I inched my way up the wooden steps to the front door.

After following my aunt inside, I closed the door tightly behind me. Brit walked past me, slipping the chain lock into place then peeking outside as if she were expecting to see someone else peering back at her.

I took a deep breath. The place smelled like vanilla, and I noticed two little votive candles burning on either side of a picture. The photograph was that of a very young Marvin Clegg and the young woman who had been his wife. The picture was lovely, and I would remember it later, but at the moment, the sickeningly sweet smell of the candles was making my stomach fold over onto itself.

"Can I offer you guys some coffee or maybe a glass of water?" Brit sounded much calmer, nicer, to my surprise. Aunt Astrid could work wonders on people.

"I'd like water," I said, shocked at the weakness of my own voice.

My Aunt Astrid looked at me sternly as if to say, "Just hold on."

We were there to get information then get out. It seemed odd that my aunt had focused on me as if she had just seen me. I had never seen that look from her, and it was a little unnerving, like seeing someone who'd had long hair all her life suddenly show up with her head shaved... still the same person yet not.

Brit went into the little kitchenette, grabbed a bottle of water from her fridge, and quickly handed it to me.

Twisting off the cap, I took a quick, cold sip and felt a little better. Holding the cold bottle to my forehead, I followed them into the sitting area.

"Are you all right?" Brit asked, looking me up and down with what I could only perceive as reluctant concern.

"Yeah, um... I think it was just something I ate. I'll be fine." I tried to brighten, smiling and nodding as I spoke.

"Brit, we don't want to take up too much of your time but... well, we need your help," Aunt Astrid said.

"I can't help you." Brit sat down on the edge of a rose-colored recliner. She looked around at the windows, stood, peeked out between them, then pulled the curtains tightly shut. She took her seat again on the edge of the chair.

"What are you looking for?" Aunt Astrid asked. "Are you expecting someone?"

Brit looked at us as if we had lobsters coming out of our ears. "Don't pretend you don't know she's out there."

"Who?" Aunt Astrid asked.

"Look, you said you needed to tell me something important. You said it had to do with my father and that you knew his heart attack wasn't... natural."

"You're afraid of something, Brit. Please, tell us what, or who?" My aunt took a seat on the edge of the couch closest to Brit and stretched out her hand to touch Brit's gently.

Brit swallowed, and tears filled her eyes. She stood up and walked to the door. For a second, I was sure she was going to rip off the chain, yank it open, and tell us not to let it hit us on our backsides on the way out. But she didn't. She peeked out the peephole then turned to face us, rubbing her hands together.

"She's constantly loitering around, and if it isn't her, it's her disgusting toady." Brit's voice was a harsh whisper. "I tried to like her. I tried to be nice to her, but something is wrong. Really wrong." Brit tapped her temple, her voice still low and raspy.

Aunt Astrid straightened her back and spoke low but confidently. "Brit, my daughter Bea's husband works for the police department. He's a detective and was at your father's house after you had called for help."

"Was he the really good-looking guy? Detective Samberg?" Brit asked, her eyes tired but twinkling a little.

I couldn't help but cough as a little water went down the wrong pipe when she mentioned Samberg as the really good-looking guy. I suppose Blake could be kind of handsome, in a brooding, pensive sort of way. He had the ability to look at a person and make them feel as if they were the only person in the room, and that could be quite terrifying if you were being interrogated for murder.

"No. Detective Jake Williams," Aunt Astrid said.

Brit nodded but didn't say anything more.

"Brit, he said he saw writing on the walls, symbols and weird letters. His gut told him there was more to the story than you were letting on. But he didn't have any proof, so the case was ruled natural causes and closed. But it wasn't natural, was it, Brit?"

Her eyes filled with tears. She shook her head.

"Can you tell us what you think is going on? Who did you try to be nice to?" I asked, my curiosity overcoming the nausea.

"That writing isn't on the walls anymore." Brit looked down at the carpet as if she were seeing her father's house in her mind. "It fades away. I don't know what it says. I think she just does it to mess with people."

"Who?" I was nearly begging. I wanted a name and preferably an address, then I wanted to get out of there and start feeling better. Aunt Astrid seemed totally unfazed.

Brit crossed the room, pulled back the long, heavy curtains, and peeked out the sliding glass door. I noticed a line of white along the floor. She had poured salt there.

"This is what I do. I don't have any schedule because she'll see me, and I don't want her to know I'll be at any certain place at any certain time. So every day is different. Every day is confusing and messy. I can't even get into the house I grew up in to tie up the loose ends because she'll eventually come by."

Wiping her eyes as she spoke, Brit seemed to have transformed from the woman who stole my cat into a girl who was alone in the world.

Aunt Astrid produced a beautiful lace handkerchief from her purse and handed it to Brit.

"This is so pretty." Brit said with a little smile. "I don't want to ruin it."

She tried to hand it back, but my aunt shook her head. "It's okay, honey. I've got hundreds of them."

Whatever was in those eight words was enough to break the wall Brit had built around herself. She broke down and sobbed.

"I miss him so much. I didn't even get a chance to say goodbye. It didn't have to happen. She did this. I don't care what the police say, or what the funeral home says, or what you people say! She killed him! And now, she's coming after me! And I'm all alone!"

Aunt Astrid pursed her lips together and took hold of Brit's hand. "You are not alone, Brit. Please, tell me her name."

Brit looked at Aunt Astrid then at me as if she suddenly realized we were in the room. Swallowing hard, she spoke barely over a whisper. "Jennifer Skala. That is her name."

High Priestess

Neither my aunt nor myself had heard the woman's name before.

"My father said he knew her from years back before he met my mother," Brit said. "He said they had gone on a couple of dates, but that she was always a little too clingy, you know? The kind of girl who always had to be told she was pretty. We've all met that kind."

Images of Darla Castellan flipping her hair at the café and getting that poor schmuck she'd just met to carry her bags popped into my head. Yes, Brit. We had all met that kind. I felt my stomach grind over on itself at the thought of my own high school nemesis.

"So, she showed up again at my school a few years after my mother had passed away. She came up to me and asked if I was Marvin Clegg's daughter. She made it sound like they had kept in touch over the years. I talked with her on the phone. I went to lunch with her. She told me about places she had gone and things she had done and that she was a high priestess in some Wiccan group. I don't know. I just laughed it off." Brit wiped her nose and stared at the carpet.

"What did your father do when you told him you were talking with her?" I asked.

Brit chewed her bottom lip. "He didn't seem to mind at first. He told me she was a little on the crazy side when he knew her, but that she had probably mellowed by now. I liked her, sort of. We'd go shopping sometimes, and she'd ask me all about him. When I look back on it, I don't know why I didn't see it before. But she was really intrusive, you know?"

Still sweating and hoping my stomach would hold still if I did, I slowly leaned in a little closer as Brit continued her tale.

"She wanted to know if my father was dating. She wanted to know if I thought he'd like her to visit. And she was always asking me to tell him stuff like she had her boobs done and that she wasn't seeing anyone and had never been married. How could I have missed all this? I just repeated it all to my father like a parrot. I don't even know what I was hoping for. I didn't want my father to date this woman. But yet, I kept doing what she said."

"It's not your fault, Brit. Some people can be very persuasive, manipulative," Aunt Astrid said seriously. "Good-hearted people often have to learn the hard way how to spot these kinds of people." My aunt's face was getting angrier by the minute from the story she was hearing.

"Well, I decided to stop talking to her when I caught her with Lucas."

"Who is that?" I murmured, quickly sipping a little more water.

"I don't know what their official story is, but not long after I started communicating with Jennifer on a regular basis, I saw this guy with her all the time. He was a weird, gothic dude in his late forties. Too old to be wearing eyeliner, that's for sure. How cliché."

I rolled my eyes, thinking the exact same thing.

"He started coming with us to lunch or shopping. It was just plain creepy. Sometimes, when he thought I wasn't looking, I'd catch him staring at me. He looked at me like I was a steak on a platter." Brit shivered as she spoke.

"Did he speak to you?" I asked.

"No." Brit straightened up in her chair. "He'd mumble and whisper things to Jennifer but never directly to me. I thought... and this is totally gross, but I thought they were swingers or something and were sizing my dad up for something weird. Now, I only wish they were just pervy instead of..." She started to cry again.

"What happened between her and your father?" Aunt Astrid asked, trying to keep Brit going with her story.

"Jennifer showed up at my apartment by the school. I had never given her my address. I always met her somewhere. She had my phone number, but that was all. And she started calling me first thing when I got up and a couple times a night after I got home from school and work. When she showed up all dressed in black, with bright red nails and lipstick, and her hair all wild and hanging down her back, I told her no way. She looked ridiculous. Like she was dressed up for Halloween a couple months early. And Lucas was just as bad. I honestly didn't want to be seen with them."

Brit stood and peeked out the peephole of her front door.

"Jennifer said it was time she paid my father a visit. That she had been wanting to see him for such a long time. That he was this great guy she never forgot. Blah, blah, blah. I told her to do what she wanted. I was getting tired of her. She begged me to go with her to see him, but I said no." As Brit sat back down again, she clenched her hands into fists. Her voice dropped to an angry drone. "That was when she told me she wasn't just a Wiccan high priestess. She started going on and on about being some divine messenger, untouchable, a super-powerful, centuries-old witch. It was just crazy talk."

"Oh, Brit, you poor thing." My aunt was very upset. Those kinds of people were horrors to her because the Greenstones worked so hard to dispel that kind of thinking.

"She told me that my father and I had been chosen to be her new family. And we'd be powerful and feared and all this other crazy stuff that I couldn't believe I was hearing. Who talks like this?"

I shook my head in disbelief.

"So I told her that sounded insane, but if she wanted to see my father, I couldn't stop her. So off she went in her Elvira Mistress of the Night gown and tacky jewelry with Lucas strutting along behind her like the guy who scoops poop up behind an elephant in those old cartoons."

Despite my queasiness, I let out a chuckle.

"You know what I'm talking about?" Brit asked, looking at me with the first sign of joy I'd seen on her face since we met. I nodded, and even she had to chuckle.

"Of course, I called my dad to warn him," she continued. "He said not to worry, and that he'd deal with her. He said she was always a little weird. He told me that part of the reason he couldn't continue dating her was that aside from her insane insecurities, she started playing with Ouija boards, reading all kinds of stuff on the occult. I mean, if you knew my dad, you'd know this wasn't his style."

Brit's eyes shot to her father's picture on the little altar with the burning vanilla votive candles. "We're just plain people. He went to church. He liked to play solitaire and watch old cowboy movies and make candy. That was about it. Nothing fancy. Nothing weird. He was just my dad. And when he shot her down, when he refused her... she went insane."

"When did this happen? When did she go and see your father for the first time?" I asked, wishing I could just go outside and kick all those vials far away from me.

"Maybe six months ago. From then on, she kept driving by his house. She'd leave notes at his door, but when my dad would try and show them to me, the writing would disappear right in front of us. He said he'd seen her parked across the street from the candy store. She'd peek at him around corners if he were grocery shopping or going for coffee. I told him I didn't like any of it, but he said it was just to get attention. If he ignored her long enough, he thought she'd get bored and leave."

"But she never did," my aunt said.

Brit shook her head. "It made her madder. One time, I came home from school to stay with Dad for the weekend and found her sneaking around my father's house. She was putting weird dried things around and strange trinkets and crystals. When I looked it up online, I found out that those things were supposed to start a fire if a person said some kind of chant. I told my dad, but he said he didn't believe in that stuff, so it couldn't hurt him."

"What did she do when she saw you?" I asked, wiping sweat from my forehead.

"She looked at me and walked slowly back to her car then sped off." Brit took a deep breath. "I should have called the cops so there would at least be a record. But Dad said no. Then I saw her doing the same kind of thing around his shop. When I stayed overnight at my dad's house, which became more and more frequent, I'd hear things outside. I'd hear footsteps and mumbling and laughing. And then the cats started to show up."

"Is that why you took Treacle?" I asked.

"Treacle? Is that your cat's name? That's pretty. I was calling him kitty when I had him." She looked up at me as if she were ashamed of herself. "I am so sorry about that. I love animals. I do. But with her doing all the things she was doing, claiming to be a witch or priestess or whatever she thought she was, I started doing some research and, well, a black cat can be a lucky talisman for someone like me. It can also be quite a power shot for someone like her. Because I believe she is a witch. You can go ahead and think I'm crazy but..."

With trembling hands, Brit pulled her hair away from her face and let out a deep sigh. "Jennifer Skala is evil. She's got a blackness around her, and she's made friends with it. I've seen it. It peeks at me from around corners and knocks on my door and rattles the windows at night. It would at my father's house, too. That was why I was looking at getting him into a community. I thought with people around, cameras, a security guard, and a few trinkets planted around, I could keep him safe. It was a long shot, but I was desperate. I just wanted the old man safe, you know? Turns out he had nowhere to run to even if he did want to go."

It seemed as if getting this story out, even to two relative strangers, was helping Brit. She leaned back in her chair. "So the cats started showing up. They'd stare at the house and watch my father and I as we came and went. They'd be sitting outside the candy shop. They'd be at the library. They'd show up if we went to McDonald's or did the grocery shopping. They'd show up here and stare at the trailer. Sometimes, they'd howl and fight. Have you ever heard cats fighting? It's a very unnerving sound. The things were everywhere, and the saddest part was I don't think they wanted to be doing what they were doing."

"What makes you say that?" Aunt Astrid asked before I could.

"Normal cats study people. These cats seemed to have a begging quality behind their eyes. Such independent animals should never be forced to sit still. And that's what she was making them do. I believe she was making them do this. Jeez, I sound like I'm off my rocker, but it's true.

"The cats kept showing up, and they'd get skinnier and skinnier, like whatever she was doing didn't allow them to eat. Then one day, one of them would be gone, and another one would have taken its place until it got too skinny and disappeared. And sometimes, I'd see Jennifer peeking around the other trailers, staring at the black cat. Your Treacle.

"I would be inside, scared to death that she'd come break in. She'd talk to herself or to Lucas, saying things like 'I want that cat' or 'that cat will be mine.' Every couple of days, once she knew I had him, she was sneaking around. I don't know if the vials really work, or if she's just cowardly, but after I put them out and poured salt, she had to keep her distance. That was all after my father died. My father who never had a health problem in his life dies of a sudden heart attack."

"Where is your bathroom?" I asked desperately. I'd like to say I held my own and just needed to splash some cold water on my face.

Brit pointed behind her, and I dashed off, slamming the door behind me. The power of the witches' vials, compounded by Brit's tale, was getting to me. The horrible abuse being inflicted on cats—the creatures witches considered valuable and powerful companions— was too much for me to bear.

I'm not sure how long I was in the bathroom. My mind kept saying 'get up, they're waiting for you,' but my body said 'don't try to move, or you'll regret it.' I moved. I regretted it. But I managed to pull the door open and step back into the living room.

My aunt stood up and came to me. "You poor dear," she whispered, pushing my hair away from my sweaty face. "We're almost done." She turned to Brit, who was also standing and wringing her hands nervously.

"Brit, do you have any idea where Jennifer is staying?" Aunt Astrid asked.

She shook her head. Suddenly, her eyes popped wide. "No, I don't know where she's staying, but I've got a picture of her I can show you. I took it on my phone just so she'd know I saw her. I also read I might be able to stop her by using a picture and a spell and, well... it can't hurt, right?" She pulled her phone from her pocket and showed us the picture.

"If she's sneaking around," I said with slightly slurred words, "why haven't you told the police?"

Brit rolled her eyes. "What would I tell them? This woman says she's a witch? She killed my dad with her witchy powers, and now she's after me?"

Aunt Astrid shook her head then took Brit's hands. "You have no idea how much you've helped us, Brit. Your father would be very proud of you." Aunt Astrid hugged the girl then let go, took my hand, and began heading toward the door.

"I don't mean to be rude, but what do you guys think you can do against her?" Brit asked. "I think she *is* a witch. I think she can hurt people without touching them, and I think she likes doing it. I'd suggest getting some witches' vials and salt for your homes. Because if she didn't know you've been here before, she knows you've been here now."

"Oh, uh, like I said, my daughter's husband is a detective," my aunt said quickly. "We might be able to help."

Brit peeked through the peephole, and after deciding the coast was clear, opened the door. The cool night air felt great, and I inhaled it deeply.

"I am sorry I took your cat," Brit said. "But please, guard him with your life. At the risk of sounding even crazier, don't let her get her hands on him. She'll use him up and then kill him."

My body shivered at the thought. "I won't. I promise." I hobbled weakly down the wooden steps. Before I could turn around, Brit had the door closed, and I heard the lock slip back into place.

"Do you need me to drive?" my aunt asked as I limped pitifully to the car.

"No. No. I can do it. You better uncover her jars. From the sound of it, she needs them. They work quite well... at least, on me they do. They didn't seem to have any effect on you."

My aunt waved her arms and sent the sheet and towel back to their places on the neighbor's clothesline. Once both of us were in the car, she spoke. "I couldn't see."

"What?" I gasped. "What are you talking about?"

"I couldn't see, couldn't see a thing but a few shadows and

shapes moving around the room. Those vials took away my vision. I couldn't see the past, the future, another dimension, or even this one."

"You sounded different." My legs felt stronger as we drove away, but my head was pounding.

"It was the first time in my life that I didn't see a dozen things taking place at the same time. The first time I was almost like everyone else. I enjoyed it. The simplicity of it." She turned her head and smiled at me.

"Well, it made me puke, literally. I didn't enjoy it."

Aunt Astrid patted my arm, and as we got to the road that led back to Bea's place, we were both feeling much better. But Bea had been correct—the psychic backwash we were going to swallow was going to be hell to pay tomorrow.

Walona Motel

As soon as I pulled the car into Bea's driveway, she came running out of the house, slamming the door shut behind her. She was waving and shouting, and her eyes were wild. My first thought was that something had happened to Jake or Blake.

"You won't believe this!" she called before the car was even in park. "Hurry! Hurry!"

"What?" I asked, a little annoyed due to my upset tummy.

"Jake called."

"Yeah, and?" I got out of the car and slowly walked toward the house with Aunt Astrid at my side.

"He reported to a scene at the Walona Motel."

"Eww, gross. He was just over there the other day. That place right by the expressway, right? Do I want to hear this? The Walona isn't exactly known for high-profile celebrity clientele, I hear."

"Right?" Bea nodded in agreement. "But Jake said there was a woman there answering questions about the noises she'd heard in the room next to hers. Apparently, the man there was dealing with some shady people, had a big argument, and then bingo—this woman said he had a heart attack."

"So? Maybe this person just had a good old-fashioned heart attack," I said with about as much tact as a porcupine in a room full of balloons.

"And what makes her so special that Jake had to call you?" Aunt Astrid asked.

"He thought that he was being funny when he said she was dressed all in black. She had this whole gothic theme going on, including wearing a pentagram in rhinestones on a big, gaudy ring. He wanted to know if I'd like him to introduce us, you know, like a joke. If we wanted to add anyone to the coven, are his exact words. He thinks he's so clever. I told him... Cath, what's the matter?"

My heart stopped beating, and for a split second, I thought I was going to have a heart attack myself.

"Did you say a ring with a rhinestone pentagram on it?"

Bea repeated herself and described the woman as Jake told her. Aunt Astrid and I agreed that it had to be the woman Brit had shown us a picture of, complete with that ring of horror and tackiness from my dream.

Quickly, I told them about my dream—the fog and the thing crawling through my window just before I snapped awake—and how it came true, with the threatening notices, the cats that started showing up, and all that other witchy business.

"Did she give the woman's name?" I asked.

"Yes, Jennifer something, I don't remember."

Close enough. I was feeling as though we had her trapped. It would take just a day or two, maybe just a matter of hours, before we would have her cornered and begging to go to jail. She would wish she didn't even know how to spell the word *witch*, let alone pretend to be one.

"So, who was the man?"

"She said she just met him at the motel when she checked in. She was in town visiting friends. She said she didn't know what he was doing there. Living there, perhaps. But she felt sorry for him since he was all alone."

"She sounds very charitable," I said sarcastically.

"Yeah, well, Jake said she was coming on strong with him even as the ambulance was wheeling away her neighbor under a white sheet on a stretcher. You don't act that way when death is that close to you."

And you don't act that way with Bea's husband, I thought.

"Lucas. That was the guy's name. I don't know if that was his first or last name, but that was what I heard Jake say to Detective Samberg before he hung up the phone with me."

"So we've got her." I rubbed my stomach to try to help the queasiness out of my system. Bea nodded with excitement.

"Not quite, girls," Aunt Astrid said as we made our way to Bea's kitchen. My aunt took her seat on the stool at the end of the counter. "Yes, in the world of witches, she has committed horrible crimes against the universe. But in Wonder Falls, she hasn't done a thing. Nothing that could be pinned on her at any rate." She pointed to the kettle, letting Bea know she wanted some tea.

I grabbed a step stool and pulled down the Doritos from their hiding place that Jake had revealed earlier. But one whiff of the processed cheesy goodness made me weak in the knees and light-headed. I put them back, swallowed hard, and pulled up a stool next to my aunt.

"Maybe we should sleep on it." Bea yawned. "It's already past ten o'clock, and we still have to work in the morning."

"I think that's a good idea," Aunt Astrid said, still pointing at the cold, empty kettle while looking at Bea.

"Oh, you want some tea, Mom? Is that it?" Bea rolled her eyes and smiled, snatching the teapot and quickly filling it from the tap. "It's not like you don't know how to make tea," she teased.

"It just tastes better when you do it." They both laughed.

I was sure Bea's tea would sooth my stomach, but the thought of trying to get it down was too much. I just wanted to go home and sleep in my own bed.

"Are you sure you think it's safe? We've got lots of room and love having everyone around," Bea said.

"Yeah, I'm sure. That trip to Brit's really knocked me out, and I think I'd really just like to be around my own things. Plus, I have the feeling I may be up and down a couple times during the night. The last thing I want is an audience."

I looked at Treacle who was sitting up straight, looking

out the back door. His eyes were little green slits, but I knew he wasn't sleeping. He was studying.

"I think you should stay here," I said to him in my mind. *"You're safer here than with me."* I walked over to him when he didn't respond. *"Treacle? Are you all right?"* Stooping over, I felt the world spin again but picked the big furry ball up in my arms. He let out a little growl like he used to when he was a kitten and watching a bird hop near the windowsill… as if he were trying to coax it closer and closer until he could catch it.

"Something is out there," he thought to me.

I held him close and looked out into the darkness. *"Are you sure?"*

"Yes. But whatever it is, it can't get closer. It has a weakness, and it can't get closer."

"Is it another cat?"

"No. It's what the cats see for."

I stood there, rocking the cat in my arms, letting the heat from his body soothe my aching belly. I strained to see some kind of movement, some ghoulish face, or a pair of eyes blinking back at me, but all I saw was darkness.

"We will take care of him," Peanut Butter said, wrapping his body around my leg and standing bravely at the door, looking out.

"Yes, we have a plan of our own should anything find its way in," Marshmallow said, prancing up to Peanut Butter and nudging him gently with her head.

"Don't you guys take any risks. If anything happens, run and hide," I said to them.

"Run and hide. Only after we teach whatever that is out there a lesson that you don't mess with our family." Peanut Butter quickly licked his front paw then resumed his vigil.

I contemplated telling them about what Brit had said about this woman's abusive treatment of cats. I don't know what she could have done to get inside their heads, to control them so cruelly, as though they were replaceable tools to be thrown away when she was done with them. I didn't. I couldn't bring myself to tell them. *"This thing is dangerous. Just do me a favor, and don't take any chances. Okay?"*

They all looked up at me and meowed in unison.

Meteor Showers

As I drove, I began to feel as though I really wanted to talk to someone about anything but witchcraft. It was late, but I wondered if Min was around. I decided to drive past his parent's house and see if his car was in the driveway.

As the familiar roads wound and weaved around, I let out a big sigh. My stomach was starting to feel better. I thought of a double cheeseburger and didn't feel the need to pull over and gag.

I knew Treacle was unhappy but safe for the time being. My blood boiled to think of that woman torturing cats. Even the alley cats had their own ways of doing things. Her treatment was cruel, like slave labor.

So, this Jennifer person was a woman scorned, as if none of us had ever had our hearts broken before. I hated to admit it, but I thought of Min and Amalia. It would have been easier if she were a crackpot, but she wasn't. She was probably more normal than me, and I consider myself a pretty down-to-earth person, with a few extra talents no one can ever know about.

I was seriously starting to depress myself when I looked in my rearview mirror and noticed the guy behind me had his high beams on.

"Jeez, thanks, pal. I don't have a bad *enough* headache," I grumbled, flipping the mirror to tint in an attempt to tone down the brightness.

I turned off down a side street that was home to some of the wealthier people who lived in Wonder Falls. Darla lived in a mansion high up on a hill around there, but it was easy to avoid. I decided to do just that.

These were homes for families. I wouldn't know what to do with so much space, but it sure would be an awesome challenge to imagine. As I looked through some of the open windows, I saw beautifully decorated rooms painted in rich reds or browns. It seemed as if the people knew exactly where to put everything to make it look beautiful.

And speaking of beautiful, I wondered what Brit meant about Blake being the really good-looking detective. Jake had always been what most women thought of as a tall glass of water. I didn't think anyone but me thought Blake was the better-looking one, not that I thought he was hot or anything. But he had some pleasing features I liked. If he would keep his mouth closed, he would be perfect. Maybe. What was I thinking? It certainly wasn't the time or place to be considering the positive attributes of Blake Samberg.

How were we ever going to get to Jennifer before she got to Brit, Bea, Aunt Astrid, and myself... and anyone else who looked at her cock-eyed? I wanted to just cruise along, but the guy driving behind me was in some kind of hurry, tailgating and weaving back and forth. I hit my hazard lights and pulled over to let him pass.

"Leave five minutes early if you don't want to be late," I mumbled as I looked in the rearview mirror. The car pulled slowly around mine. It was dark outside, but as I looked at the driver, something very unsettling looked back at me.

Suddenly, I felt like the locked car door and rolled-up window may not be enough protection for me. I could make out a silhouette by the glow of the streetlamps. It had long, wild hair, a grin like a starving animal, and white eyes.

It was her. Jennifer Skala knew where I'd come from and was passing me slowly on the street. I could feel her evil presence like you'd smell garbage from the opening of an alley. You knew it was deep in there and that it was foul without getting anywhere near it.

She drove past then suddenly hit the gas, speeding off just far enough to turn around. She flashed her lights and revved the engine. Was she seriously going to ram me?

The thing about us witches is that we could be killed by regular, good old-fashioned car accidents, too. I couldn't tell what this lunatic was thinking, but she was ready to push the envelope. She hit the gas, and her car burst to life, zooming straight for me.

I put my arms up, unable to move quickly enough to do much more, and squeezed my eyes shut. Nothing... no shattering impact, no sound of crunching metal, no glass breaking. Letting out the breath I hadn't even realized I was holding, I opened one eye and peeked around. I was alone on the street. Shifting quickly in my seat, I turned around.

Maybe she'd passed me. Maybe at the last second, her car had swerved, and I'd see her taillights getting smaller and smaller as she drove away. But there were no red taillights. No other car was on the street. I was completely alone.

"This is ridiculous," I grumbled, putting the car in gear and pulling back onto the road.

Min's house was only a few blocks away. I hoped he was there and the lights were still on. It was almost eleven o'clock —a little late to be calling, but as I rounded the corner of his street, I was happy to see his car. In fact, I was really happy because he was standing right by his car... and so was Amalia.

"Oh, geez," I groaned. How was this going to look? "Hi, Min. I know it's late, but I just happened to be in the neighborhood and thought I'd see if you had a shoulder to lean on right now." Yikes. That sounded like something out of a cheesy Lifetime movie about torrid affairs or deadly marriages.

Min and Amalia both looked up at the same time and saw me. I flashed my lights as I pulled my car to the curb and cut the engine.

"Cath! What a nice surprise!" Min smiled broadly.

"Hey, Min," I said as casually as I could. "Hi, Amalia. I hope I'm not interrupting anything."

"Cath!" Amalia almost ran up to me. "No. My gosh, it's so nice to see you. You know, Min and I were just hanging out here because he said there was a meteor shower tonight, but I could have sworn it was next week."

"Yeah, I heard about that. Sorry, Min, but the lady is correct. That is *next* week." I had almost forgotten about the meteor shower coming up. If we didn't get that lunatic Jennifer Skala in line before then, heaven only knew what she might do.

When the heavens moved through their celestial routine, us witches would experience varying degrees of power. Sometimes, our powers were stronger than other times. Meteor showers were like spontaneous bursts of energy. They were fun and exciting, enhancing our gifts and sometimes enlightening us to a new power, temporary or permanent. It was all up to the heavens.

"Oh well, you can't blame a guy for trying." He smiled down at Amalia. "So, what are you doing around here at this hour, Cath? Not that we'd ever mind a visit from you any time day or night."

"I didn't mean to break up your little stargazing party. Actually, I started to get a little dizzy as I was driving and thought I should pull over for a spell." It wasn't a complete lie. I didn't have any reason to mention the witches' vials at Brit's place that made me sicker than a dog or the phantom driver, who tailgated me then proceeded to drive directly into my headlights only to disappear a split second before impact.

"You do look a little pale, Cath," Amalia said. Grabbing me by the wrist, she gave me a puzzled look. "My gosh, girl, your heart is pumping to beat the band. Come on and have a seat on the porch."

"I'll get you some water." Min dashed into the house.

"I'm really all right. Just something I ate, I think." That excuse worked before.

"You know, you don't want to be driving in traffic and feel the urge to puke, pardon my French. I had that happen to me once," Amalia said in one quick breath of air. She pulled up a small cushioned ottoman and sat down next to me. "There was a twenty-four hour flu going around the Home. It had worked its way through every patient and every nurse on staff within two weeks. I was feeling good, thinking all the orange juice and exercise I was doing had my antibodies in better shape than the rest of them."

I watched Amalia as she told her story, polishing her nails on her chest as she spoke, then rolling her eyes and shaking her head in disgust as she continued.

"I'm on my way home, traffic is moving but packed, and it hits me."

"Oh, no," I said, completely engrossed in her tale.

"Yup. I started to sweat, felt nauseated, and before I could put on my blinker to pull to the right, my whole dashboard... well, let's just say, it wasn't pretty."

I couldn't help it. I started to laugh.

"And if that isn't bad enough, home was still twenty-five minutes away."

Then I was really chuckling.

"The worst part is..."

"You mean that wasn't the worst part?" I laughed some more as Amalia started to laugh with me.

"No. The worst part was that my car was in the shop. This was my sister's car."

"Well, if you're an optimist, then perhaps that was the best part," I said, gasping for breath as I laughed.

"I never thought of it like that. I was too busy feeling awful all these years when I should have been thrilled."

By the time Min came out with a glass of water garnished with a delicate slice of lemon, I was not only feeling a world of better, but I was still laughing with Amalia.

A Thug

I didn't stay for very long, maybe a half an hour... forty-five minutes tops. Min and Amalia would never know how much good they did for me.

I listened to them tell stories about their day, and Amalia was like an open book. The poor thing was more than happy to laugh at what seemed to be a never-ending series of unfortunate events.

On her day off about three months ago, she managed to put gas in her car, drop off dry cleaning, and make it halfway through grocery shopping before someone told her that her skirt was tucked into her pantyhose.

At work, one of the new residents had received flowers from her family, and when Amalia went to fill up a vase, she spilled all the water on her shirt. Nursing uniforms are quite sturdy, built to stand up to all kinds of spills, and hers was no different. Ironically, the uniform had multicolored cats all over it. When she got home and took off her shirt, the colors of the cats had transferred onto her skin.

"I looked like I had Morgellons disease. All these goofy, multicolored lines all over me. It took over a week of near-scalding hot baths to get them off completely."

The way she told a story had me in stitches. I found myself liking her more and more. It wasn't just because she was so willing to share her misfortune with a smile and such good nature, but I saw a lot of myself in her.

She never talked about going out with girlfriends or partying or anything like that. She worked and kept to herself until Min came along… just as he'd done for me in high school.

When I finally left, I felt good. For the first time in a couple of days, I felt like myself. A good night's sleep in my own bed, knowing my cat and family were safe, was all I needed. But as I drove down the dark and deserted streets, I began to feel uneasy.

I couldn't be sure, but I thought every couple of blocks, I saw the glowing eyes of felines peering out at me from the roadside, from around mailboxes, from side streets and alleyways. I scanned the roads for any other cars but saw none.

Finally, I arrived at my house. I swear that the journey, which had only taken about ten minutes, felt like it had slowed down. I was shocked to see it was only a little after midnight. I had been sure it was at least two in the morning.

Climbing out of my car, I listened and heard nothing. As I walked up the steps to my house, my footsteps echoed loudly.

The key slipping into the lock sounded like an explosion against the quiet neighborhood. Again, I listened but heard nothing. Shrugging, I slipped inside, locked the door behind me, and let out my breath.

Without Treacle, the house was very still. Just to be on the safe side, I checked all the windows and the back door and found everything to be locked up tight, just as I had left it.

Even though Bea's home was spacious and lovely and always smelled of a soothing spice or flower, I loved being in my own little house. Sage hung in the air, my crystals hung from the corners of the ceiling, and my clothes, notes, magazines, and books were scattered wherever I set them. Even the most skilled witch should appreciate her own sacred space.

Letting the water heat up in my shower, I thought of Amalia's story and began to chuckle again. The shower felt good and helped clear my mind. When I finally emerged, my fingers were prunes and my internal temperature was raised, so the cool air outside the bathroom felt invigorating. Slipping into flannel pajamas, I checked all the doors and windows again, left one light on in the living room, crawled into bed, and snapped off the light on the nightstand.

Then it hit me. There was no sound outside. No sound of any kind. No crickets. No hum from the busy streets a couple of blocks down. There was no wind rustling the leaves.

My eyes popped wide open, and I held my breath.

"Meow-er-eow!"

A layer of sweat instantly broke out all over me. Not

wanting to look but feeling an invisible pull turn my head, I turned to the window and saw not just one but three sets of glowing eyes staring in at me from behind a tiny slit of open curtain.

The cats banged and scratched viciously at the window with a feverish determination. What they would have done to me had they been able to get in, I don't know. But I saw nothing in those glowing orbs that would make me think they were anything other than fully consumed by the beast that had chosen them to do her dirty work.

I got out of bed carefully and looked at them. I tried to talk to them, to hear their thoughts, but I couldn't. All I could hear was screaming.

PING! PING! PING! The light, bouncy sound of my cell phone ringing made me jump and clutch my chest.

I walked over to the phone, expecting it to be my aunt or Bea calling to tell me it was like a crazy cat lady's dream come true at their house, with a couple of dozen felines howling and meowing in their yard.

Instead, when I answered, I felt an ice-cold breath across the back of my neck.

"Cath? Why do they call you that? You have half a name because you are just half a person. They all know that. Don't you?" The voice on the other end of the phone was hypnotic. I began to tremble, but I couldn't put the phone down. "I can see you." Her sing-songy voice reminded me of the condescending way Darla used to insult me in high school, with her voice sounding kind, even though the words were anything but. "Did you like my driving tonight? You looked like you did."

"What do you want?" I managed to squeak, angry with myself for not sounding tougher.

"You know what I want. I want your cat." She sounded frustrated. "You don't even know what he's capable of doing. You have no idea what kind of power he could radiate because you just want him as a pet. A companion because you don't have a man."

"You can't have him."

"Oh, says you?"

"Yeah."

"You know, Cath, you might know who I am now, but you don't know what I am."

"I know what you *think* you are. You think you're some kind of witch. It takes a little more than black clothes and a bedazzled pentagram to make a witch."

The other end of the phone was quiet for a moment. I was hoping she was embarrassed over that tacky ring.

"I'm not just a witch. Brit's little trinkets won't be able to stop me once I have the power of your black cat at my disposal. Don't worry, once he's mine he'll probably forget all about you."

"It'll be over my dead body before you get my cat," I growled into the phone, wishing I could reach through the line and strangle her. Especially when she laughed at me.

"That sounds about right. And the beautiful thing is I can do it. To you. To that old hippie. To the one married to that handsome detective who would inevitably need a shoulder to cry on... or more."

"You're disgusting. You're a slob. We've seen your work. You got lucky a couple of times, that's it. Anyone could make a mess like you did. You're a hack." When I genuinely laughed at Jennifer, she said nothing. "I'll tell you what, Jennifer, if you knew anything, you might have tried a love spell on Marvin to get him to notice your softer side. But see, you didn't even have the smarts to do that. You just resort to violence. Like a thug. Like an ignorant thug."

"I'll show you a..."

"You won't show me anything. Oh, I take that back. You'll show me a bunch of cats who will do what? Scratch my furniture until I beg for mercy?" A surge of positive energy coursed through me. I suddenly realized what was happening. Jennifer, having chosen to learn from those darker shadows and beasts in other dimensions, could not maintain the upper hand for long if her victim wasn't afraid. My gosh, how terrified had Marvin been for her to do what she did to him? "Tell me, Jennifer, what was your plan for Lucas? Did he know you were just using him? Or did he..."

"Shut your mouth, subcreature!" she screamed into the phone. Her voice was like a growl and a scream all at once.

I think I had just gone one step too far. "Yeah, okay. You're real tough over the phone, Jennifer, but how would you be if I was right in front of you? You think I'm scared of a voice? You think I'm scared of someone who has to stick to the shadows and uses cats because she's so horrible, she knows no one wants to even look at her?"

I was shaking as the words came out of me, especially when the other end of the line had gone silent.

Then I remembered something Jake had said about the notes we received. Jennifer could do parlor tricks. She could make cats act crazy to freak us out and deliver notes, but she was still using the things in this world for most of her scare tactics. And her psychic attacks were as chaotic as her own mind was. She was no match for the Greenstones.

"Jennifer, are you still there?"

"Your whole world is going to become very dark, very soon." Her voice was low and gravelly.

"Yeah, yeah, well, that may be. But let's just say we handle this like big witches. You meet me by the waterfall tomorrow at one in the morning. Do you know where that is? There's a clearing where the water begins to fall. It's out of the way. Quiet. No way for an ambush. And let's settle this. If you win, you get Treacle, and I'll step aside. If I win..."

"Deal," she said without listening to me, then the phone clicked and went dead.

I looked at the phone. The number was listed as unknown, which I thought was kind of creepy. But the decision I had made, this duel I had arranged, felt oddly comforting.

Until I remembered I had to tell Bea and Aunt Astrid.

Fight

"Are you out of your mind?" Aunt Astrid asked me the next morning after we had opened the café. "How could you just challenge her to a duel without even discussing it with us?"

I stood with my hands thrust deep in my jeans pockets as if I were back in high school and being questioned about a failed exam. I shrugged, not looking up.

"She makes people's hearts explode!" Bea hissed so as not to be overheard by the patrons who were seated in the café, drinking. "Did you forget about that?"

"No, I didn't forget," I mumbled.

"Then what? What made you think this was a good idea?" Aunt Astrid asked, not caring about the people who turned to look at her. "I lost my sister because she went into something unprepared. I don't plan on losing my niece the same way."

I looked up at my aunt. "What do you mean my mom wasn't prepared?" I asked quietly.

"Don't try and change the subject. You might be in your own house, paying your own way, but Cath, you are still my responsibility. You can't just assume you can handle anything thrown your way. Sometimes, you need to let the universe tell you what to do."

"I thought I was. I have a hunch. I have a gut feeling that meeting her up there is the answer."

"The answer to what?" Bea asked.

"The answer to getting her to stop."

Aunt Astrid looked at me gravely.

"Aunt Astrid." I leaned in to whisper in her ear. "Jennifer Skala is just a big bully. When you take away the gruesomeness, she's no different than a punk in school."

"I hope you're right."

"I think I am." I smiled weakly at both of them.

"Mom, there's got to be some kind of passage we can find to help with this," Bea said. "Somewhere in one of your books, there has got to be something that would help."

Aunt Astrid planted both hands on her hips and looked around the café. "If there is, I can't think of it offhand."

Bea scooted gracefully around the counter, wiping her hands on her apron. "Sorry, folks, family emergency. We're closing for the day."

A chorus of groans went up as chairs began scraping the floor. Papers rustled, and the bell behind the door jingled as the customers slowly exited.

"We're sorry. So Sorry. Some things just can't be helped. But come back tomorrow for a free coffee or tea and a slice of apple pie."

"What?" I asked. "They don't need to get a freebie for this, do they?"

"Compliments of my soul sister here. She'll be buying your coffee for you tomorrow. Thanks so much for understanding." Bea continued to usher people gently toward the door, winking at me as I felt my paycheck totally disappear before I'd even earned it.

I locked up the front door and flipped the CLOSED sign. We told Kevin he was welcome to go home, but he insisted on staying and getting a jump on those free pies we'd be giving away the next day. He said he'd be sure to lock up when he left.

"We need to get the cats," I said as everyone piled into my car. We drove to Bea's place, then all of us, each with a cat in her arms, got back in the car.

Treacle, who was usually quite at ease in the car, was trembling in my arms. *"Don't you hear it?"* he said to me. *"It's like someone keeps calling my name. I keep hearing it and wanting to go there, but..."*

"It's not what you think it is, Treacle." I looked at the other cats. *"Marshmallow, Peanut Butter, how are you guys feeling?"*

"We hear it, too." Marshmallow shifted in Aunt Astrid's arms. *"But it's not calling Treacle. It's calling me."*

"No," Peanut Butter said. *"It's me. I told you it was me. I heard it first."*

I felt the blood drain from my face. She was starting already. Jennifer was going to get to me by getting to my cat first. We had to find something to stop her.

I backed out of the driveway and quickly pulled onto the street. Before I'd gotten ten feet away from the house, I slammed on the brakes, causing everyone to lurch forward.

"Look! Over there!" I pointed to a long-haired woman getting into a silver car and speeding away. She was wearing all black.

"Is that her?" Treacle asked.

"I'll bet it is," I said. *"We have to hurry. Who knows what she'll try to do to us while we're on the road."*

I was right to be concerned. But instead of using forces around us, like trees falling in our path or birds swooping into the windshield, the person in the silver car drove like a maniac.

She pulled in front of us then slammed on her brakes. Turning down a side street, we thought she was going another route until she made a complete circle and sped up behind us. She kept up with us for several blocks, weaving and swerving, speeding up then slamming on her brakes.

I couldn't panic. I whispered into Treacle's ear, keeping both hands on the wheel as my cat stared with wide green eyes out the window.

Finally, the silver car pulled away, and I hit the gas to get to Bea's house. It seemed like every car ride I took recently managed to take a couple of years off my life. This one was no exception.

Finally at my aunt's house, we all piled out of the car. Looking around, I noticed the street was quiet. Treacle strained and cried, trying to tear free of my arms. I knew he wanted me to let him go. I knew he missed prowling around on his own, but I couldn't be sure whether it was his idea or Jennifer's. I wasn't taking any chances. He had to stay with me.

"I know, Treacle. It won't be much longer." I held his big, squirming body as I tried to get to the front door.

"MEOW-MEOW-EROW!" He hissed, swiping at my face and clawing a long scratch down my neck. The mark quickly turned from a hot pink to a thin thread of bright red as blood surfaced.

I lost my grip on him, and he landed on the ground. With one push of his strong back legs, he was off, darting into the neighbor's yard, scooting underneath a car then out the other side to squeeze through a row of Yucca trees. Treacle had made his escape.

"Treacle!" I cried. My eyes burned instantly with tears. I took a few pathetic steps in the direction he'd run but knew I'd never be able to keep up with him, let alone catch him. "Oh, no! She's going to get him! She told me she would. She told me what she was going to do to him. To all of them. This is all my fault!"

"Come on." My aunt grabbed me by the hand. "She's doing this to distract you."

"No," I said pitifully. "She told me on the phone. She said

what she wanted and what she was going to do. She's calling him, and he's going to go to her. What have I done?"

Bea hurried and opened the door to her mother's house, tossing in a skinny and high-strung Peanut Butter. She quickly came back and scooped up Marshmallow.

"Cath, I know you're scared, but we don't have much time. If Treacle does go to her, then we need to find a way to get him back and get her in check. She's not playing by the rules. If she has your black cat, this might be a bigger fight than we anticipated."

"We?" I asked. "You guys can't come."

"Oh, right." Aunt Astrid stomped her way toward the house. "Bea, get the books from my nightstand. Cath, in the pantry behind the cans of soup, you'll find *The Outpost of the Enderton*. Grab that and—"

"I mean it. You guys can't come. I didn't tell her I'd meet her at the waterfall with my whole family. I just said me." I stood on the porch as my family stepped inside then turned to look at me. The image of us right there couldn't have been more perfect. Bea and her mom were inside the house, and I was standing at the threshold, on the porch but not in the house. It was so clear, I almost began to cry.

I didn't want to admit it, but although I'd never felt unloved, I would always feel as if I were just outside the threshold. I don't believe my family made me feel that way. I chose it. I knew I would always feel like that, and I had taken a stick to that snakes' nest and poked and poked until every one of those tails rattled with hatred and aggression.

I couldn't risk my family. They'd have each other. How awful would I feel if I left one of them feeling like I did? What if I left one of them feeling incomplete, unfinished? I couldn't even think of it. It was too much.

"Do you think she's going to abide by that?" Aunt Astrid scowled. "Do you think she even knows the meaning of the words 'fair fight'? She killed a man for not being in love with her. How unreasonable is that? There is no telling what she'll do to you if she gets the upper hand."

I swallowed hard. "She won't."

"What time are you meeting her?" Aunt Astrid asked.

"I told her one in the morning. No one will be up there. Anyone around Lover's Lane would be long gone by then. No one else would get hurt."

"Fine," Aunt Astrid said. "Let's get to work, and no more talk about going solo."

I nodded without smiling or making eye contact. I stepped over the threshold and felt a strange feeling of unfamiliarity. I wasn't sure if the feeling was real, or if Jennifer was getting her talons in me from a distance, or if I had just gotten myself so worked up that I didn't know what to feel.

Either way, I needed a plan, and hopefully there would be something in one of Aunt Astrid's books to help me. I hated the sense of loneliness I felt. Yet if I could prove to my aunt and cousin that I was capable of handling myself then maybe...

What was I thinking? Maybe this would somehow bring my parents back? Maybe all my years of growing up surrounded by oddities, curiosities, and just plain weirdness would pay off? Maybe this fight would prove I had the ability to get whatever took my mom and do what? Beat it up?

I was having trouble focusing. Why was I so distracted? I turned around and faced the street. In the distance, I saw a Wonder Falls police car cruise slowly by. Why wasn't Blake Samberg there to help?

What? Where in the world had that thought come from? I felt as though I'd spoken the words out loud, and both Aunt Astrid and Bea had heard me. I turned back to face them, my face beet red and my nerves a mess. This had to be some kind of inter-dimensional warfare. She had sprinkled some kind of fairy dust my way and was trying to get me so wrapped up in the wrong thoughts that I'd never be able to fight her.

"Cath, honey, she's working on you already. Come on." Bea took my hand like she did when we were little girls. I let her lead me into the house. Once Aunt Astrid shut the door, I looked around, almost surprised I was inside of the house. It was time to get to work... if I could just focus.

Dirty

❧

After several hours, I found myself starting to doze, which was not good considering I was stretched out on Aunt Astrid's couch, holding a four-inch thick book in front of my face.

Outside, the sky had gone from blue to violet to black, and the clock struck once, indicating ten thirty.

"Are you sure a good, old-fashioned binding spell won't do the trick on this one?" Bea asked, wiping her hair away from her face. She and my aunt had gone through two kettles of tea, and I had eaten three brownies I'd found in the back of the freezer.

"I'm just positive she'll be expecting that," Aunt Astrid said. "She has probably already put up her defenses and psychically bricked them over by now. We need to find something that will enable Cath to fight fire with fire. And since Miss Skala has crossed so far into sorcery with no real knowledge of what she's doing based on her past handiwork, she's going to play dirty. Very dirty."

Dirty. The word stuck in my head, and I quietly got up, setting the big book down. Tucked on a shelf between some bigger books was just what I was looking for. I'd seen it before. It was about thirty pages long and reminded me of the CliffsNotes some kids used in high school when they didn't want to read a whole book. It was a classic witches' spell book called *Light Magic*... because it was so small.

I stuffed it into my back pocket, yawned, stretched, then shrugged. "Oh, geez!" I thought fast on my feet. "I think I'm still a little nauseated from those witches' vials." My lie was lame, but it was all I could think of.

Both Aunt Astrid and Bea looked at me as if I'd suddenly turned green.

I didn't say anything. I was sure they saw right through me. Then suddenly, my aunt jumped up from her seat, pushed aside the big book she was reading, and rushed over to me.

"You poor thing. You've got to rest. You can't have any distractions. It wasn't smart of you to challenge this woman, but I know your intentions were to save Treacle and us." My aunt tucked a few stray hairs behind my ear. "That's why we're going to help you. We'll find a spell that will work, something that will keep you safe and maybe, just maybe, knock her out of the game."

I looked deep into my aunt's eyes and saw how worried she was. It tore at my heart. I never lied to her. It made my stomach fold over on itself, and I thought I was going to start actually feeling like I did at Brit's place.

"Go lie down in my room. I'll have Bea bring you some special tea and—"

"No. I don't want any tea. Just a little rest. Maybe twenty minutes or so."

"Take a little longer than that if you need to," Bea said. "We'll be ready when it's time to go."

I couldn't look at them anymore. The guilt was too much. I looked down at my feet, smiled, and headed off to my aunt's room. Along the way, I grabbed a white candle and a book of matches from the side table in the hallway.

Once inside her room, I pulled out the little booklet and found exactly what I was looking for.

I said the words quietly over the tiny flame, lifting the spell to the four corners of the Earth and calling to my side a few familiar souls to walk with me on this scary journey.

I was scared for my family. More than that, I was scared for Treacle. He was out there, and I couldn't tell if it was because wandering was his nature, or if it was the hocus-pocus that Jennifer had cast on the felines around town. He was a tough kitty, but he was no match for that kind of black sorcery. He didn't stand a chance. And when it was all over, if she got a hold of him and did the horrible things she had threatened, he would just be left there, alone, dying, suffering, and wondering where I was.

My eyes clouded up with tears, but I continued my vigil, requesting the simplest assistance.

Once I was finished with part one, I tiptoed to the door and listened.

"Hmmm," I heard Bea mutter. "What about this? It's a chant to induce a sort of hologram. Cath wouldn't even have to actually go to the clearing. She could stay here in a circle of salt, but Jennifer would see her, hear her, yet not be able to touch her."

"Yes, yes, that sounds good. And here, look here," Bea said. "Since her strength would be at a lesser level, she could summon a simple silencing spell that would shut that girl's mouth for almost seventy-two hours. That would be just enough time for us to get a hold of her and make that muteness permanent. She wouldn't be able to summon a waiter, let alone a cessation spell."

"Do you think that would be enough? She is a murderer."

"We just have to stop her and trust that the universe will deal with her in an appropriate manner. It will be out of our hands by that point."

I shook my head. Why didn't I know about this omnipresent spell when I was taking gym class in high school, where it really would have come in handy? But this was a different situation.

Jennifer had threatened my family but had singled me out because of my cat... just like Darla had singled me out because something about me rubbed her the wrong way. I couldn't just send my shadow to fight. I had to be there no matter what my chances were. Anything other than a physical confrontation wasn't going to stop a person like Jennifer Skala. She thrived on inducing fear. Taking away her voice, even permanently, wasn't going to deter her. I had no doubt she would retaliate.

I looked at the clock and saw it was nearly eleven. I had to prepare, and if I was going through with meeting the class bully at the clearing by the top of the waterfall, I wanted to get there first. Hopefully, my little plan would work, and I could be back at my aunt's house soon and tell Aunt Astrid and Bea that Jennifer was no longer a problem. I quietly cracked the door and listened again.

"Why would Cath accept a fight like this? Without us? Without our help? She's never done anything like this before?" I could hear the hurt in Bea's voice. It made me feel worse than the lying did.

Aunt Astrid replaced the teakettle on the stove for the third time. The click, click, click of the burner kicking on sounded like a cricket from where I was standing.

"I don't know what she could be thinking, but we have to respect it. Although we're all family, she is still an orphan, and I don't think she'll ever not feel that desire to prove herself."

"She doesn't have to prove anything to us," Bea said. "Why would she think that?"

"Because she's so good. She doesn't want to be a burden or a victim or anything less than a true Greenstone woman. No matter how stubborn that may make her."

I'd heard enough. I had to leave and do this on my own. I quietly slipped out of the bedroom door, down the hallway, and to the front door.

Waterfalls

Before I could leave, I was confronted with Marshmallow, who stood there in all her puffed-up glory looking right at me. Behind her, Peanut Butter chased a rainbow prism on the ground that came from the lamp on my aunt's roll top desk.

"And where are you going?" Marshmallow asked.

"I'm going to get Treacle."

Marshmallow purred quietly. *"Take me with you."*

"No. And don't sound the alarm until I'm good and gone."

"Is it dangerous... what you're doing?"

"Yes."

"Will you come back?"

"I sure hope so."

Marshmallow rubbed up against my leg then stepped back, sitting on her haunches and looking at me through little slitted eyes. *"I'll be right here when you and Treacle come home."*

All I could do was smile. I opened the front door, slipped out, and pulled it tightly shut behind me.

The air felt colder than usual, and I wished I had a jacket. I would like to think the cold was what made me shake as I got into my car, started it up, and pulled out of the driveway without turning on the headlights. Once I was three houses away, I hit the lights and the gas and began my journey to the waterfall.

I saw a calico cat peering at me from the area of the woods where Treacle had run. Was the calico just a stray, or someone's furry companion out for an evening adventure? Or was it one of hers?

"It's not Treacle. There's still hope. That isn't him, and as long as I don't see him around, I can assume she doesn't have him. And if she doesn't, then she's just a hack witch with a bad attitude." The words sounded braver than I felt.

The dark street unfolded in front of me like an innocent set of rollercoaster tracks… the ones that led you up, up, up. They weren't threatening. There was nothing scary about those bits of track. The view was usually very pretty until you realized those tracks had led you to terror.

"Come on, Cath. You've got a plan. Stop freaking yourself out," I said out loud, hoping I'd listen to me and toughen up.

It usually took about twenty minutes to get to the waterfall clearing by car. If I wanted to play it extra safe, I'd park the car and take the path that, in the daytime, took about thirty minutes to maneuver. It was wide and well-marked, so I was pretty confident I would still get to the clearing before Jennifer with enough time to prepare.

I parked the car at a gravel turn-in where Wonder Falls Water Works vehicles and Wonder Falls Department of Streets and Sanitation trucks would park for their surveys and sometimes to nap. My car was barely visible from the street.

I grabbed a bottle of water that I had in the car and began to walk. The path was just ahead, and I was able to find it easily by the light from the streets. Once I was on it, though, the path became very dark, very fast.

The night was perfectly clear, and high in the sky, a beautiful third-quarter moon seemed to welcome the millions of stars around it. Stopping for a moment, I listened and heard a wild and comforting choir of crickets. I was ready to start running if the sounds of nature stopped, but so far, it was just a regular night. Within minutes, I heard the sound of the waterfall in the distance. With each step, it grew louder and louder.

Finally, I saw the slope in the path begin to level out, and up ahead was the beautiful, flat clearing where the river lazily drifted past only to pick up speed in the distance in its hurry to get to the waterfall. The water wasn't that deep along the edges. Many people would stand on the bank in waders and fish. But the river did get deep in the center and at times, after the rains, the undertow would try to claim a victim or two.

Arriving at the center of the clearing, I knelt down. I began to finish the chant I had started at my aunt's house.

This was part two, and I needed my hands in the dirt of this place, some water to mix, and just a couple of ancient words that were pretty to say and simple in concept. I wasn't looking for complicated.

I stood up, again greeting the four corners of the Earth with my hands covered in what was then sacred mud. I had one more step to complete but stopped dead in my tracks.

"Hey, who's over there?"

I knew that voice.

No.

Defensive

Of all the times and places, Blake Samberg had to show up then.

"Blake?" I said in a hushed voice. "Is that you?"

"Cath Greenstone?" I heard his voice and suddenly saw a spot from a small flashlight not twenty feet from me. "What are you doing up here at this hour?" he asked, strolling my way.

"I thought there was supposed to be a meteor shower tonight. I came up here to get a front row seat, so to speak," I said nervously as the flashlight lit up almost everything around me. "But you can't see a thing with that flashlight. Maybe you should douse it, you know?"

"No, you won't miss anything. It's next week. Actually, Jake said this was a good place for stargazing. I didn't know you were interested in astronomy." He shifted from his left foot to his right as he stood close to me. The soft glow of the flashlight lit his face, and I noticed what looked like a smile on his face.

"You have no idea." I looked up at the stars that had helped me find my way home on more than one occasion, as well as fight a demon once. That was another long story for another time. "I think I'll be going now."

"I didn't see a car pull up. Did you take the path up here?" Blake asked. He sure was talkative.

"Yes. I felt like walking, sort of taking the path less traveled, you know? But I think I'll be heading back now."

"Well, let me give you a ride."

"No. That's not necessary."

"You don't want to walk that path in the dark. You could slip and fall." He shined his flashlight on me and saw my hands covered in mud. "Or did you already?"

I held them up in front of me, shrugging.

"Yeah, you know how clumsy I am. Just ask Bea." It was all I could think of to say.

"All the more reason you shouldn't walk back."

"Look, I know you're trying to help, but I don't need any help."

"From the looks of it, you really do."

"This isn't the time or place, Blake, for you to get all police-y on me. I'm a big girl. It isn't a crime to fall in the mud."

"Why are you getting so defensive?"

"I'm not defensive."

"You sound like it."

"Well, that shows how much you know. Now, if you don't mind, I'd like to wash my hands in the water and be on my way."

"Leaning over the banks at night is also dangerous. Let me get you a bottle of water from the car, and you can wash your hands with that."

"Fine. If it will make you happy."

"It would. Just wait here."

I watched as Blake's flashlight bounced along the ground a good couple of yards from where I was standing. Quickly, I hurried to the water's edge. No sooner was I on my knees, bent down, and reaching for the water, than I heard another familiar voice.

"Isn't this nice?" Her voice was low and menacing, like the growl of a hungry animal. "You get here early and bring the police."

I whipped around and got to my feet. My hands were still caked with mud. I just needed a drop, one single drop from the river to complete my spell. But Jennifer had other ideas. I quickly stepped to the side to get myself in between Jennifer and Blake.

"He was here when I got here. Leave him out of it." I tried to appeal to her logical side, if she had one. "He's a cop. You don't want to be known as a cop killer," I said, making a design in the dirt with my foot.

"What is that you're doing? Some kind of binding spell?"

If I lived through this ordeal, I'd be sure to tell Aunt

Astrid she'd nailed that one. Miss Paranoia would have sniffed out a binding spell from thirty miles away.

"No." I quickly glanced behind me in the direction Blake had walked. I still saw the light from his flashlight aimed away from me and in the trunk of his car.

"What are you looking for? Did you bring other people here, too? Maybe Brit is with you or your aunt. Who's back there besides that cop?"

I didn't say anything. I was trying to concentrate and find the right words. But when Jennifer stepped closer to me, I saw her face clearer than I'd ever wanted to.

Her cheeks were high and chiseled. Her mouth was covered in thick, red lipstick, and her eyes were plain, milky white holes in her face. I couldn't help but gasp.

"I'll tear you to shreds," she hissed.

"Cath? You okay?" Blake yelled.

"Do not keep until the frost. Time to sleep when time is lost," I muttered quickly, pointing in the direction Blake had called from. Within a few seconds, I heard the gentle thud of a body hitting the ground. He was asleep. His catnap would last a little while and buy me some time.

"Your boyfriend?"

My cheeks flushed. Anger surged through me because I knew even in the dark, Jennifer could feel my embarrassment, and she enjoyed it.

But I had to stay in control. My plan was so simple, and all I needed was some water and a little luck.

I started to inch my way toward the riverbank but was

frozen in place when Jennifer grinned a wide grimace of sharpened teeth. The moon bounced off of them and gave her an almost translucent look. She growled a low, feral-sounding grunt, and I began to shake.

"I'll tear you apart, but only after I have my fun with that man married to your cousin."

Jake. No!

"I'll drive his wife mad. Hearing noises, seeing things, and late-night visitations from some of the more aggressive entities should send her off the deep end quite nicely."

"You stay away from my family!"

"Well, aren't you scary?" She waved her hand, and I felt as if I had just been punched in the gut. I reeled backward only to lose my balance and fall on my butt. I coughed and gagged. She came at me again, clenching her fist. I felt my hair being pulled by the handfuls, and I was dragged up to Jennifer's face.

"Is this all you've got?" I asked. "I thought you were supposed to be some kind of super witch. All you're doing is beating me up without using your hands. Any sixth-grader could do that."

She snarled at me, her lips peeling back from her horrible teeth. Why had she done that to herself? I was reminded of the before and after pictures of drug addicts, except Jennifer depicted what sorcery did to a person. It was black, no matter what anyone said.

If Bea were there and took Jennifer's hand, she would probably see the black legions in her brain... layers and layers of filth, clogging up her arteries and coating her organs like a parasite. But unlike a cancer or a tumor, paranormal infections are invited in. Jennifer had made an intentional transformation, and she was enjoying herself.

I was tossed another fifteen feet across the grass. I lay there panting, wondering what time it was and why the hell I hadn't allowed my family to come and help. I almost laughed out loud at the thought, but it couldn't get past the lump in my throat when I heard the most horrible sound.

Trying to gulp in air enough to speak, I croaked out the word. "Treacle?"

It was a quiet meow, but I heard it.

"NO!" I screamed in my head. *"Run, Treacle! Hide. Don't come here!"* But I got no answer.

"Aren't you going to even try and fight back? Don't you have a power of any kind, or are you one of those witches who can only make flowers grow or talk to animals?" Jennifer laughed. Her white eyes scrunched into half moons as her cheeks pushed them up.

I tried muttering a spell of confusion to get her lost for a few minutes, even seconds, so I could get to the water. My head pounded, and my stomach and ribs ached terribly. But when I muttered the words, I felt the psychic vibration as it bounced right off of her. I tried a binding spell again, which was all I could think of at the moment, but it also rolled off of her like raindrops on a windshield.

Suddenly, I was yanked to my feet. Jennifer held me by my

collar with one hand. She walked toward the riverbank, and my feet dragged clumsily along the ground.

"Your family will probably find your body in a couple days. And you know what the autopsy will say? Natural causes. Who would have thought someone so young, so full of life, would have such a bad ticker." She swung me over the edge, bending my back at an unnatural angle.

I looked around as best I could and saw a sleek, black form moving along the grass.

Three Flashes

"G*et away, Treacle!*" I screamed in my head. *"Run home! Just get home where it's safe!"* I then saw him rub against Jennifer's leg. My eyes swelled with tears. She had him, and she was going to kill him, slowly and cruelly. My mud-crusted hand clutched her, and I sank my nails in as far as I could. *"Fight her, Treacle! Remember me? I wouldn't hurt you! Fight her!"*

"Oh, I see. I got your cat," Jennifer said. "He's been lurking around here for a little while now while you've been doing anything but fighting back. He's seen you give up. Now he's mine."

I coughed and cried, still clawing at her hand around my neck. I was starting to feel light-headed. With one last try, I screamed in my head, *"One good swipe, Treacle!"*

I think the balance between the light and the darkness

had been tipped because just as I thought I was going to pass out, I heard a fierce *meower-er-eow*.

My cat hissed and arched his back with all his fur on edge. In one sudden movement, he jumped up at Jennifer's face.

She screamed out a stream of obscenities as Treacle scratched all the way down her cheek. She dropped me to the ground, and I landed on the hard, bumpy rocks that were along the banks of the river. Just as I looked up, she waved her left hand, and my poor cat went flying into a tree, dropping to the ground with a thud.

As much as my gut pulled me toward Treacle, I reached out to the water instead. I just needed one lousy drop. Then I heard Jennifer again. She just wouldn't shut up.

"I'll kill you both! I'll tear you apart! You'll explode from the inside out just like the others!"

I scrambled with all my strength just to get a couple more inches, but Jennifer had me in her invisible vise. I felt my breath catch in my chest. My whole body was in pain, and my chest was burning.

I arched backward, and with my last ounce of free will, I stretched toward the water only inches away, but it seemed like miles. My muddy hand came closer and closer to the slow-moving ripples. Finally, I felt the cold water gently kiss the very tip of my fingers, and I muttered the words, *"Coerce an unblemished soul for infinity, and let this be washed away*."

The water in the lake shot up into a fine spray. It seemed as though it went all the way up to the stars, but that may have been because the oxygen had stopped going to my brain for several minutes.

Jennifer was soaked from head to toe, and so was I. But I saw what I'd hoped to see. The Maid of the Mist.

The thing about the Maid of the Mist is that she didn't always show up when you needed her. She showed up when she felt like it, when the cause was worthy, and when her absence would cause more harm than good.

With each drop of cold water on Jennifer's skin, the residue of the black magic she'd been wallowing in was washed off. She didn't know it. She didn't feel it. But the enchanted water of the Maid of the Mist had the power to wash away what had been accumulated through false and misguided methods.

If Jennifer were a real sorceress, someone with a bloodline tied to it, then this cleansing ritual wouldn't have worked. But she was a wannabe, a hack, a freshman self-taught in the diabolical. And the diabolical had no real use for an amateur witch.

"Great! You splashed me!" Jennifer said, unaware her powers had left her.

Her eyes were still filled with hatred for me. She waved a hand, expecting to see something. When she did it again and nothing happened, her eyes became wild. She looked as if she had just emerged from a cave, with her hair straggling in a hundred different directions and her teeth gritted together.

I slowly regained my composure and looked toward where

Treacle had smashed into the tree. I began to hobble in that direction.

"Stop!" Jennifer yelled. I paid no attention to her. She was just a person... a regular person with no special talents for causing heart attacks, or making people fall to the ground, or punching someone in the stomach with invisible fists.

I wanted my cat to be all right. I wanted Treacle back to the way he was.

"Stop!" she yelled again. As if something snapped, she began swearing and stomping her feet. Waving her arms, she found no magic there. She looked like a person suffering from an epileptic fit of some kind. I couldn't watch. Instead, I carefully got down on my hands and knees. Crawling through the grass, I felt for Treacle. In my head, I was screaming for him. Tears rolled down my cheeks. Then I heard it.

"I'm here." His voice was so little, but I heard it. Within seconds, I felt his warm fur beneath my hand.

"Are you hurt badly?"

"I don't think so," he said weakly, letting me scoop him up into my arms and hold him close. *"It was like a nightmare in there. Her mind pushed into mine. It hurt. It was so black."*

"I'm so sorry," I said aloud.

"Do you think I care if you're sorry?"

I whipped around to see Jennifer standing just a few feet from us. In the moonlight, I could see she had one thing no witch could stop with just magic. She had a gun. I couldn't speak.

"What have you done to me? I'll kill you for this! I don't need witchcraft for that! I'll kill you and—"

"Put the gun down!" I heard Blake call out.

Jennifer's face was shadowed, but she looked nervously to her left where Blake's voice was coming from.

"Just put the gun down, Miss."

He approached with his gun drawn and his flashlight trained on Jennifer.

She began to wave her hands and utter spells in long-dead languages that I wouldn't dare say out loud. Without knowing what she had done, she had allowed the blackest sorcery into her body and soul. When it was removed, the damage had already been done. She was insane. "You deserve to die like Marvin! Like Lucas! Like Bob and Regina! You'll pay for this, too."

"Who's Bob and Regina?" I asked, clutching Treacle close to me, feeling his warm, purring body and stroking his fur nervously.

"Put the gun down!" Blake cried out.

"...deserve to die."

"I'm not going to tell you again!"

"I'll kill you!"

"Miss! Put the gun down!"

It was then that all the crickets stopped. I saw three flashes—one from Jennifer's direction and two from Blake's.

My shoulder felt as if it had burst into flames, and Treacle jumped from my arms. I collapsed to my knees then fell over. Everything was so quiet except for Blake's voice. I heard him request an ambulance. I heard him say two people were down. Was I one of them?

The grass was cool against my cheek when I turned my head. My shoulder felt hot and cold at the same time. And it was wet. Something hot and wet was seeping through my shirt. My mind wasn't thinking correctly. I should have just kept my mouth shut when Blake came to me.

His strong arms slipped underneath my head and back. He held my shoulder tightly. It hurt yet felt comforting. "You're okay, Cath. I promise. You're okay," he said softly. "The ambulance is on its way. You're going to be just fine."

"I'm glad you're here," I muttered as I looked up into his face. I saw what looked like a kind smile. "I'm always glad you're here." I would remember seeing all the stars behind his head.

"I am, too," he said.

After that, it was darkness.

Celestial Delights

When I finally woke up, I was in a bright room with flowers and wolf bane in pretty vases all around. I blinked my eyes a few times and tried to sit up, but my shoulder screamed out in a sharp, jagged pain.

"Ouch," I whimpered.

"Oh, my gosh! For heaven's sake, don't move! You've been shot. Take it easy," Bea said in her most motherly voice. Had I closed my eyes, she would have sounded just like Aunt Astrid. I looked up to see she had been crying.

"What's the matter? Did I almost die?" I asked with a mouth as dry as the desert.

"What's the matter? You hear that, Mom? What's the matter? You go off and fight the Wicked Witch of Insanity all by yourself and get shot and then ask what's the matter?"

The whole ordeal came rushing back. Not only had I been

shot in the shoulder, I had one heck of a magic burnout, too. "Yeah, in hindsight, I guess it wasn't such a great idea."

"No, it wasn't," Aunt Astrid scolded. "However, a cleansing ritual—how practical. We were too busy trying to stoop to her level, and here you were taking the high road. You made us very proud."

"I don't feel proud. How is she?"

Neither Bea nor my aunt needed to answer. I saw the looks on their faces and knew Jennifer had died.

Bea climbed onto the side of the bed and took my hand in hers. "She was sick, Cath. There was no medicine that was ever going to cure her. No therapy that would have brought her back."

"Detective Samberg doesn't realize it because he is such a good man, but he helped her more than any one of us ever could have," Aunt Astrid said. "Before she got to Marvin, she was wanted in New York City for the murder of a ten-year-old boy and his mother. She drove right into them at a crosswalk. Video footage makes it look like it was deliberate."

"How awful. A sacrifice obviously." I winced at the pain in my shoulder.

Bea nodded, still holding my hand and patting it as though I were a child with a fever.

"It was really divine intervention that Blake was there to begin with," Aunt Astrid said. "How lucky for all of us that he was."

I felt my cheeks blush as my aunt talked about him in such glowing terms.

"And..." Bea grinned like the cat that swallowed the canary. "He said you said you were glad he was here in town."

"I didn't say that."

"Sure you did."

"No, I said something like 'glad you're here to help me with this bullet in my shoulder.'"

"That's not what Jake said Blake said."

"No. I said I was glad he was there at that moment. Otherwise, well, I'd be dead."

Bea looked suspiciously at my aunt as if they had some insider knowledge about me.

"Blake needs to get his ears cleaned out," I muttered, my eyebrows pursed together in aggravation.

"Knock, knock!" Jake said, as he walked in carrying a big box of chocolates and some crossword puzzle books. "How's our girl feeling?" He leaned down to give me a kiss on the forehead then quickly peck Bea on the lips.

"I'm doing fine."

"That was quite a stunt you pulled. Your aunt and your cousin won't yell at you because they're just happy you're all right, but you had all of us worried sick. Bea called me up half-hysterical that you'd left the house without telling them."

"I'm sorry?" I said as more of a question than a statement because I wasn't sure if Jake was serious. Not until I looked into his eyes and saw the tears. Then I proceeded to feel horrible.

"You better be," the big man said, folding his huge arms in front of his chest.

"I promise I'll never go out and engage in a conversation or beat-down with anyone who is mentally unstable."

Jake nodded then gave me a wink.

I smiled back and tried not to move too much.

"They told you the news about Jennifer, right?" he asked.

"Yes."

Just then, there was another knock on the door.

"Oh, come in, Detective!" Aunt Astrid rushed across the hospital room to the door. "Please do come in."

I saw that Blake was carrying a paper bag with some big thing in it. He must have been there to visit someone else and was bringing that person a package. He didn't smile, even when Aunt Astrid hugged him. Instead, he looked around the room as if he were planning his escape.

"Hello." He nodded.

Jake walked over to shake his hand and pull him a little farther into the room.

"Hmm," Bea said quietly in my ear. "I feel your pulse has gone up. What could possibly be causing that?"

I pulled my hand away from Bea and wrinkled my nose at her.

"How are you feeling?" Blake asked, still standing almost in the doorway.

"I'm okay."

"You shouldn't have been out there alone. Statistics show women who are out past a certain time of night are seventy-five percent more likely to—"

"Well, I'm a big girl. I can go out when I want to."

"You might want to consider purchasing some Mace."

"I'll take that under consideration."

"There are also self-defense classes at the station."

"Will you be there?"

"No."

"Well, then maybe I'll check it out."

"That would be wise."

"Okay."

"Okay."

"Fine."

"Okay."

After Blake and I managed to make everyone in the room uncomfortable, they all decided to head down to the cafeteria for a snack and some coffee. Blake hung back for a few minutes. "I picked this up for you. The doctor said you'd be out in a day or two, but you should probably rest as much as they'll let you."

"Well, you didn't have to do that," I said, trying to be nice. "In fact, if anyone owes someone a gift, I owe you."

He stood a little closer to the bed, looking down at his shoes and gently touching the edge of the blanket by my feet. He kept shaking his head, but I continued.

"Look, I know you don't really like me. I'm a little prickly, I know. But from the bottom of my heart, thank you. I owe you one."

"No, you don't."

"Yes, I do."

"No, really, I was just doing my job."

"I know, but it's hard on you, too."

"It's okay."

"Really."

"You're welcome." He stood around for a few more awkward minutes then turned to face me. "I've got to get back to the office. I've got a lot of paperwork."

"Oh," I said, reluctant to admit I felt a little disappointment. "Well, thanks for stopping by."

Blake nodded. Without a smile, he handed me the package in a paper bag that he'd been carrying, then in three strides of his long legs, he walked out. I waited, hoping that maybe he'd come back. But he didn't. I was all alone.

I reached in the bag and pulled out the gift inside. It was a book.

Celestial Delights: The Best Astronomical Events Through 2030.

About the Author

Harper Lin is the *USA TODAY* bestselling author of 6 cozy mystery series including *The Patisserie Mysteries* and *The Cape Bay Cafe Mysteries*.

When she's not reading or writing mysteries, she loves going to yoga classes, hiking, and hanging out with her family and friends.

www.HarperLin.com

www.ingramcontent.com/pod-product-compliance
Lightning Source LLC
Chambersburg PA
CBHW031019030726
47497CB00004B/922

* 9 7 8 1 9 8 7 8 5 9 5 4 6 *